HUNTER
CHRIS ALLEN

By Chris Allen

Black Ops Intrepid

Defender
Hunter
Avenger
Helldiver

For my boys, Morgan and Rhett, for whom I write every word.

Vinci Books

vinci-books.com

Published by Vinci Books Ltd in 2025

1

Copyright © Chris Allen 2024

The author has asserted their moral right to be identified as the author of this work in accordance with the Copyright, Designs and Patents Act 1988.
This work is a work of fiction. Names, characters, places and incidents are the product of the author's imagination or are used fictitiously. Any resemblance to actual persons, living or dead, places and incidents is entirely coincidental.

All rights reserved. No part of this publication may be copied, reproduced, distributed, stored in any retrieval system, or transmitted in any form or by any means, including photocopying, recording, or other electronic or mechanical methods, nor used as a source for any form of machine learning including AI datasets, without the prior written permission of the publisher.

The publisher and the author have made every effort to obtain permissions for any third party material used in this book and to comply with copyright law. Any queries in this respect should be brought to the attention of the publisher and any omissions will be corrected in future editions.

A CIP catalogue record for this book is available from the British Library.

Paperback ISBN: 9781036703424

Printed and bound in Great Britain by Clays Ltd, Elcograf S.p.A.

The Sword of Interpol

When extremists plunged the world into dark decades of war and nations mobilized for vengeance, the shadow of remorseless terror and unrestrained violence called for a new generation of crime fighter.

The UN Security Council turned to INTERPOL - the International Criminal Police Organisation – to raise a new division of elite men and women, hand-picked from across the globe.

Skilled, fearless and unrelenting - part police officer, part soldier, part spy - they would be international in every way, ordained to fight fire with fire, no matter how dreadful the crime nor how treacherous the adversary.
So it was that INTREPID - the Intelligence, Recovery, Protection and Infiltration Division – came to be.

For justice to be meaningful it has to have an impact outside of the courtroom too.

—Judge Carmel Agius
Vice-President - ICTY
Zagreb Regional Legacy Conference, Zagreb, Croatia
7 November 2012

PART I
Whatever It Takes

Chapter One

CORFU, IONIAN ISLANDS, GREECE

Reaching the summit of a treacherous climb and cautiously stowing gear he'd need later, Alex Morgan pushed through a wall of coarse bracken that surmounted the sandstone cliff's edge. It was pitch black, the light breeze that had accompanied his climb had become a strong wind and the high branches on the elms and oaks were beginning to sway. A storm was coming. The noise would be both a help and a hindrance: masking his movement while also impeding his ability to identify incoming threats. A situation only exacerbated by that other double-edged sword: darkness. Wasting no time, Morgan made straight for a long corridor of olive trees and, using them for cover, crept furtively through the shadows, edging closer to the house.

His mission had begun.

With his anonymity ensured beneath a black balaclava and his body wrapped in a sheath of combat fatigues, weapons and tactical equipment, he moved quickly, deep into the grounds of the secluded Villa Prinkípissa, which, for almost five years, had harbored his target. But there were no princesses to be rescued from this cliff-top hideaway. The villa was a jumble of aging yet well-restored buildings of Mediterranean design, located in the north-east of Corfu island beyond Agnitsini. It was remote, private and protected. With views across to Albania, the main house, stables and servants' quarters were surrounded on three sides by huge stone walls topped with fat fingers of jagged glass set into cement. The fourth side of the compound was wide open, totally exposed but for a sheer 60-foot drop straight down to Ipsos Bay. That had been its weakness. Complacency had allowed them to believe it was impenetrable. It wasn't.

Morgan's target, Milivoj Šerifović, was a former senior officer and counterintelligence specialist of the State Security Service of the Ministry of the Internal Affairs of the Republic of Serbia. The old Serbia, circa early 1990s. Born in 1950, Šerifović would now be sixty-two. According to Interpol and the arrest warrant issued by the ICTY—the International Criminal Tribunal for the former Yugoslavia — Šerifović, among others, had planned, ordered and personally carried out the execution of Bosnian Muslims—Bosniaks, Bosnian Croats and other non-Serbs—within Bosnia and Herzegovina between 1992 and 1995. He was a killer on a grand scale, a very big fish, and had eluded authorities for more than fifteen years until the recent whisper of an Interpol informant reinvigorated the hunt for him. At that point, the intelligence analysts in Lyon had connected the dots and, in accordance with protocol, responsibility for the recovery of the fugitive war criminal was handed across to Intrepid: the Intelligence, Recovery, Protection and Infiltration Division – the ultra-secret, clandestine sword of Interpol.

Šerifović's time had finally come. Morgan just hoped the

man would survive the arrest so that he could be dragged in front of the ICTY and answer for his crimes. Personally, Morgan was happy to be the one doing the dragging.

Morgan's point of access would be via the old servant quarters, which now served as a guest annex. It was connected to the main villa by a long, narrow passageway. Taking a final deep breath before committing to the breach, Morgan moved in from the olive trees. He crept forward in stony silence and, reaching out, tried the handle of the ancient wooden door. Then, just as his fingers closed around the handle, one of Šerifović's bodyguards, a huge man, barreled out through the door. He hadn't even known Morgan was there, but in that split second when their eyes fixed upon each other, the magnitude of their unexpected confrontation was grasped by both of them.

As the bodyguard pushed the door open into the quiet darkness, the light from within momentarily dazzled Morgan. Nonetheless, the Intrepid agent exploded into action. There was no other choice.

Fortunately for Morgan, the bodyguard's gun, a Heckler & Koch 416 N, was slung across his back; convenient for carrying but totally useless if needed in a hurry. The weapon's sling, belted tightly across the man's chest, also impeded access to the automatic Morgan knew would be sitting beneath his left armpit. Sloppy. But he hadn't been employed for nothing: the guy was a monster. Just shy of 7 feet tall, he was a good 30 pounds heavier than Morgan. From the instant the two predators engaged, their faces just inches apart, Morgan knew the monster wouldn't get to his weapons in time. But that was no matter to this guy. He would default to brute force. Morgan, the apparent David in this David and Goliath scenario, knew it had to be quick and quiet. He could not lose time or, worse, attract the attention of others this early on.

Without hesitation, Morgan launched himself inside the guard's immediate space, driving his cupped hands upward and inward, managing to strike both ears simultaneously, bursting the man's ear drums with the ferocity of his attack. The bodyguard wailed in agony, staggering, momentarily disoriented, amid the howl of the winds high in the treetops. Morgan made the most of it, grabbing the bodyguard by the lapels of his leather jacket and pulling him down while driving a knee into the man's crotch. Once, twice, three times Morgan mercilessly pounded with everything he had. The big man was teetering like a large, mortally wounded animal but he was not going down easily. His huge arms were swinging blindly around in the darkness, each with the power of a wrecking ball on the end of a crane arm. Morgan dropped, narrowly missing one arm, then another, then side-stepped awkwardly around to the side and managed to get his right forearm up around the man's neck and chin. Clinging to the bodyguard's back, avoiding the slung weapon and fighting hard to bring him down, Morgan went for the classic blood choke, or sleeper hold, maneuver. Using his left hand, he pushed his right arm tight into a narrow V, compressing the carotid arteries and jugular veins on both sides of the guard's tree-trunk neck.

Enraged but weakening, the big man dug in hard and stood to his full height, lifting Morgan from the ground. With all his weight and strength, he pushed backward, slamming Morgan hard into the wall of the outbuilding, crushing the air from his lungs.

The Intrepid agent's grip on the blood choke loosened and the tables turned. The bodyguard clawed for Morgan's forearm with both hands and when he found it, held firm, then violently jerked his head backward, headbutting Morgan and splitting the agent's eyebrow. Snapping his upper body forward, the man flipped Morgan over his right shoulder to the ground.

Morgan slammed into the hard ground like a thrown safe, only to be grabbed by the throat, lifted off his feet and pinned against the wall. The monster's massive hands closed hungrily around Morgan's throat. Giant thumbs crept expertly across his flesh like blood-fattened slugs until they found just the right spot to squeeze. Morgan fought desperately to wrench the G-clamp hands from his neck. For seconds that seemed like minutes, Morgan went like hell for the other guy's eyes, nose and ears but his attempts were all in vain. The man had him.

Finally, with just a gasp left in his rapidly failing lungs, blood streaming from a deep gash above his left eye and the physical exertion of the affray threatening to conquer him, Morgan reached for the SIG Sauer P226. The big man's massive thumbs were closing down on the Intrepid agent's windpipe with the power, precision and finality of a hydraulic press. A victor's grin split the man's battered features. Morgan could sense rather than feel himself lifting the SIG the last agonizing fraction of an inch clear of the thigh holster. But his fingers were numbing. There was no power in his hands. The oxygen supply to his limbs had depleted. He fumbled. The thumbs around his throat tightened more. The gun was slipping. His lungs were screaming for air. Every bit of the man's weight was behind the squeeze. Morgan knew the gun was going. He felt his life draining from him. Then disaster – the SIG fell from his grasp. The grim reality that his last vision on earth was to be the hideous face of a gangland thug flashed through some still-functioning corner of his subconscious.

A surreal euphoria overwhelmed Morgan, taking control of the last moments of his life. Sight and sound were abandoning him. His body became a dead weight under the crushing assault of the bodyguard's pressure.

The monster saw the transition washing over the face of the dead man in his hands. He'd seen it before – strangulation had been his signature and even though the exhaustion of this particular struggle had taken an equal toll, he had finally prevailed. This guy was done.

With a final, utterly exhausted expulsion of air, he released his grip.

Alex Morgan felt himself falling, descending headlong through an endless tunnel of brilliant light, slowly at first, gently rolling and tumbling without a care. Then the hammer fell. He was hurtling at breakneck speed. On and on – the momentum intoxicating. Flashes of his death struggle with the bodyguard raced past as he plummeted down, down, down. Yellow teeth. Black eyes. The stench of putrid breath. The animal sounds of survival in the midst of brutal hand-to-hand combat. He submitted to the power of his primal subconscious.

Suddenly, everything changed. His descent slowed, stopped and then, with the force of a medieval catapult, Morgan hit a bend in the tunnel and was fired with crippling speed in the opposite direction, called back by the siren cry of the storm. Back the way he had come. Back to the beginning of the tunnel. Back to life. Back, back, back, until his vision was consumed by nothing but the face of his killer.

The man had made a deadly mistake. He had assumed

success rather than ensured it, releasing his grip on the Intrepid agent's throat a moment too soon.

With his gun far from reach and clinging to life his only objective, Alex Morgan's left hand closed around the SOG Force SE38 knife on his belt. His thumb popped the restraining strap across the top of the knife and his palm and fingers closed gratefully around the familiar serrated scales of the handle. With a sharp intake of air that momentarily stunned his assailant, Morgan's body erupted in an explosion of adrenal overload.

The bodyguard's face registered the transformation but it was too late. With the same animal ferocity that had beckoned him back to life, Morgan tore the knife from the sheath and drove it upward in one fluid movement, through the chest, deep into the man's heart. Both hands clasped around the handle, he pushed with everything he had left and held the blade firmly in place. Except for a last wretched attempt to reach for Morgan's throat there was no further resistance from the huge man. It was only a reflex. His knees buckled and the bodyguard crumpled to the ground, dead.

Morgan staggered, almost falling down with him, but he knew he couldn't afford to. If he was to collapse, loss of consciousness would be a certainty in his current state. Swaying, he slowly extended to full height in primal triumph and sucked air back into his grateful lungs. After those ferocious, agonizing few minutes, all was quiet again.

With his breath rasping deep in his lungs, he looked down at the blood on his hands and tried to wipe it clean against the fabric of his combat fatigues. But there was no use. Blood never came off easily.

His gaze shifted an inch, beyond the hands to the body of the man at his feet. The heart had stopped and blood was oozing rather than pouring from the chest wound. Morgan checked his watch, the battered old Tag Heuer had sat on that wrist for years. Fuck! The man had had to be killed, there'd been no alternative. The clash had only been brief, but still he'd lost precious time. Time he could ill afford.

Mechanically, Alex Morgan retrieved the knife from the chest of the dead man and, wiping the gore across the man's jacket, returned it to its sheath. He reached with bloody fingers into a pocket of his combat trousers and withdrew a small GPS tracking device, which he clipped to the body. The GPS unit would guide the local Interpol liaison officer, along with the Greek police, straight to the location of the body when Morgan remotely activated it. Of course, his intention had been that the device would be attached to a live body, not a dead one.

He found his SIG, checked it, and headed for the door.

One down.

Chapter Two

SUNSET HILL, SEATTLE, WASHINGTON, USA

Madeline Clancy was in need of fresh supplies. It had been a few days since she'd ventured out, for no other reason than she'd had enough to get by on and had been enjoying the peace and seclusion of her home. The local police had been incredibly attentive and while she'd resisted their attempts to maintain a permanent presence outside her home, she had diligently followed their instructions concerning regular call-ins and carrying her personal duress alarm at all times. But, judging by the state of the fridge and pantry, the time had finally come. Reluctantly, she closed her book, *The Bridge Betrayed: Religion and Genocide in Bosnia* by Michael A Sells, and peeled herself away from the view looking across Puget Sound to Bainbridge Island and beyond to the snow-capped Olympics, although the overcast conditions today didn't really allow for a clear view of those breathtaking mountains.

It was only 14 degrees Fahrenheit outside, so she zipped into her Marmot Chelsea coat hanging by the front door and stepped out into a chill breeze coming in from the Sound.

Normally she would have worn more, but she didn't plan to be out long so the jacket would do. Of course, locals knew that the trick to living in Seattle was layers. Learning to layer your clothes was just a normal part of life in a climate like this. She just hoped that she'd make it back home before the rain arrived.

Folding her jacket and climbing into her car, Madeline reversed her Range Rover from the garage and pulled out into the street. She drove the familiar route along NW 68th, eventually working her way across to NW 15th Avenue, heading downtown. She didn't notice the compact VW Golf that joined her near the junction and was completely unaware that it stayed close all the way to Pike Place Market.

Arriving at the market, Madeline found a spot in the small car park nearby and strode purposefully into DeLaurenti's armed with a shopping list. The driver of the VW wasn't so lucky at the car park and pulled over 50 yards further on, dropping off his passenger: a young man, rangy and unsure of himself but carrying the bluster of many younger types with something to prove. He was anonymous-looking enough to easily blend into the background of other shoppers but managed it by luck rather than actual skill. At one point, when he'd attempted to cross the road to follow her into DeLaurenti's, he'd just managed to avoid being hit by a King County Metro bus and so opted to keep his eyes on her car rather than shadowing her. After all, she'd have to come back to it.

It took Madeline half an hour to get what she needed and before long she had loaded up the Range Rover and escaped the town traffic, heading home. Behind her, a shriek of burning rubber and honking horns heralded an unexpected U-turn by the VW. Once again her furtive pursuers were following at a careful distance. Inside the Golf, the two men, the young passenger and a slightly older driver, were agitated.

They were new to the game they were playing and not sure how it would pan out. It had sounded straightforward at first – but killing a judge was a whole new level.

On a whim, Madeline decided to stop off at Picolinos and pick up a coffee and one of Manny's pastries to take home. She arrived near the junction of NW 64th Street and NW 32nd Avenue and, turning onto 64th, parked alongside Green Market. As she got out of the car, a gust of wind raced up from Puget Sound, forcing her to pull up the hood of her coat. *God, it was a cold one today*, she thought. A strong, hot coffee was definitely required.

Watching the back of the woman disappear into the café, the men remained in the VW parked outside an accountant's office 50 yards away on the opposite side of the road. They sat silently for a minute before the passenger, shaking, blurted, "I can't do it."

"What?" the driver demanded. "You can't do it? Any minute now this bitch is going to walk out of there, walk straight past us, get in her car and in two minutes she'll be back at her house. You couldn't do it before. So we drive all over Seattle to stay on her back until you got the balls to do it. And still you won't do it. Fuck! Give me the gun. I'll do it."

"No, I will but …" The passenger, no more than twenty, was sweating profusely, his knuckles white and eyes wide with fear and anticipation. "I just need to work it out in my head, you know?"

"There's no time for that, you useless fuck!" said the driver. "Here she comes. Give me the fucking gun."

"No!"

"Give it to me!"

The two men grappled wildly for the gun that lay on the floor at the passenger's Nike-clad feet.

Chapter Three

CORFU

Escaping the winds and moving deftly into a combat stance inside the door, Morgan took a moment to, in his terms, reboot. Raising the P226, he allowed his vision time to adjust to the darkness and uncertainty of the long, dimly lit passageway that connected the guest annex to the main villa. Under the feeble flicker of a single, insect-encrusted bulb halfway along the ceiling, he could barely distinguish any detail other than more shadows that only told of depressions along the walls: mostly window recesses and at least, he noted, one other doorway. It was too dark to even see the end of the passage.

Morgan's left hand returned to his throat, massaging the muscles. *The bastard was a second away from crushing my windpipe*, he mused. He wondered what it would have been like to spend the rest of his days sounding like a gravelly Clint Eastwood parody if the guy had done any permanent damage. Not good, he decided. For one thing, his Intrepid cohorts, especially Dave Sutherland, would never let him live it down. Remaining in the crouch with his gun arm still locked out in front of him ready to fire, Morgan took a series of deep breaths, slowly but surely getting his body's machinery back online.

Back in 2010, as Serbia clamored for inclusion in the European Union and with a number of the old key leadership figures still on the run, Intrepid was charged with the responsibility for the capture of all outstanding ICTY fugitives. That particular task carried the added weight and personal mandate of Intrepid's chief, Major General Reginald "Nobby" Davenport. Davenport, a legend in international special operations and intelligence circles, had served in the Balkans at the height of the troubles in the 1990s. He was only too familiar with the legacy left behind by the likes of Milivoj Šerifović. With the objective of testing old loyalties and putting the squeeze on those who had been harboring the war criminals, Davenport had lobbied, successfully, for rewards to be raised on the heads of the fugitive leadership of the old regime. The Serbian Government, with some encouragement – and assistance – from other nations, was only too keen to oblige. There were now five million euros on offer for information leading to the arrest of Šerifović.

Disconsolately pondering the fact that he wouldn't see any of those five million euros, Morgan considered how Šerifović and his confederates had managed to dodge authorities for so long. Of course there'd been absolute sanctuary under Milošević until 2000. After that they took refuge under the protection of the Serbian mafia, many of whom were former members of the security forces themselves and therefore predisposed to treating the old leadership as war heroes. But the arrest of Karadžić in 2008 was the beginning of the end. The tightly bound circle of protection that the fugitive hierarchy had enjoyed since going to ground all those years ago began to unravel. It was apparent, judging by the transcript of the Interpol informant's statement, that those old loyalties, even old fears, were tiring. A healthy reward was a great incentive, too.

The Davenport Strategy, as it became known in select circles, had worked.

There was definitely no honor among thieves or killers. Where had he heard that before? And while Šerifović in custody would be a huge coup for Intrepid, it was hoped that his arrest would precipitate the capture of an even bigger fish: Davenport's ultimate target, former brigadier general of the Serbian Security Forces Dragoslav Obrenović – Drago.

But Drago would have to wait.

There was a change in the shadows, just the slightest thing. Morgan sensed it rather than saw it as he began to move from his position by the door. Nothing more than the most minute tremor on the edge of the web, but it was enough to warn Morgan of danger. *Move!*

Instinctively reacting to the familiar thud of an M84 stun grenade, Alex Morgan threw his body upon a deep window ledge a split second before the blast. It was the only reachable space that could diminish the direct impact of the flash and noise. He cupped his hands over his ears, opened his mouth wide to avert pressure build-up and clenched his eyes shut to protect his vision from the magnesium-based flash. The roar of the explosion tore through the passageway. The flash of its subsonic deflagration stabbed at every surface and corner with blinding, ferocious intensity.

The sound ricocheted from wall to wall, escaping through the warren of his target's hideaway with the familiarity of a retreating thunderclap until it was nothing more than the faintest echo. Seconds later, but for the rattling windows and doors, it was quiet again, quiet and black as pitch. The blast had smashed the light bulb and now the shadows offered only uncertainty.

Straining against the ringing in his ears, Morgan remained frozen, not willing to even flinch lest he should give his position away. But there was nothing, just unforgiving darkness and the eerie taunts of the escalating wind storm outside. They were onto him. The battle with the monster had obviously given him away and now others had rallied. It would be a fight all the way to the target. *Well, if that's the way this is meant to go.* Then he thought of the dead man. He stole a glance from his perch on the window ledge and saw the body lying face down outside. No, this wasn't the way this was supposed to be going down. Davenport was clear in his philosophy on the use of force. Leaving a trail of dead bodies across the Greek Islands was not consistent with that philosophy, nor was it consistent with Morgan's own values. He hadn't joined Intrepid to be a killer. That said, on those occasions when he'd had to, he knew he had the stomach for it. Sometimes, there was just no other choice.

There came a sound. Footsteps? Despite the diminishing tinnitus and background noise of the winds, Morgan could make out the crunch of hard-soled shoes on the rough-hewn cement floor. Leather soles. Dress shoes? Another step, and then another. Closer now. More crunching. Definitely dress shoes. Not the preferred footwear of a professional bodyguard paid to be ready for trouble.

So, they hadn't been expecting him. That was good; it explained the monster's shock at the sight of him. It also explained the stun grenade. It was the action of a desperate man. No investigation. No escalation of force. No training. His use of the weapon suggested that he was either a scared, inexperienced underling who'd been directed into action or he was simply lazy. Made sense. The dossier said that Šerifović was protected by a bunch of overpaid local gunslingers who'd become complacent over the years because their boss thought he was safe. Too much booze, too many drugs and far too many women, apparently. Well, the good life had finally caught up with them all. Especially Šerifović.

There came another crunch on the cement, this time accompanied by the ratchet-click of a cocking lever being released awkwardly on a Heckler & Koch G3A3. The weapon sounded dry. Not well maintained. Morgan straightened the balaclava on his face, and with painstakingly slow, deliberate movements returned the SIG Sauer P226 to the tactical thigh holster on his right leg and withdrew instead the ASP expandable baton from its sheath.

Stand by.

The crunching footfalls of the reluctant bodyguard drew closer. Alex Morgan could almost visualize the man down the corridor, creeping forward on his toes, shoulder married to the wall, eyes on stalks, searching the darkness. Morgan readied himself. He could almost smell fear in this man – it was palpable. But it wouldn't do to go in half-assed. The man had a gun and he was nervous; the stun grenade proved that. That made him impulsive. His approach continued. With every reticent step, Morgan was able to calculate the distances and timings. Closer. Closer.

The guard fired a burst haphazardly through the blackened space of the corridor. The 7.62mm NATO ammunition filled the air, every molten projectile searching for a target – no surface was safe. The echo was deafening and shards of plaster, wood and glass burst from the walls and ceiling.

Then, as abruptly as it had begun, it ended. The weapon fell silent. Only the exasperation of the shooter, the torrent of his obscenities, told of his predicament; the weapon rattled unmistakably as he tried clumsily to rectify a jam.

Morgan launched from the ledge.

Even in the poor light, Morgan saw dinner-plate eyes and a wide-open mouth, full of surprise and panic. The gun was in the man's hands and, despite the shock, his defense mechanisms were instinctively bringing the assault rifle around to fire again. If he had managed to clear the jam and get off a burst at this range, Morgan would be finished. But Morgan knew he hadn't and the unmistakable waft of alcohol told Morgan he was less than at his best.

Exploding from the window ledge, Morgan snapped the extendable ASP baton out until it locked and then, in a flourish Dumas's d'Artagnan would have been proud of, brought the weapon down hard upon the guard's left forearm, just above the wrist. The blow snapped the ulna easily and the man screamed in pain. His arm spasmed and the gun clattered to the floor as he automatically grabbed for the injury with his good arm. It was nothing for Morgan to continue the flow of his assault. He swept the baton up again in a short arc and brought it back with shattering speed and accuracy on the exposed left-hand side of the man's neck. He was unconscious before his body wilted to the cement floor.

With timing and precision equaling the alacrity of his baton assault, plasti-cuffs, duct tape and GPS tracking device were all withdrawn from Morgan's pockets and equipment pouches and affixed to the limp figure crumpled on the floor at his feet.

Two down.

Chapter Four

SUNSET HILL, SEATTLE, WASHINGTON, USA

Madeline eased out of Picolinos' door, shuffling onto the sidewalk with her coffee and pastry. In a calm and contented frame of mind, she was looking forward to returning home to her books and views of the Sound. Despite the circumstances, the enforced solitude was a welcome respite from the pressures of international law. And sometimes a lack of company was good for the soul.

She became aware of a commotion going on in a car not too far ahead of her: two men were arguing with raised voices and the disagreement seemed decidedly hostile for sleepy old Sunset Hill. One burst from the passenger side of the car, tumbling onto the sidewalk as he did so and then all was quiet. Eerily quiet. Instinctively, Madeline quickened her pace, as it appeared he was crossing the street and heading straight toward her. She juggled the car keys within her right hand, managing to bring the personal duress alarm attached to the keyring around into her trembling palm. She noticed the man's right hand was reaching beneath his sweater and her heart rate skyrocketed. His dark eyes were fixed upon her and his body language was aggressive and wild. A gun appeared, pointing at her but – strangely – it was shaking in his hand.

She froze. She pressed the activate button on the duress alarm and kept pressing, again and again.

The gunman's hand tightened around the automatic but nothing happened. He stopped walking and stood dead still in the middle of 32nd Avenue, both hands clasped to the gun. She could see his finger squeeze, but still nothing.

Madeline ran to some nearby trash bins and cowered among them, screaming for help, frantically continuing to press the button.

In the middle of the road she could see the gunman fumbling with the weapon. He was full of anger and frustration, looking back and forth between her and the gun, his eyes blazing. She could hear someone calling, "Cock it! Cock it!" and saw the unmistakable movement, so familiar from films and TV, as the man pulled the slide back and released it and the weapon was brought back to life. It was up again, pointing at her. This time the gunman was smiling.

Gunfire erupted and the normally serene setting of her home town was shattered by confrontation and violence. There was a squeal of tires and a loud crash. Then more yelling. Madeline fell to the ground amid the trash cans with her arms up over her face and head, knees up to her chest, gritting her teeth – awaiting death.

The shooting lasted just seconds, then silence. Madeline didn't move.

"Oh my God. Judge! Judge! Are you OK, ma'am?" A large, warm hand rested upon on her shoulder protectively.

"Ma'am, it's Officer Connelly from the Seattle Police Department."

Judge Madeline Clancy looked up slowly at the man leaning over her. Gradually her tunneled vision cleared and the policeman's cap, leather jacket, radio gear and the SPD shield came into view. The face of a concerned, determined and, above all, familiar-looking young man came into focus beneath the cap.

"Michael? Michael Connelly?" she asked, hardly believing that she was still alive. "Is that you?"

"Yes, ma'am. It is. Are you OK?"

"My dear boy," she whispered, shaking and in shock. "How is your mother?"

"She's fine, judge. Listen, I need to get you away from here," he said, lifting her to her feet. Madeline responded mechanically to his assistance and Connelly helped her up and led her back to the café.

"What on earth just happened?" she began. "I mean, I was just getting coffee. This is Sunset Hill. I was … just getting coffee." Leaning heavily against the police officer, Madeline looked back and saw the body of the young gunman lying flat on his back with blood, lots of it, across his sweater and face. Beyond him she saw the VW Golf crashed into the front of a Seattle Police Department squad car and another man face down on the road, a police officer restraining him.

"Ma'am," Connelly began as they reached the doors of the café, "I need you to go back inside the café with these folks while I assist my partner. More officers are on the way and will be here any second."

Madeline became aware of welcoming hands reaching out and leading her inside to the warmth and security of the café. She sat down at a table looking out on the street, all flashing lights and chaos. Fresh coffee was poured and as her head fell into her hands, shock threatening to cripple her, the face of her beloved only daughter appeared in her mind.

Chapter Five

CORFU

This final phase was always going to be tricky. Morgan knew as much before he went in, although he had hoped to at least make it past the second guard before the others became aware of his presence. But to ensure that the plan to conduct a covert capture of Šerifović remained absolutely top secret, it was imperative that Intrepid took full carriage of the arrest and, as a result, participation by outsiders had been kept to a minimum. At this point even the Interpol liaison officer had been kept at arm's length, only aware that a high-risk arrest was being made and that he – along with members of EKAM, the Hellenic Police Anti-Terrorist Unit – was responsible for cleaning up the underlings. As far as the local Greek police currently on standby in helicopters at Corfu airport were concerned, it was just another drug bust. Exactly who was being arrested and why had not been disclosed beyond the walls of General Davenport's office.

Morgan knew that Milivoj Šerifović was not afraid to kill, his record in the Balkans vouched for that, and right now he was a caged animal. With his third bodyguard for backup, he would be ready to kill to extend his tenuous freedom, no matter what. Worst of all, Šerifović was now alerted to Morgan's incursion and would be ready.

So it was that Alex Morgan found himself solo, again, penetrating deep into the lair of a fugitive war criminal, mass murderer and rapist. Quite a CV, he noted wryly. In theory, flying solo on a job like this had its benefits in terms of ensuring operational security, but fuck, it had knobs on when it came time to actually be on the ground, especially when the intelligence pencil necks failed to identify that one of the three, quote, "lazy, poorly trained, shouldn't be a problem", unquote, bodyguards was built like an Abrams tank. "Thank you, intel," he whispered while reflexively massaging his neck.

Having tagged the second bodyguard with a GPS tracking device – and pilfered a couple of items he thought might come in handy – Morgan exited the corridor through a smashed window and made his way toward the main villa via an alternate, less obvious, route. Approaching through the darkness to the side of the villa, he became aware of shouting, just audible above the blustery din of the wind. Male voices at first, aggressive and demanding. One voice was dominating the other when the exchange was joined by a woman's voice. She sounded young. Whatever was going on, whoever she was, she was desperate, shouting in terror and panic.

Moving quickly, Morgan pushed through an assortment of wild herbs growing up against the house and the smells of rosemary, mint and garlic enveloped him. He found a discreet window nestled in a dark corner and peered inside. The small, ornate window gave him a clear, albeit angled, view of a long, luxuriously appointed room. From the artworks to the furniture, fittings and features, the interior of the villa was dripping with cash. The stench of far too much money and not enough taste permeated the scene, all paid for from the proceeds of a life of crime, violence and death. Jesus! Morgan thought with incredulity. *I sure chose the wrong side of the trade.* He edged closer and carefully pressed his face up against the glass. Yep, there they were. Target confirmed. Older and thinner and with much less hair, but definitely him. Morgan let out a tight hiss through clenched teeth. The man Morgan knew to be Šerifović was standing over a girl who looked like a tourist. Young, lithe and dressed to impress, she'd obviously been coaxed up into the mountains on the promise of a good time. The girl had no idea who she was dealing with. Flashing lots of cash and drugs, it wouldn't have been too hard for Šerifović to entice her enough to overlook the fact that he was in his sixties. But now the party was over. She was cowering helplessly on the floor and Šerifović was rough-handling her, slapping her and yelling at her to be quiet, while barking orders at the other man, the third bodyguard, to cover the door that led to the corridor. Morgan's blood boiled.

They were expecting him from entirely the wrong direction. Good news for Morgan. Not so good for Šerifović.

Urgently, Morgan surveyed the scene to ensure that he was absolutely clear on where each of them was positioned in relation to everything else in the room. He would not have time to become embroiled in another hand-to-hand confrontation with either Šerifović or his bodyguard – he would end up with a bullet in his back within seconds. Taking one last moment to scan the room, Morgan saw his opportunity. He knew what had to be done.

Despite the modern restoration of the villa, local builders had made use of the original tiles. They were of the classic terracotta, convex design, loosely stacked in columns and regimented rows across the pitched roof. The strong winds of the looming storm were screaming through the huddle of buildings now and rustling the ancient tiles like canvas sails upon rough seas. The entire surface of the roof was an enormous, vociferous wind charm.

Clambering across the roof of the villa, his movements covered by the volume of noise, Alex Morgan reached the spot he knew would provide the most direct access to his target inside. Extracting the still-bloodied SOG Force SE38 knife from his belt, he made quick work of a number of tiles, levering them off steadily before throwing them clear of the house. Then he took to the waterproof membrane and insulation beneath the tiles, making a hole just large enough to squeeze through.

Inside the roof, with the aid of his SureFire tactical flashlight, Morgan made his way cautiously across the roof trusses, listening for voices and activity below him. He did not have far to go before he reached the service access panel in the plasterboard ceiling he'd noted from the window. The muffled voices from the living area below became clearer. He could hear heightened levels of uncertainty and anxiety in the voices of the men. The girl was relatively silent, only now and then offering a whimper or cry of fear. Poor thing. "I'll get you out of this mess shortly, darlin'," he whispered. "Sit tight."

Steadying himself across the top of the access panel, Morgan bent his ear to the crack in the joinery and listened intently. His Serbian was scant, but he recognized enough to know they were perplexed and more than a little agitated. They'd expected him to come blundering in from the corridor minutes ago, but there'd been nothing and now, they had no idea.

It's now or never, he thought.

Just as Morgan prepared to assault, he shifted his weight across carefully to his left foot and the change in his balance caused a rippling creak along the latticework of trusses. The sound was a thunderclap in the confined space of the ceiling and the room below. It was too loud even for the wind to mask it.

Pinpricks of light instantly appeared in radical patterns through the ceiling plaster as a barrage of 9mm rounds peppered every square inch around him, pelting the layer of insulation above his head with the force and frequency of heavy rain upon a tin roof. The narrow space was filled with the fine powder of shattered plaster, splintered wood and ricochets. Morgan had no time. He was seconds away from being riddled by bullets from the submachine guns and falling dead, or worse, fatally wounded to the floor.

Alex Morgan jumped straight through the access panel, splintering the square of plaster while simultaneously hurling the M84 stun grenade he'd taken as a souvenir from the second guard. The flashbang landed perfectly in the center of the three of them. The shock of his appearance and the sight of the grenade at their feet stunned the two men and sent the girl into hysterics. Morgan dropped behind a natural barricade of lavish furniture – hands to ears, mouth open and eyes clamped shut – allowing the detonation to do its thing.

The instantaneous combination of the one million candela flash and 170 decibel bang of the 84's eruption brought the room under Morgan's power. Without hesitation, he was in action, leaping across the furniture and heading first for the bodyguard.

Once again, Morgan resorted to the baton. His targeted first strike of the telescopic high carbon steel blade at the side of the man's neck missed, but the baton still struck hard, crashing down upon the collar bone and shattering it. The guard screamed in agony. He teetered forward, grabbing for his shoulder, and Morgan followed through determinedly with a pulverizing knee strike to the face. The impact and pain of it all reduced the man to blithering semiconsciousness and Morgan immediately carried out the plasti-cuffs, duct tape and tracking device routine again.

Three down.

Morgan flashed across the room, responding to the sudden, but dazed, recovery of Šerifović. Beside him the girl lay silent – she'd fainted. For her it was a blessing; for Morgan it was one less thing to worry about. The Interpol liaison officer would ensure that she was identified and properly taken care of. Then Morgan saw clearly the bruising around her eyes and the splits and swelling of her lips, the results of being worked over by her host. The cold objectivity of his profession morphed into a primal revulsion of the coward – any coward – who would take to a woman with his fists.

Morgan's anger turned upon Šerifović but he forced himself to refrain from beating the man senseless. The disturbing strength and menace captured by those grainy file images that had become so familiar to Morgan back in London had all but left the Serb. The file pictures, the only official record of his appearance, dated back to the early 1990s. Seventeen years later, all that remained was a gray, emaciated-looking wretch. The old man was finally beaten.

Morgan kicked an MP5 far away from Šerifović's reach and hoisted him unceremoniously to his feet. He was groggy, a mix of the alcohol he'd consumed, the effects of the flashbang and shock, but he was coming around.

"Who are you?" he asked in Greek, finally looking into Morgan's eyes.

"Turn around," Morgan demanded in English, spinning the man on his axis.

"Not Greek police then," Šerifović said. "Interpol? No, you are no policeman. I can see that in your eyes. You are a soldier – a mercenary after the bounty on my head?"

"Consider me a facilitator. Nothing more," Morgan answered bluntly, as he pulled the man's arms behind his back and applied plasti-cuffs. "And you are to consider yourself officially under arrest. Move," he barked and frog-marched Šerifović hurriedly toward the door. Šerifović did not attempt to escape or resist but he was committed to making the task of removing him hard work, constantly tripping and stumbling as the Intrepid agent hurled him outside into the middle of the wind storm.

"Where are you taking me?" he yelled. "You know, wherever it is, they will come and get me. My friends. They will come for me and when I am free again, they will come for you. And they will find you. You should think about that before—"

Šerifović's taunts were abruptly ended by a punishing blow from Morgan, an expertly placed blunt trauma punch to the solar plexus. He crumpled to his knees, gasping horribly for air while his diaphragm went into spasm. Morgan stood over him, unemotionally, waiting for the man's breathing to recommence while he scanned their immediate surrounds. Even in the darkness he was vulnerable. Morgan was not about to assume he was home and clear. There could still be some other layer to Šerifović's protection that intel had missed. That was why Morgan had decided upon a completely unexpected form of extraction.

Finally, Šerifović regained his composure. He took in a series of long breaths, underscored by the smoker's phlegmy rattle, and then retched vilely before rolling onto his back.

Morgan dropped to a knee beside his prisoner. In the darkness the man's features looked ghoulishly stricken. Calmly, authoritatively, the menace of his words chillingly discernible through the screaming winds, Morgan said, "Old man, if you think you're going to fuck with me all the way out of here, think again. You were right before – I'm not a cop. You should remember that. And where I'm taking you, no-one will ever find you."

With that, Morgan heaved him to his feet and dragged him to the cliff's edge. Manhandling him and cutting him from the plasti-cuffs, it took only minutes to wrestle the utterly perplexed war criminal into the equipment Morgan had stashed earlier.

"What the fuck is this?" Šerifović cried. "What are you doing? Is this a parachute? I'm just an old man, you can't do this to me! Who are you? I demand to know!"

The fear and uncertainty spilling from him in every word and gesture found no solace in Morgan's stoic silence. Šerifović grabbed at the buckles and zips, trying desperately to work out what it was that Morgan had strapped him into and what was about to happen. The bravado and arrogance of the man who had eluded international authorities for a decade and a half, living a life of absolute luxury financed entirely by crime, had evaporated. Milivoj Šerifović, the former Serbian colonel of intelligence, was no more. All that remained was Šerifović, the 62 year-old man suffering the onset of lung cancer, who had been stripped of his money, his power, his privilege and influence and, above all, his protection in a few minutes. Now, he was just a frail and scared old man, as vulnerable as every one of the hundreds of poor souls over whose deaths he had presided in his glory days. Glory days. Christ! Morgan's loathing surged.

In one swift, deftly executed maneuver, Morgan had

Šerifović flat on his face on the ground. Placing a foot across the back of the man's neck, Morgan prepared himself for the extraction. In less than a minute he, too, was ready. Once again, he pulled the other man to his feet.

"You are wearing a Freedivers Recovery Vest," Morgan snapped coldly. "Designed to inflate once you are in the water. Yours is already set."

"Set? Water? What the hell do you mean? Are you crazy?"

The whites of Šerifović's eyes showed clearly all the way around his irises. His breath was shallow and strained. Panic had consumed him, but he knew that there was no way out. Not with this man. "What am I to do? What if something goes wrong? Tell me! Tell me something! You can't just—"

"OK, I'll tell you something." Morgan's hands suddenly locked on his prisoner: one onto the collar at the back of his neck and one onto the waistband of his trousers. "Mind the step."

Alex Morgan hurled the man from the cliff and off into the darkness.

Chapter Six

LOCATION: UNDISCLOSED

"Who the fuck decided to send those useless fucking assholes to do this?" The virulent, heavily accented Slavic voice crashed through the room. The three other men remained rigidly silent. "Who was it? I want a fucking answer!" A huge fist pounded emphatically upon the desk.

"One of our American chapters, *šefa*," was the only reply – self-assured, cocky but respectful.

"You did this?" The man's eyes blazed with betrayal. "No, tell me it was not you, my own son."

"No, *šefa*. It was not me," the young man answered.

The older man's attention turned to the other two, his dark brow heavy with anger.

"I made inquiries, *šefa*," said one of the others nervously. "I was assured they could do it."

"You made inquiries!" the voice boomed incredulously. "You did this and did not think to ask me! All you have done is scare that American bitch and the rest of those fucks into hiding."

The man, the one they called *šefa*, or chief, was pacing

the room. It was a big room, masculine, with no windows, luridly furnished with rich decor and dark, heavy furniture. There would normally be row upon row of ceiling-high books in this kind of room, but no such irrelevances existed here. Instead, a series of large television screens, half-a-dozen or more, were affixed to three walls at head height. Most of them were set to international news broadcasts. Where there were no screens there were oil paintings on large canvasses depicting female nudes in various displays of eroticism. Among them hung faultless reproductions of the *Three Lovers* by Théodore Géricault and Goya's famous *La maja desnuda*, alongside numerous darker, more explicit scenes.

The chief paced back and forth behind a huge Alexander Roux desk, patinated by age and lavishly ornamented in ormolu. It was grand and completely over the top. Set high upon the wall behind the desk, glowering down upon the three obedient servants, was an enormous portrait of the chief as he once was, wearing the uniform of a brigadier general of the Army of Republika Srpska, more widely known as the Bosnian Serb Army. The portrait was an indulgence in the extreme. Commissioned by its subject, it was designed to awe and spoke volumes of the chief's conceit and sense of personal historical significance. The painting depicted the man in his mid-forties, powerfully built, square-jawed with prominent cheekbones, a long slender nose and cold eyes looking into the future with absolutely no humanity to be read in them. Thick graying hair showed around the temples beneath a cap that sat like a crown upon his large head. Golden badges and buttons and the vibrant colors of a general's embellishments and medal ribbons had all been presented against the olive drab dress uniform for prime intimidatory effect. This was a man of power, a decorated man of uncompromising motivation. A man apart from other men. One to be feared.

Now, a decade and a half later, pacing beneath his portrait, General Dragoslav Obrenović was an affectation of his former self. The cruel realities of decline and excess had begun to take their toll. The square jaw was now a jowl disguised by a dense steel-wool beard that jutted from his face like the prow of a Viking longship. The nose was fleshy and red and the hair, white and long, was gathered in a band behind his neck. Of course, the uniform was gone. No more gold braid or ribbon bars to draw attention away from the heavy weight at the waist, although he did have his clothes tailored to hide it as much as possible. But despite all the changes that so encumbered the man's journey into his later years, the cold, lifeless eyes remained. They were blocks of glacial ice, buried deep within the dark fissures of his face. They had seen too much to be even remotely altered or softened by age. The eyes told the story of the man's terrifying reputation. It was not one built on folklore: he'd earned it. And he was as brutal today as he had been twenty years ago. If that was possible.

Dragoslav Obrenović, or Drago as he was more commonly known, was a cold-blooded butcher; a murderer of such magnitude that the common laws of man could barely accommodate his depravity. In 1994, Radovan Karadžić personally promoted Drago to the rank of brigadier general. Fiercely loyal and answerable only to Karadžić, his šefa and mentor, Drago immediately assumed command of the largest body of ground troops committed to perpetrating the Siege of Sarajevo, a responsibility he retained until the very end of the Bosnian War. He willingly took responsibility for the Srebrenica massacre in July 1995, a genocide on a scale not seen since the Second World War;

more than 8000 Bosniak men and boys were mercilessly exterminated and over 30 000 Bosniak women, children, elderly and infirm forcibly deported.

With the arrest of Karadžić in 2008, Mladić and Hadžić in 2011 and their subsequent detention by the International Criminal Tribunal for the former Yugoslavia in The Hague, Drago then assumed absolute control of the forces remaining loyal to the old Serbian leadership. Now Drago was chief of the darkest arm of the Serbian mafia known only as *Zmajevi*, the Dragons; a name adopted in deference to the paramilitary force who, under Drago's personal direction, carried out some of the most heinous crimes of the war. As their commanding general, Drago was held in such high regard by the *Zmajevi* that he accepted the rare honor they bestowed upon him: to be tattooed with their unit crest, a blood-red dragon, on his left breast – above the heart. Now worn by all members of Drago's immediate circle, the mark of the *Zmajevi* was becoming a much-feared symbol within the European underworld.

Drago's office, the heart of the Dragon empire, was located in the very center of his fortress-villa. It was his bunker, his war room. It was the platform from which he'd wielded his menace under the very noses of the international community and it was absolutely impenetrable. But somehow, in the bosom of all this protection, he felt exposed. Interpol had raised the reward for information leading to his arrest, while Karadžić, Hadžić, Mladić and his old comrade Šerifović were already rotting in the UN detention center in Scheveningen. Now his plan to devastate the ICTY was in jeopardy with this failed attempt against its presiding judge, the American bitch Madeline Clancy. Drago could feel the long arm of the law reaching for his collar. With the reward for his head now sitting at ten million euros, who could he trust?

His piercing gaze turned upon the three men standing in front of him. His loyal and trusted lieutenants. One was his son. No, he had nothing to gain and everything to lose by selling out his father. Drago looked at the other two as a hungry lion looks at a herd of unsuspecting wildebeest. One, no doubt with the support of the other, had showed his true ambition by instigating the attempt on the American woman without approval. The ten million euros Interpol had put on Drago's head was a lot of money. How long would it take before one or both sold him out again? How long before Interpol finally caught up with him because of their direct or indirect actions? Paranoia coursed through his body like molten lava. Coldly, mechanically, he reached to the waistband of his trousers, withdrew an automatic and shot the two men dead.

He dropped the gun on the desk and walked around to his son. His open right hand came up and struck his son across the face with a slap that would have knocked anybody else to the ground. Then, he grabbed his son's face with both hands and held his head steady so that the two of them were just inches apart, each staring intently into the other's eyes.

"My boy," Drago began, "if you want to inherit this from me then you must show me you can keep these fucks under control. Do you understand me?"

"Yes," the son answered, nodding despite his father's vice-like grip.

"Yes, what?" Drago growled. "Yes, *šefa*," he answered.

"That's better," he said, releasing his son's face. He walked back around his desk and sat down. "We have to deal with this quickly before I have half of Interpol crawling up my fucking ass. I want those fucks in The Hague to shit their pants if they dare even mention my name!" Drago spat the words across the room, thumping the desk to underscore his fury. "Where is the Wolf?"

"I don't know, šefa," replied the son honestly. "He is impossible to keep track of lately."

"Well, fuck him. You find him. I want him here; he works for me. Remind him of that if you have to."

"Yes, šefa."

"He told me he was working on a backup plan to get at the American. I want to know what it is. I want some action from the Wolf. No more fucking talk. Get him now and get those two pieces of shit out of here!"

Chapter Seven

THE RED LION, WHITEHALL, LONDON

"We always seem to find our way back here," remarked General Davenport. "Why do you think that is?"

"It's pretty simple, sir," replied Morgan good-humoredly. "We're not office types. Occasionally we need to escape. And the promise of good single malt scotch like this is its own reward."

"Well, there is that, of course," Davenport conceded with a smile. He took another drink, savoring the bite of the liquid as it warmed his chest, casting an appraising eye over his agent. "I must say, my boy, I'm pleased you've finally acquainted yourself with my tailor. You are looking decidedly less scruffy these days."

"Well, I hope you don't expect a thank you for that backhanded compliment," Morgan said with mock indignation and a broad grin. He straightened within his expertly tailored worsted suit of blended gray, complemented by a pristine white shirt, a black tie and a white pocket square folded precisely to provide the merest strip of white across the top of the pocket. All thanks to the impeccable workmanship of Davenport's personal tailor, Somerville & Son, who had rooms just off Savile Row on Conduit Street. "Anyway, it was time for an upgrade."

"Mr Somerville has done an outstanding job. It's important to look the part as much as be the part in this game, Alex. Where I'm likely sending you in coming weeks, I can't have you turning up looking like a bloody drifter."

They laughed. Morgan was happy to acknowledge his previous "comfortable" standard of dress, as the general once referred to it, and while he still preferred jeans and sports coats when off the clock, he had begun to enjoy his new bespoke wardrobe.

"What do you have in mind for me next, then, sir?" Morgan asked, reaching for his scotch. He had only recently returned from delivering Šerifović into the custody of the ICTY. But Morgan already knew that the attempted assassination in Seattle overnight of an ICTY judge would have a direct implication on his next assignment.

"I want you to stay with the Serbs. I'm scheduled to attend a meeting in New York tomorrow with Interpol, and I'd like you to join me," Davenport replied dryly.

"Of course," Morgan replied. "Anything specific?"

"This attempt on Judge Clancy, the presiding judge of the ICTY, was obviously a move to derail the tribunal and Interpol's investigations into the last remaining fugitives of the Balkans War Crimes indictments. I've arranged for her to join us in New York. I'd like to get as much detail as possible on exactly why these ICTY judges have been sent into hiding."

"I heard all the judges had been sent off on indefinite leave; something to do with threats the tribunal had received, targeting them specifically. Is that right?" Morgan asked.

"Yes," replied Davenport gravely. "The threats implied an attack upon the judges while in session at the tribunal in The Hague. The decision was made to close the court under the pretense of technical difficulties with equipment, and the judges were all given an indefinite leave of absence. They opted to return discreetly to their private residences until the all-clear was given. Madam Clancy returned home to Seattle."

"So, what have they done with the others now? Have they all been recalled to The Hague?"

"Not yet." Davenport looked genuinely concerned. "I imagine the tribunal's chief of security will be attempting to make contact with them all and Interpol will be making arrangements with police in the various countries to provide additional protection while they are at their homes. But short of just locking them all away, the best solution has yet to present itself."

"Which way do you think they'll go?" Morgan asked.

"I think they'll upgrade security arrangements at court and at the judges' residences back in The Hague. Meanwhile, they have little alternative but to allow them all to remain at home – under strict security, of course – until arrangements in The Hague have been finalized."

"Makes sense," Morgan said. "I guess that means we need to leave it in the hands of tribunal security and Interpol for now. In the meantime, where do you want me?" He took a drink.

"Making a hit on an ICTY judge near her private residence sends a message. It says: We can get you, wherever you are. It scares the hell out of witnesses preparing to give evidence before the tribunal and it strikes the fear of God into the remaining judges. But you don't arrange a hit like that without a reason."

"Drago getting nervous?" Morgan suggested.

"Precisely, which is exactly why the chief prosecutor of the tribunal and Interpol's secretary general are adamant that the investigations and ongoing hearings must get back on track as soon as possible." Davenport took a drink. "We have Karadžić, Hadžić, Mladić and now, thanks to you, that other delightful creature, Milivoj Šerifović. We're closer than we've ever been to finding Drago's exact whereabouts. So, I need you to familiarize yourself with him, Alex. You have to get to know everything there is to know about this man. Because, when the time comes, there won't be any margin for error."

"I'm across his background, sir," Morgan replied. "Drago is the subject of an Interpol Red Notice and he's the last remaining fugitive of the 160 or so indicted by the tribunal since 1993. Interpol suggests he's been able to elude capture for so long by operating under the protection of the Serbian criminal grid and there's strong intelligence indicating that he heads an arm of the Serbian mafia made up exclusively of former members of the security forces who operated under his command during the Balkans War."

Davenport nodded. "The assassination attempt on Madeline Clancy was undoubtedly on Drago's orders. The fact that it occurred at the very time you were arresting Šerifović is of interest, though. The would-be assassins could not have known we were moving on Šerifović."

"Perhaps Drago's intelligence was a bit off," Morgan surmised. Davenport raised his eyebrows. "Well, it's possible his network reported that Interpol was closing in," Morgan continued. "Thinking it was him they were closing in on, Drago takes immediate pre-emptive action against the tribunal; sending in people to kill one of the judges. But in reality it was Šerifović we were arresting, not Drago Obrenović."

Davenport nodded his agreement and both men fell silent for a moment, drinking and considering the possibilities.

"According to Interpol Belgrade, Drago wouldn't risk exposure under any circumstances, not even for one of his most trusted comrades. Which suggests that he was not actively communicating with Šerifović," said Davenport. "If he had been, he would have warned Šerifović that Interpol was closing in. Šerifović would have been prepared."

"Šerifović wasn't prepared," said Morgan. "Although that big bastard, Zupan, certainly gave me a run for my money. I could really have used our new guy. What's his name? The German."

"Braunschweiger. Austrian, actually. Hermann Braunschweiger; built like a tank," Davenport replied. "You know, they had a nickname for him in the GSG 9. They called him *Der Schlüssel*."

Morgan's quizzical expression asked the question.

"It means 'the key.' Considering the man's size, it's a rather delicate nickname, don't you think? Some eccentric Germanic humor, no doubt, but according to the head of GSG 9, if they needed to get into anywhere, he could open the door simply by putting his shoulder to it. Hence, the key." They both smiled at the idea. "But, all that aside for now, you can see why I've had to keep our involvement strictly out of the mainstream," he said. "I know it limited your backup options, Alex. But the mere suggestion that Drago is able to gather intelligence on the progress of Interpol investigations is enough to warrant my precautions."

"I understand, sir." Morgan trusted the general's judgment completely, despite certain implications in the field. But more than that, he could see that there was something else troubling his chief. He allowed Davenport to gather his thoughts.

"The attempt on the ICTY judge was a warning. That's obvious," Davenport stated. "And we know that the arrest of Šerifović will send Drago into survival overdrive. He'll be looking at any means possible, whatever it takes, to keep himself clear of authorities and prolong his freedom."

"So, you're expecting him to ramp up his counteroffensive."

"I have no doubt of it," Davenport replied. "But are we thinking about this coldly and objectively, or are we allowing Drago's obvious counteroffensive strategy to limit our consideration?"

"You think we're being played?" Morgan asked.

Davenport took a long pull at his scotch and leant heavily against the wide ledge directly beneath Lord Stanley's portrait. He remained silent for a while, absently stroking his beard, the lines of his face set deep in contemplation. Morgan respected the general's silence and, easing his way through the rest of his own scotch, watched the traffic going past on Whitehall.

"The more I think about these recent successes – Mladić, Hadžić and Šerifović – the more I am drawn back to the common denominator in all of them."

"The informant?"

"Precisely, my boy," Davenport replied emphatically. "Precisely. The informant."

Chapter Eight

BORDEAUX, SOUTH-WESTERN FRANCE

La belle au bois dormant, the sleeping beauty! Guillaume René de Villepin loved this graceful city, his home that lay serenely upon the banks of the Garonne. Her history could be traced for millennia and, for those who elected to pay no heed to the centuries of bloodshed or even the discovery of Neanderthal remains at Pair-non-Pair, it was a history written exclusively in commerce, culture and the arts. Her streets and architecture, Place de la Bourse, Rue Ausone, Cathédrale Saint-André, all conjured so many memories. And, of course, the wines. The wines! A quarter of a million acres of the world's finest grapes grew here. How he loved to come home. It was his life, his sanctuary. His heart resided here. Here he was a citizen. Here he was anonymous. Here he could be himself with none of the responsibilities, scrutiny or stresses of his real life – his life under the spotlight in The Hague.

Guillaume, or simply Guy to those who were close enough to be invited to call him that, walked briskly but relaxedly along the Rue Sainte-Catherine in search of coffee. The de Villepin family had lived in the Aquitaine region for many centuries and if truth be known, there was a time when the Bordeaux de Villepins were considered noblesse de chancellerie, landed gentry, much favored by royalty. Of course, La Révolution française had changed all that.

Soaking up the beauty and promise of his homeland, Guy de Villepin took a seat on a rickety metal chair and rested his arm on an equally rickety metal table just outside the entrance of his favorite café. He ordered coffee and, with little genuine interest, thumbed through a copy of *Le Figaro* that had been left on a seat nearby. From here he could watch the world go by, basking in the peaceful enjoyment of his brief leave of absence. *Liberté!*

Despite the joy he felt at being back in Bordeaux, de Villepin could not help but turn his mind to what he had left behind. To be so threatened – with death – and to constantly live under its power and menace was taking its toll. Not only upon him but also upon his colleagues. The work was so important and to consider the possibility that these threats could be realized made him cold to the bone. Theirs was much more than a mere job of work. It was a vocation. He, like his colleagues, was committed. He had sworn an oath to carry out his duty and now he'd been forced to flee. He and the others had been ordered into hiding, scurrying like frightened mice. How could this be happening? He suddenly felt ashamed that he had acquiesced to the decision. Still, he was here now and nobody knew him.

Further along Rue Sainte-Catherine, a man – tall, dark, with striking good looks and impeccable dress sense – stood quietly examining a shop front. There was nothing particularly out of place in either where he was standing or what he was doing. A dozen other men could easily be observed striking similar poses in both directions, perusing the various stores of the famous shopping strip. What was not obvious was that this man was watching a reflection. The reflection he was watching was that of Guy de Villepin.

The man at the window casually reached into the pocket of his designer jeans and extracted an iPhone. He tapped the screen and placed the phone to his ear. He made a play of speaking as if to a wife or girlfriend, seemingly describing items he was looking at in the window. In fact he was providing the listener with a very different description in fluent French.

"It's him. He's on his own, sitting right in front of the café diagonally opposite me. He's about sixty. Medium height. Skinny. Gray hair, well groomed. He's wearing a light overcoat with a red scarf, dark pants and black boots. Good-quality stuff, not cheap shit. Walks quickly but with a bit of a shuffle. He's wearing glasses. He needs them to read but not for walking around. Can you see him? Right, get as many pictures as you can and stay on him. I need to pull back, I've been on him for too long already. Now that you know what he looks like, don't fucking lose him. Report back to me as soon as you have him returning to his home and stay there until I reach you. Got it? Good."

The phone was returned to his pocket and the dark figure disappeared into the milieu.

Chapter Nine

OFFICE OF THE SPECIAL REPRESENTATIVE OF INTERPOL TO THE UNITED NATIONS, MANHATTAN, NEW YORK, USA

Brett Tappin, assistant director responsible for the Judicial Security Division of the United States Marshals Service, wasn't happy about the meeting, but he had no choice. The director wanted him there, and when she said jump, everyone in the Service knew better than to ask "How high?"; they just jumped as high as they could first time and hoped it was enough.

Tappin, with elbows on the arms of his chair and chin resting atop steepled fingers, surveyed the others around the table with a marksman's critical eye. A former Marine sniper with service in the first Gulf War, Tappin had been with the Marshals Service, the USMS, for twenty years.

His attention was drawn to the man closest to him. He was younger than all of them, Tappin observed, about thirty-five and, by the look of him, extremely fit. He had dark hair, cut short and neat, a tanned complexion, and looked like he weighed about 200 pounds. The young bastard exuded health and vitality along with that particular quality that can't be faked: a comfortable indifference to danger; it was written all over him. Tappin could spot it because he'd been exactly the same, back in the day. The guy was a gunslinger, no doubt about it.

As the meeting was getting under way, Tappin's attention turned to the head of the large oval-shaped conference table where the meeting's chair, Peter Vallincourt, was going through the usual round of introductions and pleasantries. Vallincourt, special representative of Interpol to the United Nations, was exactly what you'd expect of a former NYPD commissioner: tall, broad-chested, with a thick, walrus-like moustache, boxer's nose and eyes that sat like telescopes beneath a heavy, determined brow. He'd been around a long time and was renowned among senior figures in the US law enforcement fraternity as a total old-school hard-ass. He was the host of the meeting and this was his turf.

To the left of Vallincourt was Madeline Clancy, presiding judge at the International Criminal Tribunal for the former Yugoslavia. Tappin placed her in her mid-fifties. She was tall, slender and elegant, in contrast to her business suit, which was dark gray and masculine, with a fine pinstripe. She had light brown hair with a reddish tinge, worn in a neat bob. Judge Clancy was the reason they were all there.

As the discussion began, Tappin continued his scan of participants, shifting his focus to the man addressing the judge, FBI Special Agent Pat Ryerson, deputy director of Interpol Washington, or more formally, the US National Central Bureau of Interpol. Ryerson was the senior Homeland Security guy with day-to-day coordination responsibility between Interpol and over 18 000 law enforcement agencies across the United States. If there was any interagency cooperation required, he was the man to make it happen.

"So, Your Honor," Ryerson was saying, "as I see it, you were on your way home and stopped for coffee when these guys made their move. Is that right, ma'am?"

"Yes, Mr Ryerson," Judge Clancy replied. "I had already collected my coffee and was walking back to the car. I know it sounds like a cliché, gentlemen, but it all happened very quickly."

"I understand, judge," said Ryerson. "I noted in your statement to the Seattle PD that you had your personal distress beacon on you at the time."

"I have it attached to my keyring, just as I'd been advised by the police when I returned to Seattle from The Hague. If I'd pressed it any damn harder I think I would have broken my finger." There were smiles around the table.

The fourth person to fall into Tappin's sights was someone he knew only by reputation. Sitting to the right of Vallincourt, he was also tall and solidly built. Late fifties, impeccably dressed, salt-and-pepper hair brushed straight back and beard precisely trimmed. Major General Reginald "Nobby" Davenport, chief of Intrepid. Davenport carried himself in a way Tappin could only put down to absolute, unequivocal self-assuredness. A former British SAS officer injured chasing Scuds across Iraq during Desert Storm. Rumor had it that he led the SAS assault on the Iranian Embassy at Princes Gate in London back in 1980. *Nobby,* he thought. *Where the hell do the Brits come up with these nicknames?*

"Well, it's important that you were carrying it, Madeline," Davenport said, "and that your instincts told you to use it." Tappin noted Davenport's use of the judge's first name. It was familiar, almost intimate, indicating they knew each other well.

"The activated beacon was picked up by Seattle dispatch," Ryerson added. "But it was pure coincidence that there was a squad car so close at the time. I think you know already, judge, that those officers responded to what they saw. If they hadn't been there at that moment … well, I don't mean to belabor the issue."

"I'm absolutely aware of how lucky I was to have those officers nearby, Mr Ryerson. And, of all things, one was the son of one of my oldest friends, no less. Still, what more could I have done?"

"Don't get me wrong, ma'am," said Ryerson. "You did everything that you'd been advised to. And, that's my point. This attempt on you, coming in so close to the arrest of Šerifović and the threats against the tribunal and all, necessitates that we make drastic changes immediately to ensure your safety while you're back home on US soil."

"What do you have in mind, Pat?" asked Vallincourt.

While the general discussion between Vallincourt, Clancy, Davenport and Ryerson continued, Tappin turned his attention back to the last person at the table, the gunslinger. So far, he'd been introduced only as Major Morgan, nothing more. Morgan had arrived with Davenport, quietly taking a seat toward the end of the table, to the right of his chief and left of Tappin. An Intrepid agent? Had to be.

Tappin had only heard conjecture about this new covert arm of Interpol; in fact most of the anecdotal intelligence getting around on the law enforcement grapevine was all rumor and speculation. Some kind of black ops outfit, apparently – the existence of Intrepid had never been officially, or unofficially, confirmed by Interpol and there was no evidence of it on any reports or documentation that he could find. As a professional courtesy ahead of this meeting, Vallincourt had given Tappin and Ryerson the most cursory overview of Davenport's role within Interpol, but nothing more. As Tappin's eyes came back around to survey Morgan, he realized that the Intrepid agent had been watching him the entire time. When Tappin saw he'd been caught out, Morgan simply gave him a knowing nod, as if to say, *I know what you're doing.* But there was more to it than that. The look also said, *Don't worry. I've been doing exactly the same thing.*

"So, I'm very interested to know what the United States Marshals Service has in mind." The voice that broke in on Tappin's thoughts belonged to Davenport. "Mr Tappin?"

"Ah, well, general," he began slowly, catching up on the threads of the conversation he'd been monitoring. "With respect to everybody present, we normally do things our way, you know. We're not keen on a committee-style approach to making these kinds of arrangements. It makes things complicated and when we have too many chiefs – well, things get missed, big holes start appearing in the plan and things go pear-shaped real quick. My director asked that I put that on the table from the get-go."

"I couldn't agree more, Mr Tappin," said Davenport diplomatically.

"What do you have in mind, marshal?" asked Vallincourt bluntly, not wanting to get bogged in a jurisdictional pissing competition.

"OK." Tappin shifted in his seat. "We'll be providing rotating teams of US marshals for round-the-clock protection of the judge." Turning to Madeline Clancy, he said, "That'll include whenever you're at your residence, ma'am, away from the residence, or when you're in transit to or from the residence, even if you're only going for coffee, until you're required back in The Hague. As far as I can gather, we're talking about a month or so. We currently have a team of technical specialists on standby in Sunset Hill, ready to install a new home security and duress system that will be patched directly through to our field office in Seattle. And as soon as you arrive on the ground at Sea-Tac Airport, the senior US marshal responsible for coordinating the protection details will be there with her team to meet you."

"I'm really very grateful, Mr Tappin," said Madeline Clancy. "I'm just sorry to be such a bother to everybody."

"This is what we do, Your Honor," replied Tappin. "The marshals will collect you and your luggage and will drive you home from the airport. It's about a forty-minute drive from Sea-Tac to your home, so you'll have ample time to get acquainted and to go over all the details."

"I very much appreciate you all allowing us to be involved, particularly the US Marshals Service, Mr Tappin," Davenport said. "I have absolutely no intention of stepping on anyone's toes, and I offer my full support for the protection strategy you've just described. With that in mind, I would like to take a moment to clarify our involvement."

Davenport received a number of nodded responses of agreement. "We will remain at arm's length, nothing more than observers. But we will be looking with great interest for any opportunities that Dragoslav Obrenović or his confederates may present. It's clear that he is feeling uncomfortable as a result of the endeavors of our colleagues at Interpol and through the excellent work of the tribunal." He nodded respectfully to both Vallincourt and Clancy. "And should his discomfiture cause Drago to act in such a way as to present us with an opportunity, our involvement will immediately move from the sidelines to the playing field. My intention will be to insert Major Morgan here at the appropriate juncture to exploit those opportunities and apply pressure to best effect. Madeline, one final thought has occurred to me. Perhaps we could discuss your daughter?"

Chapter Ten

SAINT SEURIN-FONDAUDÈGE, BORDEAUX

Guy de Villepin's home away from home, *un second chez-soi*, was a luxurious, very private apartment housed within what had once been a magnificent eighteenth-century mansion. He had owned the apartment for many years and when he'd finally grown tired of its aging décor, he'd decided to have it completely renovated. Gone were the dreary wallpapers and brocade curtains that had hung too many years beyond their useful life. The dark, dank carpets were also gone along with most of the old furniture. He had kept a few favorite pieces for nostalgia's sake. For the rest, there were just far too many memories, too much sentimental clutter to constantly remind him of the highs and lows, the joy and the pain of his solitary journey through these many years. Now, as he pottered about preparing an early meal for one – lamenting the failure of the building superintendent to respond to his calls to attend to a broken electrical socket in the kitchen – he delighted in the quiet simplicity of the contemporary, minimalist design he had selected and the sense of calm and contentment he felt when he returned to it.

De Villepin strode purposefully into his living room then – drawn by some recollection – went instead to his bedroom, rummaged through his travel bags and returned to the living room with a compact disc. It was a gift from a colleague: *So proud of my little girl. Enjoy during our enforced sabbatical! Madeline x*, an attached note read. He smiled and took a moment to examine the small square cover and the face of a beautiful young woman sitting at a grand piano. Her hair, the most vibrant copper-red, was tied back from her face in a very regal way, yet had been allowed to cascade in a firestorm of wild curls and waves, just visible behind the exquisite line of her bare shoulders. Her skin was almost pure white, her eyes – deep and soulful – sky blue above pouting lips, full and wide and even redder than her hair. The style was old Hollywood and she captured it perfectly. *Pommettes charmantes*, he thought.

He placed the CD into the player and to the enchantment of the opening bars of Debussy's "Clair de lune", he wandered back to the kitchen to continue his meal preparation.

At the rear of de Villepin's apartment building, four stories down, was a small private courtyard. It was for the exclusive use of apartment owners. Of course, while the ornate, refurbished, eighteenth-century surrounding wall, guarded by clusters of maple and chestnut trees, would serve to deter the mostly well-to-do, law-abiding folk of the immediate environs, it presented anything but an obstacle to a man known in certain circles only as the Wolf.

Enhancing his deception by using a dark corner, the shadowy figure had scaled the wall and, extracting a paperback from his coat pocket, immediately affected a casual reading pose upon a mold-stained stone bench that had sat beneath a Persian walnut tree for over a hundred years. He waited there a few moments until he heard a middle-aged couple, a man and woman, returning from their evening ritual – walking their pet Shih Tzu. He'd been watching the building for over a week and had noted the strict routine of this pair and their pampered pooch. He had timed his incursion precisely to coincide with their return. As he listened carefully to the keys rattling in the lock of the external gate that accessed the courtyard from the street behind the building, he made a small pantomime of finishing his reading and blowing his nose loudly into a handkerchief; to all intents and purposes, readying himself to return inside. Seconds later the couple and their dog were scurrying past, oblivious to his presence. The keys rattled again, this time in the doorway that led into the apartment building, and with a general flurry of polite monosyllables, charm and smiles, he bundled in behind them as if he too belonged, and made for the stairs while they chose the elevator. They of course thought nothing of it. After all, only those who lived in the building were allowed within the courtyard.

Upstairs, blissfully unaware that an intruder had gained access to the building, Guy de Villepin was finally laying the table, preparing to serve his meal for one. From the CD, "Clair de lune" had concluded and Liebestraum No. 3 by Franz Liszt gently eased into the quiet, unassuming space of the apartment. He fussed over the setting of his table as was his custom, and selected a moderately aged red wine. Satisfied that everything was just as it should be, Guy returned to the kitchen to retrieve his meal.

There came three harsh raps on the entrance door of the apartment.

C'est curieux, he thought, momentarily startled. Normally, it would be a buzz from downstairs at the building's entrance foyer rather than a knock directly upon his door. Who on earth could it be? Then, with relief, he realized: *Ah, le surintendant!*

"*Un moment!*" he cried as he bustled toward the door, drying his hands on a kitchen towel.

When he opened the door de Villepin was in mid-sentence, somewhere between commending and condemning the building superintendent for finally giving his attention to the faulty electrical switch. But it was not the superintendent and it took de Villepin only a second to realize his mistake. "No!" he exclaimed. The silenced automatic fired once and a single round penetrated de Villepin's chest directly through the heart, killing him instantly. The moment the dead man began to fall, the Wolf stepped across the threshold of the apartment and caught him easily behind the back of the neck, controlling the fall of the body and easing it to the floor without a sound. Without fuss, he quickly dragged the body clear of the entrance and closed the door. Leaving the body as it lay, he strolled unhurriedly into the kitchen, found the meal de Villepin had prepared and took it to the table.

Chapter Eleven

CARNEGIE HALL, NEW YORK

The applause of the crowd erupted as Charlotte-Rose returned to the stage. Intermission was over, the second half was due to commence and the crowd of almost 3000 that filled Carnegie Hall's Isaac Stern Auditorium were in the palm of her hand. Across each of the five levels of the main hall, people were on their feet, clapping, stamping, whistling, crying out for more, hoping, praying that she might look their way. To leave with just a smile from her would mean everything and there wasn't a person in the hall who didn't feel the same way.

To her legions of fans, the woman on stage was a goddess. Curvaceous and fair-skinned with a mane of fiery red curls that fell to her waist, she was every bit the superstar, renowned for an ethereal quality beyond the reach of mere mortals. Women's magazines the world over adored her and she enjoyed a level of celebrity normally reserved for the Hollywood – or reality television – elite. But she was neither of those things.

Charlotte-Rose Fleming was one of the finest classical

pianists of her time. Performing under the name Charlotte-Rose, she emerged as an overnight sensation – despite seven years on the international classical music circuit and three platinum-selling albums – when her guest appearance at the BBC Proms, including performances of Chopin's Ballade No. 1 in G minor and Rachmaninov's Piano Concerto No. 3, catapulted her into the mainstream media. International stardom inevitably followed.

Standing regally beside her piano upon the Ronald O. Perelman Stage, with a smile that reached the back rows of the fifth-level balcony, Charlotte-Rose turned from her adoring fans and sat down to face the keyboard. Obediently the crowd fell silent and the lights of the main hall into total darkness. Everything remained so for almost thirty seconds and then, as an eerie expectancy embraced the room, a golden shimmer appeared to emanate from the stage like those very first tentative rays of the dawn. The soft lighting captured the spellbound audience and, as the gentle hue gathered and withdrew across the stage, only a single beam of light remained, focusing their attention perfectly upon their princess. With hands outstretched to either end of the keyboard, she began with one solid strike at the notes, launching straight into one of her personal favorites and a popular hit with the crowd, the Toccata in E flat minor by Armenian composer Aram Khachaturian.

Her mastery of the instrument was indisputable, showcased via a repertoire only the finest players at the absolute pinnacle of their careers could ever attempt. But it was the showmanship, a combination of unbridled energy, passion, humor and seduction, that beguiled her audiences. The atmosphere and physicality of her performances were more akin to a rock concert than a classical music recital. During some of her most demanding pieces when her technical prowess was in full flight, she could captivate an already mesmerized crowd with a private smile or wickedly seductive laugh, just as she could bring them to their feet with her head thrown back, red hair whipping about her face and eyes to the ceiling in raptures of unadulterated classical ecstasy. Despite the fact that, to date, her repertoire had contained nothing but strictly classical pieces, her popularity with non-classical audiences had critics claiming her to be the most influential crossover artist ever.

Leaving Khachaturian and giving her audience no chance to recover their composure, Charlotte-Rose moved effortlessly into *Un Sospiro* by Liszt. Meanwhile, behind her in the wings, her devoted assistant, Daniel, was being beckoned into the shadows by a tall, handsome, elegantly dressed man of about forty, holding an enormous bouquet of red roses. Dutifully, Daniel responded.

"I take it these aren't for me," noted Daniel, coyly engaging the stranger.

"I'm afraid not," the man said with a smile, his voice deep and smooth. "But I would be very grateful if you would ensure that she gets these the moment she leaves the stage at the end of her performance. She'll be expecting … well, she is expecting something, from me."

"So, you're the mystery man Charly's been keeping under wraps," said Daniel. "I can see why. Don't worry, Romeo, I'll see that she gets them."

"The moment she leaves the stage," the man said firmly, although the charm made the order feel more like a request. "Especially the note. It's really very important."

"Honey, I'll give them to her personally. And, who shall I say they're from?"

"She'll know," he replied and vanished.

A hopeless snoop, but justifying it as a result of being

utterly protective of his girl, Daniel couldn't resist the temptation. There was something about this latest suitor that just didn't add up. For somebody chasing an international superstar he was far too circumspect. Laying the bouquet down on a packing crate, Daniel gently removed the card from the envelope pinned to the clear plastic wrapping. With a little guilt he looked back out to the stage and watched Charlotte-Rose for a while, then turned his attention to its message. In a somewhat messy hand, it read: *Meet you at the helipad at midnight. Don't be late. Paradise awaits! Raoul x*

Chapter Twelve

OFFICE OF THE SPECIAL REPRESENTATIVE OF INTERPOL TO THE UNITED NATIONS, NEW YORK

Pat Ryerson, deputy director of Interpol Washington, led a slightly built, emaciated, nervous-looking man into a private room at the very back of the suite that comprised the Office of the Special Representative.

The man was in his mid-forties. He had greasy, shoulder length dark hair parted on the left and combed over lazily so that it sat in bedraggled curtains on either side of a narrow, rat-like face. The brown eyes were shifty, constantly moving and floating in deep gray craters upon a marginally less gray landscape. His patchy red and brown beard was really no more than a collection of haphazard tufts resulting from a weekly, sometimes only a fortnightly, shave. His teeth were yellowed and his breath sour from far too many cigarettes. His clothes – leather jacket, shirt, jeans and boots – were black and grungy.

The room was plain and not particularly noteworthy. It contained some chairs and a table with a telephone. It was just like any other corporate interview room in any other first-world high-rise building. Although this one had spectacular views across the East River.

Ryerson brought the man to the table and sat him down with sufficient courtesy to warrant a thank you, which he received. Across the table sat Brett Tappin. On the far side of the room, leaning against the wall to Tappin's left, stood Alex Morgan.

"Gentlemen, allow me to introduce Đurađ Lazarević," Ryerson announced before joining Tappin at the table.

"Good afternoon," said Lazarević stiffly.

"Good afternoon, Mr Lazarević," Tappin replied. "I'm Assistant Director Brett Tappin of the United States Marshals Service." Lazarević nodded in response and then looked to his right toward Morgan, awaiting an introduction. "You don't have to know who he is, Mr Lazarević," said Tappin.

The tone was set. Lazarević had sat through many similar interviews before. He was prepared. Being an Interpol informant, and the man responsible for leading investigators to Šerifović and the others, he was routinely lifted and brought in for questioning. The Hague, Lyon, New York; he was used to it. It was expected. The way he figured it, there were a lot worse things than flying around the world under a new identity, protected by Interpol. It was also the best and possibly only chance he had of survival. Because he knew that if he ever put a foot wrong or if his past caught up with him, his death would be an extremely slow and painful one. Besides, his cut of the reward made it all worthwhile.

"Now, you gotta forgive me, Mr Lazarević," Tappin began. "I'm kinda the new boy here, you know? I've come into the game a little late in the play."

"I understand," Lazarević replied. "How can I help?"

"Well, to start with, I'm very interested in how you came to be this special informant for Interpol. I hear you've helped our friends a whole bunch; I mean, a couple of your big kahunas from the old country are now cooling their heels in Scheveningen, thanks to you."

Lazarević looked quizzically from Tappin to Ryerson, even across to Morgan. He said, "I'm not sure what you mean, Mr Tappin. What are you asking of me?"

"What I'm asking, Đurađ, is what brought you in from the cold all of a sudden? The war's been over for almost twenty years; not quite, but close enough. You've had plenty of opportunity to come forward with information before. Why now?"

"Five million euros is a great incentive in anyone's language," Lazarević began. He was suddenly uncomfortable. "Where I come from, where I live now in Albania, we do not enjoy the freedom of choice that you all take for granted. These men are butchers, Mr Tappin. I've lived under their shadow before, during and since the war. I always wanted to speak up but I knew if I did, I would be cut down; if not immediately, then someday. I would be looking over my shoulder forever, knowing that any day, any moment could be my last. Even when the reward is made available to me, I will be a marked man for the rest of my days."

"Yes, that's right. I heard that the money hasn't been given to you yet," Tappin stated with a deliberately skeptical tone designed to unsettle Lazarević. "Interesting."

"I am told it will be soon, now that Šerifović is in custody." Lazarević looked up at Morgan, who he assumed was in charge, for reassurance. He didn't get it. "Is there now some problem?"

"Mr Lazarević, we believe you can continue to be of

assistance to us," said Ryerson. An old pro, his manner was deadpan, giving nothing away. "We have a number of scared judges, one of whom has been personally targeted. To protect them, we need to understand the mentality of the people we're up against and you're our best shot. I mean, who better than the guy who led us to the worst of them, right?"

Lazarević was sweating. He shifted nervously in his chair, brown eyes bouncing from side to side in their dark craters. This interview was nothing like the others. He'd been treated like royalty when he first came forward with information back in Tirana. They'd lapped it up. But now he didn't know if he was a guest at the banquet or the fatted calf. He ran cigarette-stained fingers through his greasy hair.

"I've been nothing but cooperative. You ask the Interpol man in Tirana, Lorenc Gjoka. He's my case officer; he'll vouch for me."

"Hey, now, take it easy there, sport," Tappin said with a broad smile. "We know you've been hiding out in Albania since the Balkans War – can't say I blame you for that; and, we also know that you voluntarily met with the Interpol guys there. So, yeah, we'll check in with your case officer, this Mr Gjoka. Nobody's suggesting anything untoward. In fact, it's the exact opposite. Isn't that right, Pat?"

"Sure. We'd just like to impose on you one last time, so we can really make sure we're looking after these judges. That sound OK?" asked Ryerson. Ryerson had met Lorenc Gjoka once in Lyon, long before Lazarević had come forward as an informant. He didn't like him.

"Yes. Yes, of course," Lazarević replied cautiously. "Anything. Just ask me."

"Well, let's start with something easy." Tappin gave the

impression they were just a bunch of guys sitting around talking about baseball or football with his easy manner. He was just warming up. "We'd like to start with anything you know about any folks here in the US who may be sympathetic to—"

There was a loud knock on the door, it opened and a young woman, one of the Interpol staff, appeared. She excused herself and gestured for Ryerson to join her. Pat Ryerson was immediately on his feet and disappeared into the corridor, closing the door behind him. There was silence for a few moments before he returned. The door remained open.

"Mr Lazarević," Ryerson said, "my colleague here is going to escort you to another room. I'd appreciate it if you'd wait there until I collect you. This will only take a moment."

The young woman was at the door again and ushered Lazarević outside in silence. Ryerson closed the door and came back. He sat heavily upon the edge of the table. His face was grave.

"What the fuck's going on, Pat?" asked Tappin.

"There's been a hit on one of the other judges," Ryerson said. "This one was successful."

"Who was it?" Morgan said.

"Judge Guillaume René de Villepin. Happened at his home in Bordeaux last night. Wasn't discovered until this morning. Building superintendent called it in."

"Jesus!" exclaimed Tappin. "How?"

"Bullet straight through the heart as he answered his front door," Ryerson replied. Then he turned to Morgan. "Alex, I don't really know what it is you guys do, but your boss wants you, son. Pronto. He's in Vallincourt's office. You're to go straight in."

PART II
Dead or Alive

Chapter Thirteen

THE YACHT FLORENCE, THE MEDITERRANEAN

The yacht swam upon the crystalline waters of the Mediterranean, rolling gently on the waves as sea breezes kissed her decks with secret whispers of ancient history. She sat five nautical miles off the east coast of Malta, due south of Sicily, along the maritime route between Valletta and Catania, her last port of call.

The significance of the island's strategic position in the center of the Mediterranean had seen Malta be a much sought-after prize throughout all the great empires, from the Phoenicians to the British, for literally thousands of years. While that was still true to some extent, its significance today as a staging point into southern Europe was equally as important to those who exploited its location for other reasons, human trafficking being the most prevalent.

Of course, those sorts of considerations were not an issue for the guests aboard the *Florence*

"I can't believe I ever let you talk me into this, you know," Charly said in her soft, playful, educated American accent. "I mean, seriously, we're still just getting to know each other and I'm not someone given to flights of fancy. You're very persuasive." She leant her body back provocatively from the upper-deck dining table, reclining so that her magnificent curves gave their best effect upon the broad gold and white stripes of the bench seat.

"I am ... enchanted by you," Raoul replied, openly admiring her. "How could I not wish to lavish you with luxury?"

"Well, it certainly is beautiful here. Still, why I allowed you to whisk me away from New York like that; flying me off to Rome, then Catalina, then this ..." She smiled at him, casting her eyes out across the deep blue waters twinkling under a perfect sun. "It's been an amazing week already, Raoul. I just want to thank you for taking things slowly."

"We have as much or as little time as you like, my dear," he said. "Who knows, you may even grow to like me along the way." Again, the dazzling smile. "It is my pleasure to share time with you, Charly, away from all the madness that follows, it seems, wherever you go."

"Chaos, more like." She took another sip of the exquisite champagne, chilled to perfection, while the remnants of their lunch were being cleared away by a member of the kitchen crew.

Charly gazed across into Raoul's ice-gray eyes, contemplating how she'd allowed this stranger to entice her away like this. She had never been so calculatingly seduced, which she put down to him being older than any other man she'd dated. But the invitation had been too good to refuse; the promise of escape was intoxicating and any time away from the media spotlight was good for her. Besides, that last night at Carnegie Hall had been the final night of the tour and she now had two blissful months before she needed to be anywhere. And he was starting to grow on her, just a little.

"I must go and enjoy this magnificent sunshine before Malta's spring chill finds me again."

"A splendid idea, Charly," he said, his silky smooth tone looping its way around her willpower.

"Join me, and you can slip out of that shirt so I can get a proper look at you," said Charly mischievously. "You're so modest."

"I'll be down soon," he said. "I'll keep an eye on you from here."

"Have it your way," Charly replied, feigning hurt feelings. "Don't let me get too lonely down there. I may need to ask one of the crew to rub lotion on me."

Charly slid from the bench and moved over to him. She ran her slender fingers over his shoulders and through his hair as he sat obediently, looking up into her eyes. Slowly, gently, with the promise of more to come, she kissed him on the mouth. He started to respond but then she broke away. Unpretentiously, she dropped her flowing Crystal Jin cover up to the floor beside his chair, then holding his gaze, excused herself and left the upper deck with its spectacular 360-degree views of the Mediterranean.

She made her way to the forward deck where an area had been prepared especially for her to relax while avoiding the damaging effects of the sun. Deliberately exposing herself to the risk of skin cancer was something Charly was just not prepared to do, but that didn't mean she couldn't still enjoy a little paradise.

She wore a black Cia Maritima two-piece that complemented her full curves. The pitch of the costume sat in stark contrast upon the incredible contours of her fair skin and against the volcanic effect of her lustrous red hair. Charlotte-Rose moved toward the Bedouin-like pavilion arrangement on the foredeck, complete with flanks of billowing lawn and a bed of sumptuous cushions. She conjured 1950s movie star glamor with every step and unaffected gesture.

Every crew member within view craned to watch.

Chapter Fourteen

Two miles south of the *Florence*, a large Zodiac rigid-hulled inflatable boat, powered by a 165-horsepower MerCruiser engine, was moving in fast from the direction of Marsaskala. At the wheel a man dressed in the navy blue uniform, baseball cap and orange life vest of the Malta Police Force Maritime Patrol was clearly visible. He was armed and focused intently upon the *Florence*.

The conditions were perfect. The sea was still, visibility clear and the only merchant shipping in the area was far enough away to be beyond the range of the naked eye.

Charly lounged on the cushions, a sea breeze running gently across her skin. She looked up at Raoul with a smile as he watched lasciviously from the dining deck. She allowed herself to be immersed in the trinkets of rising celebrity: the luxurious yacht; the hot, breezy Mediterranean; and, of course, the swarthy European millionaire wrapped around her little finger.

With a movement that said, "You'll just have to wait until I'm ready," the world-famous classical pianist nestled upon the soft carpet of cushions and allowed the calming roll of the sea to carry her off into a blissful daydream.

Aboard the Zodiac, a black tarpaulin was thrown back to reveal four heavily armed men crouching low behind the rounded flanks of the vessel. Unlike the policeman at the helm, they were dressed in scruffy, rag-tag clothes, with long hair and beards, brandishing an assortment of weapons from Kalashnikov assault rifles to FN Herstal shotguns to Makarov pistols. The Zodiac was now 100 yards from the *Florence*; close enough for the four hostile silhouettes to be seen from the mega-yacht.

"Everybody get below decks, right fucking now!"

The voice, full of tension and insistence, roused Charly like a slap to the face.

Wrenched from siesta, she awoke to the terrifying sight of a man brandishing a large gun on the decks above her, yelling at those aboard to get below. Charly sat bolt upright, heart racing furiously beneath her breast.

Get below? Why? What was happening? Who was he?

She tried to call out in distress, but couldn't make a sound. Her eyes darted left and right, searching anxiously through the billowing white curtains for the source of the turmoil. She reached for her cover up but realized she didn't have it. She could only hear the voices of the crew yelling and the unmistakable voice of the man with the gun barking at everybody. Why had nobody come for her? Where was Raoul? Through the noise on board and the frightened volume of her own breathing, Charly heard the sound of an approaching engine. She grabbed a large towel and wrapped it defensively around her vulnerable, near-naked body. She rushed from the marquee, calling for Raoul, calling for somebody, *anybody* to come for her, to tell her what was happening, to protect her.

"What's going on?" she yelled. But now there was no one to answer her call; no one at all.

A long burst of automatic gunfire erupted from the stern. Charly screamed. There was more, this time from the port side. There came another loud burst, and another. Within seconds an exchange was underway between security men onboard the *Florence* and the ragged figures aboard the rapidly approaching Zodiac.

Oh my God! Charly fell to the deck in fetal-like self-preservation. Gingerly, she inched to the edge of the deck and peered out. Down the port side toward the stern, the Zodiac was powering across the dead-calm sea toward the *Florence*. A security man, who Charly now recognized to be the same man with the gun who'd been yelling at everybody to get below, was at the stern of the yacht shooting ferociously at the Zodiac. With every deafening staccato burst, Charly's heart skipped and her knuckles clenched, but she could not avert her eyes from the mayhem. *This is not happening*, she thought. *This is not happening!*

As another hail of bullets exploded close by, she saw him beneath her, on the portside. Raoul had a gun and was shooting at the Zodiac. Overwhelmed, Charly staggered to her knees and then to her feet, on the verge of shocked collapse, grasping for rails, anything, to steady her as she looked frantically for shelter.

The Zodiac was closing fast and the shooting intensified from both sides. The security man at the back of the *Florence* was hit by a full burst from an AKM. The 7.62mm ammunition tore through his body and launched him over the side. He fell face down upon the surface of the water, dead.

Flattening herself against the deck, Charly cowered, not wanting to draw any attention. Terrifyingly, a recent CNN story on piracy flickered strobe-like through her thoughts.

Soon the firing had all but stopped and she could hear brutal yelling, lots of it, at the back of the boat. It sounded as bad as it could get. Dread filled Charly's heart. *Raoul!*

Charly was close to a lifeboat so she crawled under it, squeezing her body into the tiny space beneath the hull. Crying quietly and scared out of her mind, she summoned her survival instincts and laid still. There was a splash, as though someone had been thrown overboard, and screams from the crew. Voices drew closer, toward the front of the boat, toward her. *No! No!* A burst of gunfire was followed by more screaming from the crew. Then she heard footsteps racing heavily on the decks. In a panicked moment, she clamped her eyes shut tight and pulled the towel over her head, just as she had done with the bed covers as a little girl when the thunder and lightning coming across Puget Sound became too much.

Thinking of her father, Charly prayed through silent tears that the attackers wouldn't find her.

Chapter Fifteen

INTREPID HQ, BROADWAY, LONDON

"Major Morgan is here, sir."

"Thank you, Mrs Jolley," replied Davenport from his desk. "Send him in. Oh, and rustle up some coffee, please? We're going to need it."

"On the way," she said.

Margaret Jolley, the general's devoted personal assistant, withdrew from the doorway connecting her office to the chief's inner sanctum and ushered Morgan across the threshold.

"Pull up a pew; I won't be a moment," Davenport said to Morgan.

Morgan moved familiarly over to the old circular mahogany coffee table and, unbuttoning his jacket, dropped into a beautifully aged Chesterfield. Comfortable in the way men find firm, studded leather chairs comfortable, he waited dutifully as General Davenport made a final few taps on his computer keyboard. On the table he noticed a file with the title DEFENDER: 091012/43. "Defender" was the official Interpol designator for all Intrepid operations, and

091012 was the number allocated to the hunt for Drago. The numerals 43, pronounced four-three, were Morgan's official identifier and indicated that he was the agent leading the operation.

"Right, that's done," said Davenport, stepping from behind his desk, contemplatively gazing about the oak-paneled, volume-lined walls of his "war room". Framed parchments, awards, presentations and mementos adorned the room from which Davenport would launch his agents across the world. It was a room within which Morgan felt at ease. "I'm still interested in this informant, Lazarević," Davenport said. "There's something not quite right there. Something I can't put my finger on."

"Anything I can help with?"

"No, you've got enough on your plate for now. And your appraisal of him, along with the video interview Mr Tappin conducted, has been most helpful. No, I'll get to the bottom of it. In fact, I have our new man, Hauptmann Braun-schweiger, working on it for me. I want to give him a chance to fly his kite."

Mrs Jolley returned with a tray containing cups and a pot of strong coffee.

"Thank you, my dear. Very kind," said Davenport, somewhat absently. "Oh, would you ask Ms Haddad to hunt down my old case files from Bosnia? Archived among my personal files somewhere. I'd like to see her once she has them."

"Of course." She gave them both a warm smile and left without another word, closing the door quietly behind her.

"More developments, sir?" Morgan asked, pouring coffee for them both. Following the assassination of Judge de Villepin, he and Davenport had taken the first flight out of New York and spent the entire flight back to London working through the dozens of theories and various scenarios that could be ahead of them. By the time they'd landed, Interpol had already confirmed via the joint Ryerson/Tappin interrogation of Lazarević that Drago was behind the de Villepin murder and that there would almost certainly be more to come. Exactly what would happen next was unknown. One thing was certain though: the hunt for Drago was on. Morgan was already packed and ready to head to France – his bags were in his office. But somehow, by the look on Davenport's face, he guessed the situation had changed.

"Yes, but not what you're thinking, I'm afraid." Morgan watched as his chief, hands in pockets, strolled to the far corner of the office and removed a framed photograph from a shelf. In a private moment of reflection, Davenport looked at the photo for some time before joining Morgan at the circular table. He handed the frame to Morgan and picked up a coffee. "See any familiar faces?"

"Well, the tall one there on the left is you, sir," Morgan said, appreciating the camaraderie evident in the picture. It was in black and white and showed two men, a younger, clean-shaven Davenport and a comrade, not quite as tall as Davenport but more solidly built, smiling at the camera with shoulder slung Heckler & Koch MP5s, clad in the iconic black garb of the SAS counter-terrorist squadron circa the early 1980s. It was a rare photo, a candid moment, intended only for private display. "Where and when?"

"We'd not long been done at Princes Gate," Davenport began quietly, reflectively. Morgan knew the general was referring to the Iranian Embassy siege in London in May 1980. The regiment's action to retrieve hostages taken at the embassy was televised live around the world. It was the first time anybody outside of select circles had ever heard of the

SAS. "We were at Regents Park Barracks for the post-op debrief and beer. Maggie Thatcher was even there to thank us. That chap with me, Peter Fleming, was one of my closest friends. We were the only two officers involved in the assault. Sadly, he was killed not so long ago, during a task in Central America. Two thousand and six, from memory."

"I'm sorry to hear that, sir," Morgan said.

"Anyway," Davenport replied gruffly, shrugging off the reverie and retrieving the frame from Morgan. "The reason I raise all this with you is that Peter was married to Madeline Clancy."

"I see."

"Peter was a good man," Davenport said, looking again at the photograph. "He could have commanded the Special Air Service Regiment. In fact, many thought it inevitable that he would. But an opportunity too good to refuse was offered to Madeline back in the United States. So, Peter left the British Army to enable Madeline to focus on her judicial career. They left England and moved back to America. Madeline became a judge and Peter a much in demand, very highly paid security consultant. Of course, he was still able to be useful from time to time when the British Government needed an experienced pair of hands in the Americas."

"Was the Central America business one of those tasks, sir?"

Davenport nodded.

Morgan now understood the familiarity and loyalty he'd sensed between Davenport and the judge. The two had almost managed to suppress their personal connection among the others present at the meeting in New York, but not well enough for Morgan to miss it.

Davenport reached for his well-worn brown leather

satchel and rummaged through it, extracting a CD cover. He handed it to Morgan. "Recognize her?"

"Who wouldn't? Charlotte-Rose," Morgan answered, a little perplexed. "I have a couple of her CDs, including this one. She's incredible – and stunning, which makes listening to some of her heavier pieces less taxing."

"I'm sure," replied Davenport. "The Grace Kelly of our time, that girl."

"Well, you're showing your vintage, now, sir. But yeah, I guess she is."

Morgan's gaze remained fixed on the crystal blue eyes staring straight back at him from the photo on the CD cover. Her fine features exuded elegance, yet were underwritten by a natural beauty that most men, including Morgan, found hard to resist. Her trademark red hair was pulled back in an elegant yet tousled style.

"She strikes me as a cross between Scarlett Johansson and ..." Morgan was thinking aloud, "Christina Hendricks. Don't you think?"

"How the bloody hell should I know?"

"She's certainly a spectacular creature," Morgan said, almost to himself. "You're right there," Davenport agreed. "Very beautiful girl."

"So, what's she got to do with us?" Morgan asked, placing the CD onto the table. "Celebrities aren't really our thing."

"This one is very much our thing, I'm afraid. Apart from being an internationally renowned pianist, she is also Peter and Madeline's only child and, as it happens, my goddaughter," the general said gravely, "and she disappeared earlier today, off the coast of Malta."

"Jesus!" Of course, Charlotte-Rose *Fleming*, Morgan realized. He sat up in his chair and leant forward. "I recall you and the judge mentioning a daughter at our meeting in New York. I heard Judge Clancy say that she was a musician but she referred to her only as Charly and, I guess, the judge uses her own maiden name. I didn't make the connection. Weren't the FBI supposed to be checking up on Charly's security arrangements?"

"They didn't have time. She'd already headed off on holiday with a gentleman friend, Raoul Demaçi, who I understand is also missing. I've asked for details on him. So far, all we know is that he's a wealthy European businessman. They were aboard a luxury yacht a few miles off the Maltese coast. Malta Police Force detectives claim it's the work of pirates."

Morgan gathered his thoughts, considering the impact of Charly's disappearance upon their hunt for Drago and, importantly, upon his chief and mentor, Davenport. "Well, kidnapping is standard practice for pirates these days. And hitting luxury yachts or cruise ships in search of cash and jewelry or ransoms is their bread and butter. But that mostly occurs off the east coast of Africa, usually by Somalis on the payroll of the warlords. It's rare for the Mediterranean."

"Rare, but not implausible," remarked Davenport. "Thoughts?"

"In the Mediterranean, I'd have to say Algerians, most likely, or Libyans – even a combination. There are some well-organized criminal cartels operating out of North Africa. They have established pipelines in and out of southern Europe and traditionally traffic weapons, drugs, gold or people. Maybe somebody recognized her before they set off, or the paparazzi tracked her down and word filtered through to one of these local outfits. They'd be falling all over themselves to get hold of her. A ransom would be astronomical. Do we know where she set off from?"

"Catania, Sicily. They flew in from New York, via Rome and were picked up by the yacht, *Florence*, at a private marina."

Morgan read his chief's expression. "But you don't think she's been taken by opportunists."

"No, I do not. We can let the locals think that, if they like, but as you say, if she'd been sailing in East African waters then it may be a consideration. Lazarević confirmed that Drago was behind the assassination of Judge de Villepin and warned that we should expect more action against the ICTY. So, for now, we'll approach this on the basis that Charlotte is the daughter of the ICTY's Presiding Judge."

"So, locals were engaged to conduct the kidnapping, and now she'll be passed along the pipeline to whoever paid for the abduction."

"Correct. It's sure to bring further pressure to bear upon the tribunal. There is a real danger that using such a personal leverage upon a judge could corrupt and undermine the work of the International Criminal Tribunal for the former Yugoslavia at what can only be described as a critical juncture. All of Interpol's outstanding Red Notice fugitives have been captured and are on trial or awaiting trial in The Hague. All bar one: Drago Obrenović. If he can orchestrate the kidnapping of Charlotte-Rose and then threaten her safety and wellbeing, there's no doubt it will weigh heavily upon Madeline and her colleagues on the tribunal and impact directly upon their objectivity. The whole thing could be disastrous."

"So, my objective is to get Charlotte-Rose back before she disappears into the pipeline completely."

General Davenport looked across at his agent. He knew that of all of them, Morgan was the one who would act ruthlessly and relentlessly to achieve any mission objectives Davenport set for him, no matter what the personal cost.

"Alex, you know I have spent all of my adult life defending the lives of others and upholding the rule of international law. But, for the first time in all those years, the very fabric of international justice is hanging in the balance with, of all people, an appalling creature like Dragoslav Obrenović picking away at its already fraying edges. I can't allow that to go any further. If they manage to get Charlotte-Rose into Serbia, she'll be lost for good. I owe it to her father to ensure that doesn't happen."

Alex Morgan remained silent, primed and ready as his chief issued his final orders.

"The safety catch is off. Return that girl to her family and drag those bastards back to justice. Dead or alive, it makes no difference to me."

Chapter Sixteen

Charly curled back into the warm embrace and safety of the limousine, luxuriating in its splendid comfort, relieved to have successfully run the gauntlet and escaped the paparazzi again. With a confidence that comes from feeling absolutely safe, her smile beamed from the back of the car, reaching out to the faithful sea of strangers still crushed behind the security barriers, all straining to catch a final glimpse.

As usual, cameras flashed and digital images captured it all, every second, every gesture and movement. Thousands of shots taken throughout the brief appearance would already be charging across the internet to newsrooms around the planet. As the big car slowly took its place in the midtown Manhattan traffic amid the galaxy of lights along Seventh Avenue, a black curtain of security men fell upon the scene, bringing the event to a close. For the crowd, she was gone, but there was nowhere on earth Charlotte-Rose could not be found.

"Would you like any music back there, Miss Fleming? I've got your iPod up here ready to go!"

"No thanks, John. It's been a long day. I'd like to enjoy some quiet. Take me straight home, please. And could you call ahead and ask Maria to prepare a bath for me?"

"Yes, ma'am."

Charly gave him a warm smile of thanks and closed her eyes as the communicating panel between the front and rear compartments of the car hissed slowly back into place. She rested her elbow against the door and allowed her head to fall comfortably into her open hand, sliding her fingers through her thick red hair. God, she could not wait to get home and get out of everything. She would go straight to her room, drop her gown to the floor, peel herself from her lingerie and lower her tired, naked body straight into the bath. She could already feel the water pulling her down, the bubbles gently caressing her skin as she slowly allowed herself to submerge.

Blissfully away from prying lenses and eyes, and secure in the hands of her trusted and loyal driver, Charly curled a finger through the ankle strap to unbuckle her stilettos.

But the strap wasn't budging. She tried again, and still the strap didn't move. In fact, it seemed much thicker than she'd remembered. What shoes was she wearing? She tried harder but the strap was more like a fat snake coiled tightly around both ankles.

Reality returned like a bolt of lightning and Charly came spiraling back from semiconsciousness to find herself in the middle of her worst nightmare. She was lying on her side on the floor of what felt like an old four-wheel drive, trussed up like a pig, ankles and wrists locked together with heavy-duty tape, wearing nothing but her bikini and sandals. A flimsy bag was pulled over her head, but she could just see through it. With every pothole along the track, Charly was bounced painfully against the rusted metal surface of the rear compartment. Petrol fumes filled the air. A pothole caused the vehicle to leave the road and then crash back onto the uneven surface with a thump. Charly was bashed down hard against the floor and let out a gasp.

"Hey, bitch," a deeply accented, vaguely familiar male voice said, somewhere close. "It's OK. We're going to take good care of you."

A rough hand touched her and began caressing slowly, creepily along her thigh and up to the thin line of her bikini.

Charly screamed.

Chapter Seventeen

VALLETTA, MALTA

Alex Morgan stepped out onto the balcony of his hotel room at the Grand Hotel Excelsior feeling deeply troubled. The urgency of the mission and the revelation that Charlotte-Rose Fleming was Davenport's goddaughter were clawing at him. While the general's orders were clear – "Get her back, fast" – the amount of information available on her abduction was scant, almost non-existent. The scraps that Intrepid's intelligence section had been able to piece together from police reports, crew statements and the media were light on detail, heavy on speculation. And, as far as Morgan was concerned, there were too many elements that didn't add up.

The Grand Hotel Excelsior sat upon the Great Siege Road of Valletta facing north across the harbor. He preferred to stay in large hotels because they assured him a level of anonymity, a prerequisite of his profession. It was easier to be forgotten among hundreds of guests, rather than being one of just a dozen in some trendy boutique hotel.

With his first strong black coffee of the day and contemplating the imminent future, Morgan could not help but be mesmerized by the breathtaking views across the ancient Marsamxett Harbour. Biblical domes and spires filled the skyline and massive sandstone walls sat like cliffs in every direction along the length and breadth of the harborside. Gazing across at Fort Manoel, located strategically on Manoel Island to cover the sea entrance to the city, Morgan felt an eerie affinity with the old Knights of Malta, who built the fort in the eighteenth century. The fort had served its purpose nobly for almost 200 years, right up until the Second World War when it had suffered heavy bombardment. Now, instead of warships, the multi-million-dollar playthings of the rich and famous, leisure craft and tourist launches dotted the harbor's shoreline. But Morgan hadn't chosen the room for its luxury appeal. It gave him a perfect panorama of the harbor and, most importantly, a clear line of sight to the exclusive marina on the southwestern edge of Manoel Island. The very marina where the *Florence* was currently berthed.

The phone on the bedside table rang.

"Your harbor taxi is ready, sir."

"Thank you," Morgan replied. Time to get to work.

"Welcome aboard, Mr Hamilton. We received the email from your secretary. It's so very nice to meet you." The captain of the *Florence* met Morgan, operating under the pseudonym of Hamilton, with a slimy grin and a wet-fish handshake. "I apologize, as you can see, we're in the middle of some minor refurbishment, but we'll be ready for sea again soon. You were thinking of something for the end of this month?"

"That's right," Morgan replied. Dressed in a beige lightweight suit, fitted white shirt and brown suede boots, he was the picture of a successful businessman. "I have a number of associates I need to impress." He gave a thin smile. "Want to show them a good time and give them a reason to get their check books out, you know?"

The captain returned a conspiratorial look. "We often look after business investors, Mr Hamilton, with our exclusive service."

Morgan allowed the captain to lead him around the yacht while taking the opportunity to make his own critical observations. He was at times distracted by the sheer opulence of the craft. There was nothing that hadn't been thought of and provided for tenfold in terms of luxury appointments. It was light-years removed from any seafaring vessel he'd ever been on, most of which were navy boats and none of which were built for comfort.

"So," Morgan began as they headed from the staterooms back up to the main deck, "why the refurbishment? She seems to be quite young and in excellent condition."

The captain became cautious.

"Well, Mr Hamilton, unfortunately we had some trouble on board a couple of days ago. You haven't heard?" He shot a skeptical glance straight at Morgan. "It has been reported in the news."

"I recall seeing something about trouble in these waters, but I didn't know this particular boat was involved. Was it a robbery?"

"Something like that." He didn't expand. "Nothing to worry about for your trip, I assure you. We have been cooperating with the police, who gave us access back aboard this morning, and I have changed over the crew to give the others some rest. We are also upgrading our security arrangements."

"Giuseppe!" A man called for the captain from the bridge. "Can you come up?"

"OK, OK," the captain cried. "I'm sorry, Mr Hamilton. Would you excuse me for a minute?"

"Of course," said Morgan, relieved to be unsupervised. "Do you mind if I continue to wander around?"

"Be my guest. I won't be long."

Alex Morgan walked casually toward the locations from which the security guards had engaged the pirates. He went aft to where the first guard had been shot and killed and, according to the crew statements, his body thrown overboard. There was an area that had borne the brunt of large-caliber automatic rifle fire, defined by the faintest amount of blood splatter residue – not so clearly visible to the uninitiated, despite obvious attempts to clean it all away – and a narrow vertical tract across the upper area of the bow and upon the superstructure where the ammunition had impacted. The man had been somewhere in between, close to where Morgan was currently standing, he surmised. He was disturbed that there were no other signs of a firefight; considering the amount of shooting that had allegedly occurred in both directions, he expected there to have been much more. As discreetly as possible, he lifted a flimsy piece of tape that had been smoothed over a bullet hole and pressed the end of his forefinger firmly against it. The pressure formed a circular indentation upon the fleshy end of his finger. Examining it, he noted the caliber quietly to himself – "Seven six two" – and then, replacing the tape, walked back toward the area on the port side where the second man had been.

Up on the bridge, the captain turned from speaking with his number two and noticed Morgan in the area where the guard had been shot. Nervously, he brought his conversation to an end, heading quickly for the decks.

Chapter Eighteen

WEST OF SAN LAWRENZ, GOZO, MALTA

Charlotte-Rose Fleming, terrified and wretched, shrank back against the rocks like a child cowering from invisible demons at the foot of her bed.

She cradled her knees, pulling them protectively to her breast. Full of fear and anxiety, her teeth bit down hard into the coarse fabric of the filthy clothes they had finally given her, her only protection from the chilling early evening air. Too weary to attempt movement to stay warm, she endured the cold in grim silence. She was physically and mentally exhausted, hungry and dehydrated. But still her terrified eyes remained wide open, staring blankly out into the sky beyond the entrance to the cave. All she could hear was the ocean.

Her mind played over and over the events of the day – was it two days ago? Three? – when she and Raoul had been taken from the *Florence*. Everything had been so perfect. The yacht. The sea. The sun. It was idyllic. And then hell had descended upon them.

She still had no idea what had happened to Raoul. She

knew he'd been with her when they'd been bundled off the yacht and even remembered seeing him firing a gun at the pirates. But wasn't that the job of the security men who'd been traveling with them? How did Raoul know about guns? She had no idea about such things. Those were skills she definitely had not inherited from her action-man father. With great longing and sadness, she thought about him for a while. *You'd know what to do, Daddy,* she thought. *You wouldn't have let this happen to me. But I'm your daughter and, by God, I won't let them beat me.*

One thing she did know was that she and Raoul had been the only ones taken. The crew had been left behind. Whoever these people were, they'd known she was aboard. But what had become of the crew? She felt a pain in her chest at the idea that the crew had been killed aboard the yacht. She thought again of Raoul: his piercing gray eyes and thick, dark hair. A man she realized she hardly knew, but who she was now inexplicably connected to for what – life? "Oh God!" she whispered.

Charly lay dead still, contemplating her chances of survival, looking out to the only scrap of sky that she could see beyond the cave. She had no idea what the time was and her delirium had convinced her that it was already late afternoon: the sun would retreat again soon, and the stars would appear for another night. But it was only late morning. A gentle wind whispered along the cliffs as the waves of the Mediterranean crashed below. Charly was exhausted but strangely serene. She allowed herself to drift away in that moment, far from Malta, to another time, another place, another world.

Charly's thoughts were filled with memories of family and happier times. Images of her beloved parents, Peter and Madeline, floated wistfully upon her subconscious. Among them, her favorite picture – the silver-framed portrait so familiar upon her piano at home. There was her father, resplendent in dress uniform, SAS beret and medals, with her mother standing proudly beside him, clutching his arm close to her. So young and in love. Then Charly saw hands, a child's hands, her long slender fingers waltzing upon the keys through 'Cavatina', with the warmth and smell of her father sitting beside her. With the memory of his smile beaming down at her as she played it for him, Charly was soon asleep.

"You filthy white whore!" the leader screamed, tearing her from sleep. He grabbed a fistful of her hair and dragged her to her knees. "You tempt my men by showing your body!"

"No! No, I didn't!" she cried desperately, then realized that the flimsy rag of a shirt they had given her had fallen open as she slept. "No, this is not my fault. The shirt is falling apart. It has no buttons!"

Behind the leader, the one the others called only "Boss", the two men who had been guarding Charly were sniggering.

"Slut! You are lucky I don't let them have you." The boss slapped her hard across the face. Charly cried out in pain and despair as his blow landed heavily upon her already swollen cheek.

"Coward! You fucking coward!" Charly accused, full of sudden venom and fury.

Enraged, he wrenched at her hair, lifted her to her feet and placed the edge of a razor-sharp knife across the soft skin of her neck.

"Next time, bitch," he growled, close to her face, "deal

or no deal, I fucking kill you." He threw her back to the ground and stormed out of the cave, calling for the other men.

"What have you done with Raoul?" she screamed. "Where is he? You animals!"

The boss turned back and stormed toward her. Under the intensity of the sunlight behind him, his features were a death mask just inches from her. "You should not hold any hope for your Raoul," he sneered and left the cave.

Charly began to tremble, overwhelmed by a sense that her life would end in this horrible, forgotten place. Hopelessness found her. Her heart screamed for freedom. Somewhere close by there was a shuffle of activity and then the unmistakable sound of a guard laughing and relieving himself in the entrance to the cave.

With nowhere else to turn and no hope of rescue in sight, she clasped her hands tightly and sobbed.

Chapter Nineteen

VALLETTA, MALTA

Morgan was growing perplexed but knew his naturally suspicious disposition was not letting him down.

The police reports and witness statements clearly indicated that the second firing position was midway along the portside, almost exactly where he stood, yet there were no signs of a contact nor of any blood. He grasped the railing and leant over the side, looking to see if any rounds fired at the *Florence* by the pirates had dropped low against the hull. Nothing. He reversed the logic and looked up behind him into the structure of the mega-yacht, but still nothing. On an impulse, he dropped to the deck, flat on his gut, and peered into the crevices and cracks of the deck's joinery.

The captain was looking for Morgan. He went aft first and paused for a moment at the scene where the bullet holes had been covered up. The captain couldn't tell if anything had been disturbed but he knew Morgan had been there. Why? Was he curious or was there something else? The skin of his gut became taut and he felt an old, remembered sensation of uneasiness from the days when he'd smuggled just about everything in and out of southern Europe coming over him. He turned and headed amidships.

Flat on the deck, Morgan knew there was something staring at him but a blaze of sunlight resulted in a blinding glare off the yacht's pristine white salon. Then he spotted it. The most minute flicker of gold wedged within the fissure where the highly polished decking met the bodywork. Morgan reached out and grabbed it.

"Mr Hamilton! Mr Hamilton!" the captain called.

Instantly Morgan was up and on his knees. The object he'd collected was in his trouser pocket and his tortoiseshell Ray-Ban Wayfarers were in his hand.

"Dropped my sunglasses," he said casually. "Thought they were about to go over the side."

"Oh, I see," said the captain, but he wasn't convinced. His dark, scheming eyes shot from Morgan to the decks, trying to see whatever it was that had so captured Morgan's attention. "Well, if you're satisfied, perhaps we could wrap things up. I really do have a lot to be getting on with."

Ten minutes later Morgan walked casually along the road beside the southern shoreline of Manoel Island and reached The Strand. There, he took up a position in the Café Jubilee from where he could observe the vehicle and pedestrian traffic coming and going from the marina. While he waited for coffee, he reached into his pocket and discreetly removed the object he had taken from the *Florence*. The slender brass lines and expanded crimped end of a fired 5.56mm blank cartridge in his fingers taunted him. *Work it out. Work it out.* Morgan's mind raced through the reports he had read on the flight to Malta and again in his hotel room, recalling every detail he could that would place him back at the port side amidships during the pirate attack. Who the hell was firing blanks from that boat?

On an instinct he looked up and across the intersection of The Strand and the Manoel Island access road. He saw the captain emerge, walking briskly up from the marina, looking agitated. The captain's head swung from side to side, suspicious of being followed. Morgan returned the expended blank cartridge to his pocket and made a play of reviewing something on his sat phone; when deployed on ops, all agents carried them. Having selected a table toward the rear of the café, he was confident that, unless the captain came in, he would not be seen. Looking past the other patrons, Morgan realized that the captain was waiting for someone. It took only a few more moments for Morgan to see who he'd been waiting for.

A Fiat Sedici 4x4 pulled up sharply and a man wearing the uniform of the Malta Police Force Maritime Patrol leant out of the driver's window and called impatiently to the captain.

The captain got in and they sped off.

Chapter Twenty

UN DETENTION UNIT, SCHEVENINGEN, THE HAGUE

Detainee 69–54–55, Milivoj Šerifović, was escorted to the interview room by an officer of the UN Detention Unit. Šerifović had been expecting a visit from his defense counsel, in fact he'd requested it, but there'd been some problem and his appointed counsel couldn't attend personally. An alternate had been arranged.

Šerifović sat waiting in the interview room with the detention unit guard standing behind him. When the alternate counsel eventually arrived, he could not help but feel physically uneasy: the man moved through the doorway with the set and purpose of an invading tank regiment. Despite the bespoke tailoring, he looked like he was built from scaffolding, with huge slabs of muscle riveted to his superstructure. At the end of girder-sized arms, his hands swung like heavy luggage. His legs gave the impression of piledriving pistons deep within the engine room of a mammoth battleship. His hair was thick and jet black, cut short. His brow was grave and his dark eyes heavy caliber.

Not that Šerifović could see it, but there was a flicker of

recognition upon the face of the prison guard; he'd been told to expect this particular arrival and to make himself scarce when granted leave to do so. The guard was glad to see Šerifović squirm.

"I appreciate you waiting for me, officer," announced the counsel in a heavy Germanic accent. "Would you mind leaving us?"

The prison guard nodded dutifully. "No problem, sir," he replied. "I'll be right outside."

"*Danke schön*," the man replied.

"Who the hell are you?" demanded Šerifović as soon as they were alone. "You're not my appointed counsel. I've not seen you before among any of her team."

"There's been a slight change to your schedule, colonel," the man began, unruffled. "I'm not here to talk about your defense, but our conversation will have a bearing on your future."

"What the fuck are you talking about? What is this?" Šerifović spat defiantly. "You're no fucking lawyer."

"You're quite wrong, colonel," came the unemotional reply. "In fact, I have a Bachelor of Law and a Masters in International Legal Studies from the University of Vienna. I am licensed to practice in both Germany and Austria. Now, let us begin."

Hermann Braunschweiger, formerly of the elite German Federal Police special operations and counter terrorism unit GSG 9, latterly recruited to the ranks of Intrepid, removed a file from his attache case and slid a large photograph across the table to Šerifović.

"You know this man." It was a statement of fact.

Šerifović's eyes dropped for a split second, barely acknowledging the image. "I've never seen him before," he lied.

"Let me refresh your memory." Braunschweiger produced another image. This one showed the same man, albeit much younger, leaning against a military vehicle and smoking a cigarette, wearing the uniform of a soldier in the Bosnian Serb Army. "He was, at one time, your personal driver. Will you make me produce the expanded version of this photograph, which includes you?"

"What is it you want?" Šerifović exploded. "And what is your name?"

"My name is of no importance to you," Braunschweiger replied dryly. "The only name that is important to you today is his."

"Why should I give a shit?"

"Because while you trusted this man, confided in him, and even promoted him all those years ago, he is the one who led us straight to you. And he had quite a story to tell about your escapades during the war, I can assure you. For example ..."

Braunschweiger allowed the significance of his words to sink in as he expanded, in excruciating detail, on the information the man in the photographs had allegedly provided to Intrepid. He studied the face of the old man carefully as the revelation clearly made its mark. Despite his reputation as a cold-blooded killer and his years as the senior intelligence officer in the Bosnian Serb Army, Šerifović had been out of the game a long time. His ability to mask his feelings had been eroded by age and ill health.

Šerifović remained deathly silent. His jaw was clenched so tight that Braunschweiger could hear the teeth grinding beneath the gray flesh of his wrinkled jowls. The bitterness of betrayal etched across Šerifović's face told Braunschweiger everything he needed to know. The Intrepid agent remained impassively silent, allowing the prisoner to consider and process the amount of damage his accuser could possibly do, or already had done, to his defense options.

"What's this got to do with me and why would you believe a piece of shit like Petrović?" he said finally. "He was just a fucking driver."

"Yes," Braunschweiger replied. "But he was your fucking driver."

Chapter Twenty-One

MALTA

Morgan took a cab and, from a discreet distance, tracked the Fiat all the way to a side street on the outskirts of Lija. He watched the captain and the policeman park behind a Nissan Armada and walk into a semidetached terrace house, one of a row of five that stretched along half the short street.

Paying the driver, Morgan slipped deftly through an unlocked wrought-iron gate and headed down a narrow alleyway that paralleled the side wall of the terrace. Reaching the rear of the house, he searched for a way in. He found a small verandah strewn with unused furniture and discarded household paraphernalia. The back door to the house was hard to get to, protected by the mad jumble of junk and rubbish. Anyway, it was too obvious. Instead, he found a small window, unlatched and a quarter open. It belonged to what must have been a washing room – directly beneath the window was a wide bench designed for sorting laundry.

Waiting for a moment, Morgan listened to the conversation going on inside. There were definitely more than two voices. It sounded like three. He waited a few moments longer. Yes, three. They were talking in a room somewhere in the middle of the long, narrow terrace. They were speaking Maltese but he could tell by the raised tone and aggression in their conversation that they were aggrieved. He recognized the captain's highly charged voice, and registered the words *ċelebrità, famuż pjanista*, the name Hamilton and then the word *pulizija* in the midst of the excited jabbering. So, when the captain had been brought into this game, he hadn't realized that the target was, in fact, a celebrity – a famous pianist – until he was up to his neck in it. His paranoia had, correctly, driven him to the conclusion that the businessman, Hamilton, was in some way connected to the police.

Using the volume of their argument, Alex Morgan slipped into the laundry via the window.

Chapter Twenty-Two

WEST OF SAN LAWRENZ, GOZO, MALTA

When Charly opened her eyes again it was early afternoon.

She longed for water. Her throat was dry and her lips brittle and raw. Her entire body ached with the pain of being smacked around and lying on the rock floor of the cave with little or no protection from the elements. One of her eyes felt swollen with bruising and her cheeks throbbed. But she knew she must not give up hope. Inner strength was her only chance for survival and the will to live was a potent ally.

She looked down at her hands, the tools of her trade. They were scabbed and swollen. The rough stone surface of the cave was unforgiving and the bindings they'd kept her in for so long had played havoc with her circulation. She stretched her fingers wide and wiggled them, again and again, in her usual pre-performance ritual, but their responsiveness was slow and uncoordinated. Could there be permanent damage – physical or psychosomatic? Would she ever be able to play again? God, how could she even think about playing, when she didn't know if she would survive the night?

Although they'd left Charly alone most of the day, she had a distinct impression of hurried activity going on outside the entrance to the cave. There was talking and yelling among the guards and plenty of engine noises – comings and goings. It all sounded like preparation, but preparation for what? Something was going on out there. Charly felt drained and could feel herself slowly losing the drive to go on, but she couldn't let that happen.

Beyond the cave she could see the beautiful azure ocean and as she gazed longingly toward freedom, she felt a calm come upon her. She was suddenly returned to Sunset Hill and the view across Puget Sound to the distant Olympic Mountains. But only for a moment.

As she fell once again into a fit of uncontrollable sobbing, Charly knew she could not take another day of uncertainty. She could almost hear her father's voice telling her to get back in control.

If she was to have any chance of survival, she knew she had to be strong.

Chapter Twenty-Three

MALTA

Morgan edged his way closer to the three men in the midst of their altercation. His Maltese was sketchy at best but there were just enough similarities with English to get him over the line. The argument was over the issue of his, Morgan's, appearance on the boat. The captain and the policeman had been assured that the kidnapping was to be a simple issue: the daughter of a wealthy American businessman was holidaying in the Mediterranean and her abduction would fetch a sizeable ransom. The money would be paid and she would be released unharmed. For their part in it, they would receive a healthy cut. The revelation that she was famous, coupled with the death of at least one of the onboard security men, had changed everything. Now, both the captain and the policeman were agitating for more money. There was no question in their minds that the risks were greater than they had been told. The third man, clearly the point man for the operation, was not happy.

Morgan could hear plenty of tough talk, but no action. He couldn't afford to waste more time by letting them carry on indefinitely. He needed to find Charlotte-Rose and to do that he needed some answers.

Morgan stepped from the kitchen into the dark hallway. It was long and narrow, with tiles on the floor, a high ceiling and open arches leading to other rooms. He inched forward with his back against the wall. From directly behind, a door creaked open and a man emerged from a bathroom, lazily tucking his shirt back into his trousers. The two locked eyes.

Great, thought Morgan, *I bet the bastard hasn't even washed his hands.*

Morgan was catapulted into a frenzy of violence.

Chapter Twenty-Four

INTERPOL HEADQUARTERS, LYON, FRANCE

Deep inside Interpol Headquarters in Lyon, Hermann Braunschweiger was settled securely in Intrepid's Intelligence, Investigations and Communications Section. He had established his own field office within the suite of offices reserved exclusively for the use of field agents when in Lyon. He sat on the edge of a desk and was waiting on the secure line for his call to be directed to his chief, General Davenport, in London.

"Hermann, good evening."

"*Guten abend*, sir," Braunschweiger began, formally. "We've had some interesting developments today."

"Let's have it then," Davenport replied.

"Firstly, when I showed Šerifović the photographs, he referred to the informant, Lazarević, as Petrović."

"Petrović?" Davenport repeated. "Very interesting."

"Yes, sir. There was no hesitation, the name just rolled off naturally. As far as the prisoner is concerned, the informant we know as Lazarević is actually known as Petrović. It seems your instinct was correct. I've had the intelligence team here working through the files you had forwarded to us, cross-referencing with the Interpol and ICTY databases and they identified," he read from notes, "one Dobrashin Petrović, a former corporal in the Bosnian Serb Army. Lazarević is an assumed name, which he must have adopted when he relocated to Albania after the war."

"So, after all these years, he's been just another one of the dozens of nameless foot soldiers in the file photographs alongside the big fish, like Obrenović, Šerifović and company," Davenport observed. "But why, if he is so eager to cooperate, has he not disclosed to Interpol the reasons for this adopted pseudonym? What more do you have for me?"

"Well, I've been running a surveillance team in Albania to monitor the informant, formerly known as Lazarević. And when you arranged to have him flown to New York, we established a surveillance footprint within his apartment – both vision and sound – during his absence."

"Excellent. Anything yet?"

"No, nothing yet, and he is definitely covering his tracks. He doesn't make any calls from the house or meet anybody there, or even send emails from his PC. But he has been seen traveling by bus to one of the old suburbs developed by the Communists back in the fifties. It's an area similar to where he is living now, lower socio-economic, but it is on the other side of Tirana. Lots of concrete, lots of crime, not so many trees.

"We don't have a confirmed apartment number yet – it's only a matter of time before we do – but we do know the building. Most importantly, since returning from New York, he has met with a man in the grounds of the building. They've met three times so far. Their conversations are conducted innocently enough, walking around the buildings in a close huddle. We've yet to confirm the identity of the other man, as he's been dressed in dark clothing designed to obscure his features – a heavy coat, woolen hat pulled down around his ears and dark glasses. But we do know that he is tall, taller than Lazarević, and appears to be of medium build."

"And contact with this man has occurred only since his return from New York?"

"Yes, sir." Braunschweiger fell silent, allowing Davenport to consider the information.

"Very well," Davenport replied after a moment. "I've asked Commander Sutherland to follow up on the Bordeaux end of this business and, as you know, Major Morgan is currently in Malta. I have a sense that your respective paths will cross eventually. So, keep at it. Get back to Albania and get as much together as you can on this development with Lazarević and his new friend."

Chapter Twenty-Five

MALTA

The man came at Morgan in two paces.

Morgan spun around and went in low, getting a bead on his assailant as he turned. He was about Morgan's size, a bit younger, with the dark, deep-set eyes and prominent cheekbones of Central Europe. Serbian, Morgan guessed.

"Don't you guys flush?" Morgan quipped as the first blows fell. There was no reply. The hallway was just 3 feet wide and the confined, unlit space reduced the contest to a bar brawl. Both men hammered in hard and fast, punches and blocks in a constant stream. The young Serb swung at Morgan with a wild haymaker but missed, momentum carrying his body through the movement, exposing his entire right flank. Morgan responded with a driving left-handed blow to the jaw followed by a right-handed uppercut to the face. There was an eruption of blood from the smashed mouth and nose. The Serb slumped to the floor.

"What the fuck?" A clamor of voices exploded from the room ahead. All three leapt to their feet and piled haphazardly into the hallway, only to find Morgan coming at them. Morgan knew his best chance was to maximize the advantage of the narrow space and take them one on one.

The first man in, the captain of the *Florence*, struck out clumsily. A glancing blow slid across the corner of Morgan's jaw, barely making contact. Morgan hit back hard, deflecting the captain with both hands, flat-palmed, slamming him against the wall, following with a downward kick to the side of his leg. The knee crumpled under the impact and the captain screamed in tortured agony. Morgan hammered the advantage with a short, sharp punch to the side of the neck. The captain fell to the floor.

Almost simultaneously, the second man, the one the other two had come to see, attacked. He was big and heavy with thick, greasy, black hair and a thick goatee. Stumbling over the slumped, semi-conscious bodies of the captain and the young Serb, he set upon Morgan with a tall wooden stool. After taking down the captain, Morgan was still recovering his stance and couldn't block the attack in time. He took the full force of the heavy wooden legs across his right shoulder and back. The impact threw him forward against the wall. He tripped and hit the hard hallway tiles face first. Bigger than Morgan, but overweight rather than muscled, the man maintained the attack. From the floor in the midst of the affray, Morgan noted a tattoo just visible beneath the sweat-soaked armhole of the man's filthy singlet.

"*Špijun!*" the man accused – *spy*. Another Serb, Morgan noted. The big Serbian, now holding the stool by the legs, swung the rounded seat high above his head, and brought it crashing down, straight for Morgan. Morgan's hands fired upward and caught the stool just above his head. Gripping the stool with both hands, Morgan lifted his knees back and drove his feet forward with all his strength. His heels impacted with the shins of the big Serb, already off-balance, just below the knees. The man let out a cry of pain that reverberated through the terrace, but his knees did not buckle. Instead, pain contorting his face, he teetered like a column about to topple. Morgan pulled suddenly against the stool and the movement brought the big Serb crashing to the floor. Morgan launched from the ground just in time to avoid the fall and crab-walked his hands up the wall until he was back on his feet.

No sooner was he back up than a heavy punch, a king hit, caught him across the back of the head. It sent him careening headfirst into the opposite wall. He fought against the onset of unconsciousness and pushed himself back, bleary eyed, turning to address the attack of the final man, the policeman, who had somehow managed to outflank Morgan. In fact, while Morgan had fought the others, the policeman had left the terrace and come back in via the same window Morgan had climbed through.

As Morgan was turning to take on the policeman, the two Serbs recovered and set upon him again, pinning both arms behind him. The policeman seized the initiative and laid into Morgan's torso, blow after blow. But Morgan was unrelenting. Using the Serbs for ballast, he lifted his feet from the ground and kicked with everything he had straight at the policeman's chest. The impact was shattering; the heart bore the brunt of it. Gasping for breath, the policeman was thrown awkwardly backward. Sliding down the wall, his head hit the tiles with a crack.

Morgan used the momentum of the attack in his favor. He lifted his feet again, allowing his full 200 pounds to become a deadweight, dropping to the floor. Stunned, the Serbs looked at each other, puzzled. Morgan, both hands on the tiles, spun his legs in a fast 180-degree arc, scooping the legs from under the young Serb, bringing him once again to the ground. As the man fell, Morgan drove an elbow straight into his face. He hit the wall with a dull thud.

Morgan's attention turned to the big Serb, but a pulverizing blow from a cosh struck him just behind the ear. Darkness drifted over him. The big Serb followed through by kicking and stomping on Morgan repeatedly. In no time the Intrepid agent was unconscious.

"Quickly, you useless fuck, find his gun and strap him," barked the big Serb at the younger man, still recovering. "We'll take him with us."

The big Serb walked back into the room where he had been arguing with the cop and the captain of the *Florence*. He went to a drawer and removed a 9mm automatic. Rummaging deeper into the back of the drawer he found a silencer and returned to the hall. He watched impatiently as the young Serb took Morgan's gun, the SIG Sauer P226, and shoved it into the waistband of his jeans.

"Drag him in there and strap him, then bring the car around the back. And hurry, we don't have much fucking time."

Without a word, the younger man obeyed.

In the hallway, the cop was out cold and the captain was moaning in agony, his knee shattered by Morgan's assault. Standing over them dispassionately, the big Serb slowly, deliberately, screwed the silencer firmly into place.

"You two pieces of shit should have taken your money," he sneered at the captain.

"But, we—" the captain began.

"And kept your mouths fucking shut. Instead you bring

trouble to me. This guy—" his black eyes flicked toward Morgan, "—is probably fucking Interpol."

The captain was whimpering now, imploring the man for mercy. The big Serb dragged a tired hand across his face and hair, let out a thoroughly disinterested sigh and shot the captain and the policeman dead. As the blood from their fatal head wounds began to drain across the tiles, he returned to the sitting room, grabbed Morgan's limp body by the collar of his jacket and dragged him into the rat-infested alleyway through a side door.

Chapter Twenty-Six

TIRANA, ALBANIA

Hermann Braunschweiger sat uncomfortably in the back of a nondescript van parked on the outskirts of the city of Tirana, Albania's capital. Stuffed inside the vehicle, he barely had room to move. His knees sat high above a benchtop where computer keyboards, telephones, radios and joysticks for the surveillance cameras were arranged. If he extended to his full seated height, the top of his head nudged the van's high ceiling. Normally the back of the van would comfortably accommodate three people. With Hermann in the back, that number reduced to two.

"I'm with our man now," came a whispered voice over the radio. "We're on the bus, approaching the second location."

"Thank you, Four," replied Braunschweiger. "Let me know when I can switch to a visual covering that second location."

Braunschweiger's size made him less than suitable when it came to routine surveillance tasks. He avoided these types of operations, dating right back to when he was in the GSG

9. In fact, he remembered, as if it was only yesterday, one of his instructors observing during surveillance training: "Braunschweiger, no matter where in the world we may put you, you will always look like an enormous iridescent elephant sitting in the corner of a children's playground." He smiled at the memory. On this occasion, however, it was imperative that he was readily available to his team. So, he'd relegated himself to the van while his team, operatives of the Intrepid surveillance unit, conducted the field work across Tirana. Every member of the surveillance team had been deliberately selected on the basis of their physical characteristics and certain personality and behavioral traits that enabled them to blend in, unseen, within any environment. They were what used to be called gray-men and women, because of their ability to operate in the background, unnoticed.

To Braunschweiger they were his eyes and ears and he knew he'd chosen well.

Based on Intrepid intelligence on the demographics specific to this area, his team of eight – five men and three women – had faultlessly transfused into the local area. In the past two weeks they had pieced together sufficient information on the informant, Lazarević, to warrant continued covert coverage of him. Importantly, Milivoj Šerifović's unintentional identification had enabled Intrepid to confirm the informant's true identity as former Bosnian soldier Dobrashin Petrović. As Petrović, photographic evidence categorically linked him to Interpol's most wanted, including Šerifović and Intrepid's ultimate prize, Dragoslav "Drago" Obrenović. Drago was the only long-term fugitive of the ICTY who remained at large.

While General Davenport had dispatched Alex Morgan to Malta to focus on the kidnapping of Charlotte-Rose,

Braunschweiger had been given every available resource to work from the opposite direction, establishing the connection between Lazarević and Drago. Braunschweiger was absolutely clear on Davenport's position: the kidnapping of Charlotte-Rose Fleming, daughter of ICTY President Madeline Clancy, at the very time when ICTY judges were being targeted – and, so far, one assassinated – was not coincidental. Her safe recovery was fundamental to thwarting a direct and potentially irrevocable attack upon the foundations of international justice.

His sat phone buzzed in his coat pocket.

"Braunschweiger," he answered.

"Hermann, it's Dave Sutherland. You still freezing your ass off in that van?"

"Yes," he replied stiffly, still not quite used to the light-heartedness of his new colleagues.

"I still can't believe they've made a van big enough to fit you, man," Sutherland quipped. "Anyway, I've got something here that I'll send through to you. I thought you could cross-check it against your vision of this second guy that's turned up. Stand by."

Intrepid agent Lieutenant Commander Dave Sutherland, a former US Navy Seal, had been dispatched by General Davenport to work with the French authorities investigating the assassination of Judge Guillaume René de Villepin of the ICTY. There was no doubt in anyone's mind that the brazen assassin had long since fled France, but following any possible threads that could lead Intrepid to Drago Obrenović had to be followed.

Braunschweiger waited in silence until a ping from his secure sat phone told him that the image files from Sutherland had been received. Opening them, he recognized the figure on the screen immediately. He brought the images up on a larger screen within a bank of other screens running live feeds from inside the Lazarević apartment and outside the building across the city, the second location, where his mysterious contact was accommodated.

"When and where were these taken?" Braunschweiger said into the phone, his eyes glued to the screen. He urgently tapped commands into the keyboard. A number of almost identical surveillance images taken recently in Tirana flashed onto the other screens.

"In Bordeaux, during the week before and on the night of Judge de Villepin's murder," Sutherland answered. "They were taken from CCTV feeds around de Villepin's home. I can't spot anything unusual from the footage I have of the judge eating and going for coffee in town; I'll keep looking. But is this your guy?"

"Almost certainly," Braunschweiger replied. His radio came back to life.

"We're off the bus and the friend is waiting near the apartment block now. I'm dropping off here, handing over to Five. You should have visual via CCTV now."

Into the sat phone Braunschweiger said: "Dave, wait out." Into the radio he said: "Acknowledged, Four. Good work. Make your way back here. Five, are you up?"

"Roger, this is Five. Sitting across the grounds to the north. I have a clear view of them both."

"Acknowledged," Braunschweiger replied. He remotely manipulated a CCTV camera on the other side of the city, which had been covertly installed under the eaves of an apartment building just 50 yards away from the second location. He brought the lens around to target the two men: Lazarević, and the man they referred to simply as his new friend. Herman Braunschweiger's dark eyes darted between the live footage from the CCTV camera, the stored visuals that had been captured over the past few days, and the images Dave Sutherland had just sent through from Bordeaux. But this was now moot. He knew in his gut it was the same man.

"Dave, are you still there?"

"Go ahead," replied Sutherland.

"This is definitely Lazarević's friend. It has to be," Braunschweiger replied, the words underwritten with the conviction of experience. "His height, clothes, the attempt to obscure his features; they're all consistent with what we've captured here in Tirana during his meetings with Lazarević. But it's the body language, the movements and gestures, his manner of walking. Those are the things that are confirming it for me."

"Great, man," said Sutherland. "I'll keep at it for a while and see what else I can come up with. Let me know if you need a spare pair of hands down there. Speaking of which, have you heard anything from Alex?"

"No, nothing."

"No problem. If I know Morgan, he'll have everything under control … eventually."

Chapter Twenty-Seven

MALTA

With a single, long and agonizing attempt for air, Alex Morgan snapped back to consciousness. The taste of blood and bile stung at the back of his parched throat. A matted fringe of dark brown hair clung to his bloodied brow, his face hurt like hell and was caked in sweat and blood. One eye was closing over. Falling in and out of consciousness, shallow breathing barely sustaining him, Morgan couldn't see or move. Everything was black as pitch and he was overwhelmed by the stink of petrol and exhaust fumes.

He was bound, gagged and folded into the trunk of a car.

The rag that was jammed into his mouth was feral beyond words. It tasted of oil and muck and was causing him to choke and retch relentlessly while he struggled for oxygen. Instinctively recalling his resistance-to-interrogation training, Morgan focused on control: breathing through his nose, moderating his heart rate and suppressing the reflex to choke. Slowly but surely he regained composure, reminding his body that he was back in charge. With his breathing regulated, albeit under pressure, he turned his attention to the source of the problem. The gag had been poorly applied and was loose; a godsend. Whoever had done it was inexperienced, using only a single piece of material. They'd hurriedly pushed a large wad of it deep into his mouth and then tied the ends off behind the back of his neck. Slowly, patiently, still breathing only through his nose, Morgan began an awkward chewing motion, pushing the fabric forward with his tongue. Fighting the impulse to throw up with each attempt, he worked hard to dislodge the blood-sodden strip of material from his mouth. After five excruciating minutes, he spat the last edges of the filthy rag free and sucked in a huge lungful of hot, polluted air.

Clear of the gag, Morgan began an inventory of his body; specifically, what was working and what wasn't. He was lying on his right side, facing the rear of the car. His head felt like it had split open. A serious headache pounded away and he felt like he might have a couple of damaged ribs. The pain he was experiencing just trying to breathe was a sure sign of that. Jesus! They'd only just come good after his last assignment in Malfajiri.

His internal assessment turned to the extremities. Morgan's wrists were strapped tightly behind him with duct tape and his ankles were in the same state. The trunk was so confining that his knees were bent up to his chest, making it impossible for him to stretch out or get any leverage or even respite from the claustrophobic effect of the space. He returned to his regimen: control the breathing, control the breathing.

Judging by the erratic sway, the vehicle had been floating when it stopped abruptly with a huge clamor of metal upon metal, followed by a grinding, hydraulic sound. Morgan was thrown backward. His head hit hard. He fought the temptation to curse. The swaying continued for a few more moments and then all but stopped. *Christ! Think, damn it. Where the fuck am I?*

Morgan set to extracting himself from the bindings. No matter what was planned for him, he had to have his hands and feet free the moment the vehicle stopped and the trunk opened. Whatever happened after that was up to him.

The vehicle started moving again, slowly at first. Other engines nearby began to rev and horns were resounding through a closed-in area. The vehicle he was in gathered speed and bounced over a ramp. The swaying sensation was gone now and the vehicle was back on a steady surface. Had he just left a ferry?

With painstakingly deliberate movements, so as not to draw the attention of the driver, Morgan quietly contorted his body to bring his arms around from the back to the front. Within the trunk it was almost impossible but he had to make it happen. There was no other option.

Reaching down as far as he could, dangerously running the risk of dislocating both shoulders, he pulled his wrists painfully around his buttocks and the edges of his boots until they were in front of his body once again. Then he felt for the tactical folding knife he kept concealed inside his left boot. It was an M16-14ZSF tactical knife with a folding Tanto blade. Mike Fredericks had given it to him while he was recovering onboard the USS *Kearsarge* and it was a memento of their experiences in the Malfajiri evacuation. Rummaging blindly, he found it. There! It had been missed by his captors. They'd been so busy trying to bundle him into the car without anyone hearing or seeing them that they'd botched the search. Fumbling in the dark, Morgan pulled the knife from the boot and opened the blade. Spinning it back around in his hands with the tip facing upward and the razor-sharp cutting edge facing out, Morgan began the steady process of slashing through the thick, taped bindings on his wrists.

It was slow and hard going and with every stop, bump and turn in the road, the tip of the blade stabbed into the flesh of his wrists or the cutting edge slashed at his fingertips. More than once he dropped it and lost precious time in retrieving and repositioning it. Eventually, Morgan had cut through enough to pull his wrists clear. He drew in a long, much needed breath and stretched his arms out as much as he could, flexing his fingers and bending his elbows, feeling the blood flowing again.

He brought his left hand up close to his eyes and read the time from the luminous hands of the Tag Heuer: 3pm.

His mind raced through options for where he was being taken. He considered the time that had elapsed since he'd entered the house in Lija and the fact that he'd traveled over water and was now back on land. The image of a map of Malta formed in his mind's eye and Morgan studied it intently. Then it came to him. The ferry had to be the Gozo Channel ferry, connecting the main island of Malta to the northern island of Gozo. From memory, the trip across the channel took about half an hour. So, they'd left Malta via the Cirkewwa Ferry Terminal and were now on Gozo. What the hell were they doing on Gozo?

One thing was certain, the island wasn't that big. So, whatever was going to happen, it was going to happen soon.

Morgan bent his aching body again and with the knife firmly in his hand he began slashing at the duct tape binding his ankles.

Chapter Twenty-Eight

INTREPID HQ, BROADWAY, LONDON

"What do you have for me, Ms Haddad? Good news, I hope?"

"Well, it's certainly not bad news, not yet, at any rate," Ms Haddad began, pushing a thick curl of long raven hair behind her ear. She fixed big brown eyes upon the general. "We've been able to gather the financials and some background on Mr Raoul Demaçi. He's Montenegrin, has a personal fortune estimated at six million euros and if liquidated, with other shared interests – mostly real estate – his personal fortune could rise in excess of fifteen million euros."

"Go on," said Davenport.

"Well, there isn't a great deal more. Yes, I've trawled the Interpol and Europol databases, as well as the relevant security services, and have managed to find corroborating evidence of his financials and his businesses – he's made his money through long-haul transportation, trucks and shipping and so on, across Europe mainly – but there isn't much available on him personally."

"How so?"

Jamila Haddad, Mila to her friends, was executive officer, or XO, to the director general of Intrepid. She was Davenport's go-to person for anything and everything intelligence, criminal profiling or research related. A Lebanese Muslim, Mila had earned a Bachelor of Arts in Arabic Language and Literature at the American University of Beirut and a Masters in Criminology from the University of Toronto. When Davenport had recruited her on the recommendation of a colleague in The Hague, she'd been a research assistant to a judge of the International Criminal Court. Still only in her late twenties, Mila possessed a highly disciplined, analytical mind complemented by an innate ability to think boldly outside the square. She had worked for the general for just a year, but already Davenport considered her indispensable.

"It's unusual for a person to have made that much money and not have any visibility," she replied. "I mean, he has a small presence online but not much."

"I would have thought that normal, particularly in that part of the world. Not every culture is as obsessed as ours with maintaining a public profile on the bloody internet."

"I agree with that, sir. But I'd still expect to find more. Investments, business associations, trading history, government listings; there's usually something to dig into when getting a background together. There's not even a photo of him anywhere online and his passport mug shot tells us nothing; the way it's been taken, well, it could just about be anybody. Whatever the story, he's too elusive for my liking."

"Very well, keep digging. If Mr Demaçi has anything to hide, I'm sure you'll find it. Now, any more on this Lazarević creature?"

"That line of enquiry has become significantly more

enticing." A wide smile of genuine pleasure illuminated her fine features. "I was searching through your old files from Bosnia for whatever I could find on Corporal Dobrashin Petrović – aka the informant, Đurađ Lazarević – and I came across some handwritten notes you'd made on a case file back in 1994." Mila moved forward to the edge of Davenport's desk and laid open a tattered military folder, heavy with pages and the smell of old paper left in storage for too many years. With long, slender fingers, she traced her way to a place on a page and turned the file around for the general to see. "You've made these notes throughout this section, almost as an aside, mostly just question marks or 'who?' and so on." She continued to run through the pages, pointing out the general's red scrawl. "But then there's this word 'Vuk'. Which, I took to be Serbian and discovered that it means—"

"Wolf," Davenport said.

"Exactly," she replied eagerly. "It appears throughout the next thirty pages, whenever there's a reference to the unexplained deaths you were investigating. Not the mass murders. Your red scratchings were only made in relation to single unexplained murders: civilians mostly, but there were also some members of the Bosnian Serb Army, which is interesting. It seems you extracted this wolf reference as the common denominator through a number of witness statements you'd taken. But, as far as your notes are concerned, there was nothing to corroborate a connection or any sort of lead."

"My God," Davenport said, almost to himself. He was squinting through his glasses at the red-inked scribbles he'd left upon the pages sixteen years before. "How on earth did you find all this?"

"Because you asked me to," she replied matter-of-factly.

"But this is where it gets interesting. Here's where you were onto something." She leant down closer to the pages and flipped through a couple until she found what she was after. "Look at that."

In his own handwriting, in aged red ink, staring back at him beneath a perfectly manicured fingernail, he read: *Vuk: Serb enforcer?*

"It's coming back to me now," he said softly, easing the file closer and pulling his glasses down to the end of his nose. "We believed there was an enforcer at work, killing people, particularly Bosniaks suspected of collaborating with the Serbs who, for whatever reason, had outlived their usefulness. About the same time, we discovered that a number of officers of the Bosnian Serb Army were also being killed, mostly captains and majors, the odd colonel or two. In those cases we suspected that the murdered men had not been cooperating with the senior leadership. Not toeing the party line, as it were. Hence, my suspicion that an unidentified enforcer was at work."

In that moment, Davenport was transported back all those years. He'd recently been allotted to the Army Legal Services Branch of the Adjutant-General's Corps, fresh from his medical retirement from the Special Air Service, after a long process of rehabilitation resulting from a bomb blast injury during the first Gulf War. While he'd completed his law degree many years earlier, his unprecedented success in Army Legal was as much a consequence of his gut instinct – borne of a soldier's experience – as his formal education. It was a combination that saw him rocket to the top of the corps, retiring as director general of Army Legal Services before he was headhunted to raise and lead Intrepid.

Returning to the file, he scoured the pages, flicking

through them impatiently. The familiarity of his own words and deductions came flooding back.

"I never did get the opportunity to get to the bottom of this. Back then, hunting the bigger fish became the priority of the International Criminal Tribunal for the former Yugoslavia. Rightly so, of course. Still, it meant that distractions such as my speculation over a rogue killer engaged by the Serb generals to do their dirty work fell to the bottom of the pile."

"Well, I think you were onto something then that may be even more important to us today." Mila reached forward and, turning the pages, pointed to a name Davenport had underlined with a question mark above it. "One of the names you suspected of being the enforcer was Corporal Dobrashin Petrović."

"And now," Davenport hissed, "he's Interpol's star bloody informant."

Chapter Twenty-Nine

GOZO, MALTA

"There, bitch, take it and wash yourself."

The boss stood over her as one of his lackeys placed a large pail of seawater on the ground. A second dropped soap and a towel. Charly looked up at them, her piercing blue eyes defiant. Despite the exhaustion, exposure to the elements, the fear and abuse, Charlotte-Rose had regained her composure and sense of self. She was not going to spend her last days or moments as a victim. She was stronger than that; much stronger. Her fire had returned. Her parents hadn't brought her up to give in, no matter how dire the circumstances. Lying there, as she had been before they'd roused her, Charly had resolved to stand her ground. It was the only way.

"Hand me that soap and towel and get out," she said as she stood. Her eyes drew level with the boss. "And get me some proper clothes. You mentioned a deal. That means you're just the babysitter. So, whatever's going on, you better start taking care of me!"

The boss leapt forward, frothing with anger. His arm

was raised, his hand clenched into a tight fist. Charly didn't budge. Her rebelliousness checked his momentum.

Their eyes locked in seething conflict. One army pitted against another. But this time, the fortunes of the underdog, out-gunned, out-maneuvered and on the verge of defeat, had turned. Tenacity had taken on brutality and was holding ground.

"Get – me – some – fucking – clothes!" Charly demanded.

The boss, hysterical with anger, pushed his face so close to hers that his rancid breath assailed her. Spit sprayed across her fair cheeks as his breathing raged through jagged rows of clenched yellow teeth. The knuckles of his fist, still high above, showed white through the flesh of his shaking brown hand.

"Boss, no!" cried one of the lackeys, worried. "They'll be here soon."

Their eyes remained locked, neither willing to withdraw back to neutral territory.

Finally, the fist relaxed and slowly dropped to his side. A thin attempt at a smile split his pitted face and he sneered and then laughed. The lackeys joined in. Charly remained unmoved.

"Bitch, your little journey is just getting started," he said knowingly. "Be ready to move in half an hour. We will come for you." Then, without taking his eyes from her, he added, "Friggieri, give her the clothes."

The same man who had brought in the soap and towel disappeared outside and returned with clean clothes for Charly: an oversized pair of jeans, a long-sleeved shirt, sweater and pair of loafers. Much better than what they'd kept her in over the past days. He dropped them near her and grabbed the boss by the arm to lead him away. At first the boss balked at the attempt to move him but then, thinking better of it, spat on the ground at her feet and stormed out of the cave.

When they had finally left her alone, Charly's knees buckled and she fell to the ground, shaking. The adrenalin overload finally got the better of her.

In the distance she could hear an aircraft engine.

It was getting closer.

Chapter Thirty

Morgan felt every bump, pothole and divot in the road. Despite having barely enough room in the trunk of the car for his rib cage to expand and contract, he had spent the best part of the last half an hour feeling as though he was stuck in the spin cycle of a washing machine.

He was still monitoring the vehicle's movement and judging by the number of times they'd had to slow down for turns and to pull over so larger vehicles could get past and the fact that there'd been many more left turns than right, he surmised that they'd traveled mostly narrow sealed roads, heading west. The last ten minutes had been over rough, unsealed roads, hence the spin cycle. Given that they were on Malta's northernmost island, Gozo, the route suggested that they'd avoided Gozo's major population center, Victoria, and were out near the coast somewhere.

Morgan was bracing himself as best he could against the constant jarring when the vehicle came to a dead stop. He unfolded his knife and got ready.

He heard mumbling coming from the driver and

passenger as the engine shut off. The two front doors opened. One slammed shut.

"Get the bags."

Morgan recognized the voice of the big Serb, barking orders at the younger one. In the background, he could hear the ocean crashing against the coast.

"What about him?" the young Serb asked. *Yeah, what about me?* Morgan mused.

"You can come back for that piece of shit later. We'll drop him out once we get in the air."

Morgan closed the knife and returned it to the inside of his boot, listening while the young guy pulled luggage from the back of the car. There was a definite hierarchy. Obviously, the older guy was too important to do any carrying.

Without knowing exactly where they were located or if anyone else had been left standing guard over the car, Morgan's best bet was to stay put and wait for the chance to make his move when they came back for him.

Chapter Thirty-One

"What the fuck is going on?" the big Serb demanded in Maltese from inside the entrance to the cave. He'd come to collect his package, but wasn't happy about the condition it was in.

He moved closer to Charly, who was sitting on a rock, her wrists and ankles bound with rope. The bruising around her eyes and mouth was obvious. He grabbed her face with his huge paw, coaxing her to stand and turn so he could see her features more clearly. His eyes wandered hungrily over her face and body. Charly squirmed, terrified of this new arrival.

"Did any of them fuck you?" he asked her in English, loudly enough for the men to hear, although concern for her was not his priority. Charly couldn't answer, her face still clamped in the big Serb's mitt. She shook her head. "But they tried," he said, reading the fire in her eyes. "Which one of you is in charge?" he said, returning to Maltese, still looking at her. Behind him, the three local hoods remained silent.

The big Serb released his grip on her and turned slowly around to face the men. The two lackeys had already withdrawn behind their boss, betraying him, instinctively backing toward the entrance to the cave to save their own skin – self-preservation obviously outweighed loyalty in this trio. The boss remained silent. Charly couldn't understand what had been asked but she could guess. She shrank against the wall at the back of the cave, trying to make herself invisible.

"All you had to do was babysit and keep her in pristine condition until we came to collect her," said the big Serb. He was moving toward the boss with the lazy self-assuredness of an alpha male about to mark his territory. His tone remained calm and level, never rising beyond conversation volume. "Nobody said anything about roughing her up or making her sleep on the floor like a dog or trying to fuck her. Now look at her. How am I supposed to explain this?" He reached the man. A monstrous hand leapt up from his side and slapped the boss across the side of his face. The impact nearly dropped him, half the size of the big Serb. "You were paid to do a job. You agreed to the conditions but you haven't delivered. What should I do?" Another slap, this time with the other hand to the opposite side of the face. This one sent the boss to the ground.

At the back of the cave, Charly had turned away and had covered her ears to shield herself from the inevitable.

"There's nothing wrong with the bitch," the boss spat insolently from the cave floor. "We kept her here so no-one would find her, just like we were told. So she got roughed up, so what? Who is she anyway?"

The big Serb's silence was more unnerving than hearing him speak. Unhurriedly, he moved just past the boss who remained on the floor, rubbing his face. The big Serb was looking out to sea, seemingly weighing something up. Then without another word, he turned around, grabbed the boss by the collar of his shirt, dragged him back out to the opening of the cave and hurled him head first over the precipice. The man was dead before he realized that he was about to be.

The big Serb walked back in to face the two cowering lackeys as if he'd just returned from taking a piss.

"Bring her down to the pier."

Chapter Thirty-Two

Alex Morgan could hear footsteps approaching the car. He recognized the lazy shuffle of the young Serb. Twenty minutes had gone by and he felt like his legs would seize if he couldn't stretch them out soon. But he needed to be ready and finally it seemed like the time had come.

Morgan knew the young Serb would expect to find him still bound and gagged, possibly even semiconscious, when he returned, so surprise was all Morgan had on his side. What he had against him was that having been trussed up for a couple of hours, despite his wrists and ankles now being freed, his body had cramped through lack of movement within the confined space. That, coupled with the position he'd be forced to attack from and the uncertainty of whether or not the guy would be armed or arrive with backup, meant his odds weren't great.

The languid footfalls drew closer and closer, each one sliding into a crunch against the gravel surface of the unsealed road. Listening carefully for others, Morgan was satisfied that the guy was alone. Good. He braced. A dozen possible scenarios flashed through his mind. Morgan squinted his eyes to reduce the sudden impact of the sun's glare upon his vision. A key slid into the trunk's lock and turned.

Despite his precaution, the intensity of the sunlight burst into what for the past two hours had been a pitch-black void. The glare was overwhelming. But there was no time for adjustment – the threat was immediate. All he could do was react to the silhouette as the trunk opened.

In a brazen move, Morgan's left hand shot up, grabbed the young Serb's wrist and wrenched the arm inward, tipping the man over his center of gravity. At the same time, he launched his other hand for the shirt collar and, grabbing a handful, pulled the man inward hard, smashing the young Serb's face against the straight metal edge of the trunk's open lid. Morgan repeated the move twice more, splitting the Serb wide open across the bridge of the nose.

Morgan exploded from the trunk, kicking the Serb out of the way. The two of them fell in a crumpled heap. Morgan rolled onto his back, finally clear of the confined space. His legs felt like jelly as blood rushed back to them.

The back of the young Serb's head hit the ground first. Dazed, blood streaming down his face, no clue what had just happened, he turned over onto all fours to get up. A kick from Morgan's brown suede boot connected with the side of his head. Unconscious, the man slumped face first into the graveled road.

Morgan stood over him and breathed in a deep, precious lungful of fresh sea air. He spun the Serb onto his back and found his own gun, the SIG Sauer P226, tucked into the waistband of the guy's jeans. Retrieving it, he checked it was still loaded, grabbed the spare magazines that had also been pilfered and re-equipped the paddle holster and mag pouches on his belt. Rummaging through the pockets again he found his sat phone. He tapped in his security code and was relieved to find the thing still operating. He immediately called Intrepid HQ, got through to the 24/7 operations room, gave his designation number – four three – and waited to be patched through to the chief of staff.

"Alex, it's Mila," came the no-nonsense reply. "Chief of staff is still on leave. Tell me what's going on."

"OK, Mila," he began, knowing the conversation would be recorded. "Here we go ..."

Morgan gave her the headlines of everything that had occurred to date, speaking quickly to get as much across as he could within limited time: his inspection of the boat; the blank ammunition he'd found onboard; the captain and the policeman; the address of the house he'd followed them to; the Serbs; and the urgent need, he stressed, to get local law enforcement to him ASAP.

"I'm on the west coast of Gozo island, on the southern end of a large bay." He looked around, trying to get his bearings and recall his memory of the key features of Gozo. "I think it's called—"

"Dwejra Bay, the Azure Window," Mila replied. "I've just pulled it up on Google maps. OK, what do you need?"

"Wait a minute," Morgan said, hearing the piercing scream of a woman in distress, audible above the crashing of the sea along the coast.

He ran to the edge of a small cliff and then, as he strained to get a fix on her location, the splutter of an engine being coaxed to life drew his attention to the water's edge far below.

"Gotta go," he said. "Get whatever coverage you can to track an aircraft: seaplane, yellow and white with the letters HF on the tail; about to take off from this location. And send some cops. Out."

Chapter Thirty-Three

The seaplane, a de Havilland DHC-3 Turbine Single Otter, was one of a fleet normally hired out for charter flights around the islands of Malta. But today the fleet would be operating minus one. The aircraft had been commandeered, unlawfully, and a new pilot, one more familiar with illicit sorties across borders than tourist joy flights, sat at the controls. The actual owner/operator was lying dead in the Harbour Flight office on the Valletta waterfront with a 9mm slug from a Russian-made Stenchkin automatic buried in his skull.

The DHC-3 was moored next to a long concrete pier. It was out of the way, rarely used and reached far into the water from the end of a narrow dirt track that wound back up into the cliffs.

On the pier the big Serb stood lazily smoking and talking familiarly with a man who obviously spent most of his gangster downtime in a gym. He stood only 5 feet 6 inches but was a ball of steroid-induced muscle mass. His head was completely bald and he wore a thick, dark goatee.

His skintight, sleeveless T-shirt suggested he liked the way he looked, too. Muscles had flown in with the seaplane from Valletta and, on the big Serb's orders, was responsible for hijacking it, along with taking care of the loose ends at the Harbour Flight office. The Stechkin was in a dodgy shoulder holster buried under his right armpit.

The big Serb and Muscles watched with detached amusement as the two local lackeys continued their efforts to manhandle Charly aboard. It was a struggle – she was fighting them all the way. The big Serb was boasting about the captured cop they'd brought all the way up from Lija in the trunk. He was impatient to show off his new prisoner.

He laughed. "We'll drop the piece of shit onto the cliffs once we're airborne."

Meanwhile, even with wrists and ankles bound, Charly bucked, squirmed and twisted with all she had to make it as difficult as she could for them. But, despite her fierce, unwavering resistance, they managed to get her up the short ladder, shoving her unceremoniously into the plane. In a last-ditch effort to summon help before she was closed up inside the plane, Charly let out a blood-curdling scream. Muscles stepped across and pushed the lackeys aside. Charly looked up into his eyes, paralyzed with shock; recognition written all over her horrified face.

"You!" she cried. "But, you were—" Before she could finish, Muscles back-handed her across the side of the neck. The expert blow concussed her, buying the lackeys enough time to tie her into a seat.

"Hey, who the fuck is that up there watching us?" It was the pilot, troubled, pointing urgently toward the cliff top above them. He'd stepped out of the aircraft to do his routine checks before take-off and happened to look up to where the young Serb had disappeared to collect the other prisoner from the car. "That doesn't look like your guy?"

The big Serb turned around with his usual economy and realized that the man standing at the top of the cliff was not his young offsider. It was the prisoner.

In the instant that the big Serb's eyes locked onto him, Morgan disappeared from view.

"Fuck! Fuck! Fuck!" he spat; the cigarette tumbled from his lips. "You two untie us," he barked at the lackeys and, stabbing a finger at the pilot, said, "And *you* get this fucking thing in the air!"

Sprinting back from the cliff's edge, Morgan tore the car keys from the trunk and dived into the driver's seat. It was an old Peugeot and took its time to start.

"Come on! Come on!" he ordered and the old car coughed into action. He pumped the gas, revving the engine to life, wrenched the gearshift into first, stamped on the accelerator and threw the car into a tight U-turn around the comatose body of the young Serb. Gravel and dust sprayed from the spinning tires. The Peugeot fishtailed wildly on the loose rocky surface of the dirt road until the Intrepid agent tore the wheel back around, straightened the car and hurled it down the hillside. His eyes were fixed on the pier.

In the distance the sun was already hanging heavily in the sky, slipping toward the horizon. Dusk. He had less than an hour of daylight left, if that.

Chapter Thirty-Four

Aboard the seaplane, the big Serb bellowed at the pilot to take off.

"I can't. We're still tied up!" the pilot replied from the cockpit. "Those two assholes—"

"What the fuck?" the big Serb fumed impatiently. He punched the seat in front of him in frustration and then spun toward Muscles. "Sort those motherfuckers out!" he barked in Serbian, spit spraying from his mouth.

Muscles sprang from his seat, threw open the back door of the aircraft, clambered down onto the float and, with the Stechkin in hand, roared at the two lackeys on the pier to get the mooring ropes untied.

At that moment, Alex Morgan was hurtling down the ancient fisherman's track, skidding, braking and accelerating all the way. He saw nothing but the seaplane and every inch and bend in the road that lay between him and

Charlotte-Rose Fleming. His mind focused only on negotiating the car as fast as humanly possible along half a mile of dangerously narrow dirt road. There was nothing on either side but cliffs until a last-minute drop down to the pier. He had no idea what he would do when he got there or even if the plane would still be alongside. But he could see it. His objective was within reach. He knew she was onboard and nothing was going to stop him getting to her.

With sweat pouring from his brow and fierce determination chiseled across mission-hardened features, Morgan's limbs were in a state of automatic reflex, expertly responding to his subliminal instructions, manipulating gearshift, steering wheel and pedals to hurtle the aging vehicle down the rollercoaster ride of bends, sweeps and dips. At every perilous left and right turn, the Peugeot came close to careening over the edge. If it did, Morgan would plummet to a god-awful end among the rocks and crashing waves that were the hallmark of the Gozo coastline. But he couldn't think about that. If it happened, it happened. His eyes were locked onto the seaplane with the precision and singular purpose of a state-of-the-art guidance system in a surface-to-air missile.

At the controls, the pilot was anxious. He didn't know who the crazy bastard in the car was but he'd picked up enough listening to the Serbs to know he was Interpol or Europol or something. The pilot had his own reasons for not wanting to get caught: he was as desperate to get airborne as his clients. He brought the de Havilland up to maximum revs, ready to power off but the rope was jammed at the mooring and two pairs of inexperienced hands were making a dog's breakfast of it. He slid open his window.

"Come on, you assholes! Cast us off!"

Hearing the pilot, Muscles knew that two was just making matters worse – both pairs of hands were a mess of red rope. He saw the Peugeot gaining ground, rapidly – a long trail of white dust billowed in the car's wake as it screamed down the hill toward them at breakneck speed. The cop had only two or three turns left and he'd be on the direct approach to the pier. Fuck! With that, Muscles turned back to the lackeys, took aim with the Stechkin and fired. A round hit the closest one straight through the side of the chest. He toppled into the water, dead.

Stunned, the remaining lackey looked up. All he could see was the barrel of the automatic trained directly on him from backdoor of the aircraft.

In seconds, he'd unraveled the chaos and jumped into the water, clear of the firing line.

The plane was finally set free.

Chapter Thirty-Five

With a fierce burst of power, the 750-shaft-horsepower PT-6 engine of the DHC-3 responded to the release like a thoroughbred breaking away from the starting gate. The propeller bit into the wind and tore the seaplane clear with a jolt. Still leaning from the rear door, the unexpected forward thrust forced Muscles to grapple for a hold, but he missed. Dropping the gun, he fell clumsily down into the ladder, struts and tension cables that connected the port-side float to the fuselage. The pilot was oblivious, focused only on getting airborne. The big Serb didn't notice either. His eyes were fixed solely upon the looming image of the Peugeot, his Peugeot, racing toward them.

Morgan was perfectly aligned. The nose of the car pointed straight for the long concrete pier that ran along the port side of the seaplane. He was so close he could hear the de Havilland's propeller whining as the pilot headed from the bay to the open sea. Designed for short take-off and landing, the seaplane needed only 200 yards of clear water to get in the air and Morgan could see it would be a matter of seconds before the pilot would be lined up. If they took off, he would miss his only chance to reach Charly.

Morgan stamped on the gas and the Peugeot charged forward, shuddering and bouncing across the rough dirt track, hungrily grabbing at the final 30 yards, tossing each aside, one by one, until the tires gratefully reached the long flat surface of the pier.

In the cockpit, the pilot was determined to take off. A strong headwind came straight toward the coast, perfectly lined up across the nose of the aircraft. Facing into the wind would give him more lift and reduce the distance he'd require to get into the air. He set the flaps and checked the instrument panel. Oil pressure and temperature gauges read green. He lined up. Ready. He took the aircraft to full throttle. The airspeed indicator came to life: 35 knots. Keeping the long finger of the pier to his left, the pilot pumped the pedals to keep her straight, increasing speed all the way.

Morgan was running out of options. Only twenty seconds away from the end of the pier, his foot was flat to the floor. He knew the seaplane was about to fly, but he was gaining ground. The yards and seconds ticked by. Faster and faster he pushed the car, eating up the concrete that flashed beneath. He was close enough to see Muscles fumbling about on the float closest to the pier, trying to climb back into the aircraft. Morgan pushed the car harder. The needle of the speedometer leapt from 35 to 40 mph, but it felt like 60 mph. Water on either side raced past in a blur. His only tactical advantage was that the pilot had been forced to stay parallel to the pier to avoid a number of old fishing boats that sat anchored on his far side.

Morgan saw what he had to do. The most minute flash of red was all he needed to formulate a plan.

There was no time for second-guessing and no margin

for error. Alex Morgan changed down and rammed his foot to the floor. The Peugeot howled in protest but the needle flashed to 45 mph. He'd closed the gap so quickly that the nose of the car was now level with the tail of the seaplane.

Muscles, clinging to the float, looked back. He couldn't believe what he was seeing. The Peugeot was bearing down hard and the end of the pier was just feet away when he saw the driver's door fly open.

Morgan hurled himself out into thin air as the car cleared the end of the pier, crashing into the bay.

Chapter Thirty-Six

Alex Morgan surrendered to the dive, allowing the Peugeot's momentum to propel him straight at the retreating seaplane. He'd no other choice. If he failed, he was back to square one and Charly would be left to the mercy of the Serbs.

Soaring through the air, Morgan sucked in a huge lungful of oxygen and prepared for impact with the churning water. He hit it in a flat dive, scything through the aircraft's wake. Miraculously, but as planned, he caught the long red tail of mooring rope snaking behind the seaplane. Gripping on tight as the plane picked up the slack, Morgan was pulled behind, a huge bow wave forming in front of him as he ploughed through the water. He gasped for breath. Another suit ruined, he thought humorlessly.

"What the fuck just happened?" the pilot shouted. "Something rocked the shit out of us."

"Keep going," the big Serb ordered, stunned. He'd seen the car hit the water. He knew exactly what had rocked them. "Get us out of here."

Shocked by the spectacle of the car launching into the bay, the big Serb shook his head before realizing Muscles wasn't inside. He pushed roughly past Charly to reach the door. She was starting to regain consciousness. When he looked outside, he saw his compadre shouting, desperately trying to get back in.

"Give me your hand!" cried the big Serb, leaning out to him. The plane was picking up speed. The engine noise and howling wind was deafening. He could see Muscles was yelling but couldn't make out a word he was saying. "Just give me your fucking hand!" he bellowed.

Strung out behind the seaplane, Morgan buffeted across the wave tops. He was struggling. With his boots on and the fact that he hadn't waterskied in years, the odds of getting into an optimum position weighed heavily against him. The DeHavilland was rapidly reaching take-off speed and Morgan guessed that they were close to 70 knots already; the equivalent of 80 mph.

Hand over hand, against the pounding impact of the bow wave, he began the excruciating task of clawing his way along the few feet of mooring rope left between him and the floats. Morgan was unfaltering in his resolve. Every second brought him closer to the seaplane, as he methodically moved forward in a series of reach-twist-and-breathe movements. The speed picked up on the plane. The pilot was taking off.

Morgan was almost there.

The engine roared. The aircraft bounced. The pilot brought the nose up into a steep climb. As the floats lifted from the surface, Morgan was dragged from the water into the slipstream, clinging to the bight of the rope.

With 80 mph winds hammering him, Morgan twisted and turned on the rope like a ribbon on a car's radio antenna. His hands were bleeding and he felt that he'd drop at any moment. He couldn't see or hear anything but the azure haze of the sea below and the screaming howl of wind and engine noise.

The Intrepid agent locked his legs to what he could of the flailing rope and determinedly clung on with every muscle in his body. Inch by inch he pulled his way to the port-side float.

The big Serb had Muscles by the arms and was trying to pull him inside, but he was still yelling.

"What the fuck is wrong with you?" the big Serb yelled. "Get in—"

Exasperated, Muscles shouted back and the big Serb finally heard him. "The fucking cop," he said, "is on the fucking plane!"

Just as the revelation hit home, the big Serb grimaced as a bloodied hand grabbed Muscles' face. He watched, transfixed, as an entire arm locked around the man's neck, pulling him from the door.

A bizarre tug-of-war death struggle exploded between Morgan on the outside and the big Serb inside, each pulling with all their might to overcome the other, Muscles stuck in the middle.

The de Havilland was gaining height but the pilot struggled to control the ascent. Distracted by the ruckus, he'd lost his concentration at a crucial moment in the climb. The aircraft gave a splutter and began to sway.

The fight threatened to bring them all down.

Alex Morgan was at a serious disadvantage. He'd been hanging on to the aircraft with one hand while trying to dislodge Muscles with the other. Meanwhile, both the Serbs were working hammer-and-tongs to dislodge him. Faced with impossible odds, they soon got the jump on Morgan and he slipped as the big Serb hoisted Muscles inside. But Morgan never gave up easily. As the big Serb dragged his man in, Morgan came in too, firmly attached to the lower half of Muscles' tree-trunk legs.

It was then that he saw Charly, her mane of flaming red hair instantly recognizable.

Blue tear-filled eyes locked onto his.

"Oh my God!" she cried. "Who …?"

The big Serb silenced her with a slap across the face as he fumbled for a gun sitting within a holster on the back of his seat.

Muscles, trying to kick free of Morgan's grip, had spun around, bashing down hard upon Morgan's back, his clenched fists clasped together as one.

"Hang on, Charly!" Morgan managed to call out, catching a flash of acknowledgment from her eyes.

Charly could scarcely believe what she was seeing. Her would-be rescuer, a sodden, bedraggled wreck, was hanging half in, half out of a rapidly ascending aircraft, with one man beating him senseless and another about to shoot him. Charly couldn't miss the gun brandished right beside her. The big Serb had torn an old Makarov from the holster and fired recklessly at Morgan.

"No! No!" Charly screamed, thrashing against the ropes tying her to her seat.

The seaplane lurched to the left and began to drop from the sky. In a desperate attempt to recover the take-off, the pilot was forced into a drastic new maneuver. As the Makarov erupted in the back of the fuselage, the pilot pulled the seaplane through a slow arc to port, dropped the nose and headed down toward the sea. The descent enabled him to build up speed and stop the engine from stalling, which it had been dangerously close to doing. His move had extreme consequences.

One round from the Makarov punched into the seat by the door, inches from Morgan's head, and another into the wall behind him. The third shot was much lower than the others and Morgan felt the unmistakable tug of its flight path through the fine fabric of his suit coat, skimming across his back, missing his flesh by a fraction of an inch. At that moment the pilot made his move, the left side of the plane dropped and Morgan's arms slipped down Muscles' legs to his feet. Feeling the change in Morgan's grip, Muscles reacted instantly. Pulling a leg free, he kicked down hard upon Morgan's left shoulder.

Morgan plummeted from the aircraft, an indelible image of Charly's terrified face haunting him all the way down.

Chapter Thirty-Seven

TIRANA, ALBANIA

"We've got increased activity here." It was Call-sign Two, reporting in from the second location. "Our man, Lazarević, has been back and forth between his own apartment and this one all day. He's just returned from the grocery store with more supplies."

"Any sign of his mysterious friend?" Braunschweiger asked. He'd just returned from a meeting with the head of Interpol's National Central Bureau in Albania and the general director of Albania's national police force. The Head of Interpol in Tirana had paved the way for emergency backup from Albanian State Police special operations officers, if needed. The support of the ASP was critical if Intrepid needed to fire up any short-notice distress flares as a result of their surveillance operation. Braunschweiger had a feeling that time was upon them.

"No sign of the friend," came the reply from Call-sign Two. "Not for about an hour."

"OK, what's your take on our man's activity?" Braunschweiger was operating from his hotel room. It was two star and barely habitable but it was central to both apartments they were watching and, most importantly, it wasn't the van.

"Honestly, I think they're expecting company; most likely today. He's stocking up on food, milk, cigarettes, magazines."

"Well, this could be what we've been waiting for," the Key answered. "Well done on confirming the apartment by the way. Good job. When you hand over to Five, come back here and fill me in on the apartment details. We're going to need them."

"Thanks, will do. Bit strange that the friend hasn't emerged for a while, though."

"I agree," replied Braunschweiger. "Stay on it. Maybe he'll surface through another entrance. I'll recheck the CCTV coverage to see if there's anything we may have missed. The main priority is to keep eyes on the apartment block, all entrances."

"Copy that."

"Three, are you online?"

"Copy, this is Three," came the reply. "I'm on approach from the southern end of the building."

"Roger, Three. I want you to prioritize eyes on the rear entrances, vehicle and pedestrian. Find a good spot and get comfortable. Unless you're compromised, I expect you'll be there for some time."

"Understood."

Braunschweiger dropped the radio mike back onto the vinyl-topped card table that served as the room's dining area and sat on the end of the bed.

The latest was that the second apartment had now become the priority target for the surveillance teams. It had become obvious that the Interpol informant, Lazarević, was prepared for – or, at least, surrendered to – the chance that he was under observation. That made sense, given Davenport's most recent update that Lazarević was in fact a former Serbian Army soldier named Petrović and, if Davenport's theory was correct, was also suspected of being an enforcer during the Bosnian War, known only as the Wolf. Skilled at reducing the efficacy of surveillance coverage, he made no calls from his flat, sent no emails and had no visitors. Most importantly, any meetings with the friend, while initially appearing random, were clearly the result of a schedule that had been mapped out well in advance. They'd had no luck in identifying the friend, but that would come. Dave Sutherland was working that angle.

Meanwhile, his gut told him things were ramping up. He was sure there would be action at the second apartment within the next twenty-four hours. He wasn't sure what exactly. He needed to know what Morgan had managed to find out in Malta. Maybe then they could finally connect the dots.

With that, Braunschweiger reached across to the table and grabbed his sat phone. He speed-dialed Morgan's number again, having tried a number of times during the day with no success.

Once again, Morgan didn't respond.

He looked at his watch.

Time to check in with Intrepid HQ.

Chapter Thirty-Eight

GOZO, MALTA

The blast of whirring rotor blades and wailing sirens was deafening.

Alex Morgan came back to consciousness amid a crescendo of intense noise. It was dark, night had fallen, and he was lying on a gurney. But he was alive and, somehow, on dry land. A paramedic leant over him wearing a head-torch and taking his vitals. Morgan was aware of lots of people running about, lots of shouting and vehicles coming and going. The familiar Velcro-tear of a blood pressure monitor being removed from his arm jolted him back to his senses.

"Ah, you're awake," said the paramedic in Maltese-accented English, flipping the head-torch up and away from Morgan's face. "Welcome back. We were starting to get worried."

That isn't encouraging, thought Morgan. "Where am I?" he asked.

"Dwejra Bay. There are important people waiting for

you to resurface." Morgan noticed him wave somebody over. "You're very lucky, my friend."

"Lucky? Lucky how?" asked Morgan. He wasn't feeling it.

"That old man." The paramedic gestured with his head. Morgan didn't look. "He's a local fisherman. Lived here his whole life. He was coming back in with his boat, back from fishing, and heard a gunshot coming from this old pier." The paramedic was unstrapping Morgan from the gurney as he spoke. Morgan stayed on his back but tossed the blanket aside. His mouth was dry. He felt like he'd been hit by a bus. Or a boat.

"You got any water?" Morgan asked blearily. "What am I wearing?"

"The cops gave us a set of overalls for you," the medic replied, retrieving a water bottle from his gear and handing it to Morgan. "Your clothes were dripping wet. We couldn't leave you like that."

Morgan vaguely remembered. He gulped down the water.

"The old guy saw everything. Saw you water skiing behind a plane. The plane taking off. Saw you flying behind the plane. And then he saw you fall from the sky. So, he fished you out of the water." Clearly, the medic didn't believe everything the old man had been saying. "Quite a day you've had."

It was obvious to Morgan that the local emergency services people thought the old guy was out of his tree. Better it stayed that way.

"When can I get out of here?" Morgan asked, his head still spinning. "I need my phone. Have you …"

"I have all your equipment, Mr Hamilton."

It was a new voice, a woman's voice; direct and authoritative. The medic disappeared from view. Slowly, Morgan managed to get himself onto one elbow. With some effort, he progressed to sitting upright on the gurney, steadying himself with both arms.

The woman stood directly in front of him. Early to mid-forties, medium height, slender. Short, dark hair in a masculine cut. She looked fit, no-nonsense, and wore the uniform of a Malta Police Force superintendent. She was accompanied by a junior officer, who placed a plastic MPF evidence bag and a large white garbage bag down on the gurney beside Morgan and then, like the medic, disappeared without a word. The evidence bag contained Morgan's sat phone, gun, spare magazines and holster. The garbage bag contained his clothes. That'd be right.

"Mikela Pizzuto." They shook hands. She waited until they were alone. "Major Morgan, we've been contacted by your people in London. I'm the Malta Police Force Interpol liaison officer. I've spoken with Ms Haddad. We will extend you every courtesy."

"Alex Morgan," he replied, impressed by her professionalism. "I'm very grateful."

Morgan tore open the plastic bag, relieved to be reunited, for the second time that day, with his tools of trade. Everything looked OK, even the sat phone. These particular phones were designed to withstand a lot more than a swim.

"Before all this happened," he said, "I briefed my office, Ms Haddad—"

"Yes, the house in Lija. We know about that already," Pizzuto replied. "Our officers took control of the house earlier this evening. They found two men fitting the descriptions you provided; the captain of the yacht and, I believe, a police officer."

"Great, when can we question them?"

"Both were deceased when our officers arrived at the scene. They'd been shot. Formal identification will follow. We'll provide that information back to your people as soon as we have it finalized."

Morgan nodded. "What about out here? There was a guy—"

"A young man was arrested a short time ago," she began. Her expression indicated bad news. "He was pulled over by police in a stolen car, not far from here. Unfortunately, he was shot and killed in an exchange with our officers."

Jesus! The young Serb was their only lead. He'd hoped to question him, and the other two. But that option was now closed. Then he asked: "Any of your guys hurt?"

"No, thank you for asking," she replied. "We have also found a cave that appears to have been used as a refuge of some sort and another body, a man, at the base of the rocks about 200 yards from here. He looks local. He fell or was thrown from the cave. I've arranged for our forensic people to come and take charge of that area."

"So, where to from here?" he asked.

"I'm to escort you back to your hotel in Valletta immediately, where you are to gather your belongings and prepare to travel."

"Travel? Travel where?"

"I'm not able to answer that," she answered. "But I believe your office will make contact with you at your hotel."

"Very well," Morgan replied. "And how are we getting back to Valletta?"

"That helicopter is for you."

Chapter Thirty-Nine

VALLETTA, MALTA

Back in his room at the Grand Hotel Excelsior, Alex Morgan stood under a steaming hot shower, washing away the frustration and, ultimately, failure of the day. He'd been within reach. He could have almost touched her, they were so close. And now she was theirs, trapped in an underworld network she had no hope of escaping on her own. And he, the man sent to recover her, had allowed it to happen, had let her slip through his shredded fingers. At least, that's the way it felt.

After ten minutes of brooding, soaking under the therapeutic pounding of the water, he shut off the taps and stepped out into a steam-filled bathroom. Opening the door so the steam could clear, Morgan grabbed a towel and started to dry himself.

His mind returned over and over again to the image of Charly's face, lost and desperate, imploring him to rescue her. He replayed every second from when he was inside that plane. Was there anything else he could have done? Tormented by utter defeat, Morgan hurled the towel across the bathroom and leant against the marble basin. He caught the reflection of his naked black and blue body in the mirror. Christ, what a great state to be in. He was a mess of cuts, bruises and assorted other wounds and welts. Everything ached like hell, although the shower had done a heap to ease his general malaise.

Morgan walked back out into the room, found two miniature bottles of Glenfiddich, poured them into a glass, took a not-ungenerous swig and began to dress. He'd been told to await a call from London and, in the meantime, prepare for travel while Intrepid continued to track the seaplane. He'd been told that a Boeing E-3 Sentry from NATO's Airborne Early Warning and Control fleet had been diverted from maneuvers with the Italian Air Force. Intrepid would be waiting for confirmation on a definite direction or, better still, a target location from NATO before sending him to follow it. As he finished pulling on a T-shirt, his sat phone rang. He looked at the Tag. It was 9.30pm. Hell of a day.

"Morgan," he answered.

"Alex, it's Mila," Haddad began. "NATO has been tracking the Harbour Flight DHC-3 for three hours. I'm told it took a while to locate because it was flying so low."

"Where's it headed?" Morgan asked bluntly. He needed to be pointed in the right direction, and fast. "It can't be going too far, the range on those things isn't up to much."

"We've been through all that here," she answered testily.

"Fully fueled, it has a range of 1500 kays. That's a considerable area when you plot the circle over a map of southern Europe."

"OK, so where is it now?"

"Albania," Haddad answered. "We've just confirmed that it came down near a place called Himare."

Albania. Why the hell had they taken her to Albania? Hang on. He remembered something the general mentioned that the others were working on. Coming in from another angle, Davenport had said.

"What about—?" Morgan began, but Mila Haddad was way ahead of him.

"Yes, Mr Braunschweiger is on the ground in Tirana already. Without much to go on, we're banking on them taking her to a city apartment we've had under surveillance for some time. Anyway, he'll meet you at Tirana airport and brief you there."

"Great. When do I leave?"

There was a knock at Morgan's door.

"That will be Superintendent Pizzuto," Mila answered confidently. "She'll take you to Malta International Airport where a private charter is waiting for you. Wheels up at 2200 hours. You better get a wriggle on."

"Roger," he replied. "Wait, one more thing."

"Go ahead."

"The big Serb. The one who has her." Morgan's eyes were closed as he recalled an image. Something he'd seen that day. Something important. "He had a tattoo, I could only make out the tip of a wing and the end of a tail—a dragon, or something like that, high on his chest. Angry looking thing. Left side. Could you look into it?"

"Done," she replied. "Now get moving."

Chapter Forty

HIRAME, ALBANIA

Under cover of darkness the 18-foot aluminum tender cut through the surf undetected, all the way to the distant, desolate southern end of the long beach. Keeping the 115 horsepower outboard motor down in the low revs, the handler skillfully brought the vessel out of the water and onto a sandbar with hardly a sound. He was used to it.

The tender had rendezvoused with the de Havilland 500 yards off the coast. Far enough out for the seaplane's engine to be nothing more than a distant murmur out on the dark sea. Extra fuel for the plane was handed over and, while the pilot and Muscles got on with refueling, the big Serb and the boat handler transferred Charly awkwardly across to the boat. By the time they'd hit the beach, the DHC-3 was already lining up for take-off. The pilot had accepted the seaplane as part payment for his role in the abduction. He'd fly it back to Italy, not too far, and after lying low for a while, would get on with refitting and rebranding it. Piece of cake.

On the beach, the big Serb, Muscles and the boat

handler wrangled Charly from the boat into a van that sat idling on a track that led back out onto the main coast road. Nobody said a word. The van was a legitimate hire: white with two back doors and no side windows; completely anonymous.

Gagged, tied and wrapped in a dirty blanket, Charly was bundled into the back with the big Serb and Muscles. As soon as they were in, the doors were shut and the driver, one of the local hired help, got moving. He knew where he had to go. The handler returned to the boat and headed off into the darkness.

The whole process took thirty minutes.

Chapter Forty-One

TIRANA AIRPORT, ALBANIA

Hermann Braunschweiger sat behind the wheel of the surveillance team van, engine running. Even getting in the driver's seat was a squeeze, but it was better than being stuck in the back. He'd been given special dispensation to park in a space normally reserved for Albanian State Police stationed at the airport, so he could make his pick up and get going without wasting valuable time.

In the wing mirror he could see Morgan approaching along the vehicle concourse outside the arrivals hall. Morgan had been waved through the usual customs formalities and a police officer was escorting him all the way to the vehicle. While Braunschweiger hadn't worked with Morgan before, he knew that wouldn't be a problem: he'd been brought up to speed and everything he'd heard was reassuring. The rear door opened. Morgan slung in his gear, a suit carrier and a brown leather duffel bag, then followed it in.

"Alex Morgan," came the introduction from the back. Morgan stuck a hand through and they shook.

"Hermann Braunschweiger," he replied. "But just call me Key. Everybody does."

"I heard that somewhere," Morgan replied truthfully. "Care to elaborate?"

"It's a long story. Maybe I'll tell you after we've finished this." Braunschweiger reversed the van and swung it expertly back out in the airport traffic heading toward the city.

"You're on," said Morgan. A natural connection recognizing mutual respect and trust between two professionals emerged. "I got your message. Is this the gear?"

"Yes, you better suit up. I'll fill you in as we go. We don't have much time."

Morgan dragged over a large dive bag with an Albanian police crest emblazoned across the top and unzipped it. Inside was a familiar assortment of tactical gear the Key had scrounged from the special operations police: overalls, boots, gloves, holsters and, of course, tools of the trade. The weapon was an AKM, 7.62mm with half-a-dozen curved thirty-round magazines. The pistol was a Makarov 9mm. He noted that the Key was already kitted up. Morgan couldn't believe the size of the guy. The nickname was no bloody surprise. *They call him the key that opens any door*, Davenport had said. Morgan could just imagine the big guy being the point man on hard entries with the GSG 9. He didn't imagine there'd be much left for anyone else on the team once they were inside. Morgan was glad they were on the same side.

He stripped out of his civilian clothes and started pulling on the work gear.

Braunschweiger began the update.

"Driving out here, I got word that new arrivals were identified entering one of the apartments we're watching.

It's located in an old section of the city built by the Communists back in the Fifties. Three men. Two big guys," he scoffed, "fitting the descriptions you provided, and a driver. They turned up in a white van, similar to this one, and parked it in the dark around the back of the apartment block. The two big guys hauled a large bundle out of the van and took it upstairs. The driver followed them with bags, then he came back, jumped in the van and took off alone."

Morgan remained silent as he got ready, totally focused on every word Braunschweiger was saying. He wouldn't interrupt or seek clarification until the Key had finished; it was the way things were done.

"One of our people managed to get a remote CCTV micro-camera positioned in the corridor next to the elevator. Tricky job, but it means they now have a clear view of the apartment door. As the two guys were getting the bundle out of the elevator, the camera picked up a couple of feet, small feet, poking out of the end of the blanket. It's not much but—"

"It's enough," Morgan replied. "How long do we have before we get there?"

"Twenty minutes," replied Braunschweiger.

"Great." Morgan took a full magazine from the dive bag and locked it onto the AKM. "Do you have a plan?"

"Do I have a plan?" Braunschweiger looked confidently back at him through the rear-view mirror and grinned.

Chapter Forty-Two

TIRANA, ALBANIA

The naked concrete, glass and steel of the apartment complex reeked of Cold War austerity.

The perfunctory checkerboard design and anonymous facades gave an impression that the people who lived here had moved in and been forgotten. Only the occasional flicker of a television screen through a faded, weather-worn curtain betrayed the fact that anybody lived here. *Lived?* Nobody lived *here*, thought Morgan as a cold wind howled between the buildings. The hundreds forced to inhabit cesspools like this had simply run out of options.

"So, we're sure they're still up there?" Morgan asked through the black ski mask, his voice a deep whisper in the darkness.

"Yes, sir," whispered the younger man. "Three men and the woman. Sleeping like babies."

"I'm sure she's not," Morgan said. He checked his watch – its luminous hands read 2.30am. "Your men ready?"

"Of course," the policeman replied. "We're always ready!"

The Intrepid agent, smiling beneath the ski mask, knew the feeling. Every specialist group the world over considered themselves the best at their game and, most importantly, ready for anything, anytime, anywhere. Especially on their own turf. Morgan was glad to have them in his corner.

"OK, then," he said. "Let's get to it."

Morgan turned from the policeman and crept over to Braunschweiger, who was surveying a construction waste chute on the side of the target apartment building across the street. The building, identical to the one they were in, dated from the time when high-density towers emerged all over those European cities flattened by war or carved up by the Allies when the spoils were being dished out. It was an archetype of the post-war period. Concrete decay, rust and age had all but beaten it to crumbling rubble.

On Braunschweiger's orders, and in total silence, the waste chute had been lowered into place by police officers before Morgan and the Key had arrived on the scene. It was a long gray tube made of heavy-duty canvas and it hugged the wall from the roof down to the sixth floor where it then curved toward a large rubbish skip at the side of the building. The chute was located away from the street, but still visible from the stairwell where Morgan, Braunschweiger and the police commander crouched. Most importantly, it was conveniently nestled against the balcony of the target apartment.

"Happy with your little construction over there?" Morgan asked.

"Yes," Braunschweiger replied, eyes still fixed on the chute. "It's perfect."

"Done this before?"

"No, but every idea needs a chance to blossom from theory into reality," Braunschweiger answered grandly. Not that Morgan could see it, but there was a broad grin beneath the Key's ski mask.

"Well," Morgan said, "I'm willing to give anything a try."

"After you." Braunschweiger gestured to the door.

Morgan and Braunschweiger pulled black combat assault helmets down over their ski masks and made final adjustments to weapons and gear. They'd opted not to carry the AKMs, but to stick with the Makarovs. The police officers would carry the AKMs, just in case heavy fire power was required.

Moving from the shadows, the two Intrepid agents sprinted to the corner of the target building, then split. They raced noiselessly through the silent corridors and stairwells of the sleeping, crumbling building. The plan was simple: they would enter from two points, Morgan through the ceiling and Braunschweiger, no surprise, via the front door.

Up in a filthy apartment on the twelfth and top floor, their unsuspecting targets slept.

Moving as quickly as his frame allowed, Braunschweiger arrived at the twelfth-floor landing. Two Albanian special operations police officers were waiting. They would go in with him. By silhouette alone, the police could see that Braunschweiger was well over 6 feet four and easily 260 pounds.

"Do you have the ram?" Braunschweiger whispered.

"Here," answered one of the officers.

"Do you mind?" Both police knew it made sense, and handed it over. Braunschweiger grabbed the two-person, 40-pound battering ram like it was a set of car keys.

"*Danke*," he said.

Up on the rooftop, Morgan was making his way to the entry point, ankle deep in leaves. It was freezing and clouds of warm breath spun in the moonlight about his masked face. A police officer sat poised over a rooftop access hatch, rocking slowly back and forth on his haunches. When Morgan arrived, the policeman soundlessly removed the cover, laid it to one side then guided Morgan down into the black void of the roof.

"Good luck," he said.

Morgan patted the officer's shoulder, said, "Thanks, mate," and dropped into the darkness.

The policeman closed the hatch, ran to the roof's edge and located the top section of the construction waste chute. Quietly he released a slipknot in the rope that fastened the top of the chute to an ancient heating system on the roof and began to slowly lower the circular opening down until it was perfectly aligned with the top of the balcony railing of the target apartment. Satisfied, he refastened the rope. Ready.

A mile away, two unmarked black vans rolled out of a side street.

Morgan climbed down inside the roof cavity of the old building, the toes of his boots searching for the safety of a rafter or crossbeam. For a second he was transported back to Corfu, getting set to arrest Šerifović. He hoped that this roof didn't betray him like the one in Šerifović's villa had. The last thing he needed was another ceiling full of bullets. Of course, this time he had the Key for backup. He found a secure foothold and slowly lowered himself further down.

A pinprick of light caught his eye to the left. Another policeman 20 feet away was signaling through the maze of beams, trusses and other entanglements. The officer was crouched directly above what Morgan knew would be an internal ceiling access panel, providing direct entry into the target apartment. Yep, definitely déjà vu.

Morgan edged his way carefully along two parallel beams, working hard not to generate any unnecessary creaking from the decades-old wooden struts. He was conscious of his own breathing, heavy and rhythmic, as though a large animal was following directly behind, exhaling over his shoulder. He reached the policeman at the access panel, who shone a torch onto his watch – 2.48am. He held up two fingers. Morgan nodded. Two minutes.

At the front door of the apartment, less than 30 feet from Morgan, Braunschweiger was riveted to his own watch.

"Stand by," he whispered to the others.

The two unmarked vans drew to a stop down the street but close to the building. One remained where it was while the other eased silently forward, looping around in a wide arc until its rear doors faced toward the front of the building. Soundlessly, the doors opened. A police officer emerged from the shadows of the building and slowly began to twist and maneuver the bottom of the refuse chute away from the rubbish skip so that it would discharge its contents straight into the back of the van.

A dozen sets of eyes watched the sweep hands of a dozen watches as they ticked toward 2.50am.

In the ceiling, Morgan was braced and ready, with hands and feet locked against beams on three sides of the opening. He was sucking in short, sharp breaths.

At the apartment door, Braunschweiger sat motionless, coiled like a gigantic spring. His gray eyes did not flinch from the luminous face of his watch. He knew that Morgan would be waiting for the crash of the door being bashed in as his signal to move.

Three seconds. Two.

One.

The Key filled his cavernous chest with oxygen, pumping the blood he would need to power one almighty thrust at the door. His right arm drew the battering ram back like a locomotive piston rod and, channelling it forward with his left, drove the ram with a kinetic impact of 40 000 pounds straight for the condemned latches of the door.

A colossal boom rocked the apartment building. The sounds of splintered wood being torn from the clutches of its metal stanchions screamed into the silence. The door was off.

At that instant, the policeman with Morgan tore the access panel off, throwing it clear. Morgan dropped in from the ceiling, followed immediately by the policeman, just as Braunschweiger burst in from the front door. They met in the sitting room only to discover Muscles erupting from the sofa where he'd been sleeping. But he was confused, shocked beyond surprise, eyes wide at the two menacing figures that had suddenly appeared from nowhere.

"This one's mine," Braunschweiger said matter-of-factly. "You find the girl."

Morgan disappeared toward the bedrooms.

Muscles recovered his senses enough to foolishly have a crack at the Key. Braunschweiger responded good-humoredly, giving Muscles two free swings. The Key effortlessly dodged the clumsy attempts – left and right – before landing one perfectly placed flat-palmed strike, dropping the man easily with a blow to the solar plexus. Muscles crumpled to his knees, gasping for air. In seconds, Braunschweiger had him face down, tightening plasti-cuffs around his wrists and stretching a length of duct tape securely around his mouth and ears before then applying a second set of cuffs around the ankles.

Morgan ran straight into the big Serb. Silhouetted by the light he'd flicked on as he ran from his room, he was unmistakable.

Bleary-eyed, the big Serb saw Morgan's menacing silhouette within the dimly lit confines of the narrow corridor.

"What the fuck?" he yelled.

Like a lethally programmed automaton, Alex Morgan erupted into action without hesitation, emotion or restraint. Instinctively his eyes found the gun in the big Serb's right hand, held uselessly high, just like in the movies, and profiled perfectly by the light behind.

Morgan stepped left. Bracing against the wall, he grabbed the big Serb's wrist below the gun, kicked his legs out from under him and, in a perfect old-school judo maneuver, flipped the man over on his back. As the big Serb smashed into the concrete floor and the air gushed from his lungs, Morgan relieved him of the gun with one deftly executed twist that Tom Rodgers, Intrepid's unarmed combat guru, would have been proud of.

"You're fucking dead!" the big Serb croaked breathlessly. "Dead! Dead! Dea—"

Morgan stepped over him, grabbed him by the scruff of his shirt collar and drove a fist straight into the center of his face. As the punch connected, the back of the man's head slammed against the floor. With the cold economy of a professional, Morgan maintained control over the man, now dazed and disoriented. Turning him over and wrenching his limbs into position, Morgan applied the plasti-cuffs and duct tape.

Back in the sitting room everything had happened so fast that the two Albanian policemen who'd rocketed into the apartment behind the Key were left dumbfounded, like recruits watching a demonstration on how it's done. Braunschweiger unfolded back up to full height, patted the nearest officer encouragingly on the shoulder and said, "You, get that door open, and watch our friend." Then he headed off to find Morgan.

Morgan turned and saw Braunschweiger standing behind him alongside the policeman who had followed Morgan in from the ceiling. In between them both stood Đurađ Lazarević, the Interpol informant. He was cowering and submissive, a cornered, frightened animal.

"I found him hiding in a cupboard," said the policeman.

Morgan's contempt for the man knew no bounds but he resisted the temptations racing through his mind.

"Where is she?" Morgan asked. Lazarević's eyes flicked once toward a closed door at the back of the apartment. "Anyone or anything in there with her?" Lazarević shook his head. "I'll get her, Key. This piece of shit is all yours."

Chapter Forty-Three

He opened the door to the last room and fingers of light from the feeble globe in the corridor trickled inside, softly illuminating the space.

On an impulse, Morgan removed his helmet and ski mask and resisted the urge to burst in. He was sure she didn't need to be any more terrified than she already was.

He saw a single metal-framed bed with a thick gray blanket thrown loosely across it. Ropes tied to the frame at the foot of the bed disappeared underneath the blanket.

"Charly?" he said quietly from the doorway. There was a shuffle. The blanket moved a fraction, the ropes tightened and the frame and springs creaked. "Charly, my name is Alex Morgan. I work for your godfather, Nobby Davenport." He heard a muffled sob. "I'm going to switch the light on."

When the light came on, Morgan found her trembling under the covers. Her wrists were tied to the bed and a cloth was wrapped around the lower half of her face, slack enough to allow her to breathe but tight enough to stifle any screams. Charly's brilliant red hair was a matted mess and her blue eyes were poor imitations of their usual crystalline splendor – they were raw, fearful and apprehensive, but they looked up at him with hope.

Morgan moved quickly but methodically, not wanting to alarm her. He stepped across, gently unraveled the cloth from her mouth and set to work sorting out the ropes at her wrists and ankles. The instant they were clear she threw her arms around him and clung on tight, tighter than any woman had ever held him.

"You really know my uncle Nobby?" she whispered through cascading tears.

"Yes," he answered. "He served with your father. Me and the big guy out there work for him. We're here to take you home. But we have to be quick."

"You're the one from the plane," Charly said groggily as she recognized Morgan's face. "My God. How on earth?"

As she spoke the crying turned to sobbing. Her entire body shook with the intensity of the sudden release from her ordeal. She didn't move and she didn't let go.

"Plenty of time for explanations," he promised. With that, Morgan made sure the blanket was wrapped tightly around her and scooped her into his arms. "Right now, I need to get you out of here."

"Bring them over," Braunschweiger ordered, gesturing for the Albanian police officers to bring their prisoners toward the balcony. He slid back the glass door and watched as each policeman hoisted their respective charges to their feet, unceremoniously dragging tight, woolen bags over them until all three – Muscles, the big Serb and Lazarević – were cocooned from head to toe.

Morgan emerged from the back of the apartment carrying Charly.

"You OK here, Key?" he asked, noting that Braunschweiger had everything under control.

"Bound, gagged and bagged," said the Key wryly. "And ready to travel. Go on ahead."

"Roger, we'll see you downstairs." Morgan headed out. Two police officers met him at the elevator.

As Morgan and Charly descended the dozen floors, Braunschweiger wrapped things up in the flat. This was an experiment and he needed crash test dummies.

"Let's go, gentlemen," he said.

The police officers each stepped forward with their packages. The three struggling bundles were jostled out onto the balcony like thick rolls of carpet. Without a moment's hesitation, as each man reached him – Muscles first, followed by the big Serb and then Lazarević – the Key hurled them head first into the refuse chute. Their screams of terror were muted by duct tape as they hurtled down at breakneck speed; each believing in those first seconds that they had, in fact, been thrown to their deaths.

They had no clue that they had been tossed into a chute and that the chute led directly into the back of an Albanian State Police van, twelve stories below.

Moments later both vehicles pulled away into the darkness of the early morning.

It was 2.55am.

PART III
No Second Chances

Chapter Forty-Four

SUNSET HILL, SEATTLE, WASHINGTON, USA

TWO WEEKS LATER

The view across Puget Sound to the snow-capped Olympic Mountains was Charly's most enduring memory of home. It seemed that no matter how far travel had taken her away from this beautiful place, the memory of that view was so indelibly captured in her heart she could recall every aspect and color, every peak and valley, all in photographic detail. Most importantly, it was a memory so familiar, so personal, that she would retreat to it when in need of solace and calm.

She had hardly set foot outside the house since returning home two weeks ago and then only to take cups of fresh coffee to the US marshals who were guarding them day and night. Sitting in her mom's favorite chair, her shoulders wrapped in a thick blanket Gran had knitted, with a cup of hot tea and the gas fire warming the room, Charlotte-Rose Fleming looked longingly out at the Olympics. It was as if she was trying to recalibrate the image she'd so relied upon during her abduction by gazing out of the windows. Like a copy of a copy of a copy of a favorite old photograph, there was always a danger that the more frequently you tried to conjure or replicate a memory, the greater the chance of the most important details being lost.

In this room, she was embraced by the familiarity of her mother's things and comforted by the sounds of domesticity downstairs in the kitchen. During her childhood, she recalled, her mother's career limited the amount of actual at-home time they were able to enjoy together – not to mention her father's long absences on military service. Of course, playing the piano had become her comfort. Such was the irony of her life, that the thing she withdrew to during her loneliness as a child was the very thing that would define her as a woman. Still, when the rare opportunities for normalcy emerged over the years, Charly embraced them every time. But she had to admit, Mom had been excessively protective today, insisting, more than usual, that Charly remain upstairs and rest while she prepared the meal. Was she trying to make amends for all that lost time? Well, Charly wasn't complaining.

A pair of deep green eyes and a thatch of thick dark hair invaded her thoughts. Instantly Charly returned to the moment when, tied to her seat in the seaplane, the sudden appearance of that handsome, rugged face fighting furiously with her captors had given her the only glimmer of hope she'd experienced through the entire ordeal. To be given such anticipation of freedom only to have it ripped away as he fell from the plane – Charly had thought she'd never recover. And to then open her eyes later that night and find him standing in the doorway of that awful, stinking rat hole, his strong hands taking hold and leading her to safety, had conjured uncompromising emotions – then and ever since.

It wasn't the first time she'd thought about Alex Morgan since her rescue but every time she did, she found herself wracked with guilt: there'd been absolutely no news on the whereabouts of Raoul.

Charly revisited her fleeting, yet intense, relationship with the charming millionaire, about whom – she realized now – she knew so little. As she sat drinking tea in the warmth and comfort of her family home, she pondered whether the intensity of their connection might have been, in fact, entirely one way.

Raoul was charismatic and good-looking; there was no doubt of that. He had plenty of money, which he was not afraid to lavish upon her. But now the warnings of her closest friends – especially her assistant and confidante, Daniel – that his advances seemed desperate and, in some ways, contrived, had come back to taunt her. The recollection of seeing him with gun in hand on the boat came as such a shock in the midst of the terror from those moments before the abduction. She couldn't fathom why her instinct had been so alarmed at the thought of him, ultimately, trying to protect her.

Again, an image of Morgan flashed into her mind's eye. *God! This is ridiculous*, she thought.

Charly placed down her tea, unraveled herself from the blanket and strolled toward the grand piano in the far corner of the sitting room. Dressed in what she called her comfies – slippers, track pants, a T-shirt and an old rugby jersey that had belonged to her father – she sat down and placed her fingers lightly on the keyboard. It was a Steinway & Sons Chippendale with a beautiful mahogany finish. These days, her mother kept an array of special family photos on the closed top. Charly looked upon each of them with a mixture of delight and sadness as her fingers quite unintentionally began to work their way through 'Cavatina' by Stanley Myers. It was a piece originally written for classical guitar, but it was most widely known as the theme from the old Robert De Niro film *The Deer Hunter*. The film happened to be one of her father's absolute favorites and for years he would ask her to play it whenever they were together. Looking at the framed photograph of her parents that sat upon the closed lid of the piano, she could almost feel him sitting beside her now as she performed it once again for him.

When she finished, Charly turned to find her mother sitting on the seat behind her, tears of joy filling her eyes.

"That was absolutely beautiful, my darling," said Madeline. "Your dad would have loved it."

"Thanks, Mom," Charly replied with a slightly embarrassed smile. "Hang on. What's with the cat-got-the-cream look on your face? You're up to something."

"Just get showered and change into something nice," Madeline said evasively, dabbing away her tears on a tissue.

"Mom?"

"We're having company for dinner."

Chapter Forty-Five

LOCATION: UNDISCLOSED

Dressed in the tightest black satin shorts, black lace bra, fishnets and fire-engine-red skyscraper stilettos, a cropped leather jacket slung across a bare shoulder, the girl walked out of the club like she owned it. Every step she took fell to the beat of the Euro techno-pop that thumped as loudly outside as it did in. The four goons on the door, clad from head to toe in black, gunned up and built like they'd require council approval for redevelopment, fell into practiced formation and held back the long line of wild partygoers to allow her to pass undisturbed. They knew better than to let anything happen to this girl. They knew who she belonged to.

She was 6 feet tall with legs so long they could take one stride to everyone else's two. Every man and woman within reach turned to watch as she strutted out to the stretch limousine that sat waiting for her 15 feet from the club's entrance. Her dead straight platinum blond hair tickled all the way down past the dangerously straining bra strap to the small of her back. Full, sensuous lips the color of her shoes stood out on a blank canvas of porcelain-white skin like blood splatter on fresh snow.

To the casual observer, she looked to be in her mid-twenties, at least. The reality was she'd yet to reach eighteen.

Arriving at the limousine, she stopped, threw a cigarette to the pavement and turned to give the thronging masses one last look over her shoulder. The rear door of the limo opened, she stepped inside and the car drove away.

"Get in here, you little slut!" came a voice from the dark corner of the car.

"Baby, what's the matter? I'm here, aren't I? Who is this?" she said playfully, clambering over a stranger's legs. Clear gray eyes caught her attention as she struggled to get in. "Are we having a party again?"

She was answered with a slap that caught her across the entire side of her small, perfect face. The strike dropped her awkwardly to the floor between the two long bench seats and two pairs of men's shoes.

"I've been waiting," hissed the man accusingly. It was an old voice, angry and frustrated. The voice of a man used to getting what he wanted when he wanted it. He grabbed her by the hair, pulled her up to him and held her face close to his. "I took the fucking pill half an hour ago, bitch!"

"I'm sorry, baby, I'm sorry," she said, pouting. "I'll make it up to you, I promise."

As the limousine cruised through the streets of the city, sporadic bursts of street lights stabbed through the tinted windows, casting startling images of the tired, bearded old face in a stream of repulsive, ominous flashes. She knew there was only ever one way this could end if she was to avoid a real beating.

Dragoslav Obrenović pushed the girl back to the floor

and began to unbuckle his pants. She helped him. The man on the bench seat behind her casually started to unbuckle his own.

"Be patient, Wolf," said Drago. "Wait your turn."

"I want to take her from behind, *šefa*," said a deep, smooth voice. "So we can both have her together."

The girl, Jovana, could only listen like a bystander to the conversation between the men. When she ran away from home at sixteen to escape the unwanted amorous attentions of her abusive, alcoholic father, she never dreamed that her life would come to this. But now, the very thought of escape had been long abandoned. Pulling Drago's pants down to his ankles, she fought back an impulse to gag.

Drago grabbed her hair again in two fistfuls and shoved her face down into his crotch.

His eyes closed, he let out a long gasp of satisfaction and his head fell back against the head rest.

"OK, Wolf," he said. "Be my fucking guest."

Chapter Forty-Six

SUNSET HILL, SEATTLE, WASHINGTON, USA

"It really is lovely to have you here again, Nobby," said Madeline Clancy. "It's been too long."

"I'm delighted to be here, darling," replied Davenport, "sitting here again with you and my beautiful goddaughter. I can't begin to tell you how relieved I am."

Davenport turned his gaze across the table to Morgan, who was sitting comfortably, he noted, beside Charly. The general gave Morgan a nod of thanks and, raising his glass of red wine a fraction above the dining table in tribute, said: "Well done, my boy."

"Indeed," acknowledged Madeline, breathlessly. "I can never thank you enough for bringing my baby back home safely, Alex. I know if Peter was still with us, he'd consider himself greatly in your debt too."

"Very much so," Davenport added somberly.

Morgan and Charly shifted uncomfortably in their seats. Morgan waved off the accolade politely, not wanting to belittle the mountain of sentiment behind it.

"Well, it was worth it for the invitation to dinner alone,

Madeline," he said. "Lamb shanks are my hands-down favorite, and I reckon you can never go past homemade tiramisu."

"Oh, stop it," Charly piped up warmly, glad of the lifted mood. "Uncle Nobby, where did you find him? He's adorable."

"Oh, I kicked over a rock somewhere," said Davenport, "and he just crawled out."

They all laughed. Morgan was relieved by the distraction. It was good to see Davenport in this setting; it introduced a new layer to his picture of the man whom he held in such high regard. The warmth Davenport displayed in their company was indicative of his loyalty and utter devotion to those closest to him. It was no surprise as far as Morgan was concerned. It was exactly what he had expected but not yet seen in the old man.

"Now my dears, it's an opportune moment for young Morgan and I to depart and leave you both in peace. Wouldn't you say, Alex?"

"Of course," Morgan lied. The last thing he wanted to do was leave. Since they'd arrived he hadn't had a moment alone with Charly. He wanted to steal five minutes in private to see how she was doing. It looked like that chance had just passed him by. *Fuck it.*

"Oh no you don't, Davenport," Charly declared reproachfully. She stood, gathering up the last of the dessert plates. "It's only nine o'clock. I'm going to make tea and coffee. You and Mom are going to sit in there and catch up." She gestured toward a small sitting room that faced out toward Puget Sound. "And, I'm going to have some time with our guest."

There is a God, thought Morgan.

"Aren't I a guest, too?" asked Davenport, his voice full of rejection.

"You're part of the furniture in this family, Uncle Nobby," she said, then kissed him on the forehead to placate the mock hurt written all over his face. "Now, shoo. My new favorite GI Joe action figure here can help me clear this table."

Madeline Clancy and General Davenport happily acquiesced and, taking the last of their wine with them, moved into the sitting room.

"He's a delightful young man, Nobby. So noble and full of fire," Madeline began. "Exactly like you and Peter at that age, as I recall."

"He's my best man, my dear, which is exactly why I chose him to find Charlotte."

Madeline smiled, sipped from her wine glass and looked across with great affection at one of her oldest friends.

"Peter would be so grateful to you," she said, almost in a whisper. "He gave up so much for me, you know. His career and so on."

"He did it without a second thought, Madeline," Davenport replied truthfully. "You meant the world to him."

"I know, dear." She paused for a moment. "When Charly came along he was absolutely besotted; the two of them were like peas in a pod from the very beginning. Even though my work kept me away from home a lot, all those long hours and whatnot, I always knew Charly would be OK because she had Peter."

"And her music," said Davenport. "Peter was so proud of her."

"She misses him terribly. We both do. I don't know what I would have done if anything had happened to her. She's all I have."

Davenport remained quiet.

"Nobby, I'm not allowed to say this but I'll say it anyway. We've got to catch that reprehensible bastard, Drago. I know we don't have any actual proof that he was behind Guy's murder or Charly's abduction but by God we both know that he was. When I think of all those poor souls who come before the tribunal as witnesses to the atrocities of the war, what they've been through … well, he has to answer for what he's done, once and for all. It's not right that he's managed to elude us all this time. Enough is enough."

Chapter Forty-Seven

Half an hour later, Morgan was with Charly in the upstairs sitting room. She was finishing a green tea while tinkering at an old drinks cabinet, as Morgan enjoyed a strong black coffee. He stood looking out across Puget Sound, enjoying the occasional flickers of light from boats trundling past. The mountains had all but disappeared, the dark cloak of evening pulled across them. Thankfully, winds at high altitude were shunting clouds across the sky like carriages in a railway yard, allowing the full brightness of the moon to flash through the gaps, offering brief but sensational glimpses of the mountain tops.

"Beautiful," he said.

"Well, aren't you just the charmer," said Charly playfully, walking back over. "It is beautiful, though. My favorite view in the whole world is right there."

She sidled up beside him, contentedly. Morgan instantly felt charged by her closeness within the quiet privacy of the room. He looked into her eyes and smiled.

"I can see why," he said.

"Here you go, major," she said with a wink, handing him a short, fat crystal glass with ice cubes clinking within a pool of Irish whisky and cream liqueur. "I developed a taste for this in Australia during a concert tour a couple of years ago. Thought you might appreciate a nightcap."

"Ah, Baileys. I know it well. You read my mind," replied Morgan.

He put down his coffee and took the glass from her. Their fingers touched. It was electrifying. Charly caught her breath.

"You know, contact like that." She looked up at him mischievously. "You better be careful. I could take you down, right now."

"Oh, is that right?" he said, responding to the challenge in her voice. "Should I be worried?"

"Well, I haven't been sitting around on my tush all this time, Morgan. I've been getting some serious self-defense lessons from the marshals. It's been great!"

"That's fantastic," he said, genuinely. "Great skills to know and it's good for you at the same time. How did that come about?"

"I was talking to the girl who runs all these guys about what she does; she's really kickass. Anyway, I asked her about her training, one thing led to another and, now the team knows that whoever's on shift, they take it in turns to run me through some moves. Ever since the kidnapping ... well, I just want to know how to get myself out of dangerous situations, you know? I've had quite a few sessions. I'm getting pretty good."

Charly fell silent for a moment, deep in thought as Keith Emerson's "Piano Concerto No. 1" played quietly in the background. They both took a drink. Morgan enjoyed the soothing warmth of the liqueur. It was an old favorite, familiar and comforting. For a moment he was a young lieutenant again, serving with the battalion in East Timor in '99. He recalled it vividly, sitting on an ammunition box back in Dili after a few long days on patrol, tin mug in hand, drinking warm Baileys one of the boys had managed to scrounge from some aid workers. Then Charly's soft voice gently broke the silence.

"After what happened to me," she began, "you know, I felt like I just had to do more to take care of myself."

"How are you really doing, Charly?" he asked.

She didn't answer immediately but took him by the hand and led him back to a long sofa at the back of the room that would, he was sure, command a magnificent view of the Sound during daylight. They sat together, close.

"Alex, I need to ask you something but I'm a little, actually I'm *very* uncomfortable about it. God! I don't know where to begin."

"Ask me anything." Morgan replied. "Take your time."

Charly brought a hand up to her heart and took a deep breath. Morgan couldn't take his eyes off her.

"It's about Raoul, the man I was with when we were kidnapped," Charly began, blushing unexpectedly. "I know you're not allowed to talk about these things. It's your work and all …"

Her voice trailed off and she turned her eyes away from Morgan and looked out into the darkness.

"I'm afraid there's still no news, Charly," Morgan offered. For some reason, despite the fact that her boyfriend was still missing, he felt an adolescent twinge of jealousy. What the hell was he thinking? "It's clear you were separated once you hit dry land. You were taken north, of course. But, we've had absolutely no luck with regard to Raoul. Interpol has taken the lead on finding him now. Our only priority was to get you back and arrest the people responsible."

"Because of the impact on Mom?"

"Yes," he said frankly. "When an ICTY judge is threatened or somehow at risk, it's our responsibility to sort it out."

"But aren't you Interpol, too?"

"Charly, I really can't talk about that."

"I'm sorry," she said. "I understand. I just feel so guilty about Raoul and I guess I'm hoping I can get something done to find him."

"Why would you feel guilty?" Morgan asked, suddenly thinking of Arena Halls. Damn it! Was that a pang of guilt or regret over her? No. Arena had been the one to close things down, not Morgan. "Interpol is still giving it priority. There's nothing you can do."

"I know, but the further this whole shocking episode gets behind me, the less I think about him. I mean, we hardly knew each other at all. That was the whole purpose of the trip, I guess." She searched for an appropriate way to explain it all that hopefully wouldn't be completely humiliating in front of Morgan. "I mean, I'd been taking things slowly with him at first but, as much as he seemed keen to … move things along—" she blushed at her own choice of words, "—he didn't really deliver. Oh God, that sounds really terrible. I mean, nothing ever happened—"

Morgan smiled politely. "You don't have to tell me this stuff, you know."

"Anyway, now that I'm home and I'm safe and then," she looked up at him in a way that betrayed her, "—am I a terrible person?"

"Charly, it's obvious you still have genuine concern for his safety. But I suppose, based on what you've said, the two of you were in the early stages of getting to know each other when this happened." *At least I hope it had only gone that far.* "The fact that you care enough to make sure people are still looking for him is testament to your character. There's no need for you to feel guilty and I don't think you're a terrible person, at all." He meant it. In fact, in Charly's company, he realized that his own memories of Arena were retreating. That didn't mean he didn't still care for her, in some way. It was just life. Whatever the circumstances, when you have to, you move on.

"Thank you," she said, much more at ease. "You have a disarming knack for making everything seem OK. I've not been able to talk about any of it since—" She stopped, collecting her thoughts again. "I mean, I've been seeing a shrink here at the house. Mom insisted; Nobby, too, I'm sure. And she's been great. I'm beginning to feel much better. But I couldn't bring myself to just talk about it, other than how it made me feel. How would a complete stranger understand what I'd been through? But after sitting beside you at dinner, I felt like I could talk to you about all of it."

"Sometimes strangers are the best ones to talk to; especially professionals. You have no baggage or boundaries with them and they're skilled in guiding you through your thoughts." Morgan spoke from experience. "But, in lieu of a professional, I'm here. If you need to download, you can."

"I don't consider you a stranger at all."

A candle flickered and Charly's eyes sparkled, capturing every note of orange brilliance from the flame's delicate outburst. She sat less than a foot away from Morgan, resting her head on her arm, perched on the back of the sofa. She pushed a hand unaffectedly through her hair and a trail of red curls tumbled down over her shoulder, falling like scarlet silk upon her chest.

Morgan was getting seriously distracted. He was enjoying the Baileys but mostly he was enjoying watching and listening.

"When I was taken to that cave, I honestly thought I was going to die," she began. "Those men were such animals, Alex. I still can't believe the things they said to me, what they wanted to do to me, what was in store for me. Every moment I was expecting … the worst."

Morgan's eyes asked the question.

"No," she answered. "They were happy to hit me but, apart from one of them putting his hands on me when I was tied up in the back of the car—" she shuddered, "—they didn't try to touch me that way; just lots of talk. Thank God it never came to anything more." She took a drink.

"They were locals, Charly. Paid to hold you for somebody else. Of course, you weren't to know that."

"And you said a while ago that they had taken me to get to Mom. Is that right?"

"We're almost certain of it. Your mum has really led the charge against the last few guys who've been eluding the tribunal. Since she's been president of the ICTY, three of the biggest targets have been arrested, leaving only Drago Obrenović still at large. He's desperate to keep it that way and he'll stop at nothing to make sure of it."

"But what could they hope to gain by taking me?"

"When their first attempt on Madeline failed, a wall of security was literally dropped around her and the other judges overnight." He gestured outside, referencing the team of US marshals who were on protection duty out there 24/7. "Making it impossible for these guys to try another direct attempt on her, or the other judges for that matter. We believe that by taking you they would have hoped to somehow lure Madeline out from behind the perimeter. We're not sure exactly how they planned to do it – a ransom drop, or whatever – because, thankfully, we stopped it in time."

Charly nodded and gently brushed his leg in a comfortable, familiar display of gratitude.

"That doesn't mean they won't try again," he added. "That's why all this security has to stay in place until we at least have Obrenović in custody."

"I was horrified at what happened to that one the others called boss," she said. "I mean, I turned away, I couldn't stand to watch. I was terrified. But I knew what happened." Morgan nodded. "It's strange, because when I realized that he was dead, I actually felt good. In a bizarre way, I felt that I'd been protected by that big ape who came in and – took me away."

Morgan was amazed at how well she was holding it together. He was about to tell her so when she stood up, walked to the drinks cabinet, grabbed a handful of ice and returned with the bottle of Baileys. She dropped ice into their glasses and gave them both a generous top up. Charly clinked her glass against his with a wink and sat back down, closer than before.

"There's something else I was going to ask you about," she said. "But, for some reason it escapes me. Shit! It was important, too."

"Well, leave it for a moment and it may come back to you."

"Yeah, good idea." She took a sip of her drink. "When you appeared in that plane – my God! I had no idea what was going on. But something told me that you were there for me. I just knew it."

"How did you know? I must have looked like a bloody madman."

She laughed. "Oh, you did, that's for damn sure. But when I was growing up, this house was filled with my dad's closest friends. We always had visitors from his days in the army. Men like Uncle Nobby." She paused. "Men like you. I always felt so safe. So cared for and protected. I can spot 'em. I guess I just forgot what they looked like. And then you came along."

Morgan shifted self-consciously. "It's what we're trained to do, Charly."

"No, Alex Morgan, it's more than that. It's who you are. That's what I saw in your eyes." Now she was getting self-conscious. She changed tack. "When you disappeared out that door, I was sure you'd been killed. But sure enough, there you were later that night, like it was all in a day's work."

He laughed. "Working for your Uncle Nobby, it pretty much is."

Charly shuffled over the last few inches between them and nestled herself comfortably against him. Her body felt so soft and fragile and the aroma of Lady Vengeance perfume that enveloped him was seductive.

"Do you mind?" she whispered from his chest. "I just want to be held."

Chapter Forty-Eight

LOCATION: UNDISCLOSED

"So, where does this leave me now? Am I to throw myself at the mercy of the Interpol dogs or those fucks in The Hague? A noose is around my neck and the harder I try to tear it off, the tighter it gets!"

Dragoslav Obrenović's hands were clawing at his own neck, dramatizing the words to their full effect. His eyes were alive with paranoia and betrayal, heightened somewhat by the daily intake of vodka. Cigar smoke sat like a heavy fog above the simmering stench of violence, alcohol and sex that saturated the room.

The Wolf hated coming here.

The man was in obvious decline. Drago's mood was blacker than the eyes in his own portrait. He'd had too much booze and the girls had stayed too long. But they were necessary distractions. Without them the Wolf knew that there would be pointless killing. In his current state of mind, Drago didn't know any other way. One of the girls was already in a bad way from the beating he'd given her. Five more minutes and he probably would have killed her.

"It won't come to that, *šefa*," replied the Wolf in his deep rumble. He'd already decided his next course of action. He got out of Albania just in time; any longer and he would have been caught up in the Interpol raid too. He could almost smell the surveillance that he knew must have been on them while they'd prepared to receive the hostage. A quick alteration to his clothes and a well-timed exit from the apartment building – alongside an unsuspecting woman who had no idea who he was – meant that to all intents and purposes he was just an innocent resident leaving the building with his wife. He'd walked out as bold as brass. But, now he had to get back into the game if there was to be any chance of sorting out the mess. "I'll make sure of it."

"Like you made sure of that American slut?" The unexpected accusation was like a gunshot in a confined space. The echo was deafening. "And now they even have her fucking daughter back!"

Despite the vehemence in Drago's voice, to the Wolf, the dank, dark room had lost the trademark menace conjured by the total lack of natural light and the imposing ferocity of the portrait behind the desk, behind the man. Reality was very different to the legend. In many ways, the room had become a manifestation of the man himself. For years Drago reigned on the strength of his reputation, built upon his physical stature and unsurpassed record of brutality. Stories of the great general who had commanded an army, presided over massacres and tortured hundreds of Serbia's enemies breathed life into the myth like a spreading fire. He had become a beacon for the next generation of maladjusted young men looking to vent their rage against a society uninterested in the lack of opportunities it had provided them. Drago gave them their rage, nurtured their violence, made them kings, and all he expected in return was uncompromising, unquestioning devotion.

To his army of *Zmajevi*, Drago was general, legend, chief: *šefa*. But over the past year, Drago had seen his closest associates – Mladić and Šerifović – all betrayed, arrested and now rotting in cells in The Hague. Behind it all: the International Criminal Tribunal for the former Yugoslavia and, at its helm, the tribunal's president and presiding judge, Madeline Clancy.

Since Clancy had been elected president of the ICTY by the permanent judges during an extraordinary plenary session in 2010, the pressure had not stopped and Drago's allies had fallen like dominoes. In the eyes of the Wolf, they were all nothing but tired old men, out of touch and too blind to see that the winds of change were now blowing a gale through their dwindling ranks. It was only a matter of time before those winds would be tearing away the past to make way for the future.

While Madeline Clancy had come to epitomize that which Drago feared most, she was the least of Drago's problems. When the old fool finally realized, it would be too late.

The Wolf *was* the future.

"Everything was going to plan with the American when I was on the ground running it. It was only when I handed over to your cousin, Simović," the Wolf said calmly, referring to the big Serb, "that it all turned to shit. You feel you have to supervise me now with your fucking uncle's son? This is the result."

"You watch your fucking mouth," yelled Drago, gesticulating wildly across the desk. "Don't forget who the fuck you are talking to!"

Drago stormed around from his seat toward the Wolf.

His eyes blazed with anger and recrimination. Drago Obrenović was all that remained of the old guard and despite being forced to accept the unwelcome inevitability that the ICTY was closer than ever before to tapping him on the shoulder, he had an obligation to maintain the old ways and control dissidents in the ranks. The Wolf was getting far too big for his boots and the power play had gone on long enough. As far as Drago was concerned, the Wolf was still, and always would be, a subordinate.

"Let me remind you that this was your plan, Wolf. You assured me that the way to keep the ICTY at bay was to attack them. Scare them into submission, you said. Show them real fear. All you have done is stirred the fucking hornet's nest. This is your mess," he said. "And you will clean it up. Where is he now?"

"Simović?"

Drago nodded.

"I believe he is in custody, probably Belgrade."

"What about the other one? That fucking brother of yours," asked Drago with overt contempt.

"The same, I suppose."

Drago was close now, sitting on the front edge of the Alexander Roux desk, intending to intimidate with his size set against the backdrop of the portrait. It wasn't working. The waft of alcohol and body odor was nauseating. The Wolf had known him too long and was immune to the playground theatrics. It seemed that Drago had forgotten who the fuck he was talking to. All the Wolf could see was a sad, fat, scared old man who drank too much. His days were numbered. The Wolf would make sure of it.

But he had to do it properly.

To remove Drago right here, right now, would start a war among the factions that would take years to resolve. No, the construct of Drago's downfall had to be smart, surgical and, above all, impossible to trace back to him.

"You must fix this," Drago ordered, poking the Wolf's chest. "You must fix it all, Wolf. That is what I pay you to do. And you have more at stake than just money on this one, I think." Wolf remained silent, ignoring the cheap taunt and the fat, hairy finger waved inches from his face. "I want you to go to America and find this bitch, Clancy, and kill her; kill both of them, the daughter, too. That's the only way to get these fucks off my back."

"Yes, *šefa*," the Wolf answered.

"You will do this thing for me." Drago did not respond to the acknowledgment. "Because, if you don't, I will kill you."

"Yes, *šefa*," said the Wolf and he stood, came face to face with Drago, and set his deathly cold gray eyes squarely upon his former mentor. Then he turned and walked out.

Wolf knew what had to be done. If he was to remedy any of this he needed to reinsert himself back into the play. That meant recovering some lost ground and that was going to be tricky. He had survived a long time by layering his plans with as much depth as possible to remain involved but always one step removed from the center of the action. Obviously that was no longer possible.

The Wolf would fix everything, once and for all, and he would kill Clancy and the daughter.

But he wouldn't be doing it for Drago.

Chapter Forty-Nine

UN DETENTION UNIT, SCHEVENINGEN, THE HAGUE

Having finished his first meal at Scheveningen, Ivan Simović, or Detainee 93-96-69 as he was now known, was returning to his room under escort. He intended to watch television for the first time in weeks. The last fortnight had taken their toll. His age was catching up and he was less fit than the old days. It had been a while since he'd been allowed to sleep properly and he was exhausted. They had told him to expect a visit from his appointed defense counsel later that afternoon, and he knew he would need his energy; he had a lot to say.

As the big Serb approached the door to his cell, the detention unit guard dropped back, saying, "Go on by yourself," before walking back to the mess hall. Simović watched the guard's back as he disappeared along the corridor the way they'd just come. Strange. But he was too weary to question it and lazily headed to his cell.

When he walked in through the open door, he froze.

"How was lunch?" asked a young, fit and familiar-looking man in an expensive suit. He sat on the cell's only chair, legs outstretched across the tiny space, feet resting comfortably on Simović's bed. "Don't be shy, come in."

"What the fuck is this?" said Simović. "You're that fucking cop. Why aren't you dead?"

"Cop is not entirely accurate, but it'll do for now. As for being dead, well, clearly I'm not."

Alex Morgan removed his legs from the bed and gestured to the big Serb, Simović, to sit down. The look on Morgan's face made it clear it wasn't a request. Simović took the remaining few steps necessary to reach the end of the bed and sat down, feet on the floor, hands on his knees, jaw clenched.

"Excellent," said Morgan. "Now, I don't think you've been properly introduced to my colleague."

The presence of the person occupying the doorway was felt before they were seen. Simović's eyes turned sharply from Morgan and landed upon another man, similarly dressed to the cocky bastard on the chair but this guy filled the doorway.

Hermann Braunschweiger leant against the frame, arms folded and legs crossed at the ankles like he'd been kept waiting for ages. Simović had no idea where he'd come from. There'd been no-one in the corridor when he'd walked in seconds ago.

"*Guten tag*," offered Braunschweiger.

At the sight of Braunschweiger, the penny dropped. Simović recalled the feeling of being thrown twelve stories to his death, or so he thought at the time, by a guy the size of a bull elephant. When he'd slammed into the back of the Albanian police van instead, he'd already soiled his pants. His embarrassment in front of the cops had been hard to swallow. "This is harassment!" Simović hissed. "You're the ones who snatched us from Tirana. You're supposed to turn us in."

"We have turned you in," replied Morgan. "Isn't your accommodation satisfactory?"

"No you didn't, you fucks! You kept me in solitary lockdown, I don't know where, but then I just turn up here this morning and everything's rosy? You're not getting away with it!"

"We have no idea what you're talking about," said Braunschweiger. "My colleague and I arrested you last night in Tirana. Then we brought you straight here and handed you over to the tribunal."

Simović's eyes blazed as he looked back and forth between the agents for some glimmer of acknowledgment or hint of a ruse. He got nothing.

"That's certainly the way I remember it," said Morgan, then he leant forward and added menacingly, "but, if you'd prefer to be returned to our friends who specialize in looking after people like you for us – you know, spend some more time in a dark room with a bag over your head and white noise pounding in your ears night and day – I'd be happy to arrange it."

"You pieces of shit!" Simović coughed up phlegm and spat heavily upon the floor at Morgan's feet.

Morgan didn't hesitate. He stepped from the chair, grabbed Simović by the collar and forced him face down on the floor. Simović's chest fell upon the thick mess of mucus he'd spat out and Morgan took great delight in pressing the man into it until it was gone. He had Simović back on the bed in an instant, his tunic smeared with his own spit.

"You're fucked! You're totally fucked!" the big Serb yelled. "You can't do that in here. I've got you now."

"It's funny about that, Mr Simović," began Morgan,

"because people who normally come here are yet to be tried by the tribunal and so they're protected by the presumption of innocence. Which makes this place a detention center rather than a prison."

Simović suddenly lost his confidence. He had no idea what was going on. He looked up at Braunschweiger.

"No CCTV cameras," said the Key. "No record of anything that happens in here." With that, Braunschweiger eased into the cell and slowly closed the door behind him. He moved toward the big Serb in a manner that told him to shove along. Obediently, Simović shuffled to his left and the Key sat down next to him.

"Take your shirt off," Morgan ordered.

"What?"

"Perhaps you'd like me to assist you?" Braunschweiger offered helpfully.

The big Serb recoiled. He didn't need any more encouragement. Slowly he sat forward, pulled his tunic over his head and tossed it on the bed beside him.

"Just as I thought," Morgan said, extracting a folded piece of A4 paper from the inside pocket of his coat. "Exactly the same as this one." He tossed the paper across to the big Serb.

"It would appear you belong to a very select fraternity, Herr Simović," said the Key, observing the big Serb's tattoo.

The big Serb bluffed clumsily, trying to regain some ground. "You're wrong. It's just a tattoo I liked when I was young."

"Spare me, Simović, we're not here for a statement or a confession. We've got everything we need from you already. This visit was to show my friend here your ink. And now we've done that, we'll be leaving."

"What is this?" asked Simović. "It's some kind of a

setup. You guys didn't just come in here to see a fucking tattoo. You're after something and I'm not telling you any fucking thing."

"That tattoo tells us all we need to know," said the Key, pointing at it. "You're a *Zmajeba*—a Dragon. You work for General Dragoslav Obrenović, an indicted war criminal and fugitive of justice. We also know that you are related to Drago. That makes you even closer. We know that blood ties count for a great deal among your kind. So, the decision has been made. The ICTY has decreed that you are going to be indicted as an accessory to Drago's war crimes. War crimes, Herr Simović. Do you understand? You will rot in a cell like this for the rest of your days with only your little tattoo there for company. Our job is done."

The big Serb's face dropped. The color ran from his face. "I'm no war criminal!" he said. "I was just a soldier during the war."

"Just following orders, right?" said Morgan. "That one's been tried before."

"I didn't even know Drago during the war. I got pulled into the business afterward. We're cousins. I needed a job."

"Your family must be very proud of your chosen profession," Braunschweiger said, then he looked at Morgan. "What do you think?"

"I think he's full of shit. If he tries to con his way out of the war crimes charges to avoid the tribunal then he's likely to only face stock-standard criminal charges for organized crime back in Belgrade. He'd get only five, maybe ten years on criminal charges. That's getting off too lightly in my book. No, we need to keep him here and make sure he's charged with war crimes alongside his old friend Drago. The ICTY will throw the book at him and, like you said, he'll spend the rest of his miserable days in a cell."

"Yes, of course. You're right," answered the Key. "Well, that's too bad for you, Herr Simović. Thank you for showing us your tattoo, anyway. You've helped us in settling our bet. You see, I didn't believe my colleague when he told me that he'd seen the mark of the *Zmajeba*."

By now the big Serb could see the rest of his life being flushed down the toilet. He had everything to lose and nothing to gain by sticking his neck out for Drago. He wasn't the one sitting in a cell facing a life behind bars. Who knew, right now Drago was probably covered in whores with his face buried in huge tits. No, Simović was not taking the fall for anyone.

Especially not Drago Obrenović.

"What can I do to convince you pieces of shit I'm telling the truth?"

Chapter Fifty

EL DJEM, TUNISIA

Youssef Ali Hassan, the young policeman at his desk diligently filling out a report regarding a tourist being robbed, had no idea his day was about to change.

Youssef took his responsibilities very seriously. He had only been with the police, the Sûreté Nationale, a few months and was yet to become jaded by the monotony and relentlessness of compiling police reports. He happily tapped at the prehistoric computer, fastidiously checking every word, comma and period to ensure his report was submitted at the best possible standard. His station, located on the Avenue Mohamed, was a stone's throw from the amphitheatre which, Youssef loved to boast, was featured in the Russell Crowe movie *Gladiator*.

It was only 74 degrees Fahrenheit outside but the humidity level was an oppressive 83 per cent. Youssef had a small fan, decades older than the computer, sitting beside him on the desk, directed straight at his face and chest. Still, sweat dripped from his arms onto the veneered bench top and his uniform, pristine when he'd started his shift, clung to him like wet plastic wrap.

Just as he reached the end of his report, his day rocketed out of control.

There came the sudden thud of someone collapsing against the high bench top that served as the station's customer service area and as a barrier to unauthorized entry into the inner sanctum. Startled, Youssef was on his feet.

A man's muscular arms were folded upon the bench top and his head was cradled within them. His thick dark hair was matted with the white dust of the surrounding countryside and his skin was the color of fresh sunburn. He was dressed in Western clothes that, despite their obvious state of disrepair and filth, looked expensive.

"Can I help you, sir?" Youssef offered nervously, gently shaking the man by the shoulder. His clothes, like Youssef's, were also sticky and wet from the humidity. He wore no jewelry, although there was a pale band of skin on the left wrist where a watch would usually sit, and as he lifted his head to speak, Youssef saw lips red and cracked from dehydration. A pair of piercing gray eyes emerged as lids heavy with exhaustion opened. The stranger raised himself slowly, holding the bench with both arms to keep steady.

"Officer, could I trouble you for some water," he began, his voice deep, but raspy and weak. "And perhaps if I could sit …"

Youssef lifted the entry panel that gave access into the office area and carefully ushered the man in. He sat him down at an empty desk, walked to a back room and returned with a large pitcher of water and a plastic cup. Without a word, Youssef filled the cup and held it to the lips of the stranger, who gratefully relieved him of it with both hands and drank it dry. They repeated the process until he was ready to speak.

"Thank you, officer," he said. "So very much."

"How can I help, sir?" Youssef asked. "Have you been in an accident?"

"No, nothing like that," the man replied. He leant back in the chair and rubbed his hands across his face, collecting his thoughts, ready to begin.

"My name … is Raoul Demaçi."

Chapter Fifty-One

BERLIN, GERMANY

"Do you think he's ready?" asked Morgan quietly.

"I'm not sure. Do you think he would appreciate more sleep?" Braunschweiger replied. "Perhaps we should ask him."

"Good idea."

Alex Morgan walked to the center of the dimly lit, perfectly square room and took a seat at a perfectly square table. There was only one door into the room and no windows. The walls, floor and ceiling were all once highly polished concrete, but the room had lost its sheen long ago. A single fluorescent tube shone unsteadily in a rusted metal cage, fastened to the ceiling and too high to reach. The walls were light green and plastered with the graffiti of previous occupants, and there'd been plenty of those over the years. Four decades of them, in fact, before it had been closed down, because the politics of the world had changed. The Cold War was over and places such as this had become unpalatable with modern governments. Of course, that didn't mean the location could not still be useful.

Hermann Braunschweiger was familiar with this place. Berlin was his old patch. He'd pulled some strings.

The table was made of metal, like the two chairs that sat on either side of it. The table and both chairs were bolted to the floor. Directly beneath each chair, a worn D-shaped metal nub protruded from the cement floor; an old tether point for restraining subjects to the chairs. Only one of them was in use today. Around the table were well-worn scuffs in the cement, like cattle tracks, where a great deal of pacing had once occurred.

"You awake?" Morgan asked.

After a few moments the man in the opposite chair replied, "Who are you? I know your face."

The greasy hair was still greasy, hanging lower over the narrow shoulders, Morgan thought, and the scratchy beard was a bit thicker now, still the same red and brown mix of tumbleweed. But the shifty brown eyes, yellowing teeth and cigarette-stained fingers were what Morgan remembered most of all from their first sight of each other. That had been in the offices of Interpol's Special Representative to the UN in New York with Tappin and Ryerson. Unfortunately, that particular meeting had been cut short before they'd had a chance to get to the bottom of the man's past.

"Who I am isn't important," Morgan asserted. "But the questions we are going to ask and the answers you are going to provide are. Do you understand?"

"Yes," he said dolefully. "Where am I?"

The man was slumped in the seat, confused and disoriented from lack of sleep. He had been well prepped by the team, Morgan noticed. They were experts in getting subjects, especially subjects like this one, ready for interview without resorting to pain and suffering – that would be against the rules; although, no doubt civil libertarians would argue the finer points of exactly what defined "pain and suffering". It meant little to Morgan. He had a job to do and he knew the realities of what creatures like this were prepared to submit other human beings to in order to prolong their own existence.

"Would you like some water?"

"I need a cigarette," he said. "Just a cigarette, please."

"There's no smoking in here," Morgan replied matter-of-factly. "Maybe later, when we're done."

The man's fingers clenched until his knuckles whitened. He was struggling. One simple strategy Morgan knew the prep team had used was to give the subject an unlimited supply of cigarettes for a couple of weeks before withdrawing them completely thirty-six hours ago. It had worked, Morgan noted. This guy was a chain smoker and his addiction, along with some carefully managed sleep deprivation, had his nerves on a knife edge. That was helpful.

"Would you like some water?" The man nodded. "Yes."

Morgan pulled a small notepad and pencil from his suit jacket while Braunschweiger brought over a plastic bottle of water, unscrewed the lid and placed it down on the table in front of the man. At this, the man opened his eyes properly and looked at the two agents, one seated, one standing 3 feet from him. The expressions on their faces confirmed the magnitude of his dire situation.

"What is your name?" asked Morgan, the pencil in his hand poised over the notepad. His tone was deadpan, unemotional. The timbre of his voice was calm and measured.

"Lazarević. Đurađ Lazarević," he answered weakly, his voice faltering as the words tumbled unconvincingly from his lips.

"Your real name," Morgan responded.

There was a long silence. All that could be heard was the breathing of the three men in the room. The Intrepid agents waited.

"Name?" Morgan asked again, still deadpan.

The man began to fidget, nervously gnawing on ragged fingernails and looking around the cell. His head swiveled back and forth between Morgan and Braunschweiger, with the stilted, artificial movements of a child's wind-up robot, knowing all along that he'd been found out. His arrest, caught red-handed with the girl, their hostage, had taken him and his accomplices way beyond any pitiful protection assumed identities could provide. He was exhausted from the constant stress of living under the fear of surveillance and capture. He scratched his head, shuffling on the seat of the metal chair. One leg was locked in an involuntary spasm.

Looking at him, Morgan knew that his nerves were shot.

"You've got thirty seconds," Morgan said.

Beside him, the Key slowly, deliberately lifted his left arm – bigger than any normal person's leg – and made a show of observing the sweep hand of his watch.

"Twenty-five," he said.

The subject couldn't take his eyes off Braunschweiger. The guy was a monster; sounded German.

"Fifteen," counted the Austrian.

The strength of his resolve to maintain a strong silence was now inexplicably locked in a death struggle with the incessant *tick tick tick* of the sweep hand as it crept ominously toward its deadline.

"Ten."

He was shaking uncontrollably now, chewing his nails

furiously, unable to stop himself from bursting forth with whatever they wanted to hear.

"Five," announced the Key.

Sweat formed an oily slick across his forehead and thick droplets oozed from dark pores, down his face and through the scattered tussock of his beard. His wretched body wriggled and squirmed upon the chair like a schoolboy desperate to be excused but too petrified of the teacher to ask.

"Four. Three."

The fingernails were down to their quicks. The man was about to lose it.

"Two," Braunschweiger declared with finality.

As the sweep hand crashed home and the Key announced "One," the man arched back then fell forward in the chair, both hands grasping either side of his head, the chain ratcheting through the D-ring in the floor.

"Dobrashin Petrović!" he screamed at the top of his voice. "Fuck! Fuck!"

It was the first time he had admitted to that name in a very long time. The release he experienced was both terrifying and cathartic.

"Thank you," said Morgan without emotion or any other reaction to the man's obvious torment and conflict at confirming his identity. Morgan wrote it down.

"Date and place of birth?" he said.

"Come on, you obviously already know," Petrović pleaded. "Why must we do this? Give me a cigarette, then I'll tell you what you want to know."

"There's no smoking in here," repeated Morgan dryly. "Date and place of birth?"

Petrović was now looking up at the Key for support,

incredulity scratched all over his face, but getting none. He went to stand.

"Your ankles and wrists are shackled, and the chain is tethered to the floor beneath your chair," said Morgan. "Remain seated. Date and place of birth?"

Petrović dropped back down and slammed his hands hard upon the metal table. The impact crashed around the room like a dozen empty garbage cans being hit by a car. The chain rattled madly. Morgan and Braunschweiger were unmoved. They sat impassively, waiting for the frustration to abate. When the echo retreated and the room fell once again into ominous silence, Morgan simply looked at Petrović.

"Thirtieth of April, 1968," Petrović answered. "Železnik, Belgrade, Serbia."

"Father?"

His elbows sat awkwardly on his knees and his face was buried in his hands. His breathing was heavy and labored. The nervous fidgeting, head scratching and nail biting were obviously set to continue until the interview process was concluded. Morgan and Braunschweiger didn't care. They needed information and would stay put until they had it. No matter how long it took.

"My father," he began hesitantly. "My father is Branko Petrović, born Dobanovci, Belgrade, on the twelfth of January 1945."

"Mother?"

There was a long pause.

"Mother?" Morgan repeated.

"My mother was born Ljiljana Komljenovic. She was born in Pančevo, Belgrade on the first of May, 1946. Both deceased. Killed during the war in '93. And my brother—" He stopped suddenly. He'd gone too far.

This was new, thought Morgan. Simović hadn't mentioned anything about Petrović having a brother. "Name?"

"You have what you want. That's all I'm saying. Fuck you!" He slammed his hands down upon the table again.

"Brother's details? Don't make me ask again."

Dobrashin Petrović fell deathly silent.

Morgan and Braunschweiger watched him intently. Intrepid already knew the details he'd provided about himself and his parents. Mila Haddad had provided that information the moment the dubious bone fides of the informant Lazarević, now confirmed as Dobrashin Petrović, had been substantiated.

So far, the interview had been purely the beginning of what was going to be a protracted information-gathering exercise. By asking questions they already knew the answers to they would get him talking, compliant, and confirm whether or not he was going to bullshit them. Their objective was to establish links between Petrović and Drago. Morgan also had to explore the possibility of a connection between Petrović and a former Serbian enforcer, apparently known only as the Wolf, who everyone back in London was suddenly very interested in.

Morgan had not been across this Wolf development, but Braunschweiger had brought him up to speed after they'd wrapped up the arrests in Tirana. The latest word from Intrepid headquarters was that the Wolf was believed to still be operating and, as a result, had now emerged as the prime suspect in the assassination of Judge de Villepin.

That made Petrović's clumsy, unintentional reference to a brother a revelation.

There'd been nothing about a brother in any of the available intelligence summaries, nor any reference made throughout their lengthy interview with the big Serb, Simović, back in The Hague.

Simović's deposition had centered only on specific information he knew about Drago, which was all helpful in adding to the outstanding charges against Drago in the ICTY. The downside was that Simović had absolutely no knowledge as to Drago's current whereabouts. That was the most closely guarded secret of the Zmajevi and only the very inner sanctum, Drago's most trusted few, were in that loop.

Inevitably, Simović would be required to testify against Drago, which he seemed resolved to do in order to save his own skin. But it dawned on Morgan that Simović hadn't given up anything at all relating to Petrović, a brother, or the Wolf. Had he deliberately been avoiding discussion of the Petrović brothers? If so, why? Was he more fearful of them than of Drago? It occurred to Morgan that at the time of the arrests in Tirana, his gut had told him that Dobrashin Petrović appeared to be in the management role, albeit frontline, while the big Serb – Simović – and his offsider Muscles had been doing the heavy lifting stuff.

But right now, Dobrashin Petrović himself had overstepped his own boundaries and was struggling with the prospect of giving up his brother's name. Finally, they were onto something. The agents remained silent, Morgan seated with his notepad and pencil ready to scribble down the information, and the Key standing like a fortress behind his colleague.

After nearly two minutes of silence, Petrović let out a long sigh through shaking hands, his tired face full of betrayal and shame. He raised his eyes to the flickering fluorescent tube and said, "I have a brother, actually a cousin, but we were raised as brothers."

"Explain please?" asked Morgan.

"He is the son of my father's brother. He was orphaned as a baby when his parents were killed in a car accident."

He stopped for a moment, recovering the memories and details. "My parents were without children. They adopted him and raised him as their own. Two years later, I was born. Like I said, we were raised as brothers."

"Name and date of birth?" Morgan pressed on.

"Vukasin Petrović," he said. "February 27, 1966."

"Where?" asked Morgan.

"What?" said Petrović absently.

"Where was he born, exactly?"

"Same as my father. Dobanovci, Belgrade, Serbia."

"Is he still alive?"

Dobrashin Petrović's face was back in his hands. A deep, primal groan came from within and manifested itself as a series of short sobs that he struggled to, but eventually did, bring under control.

Morgan asked again: "Is Vukasin Petrović still alive?"

After a sharp intake of cold air, Petrović answered.

"Yes."

Chapter Fifty-Two

EL DJEM, TUNISIA

Under a cloudless, pale blue sky, police officer Youssef Ali Hassan raced through the streets of El Djem, heading northwest. With the red lights flashing and the siren wailing, Youssef pushed the dusty black and white Renault fast through the back streets and alleyways toward Tlesla, Ksour Essaf and onward to the coast. A stream of whitewashed walls, crumbling abandoned homes and lonely sidewalks flashed past, eventually making way for the beginning of endless miles of brown dirt and empty fields, punctuated by pockets of acacia, date palms and desert grass.

Youssef's brow was set with purpose, duty and more than a hint of excitement, on this, his very first important assignment. He was carrying a kidnapped foreigner to the hospital in Mahdia for examination and had been ordered by his officer-in-charge to wait with the man until the Sécurité Publique district director, Colonel Hamba, arrived to collect him. Youssef knew the route to the coast well – he had family in Rejiche – and estimated the trip would take an hour. He thought about how proud his father and mother would be when he would visit them later on his way back to El Djem. Finally, he had a great responsibility.

As the aging Renault finally cleared the city limits, the deep, croaky voice from the back seat interrupted Youssef's dreams of accolade and prestige.

"Officer, could we do without the sirens now?"

"Oh, yes, of course, sir," Youssef replied, reluctantly flipping the switch that quelled the siren; but he kept the lights flashing overhead.

"Is there any air conditioning? It's very hot back here."

"I'm sorry, sir," said Youssef, slightly embarrassed. "The air conditioner does not work in this car. Are you able to reach the window handle? Otherwise, I could stop and do it for you."

"That's very kind. I can manage."

"How are you feeling now, sir?" asked the young policeman, eager to make a positive, professional impression on the man.

"Fine," the foreigner replied, suddenly dismissive. "Thank you."

Raoul Demaçi shifted uncomfortably upon the hot black upholstery of the police car's back seat, grabbed the old window handle on the door he was leaning against and began to crank the window open. It came down in a series of jerky movements, steaming-hot air forcing its way into the car. Eventually, it was as open as it was going to get. It made little difference to the temperature, but did serve to provide sufficient background noise to make conversation impossible.

Demaçi preferred it that way. He had too much on his mind to get caught up in mindless chatter with a street cop.

Looking out to the north, the endlessness of the arid Saharan landscape came as a somber reminder of his relevance and place in the world. Camels, palm trees, sand and mosques. Little had changed out here in a thousand years. The world continued to turn as generations came and went. How petty and insignificant were the individual ambitions of men. The insatiable desire to conquer, dominate and exploit, so much a part of the primal genetic coding, drove some men, himself included, to do anything in order to succeed; no matter the cost. Was it worth it?

Mentally leaping the tracks to escape that particular express to nowhere good, Demaçi turned his mind instead to what was next in store for him. No doubt there would have been plenty of effort expended in searching for him. Where had he been all this time? Who had he been with? What had he been through? Why had he suddenly been released? He expected the full raft of questions by the authorities when he was eventually handed to the senior echelons; especially when they realized who he'd been with at the time of the abduction. Whatever their interest was, once he'd navigated his way through the treacle of their procedures and back-slapping, there was only one person he was focused on being reunited with.

At the thought of it, a churlish grin tugged at his left cheek.

So, the policeman, Youssef Ali Hassan, and the recently returned abductee, Raoul Demaçi, were silent and would remain that way until they arrived in Mahdia, and while fate had brought these two men together, each performing a pivotal role in the life of the other, their pasts and futures could not have been more different.

Chapter Fifty-Three

TIRANA, ALBANIA

Alex Morgan stood in Skanderbeg Square in the dead center of Tirana, taking a moment to admire the country's monument to fifteenth-century lord and Albanian national hero George Kastrioti Skanderbeg. *Or plain old Skando to his mates*, Morgan thought with a wry smile.

From where he stood, Morgan could see a variety of the city's landmarks: Tirana City Hall, the Palace of Culture and the National Historical Museum, plus a few embassies and hotels. There were people everywhere, locals and tourists moving across the square, stopping to chat, sitting on the grass or generally taking in the surrounds. It was cloudy and, despite the lateness of the afternoon, still warm, verging on hot. Morgan was glad he'd dressed practically: the polo shirt and light chinos were perfect; any more and the humidity would have him sweltering.

Morgan felt the buzz of his sat phone in his pocket.

"Morgan," he answered.

"Alex? It's Charly."

"Hey, how are you? Everything OK?"

"Yeah, I'm fine," she mumbled sleepily. There was a pause. "It's nice to hear your voice. I hope it's OK that I rang?"

"Of course it is." He meant it. His eyes continued to survey his surrounds. It was good to hear her voice too. "Jesus, what time is it over there? Must be early."

"I think it's about 5am," Charly replied. "I can't sleep. Mom's always up early, I can hear her downstairs. I hope she's putting coffee on. What time is it where you are?"

"A little after 2pm," he said, trying not to imagine her lying in bed. "Still doing your self-defense sessions with the marshals?"

"Yeah, of course. I'm totally dangerous."

He heard her laugh and pictured her smiling.

"Hey, Alex, seriously, I have to ask you something."

"Go ahead."

"Do you remember the night you were here, I said there was something I wanted to talk to you about, but I completely forgot what it was?"

"Sure, I remember. Don't tell me it's just occurred to you now."

"Yeah, random, right? Anyway, it's about that security guy. The one you arrested."

"Which security guy, Charly? I'm not sure what you mean." Morgan pressed his ear harder against the sat phone. His internal alarm bells were on the verge of going off, he just knew it.

"That muscle guy, the bald one with that awful goatee. You arrested him with those other two animals when you came and got me," she said, suddenly nervous that she hadn't mentioned this earlier. "Oh God, Alex. I thought you knew. I was just so relieved to be safe again and they were all in custody. I thought you knew." She was distressed.

"Charly, I need you to calm down, OK?" Morgan wasn't sure what he was about to hear but somehow he felt like he already knew. "Tell me exactly what you mean."

"OK, OK, I'm sorry." She was collecting herself, he could hear it. "The guy with all the muscles; he was in on the kidnapping, somehow. On the boat, I mean. I don't know how. I think he was posing as Raoul's bodyguard. They seemed to know each other, anyway. One of them was running around telling us all to get below but this guy was somewhere else. I thought he'd been shot, but then he turned up on the pier. He's the bastard who knocked me out when they were getting me into that seaplane."

"And he was posing as Raoul's bodyguard?" Morgan's blood went cold. His mind returned to his examination of the *Florence*. He'd checked the area where the second security guard, apparently Muscles, had gone down but there'd been no blood. Then, there was the round of blank ammunition he'd found on the deck. It was exactly the spot where Charly saw Raoul firing back at the pirates; firing back with blanks?

"Yes," she whispered, terrified that she'd done something very wrong by forgetting this important detail.

"OK, Charly, this is important. I'm going to arrange for one of the US marshals to come in and take a statement from you. They will guide you through everything you can possibly remember about that guy and you need to tell them."

"Yes, of course. I'm so sorry, Alex. I feel like an idiot."

"There's nothing to be sorry about," he reassured her. "You've been through a hell of a lot. It takes time for the mind to catch up on certain details that are buried after a traumatic event. We'll sort this out."

"Thank you," she said. "Thanks for being so understanding."

"Hey, nothing to thank me for. Now, do me a favor and give the marshals every single thing you can remember. No matter how petty it may seem."

After some more reassurances, they said goodbye. Morgan didn't have time to devote to that issue right now, but he knew that it was significant and needed to be followed up immediately.

He dialed a number on his sat phone.

"*Jawohl?*"

"Key, it's Alex. I need you to follow up on something. It's urgent."

"Go ahead."

Two minutes later, Morgan had completed his call to the Key. He'd given every detail Charly had provided and would now step back and leave it with him. There was nothing more he could do from here. He had to focus on the task at hand.

"One more thing, Alex," said the Key.

"Yes, mate?"

"Petrović, the brother," he began. "My Serbian is a little rusty so I looked it up."

"Yeah." Morgan wondered where the big guy was going with this. "You looked up what, exactly?"

"Vukasin Petrović," answered the Key. "The name Vukasin is Serbian for wolf."

There was a long silence as Morgan considered the possible breakthrough. Could it be that obvious?

"Morgan, listen, you leave this to me. That was just meant to be FYI. I'll get Mila to check it out. I'll brief you when you get back."

"OK, Key," he said. "You may be onto something. Great work, mate. Talk soon."

Finally, a glimmer.

Checking the time, Morgan moved away from the monument and chose a position diagonally opposite the spot where the meet was scheduled to take place. He made sure he had a clear visual of the area and the approaches to it, adjusted his Ray-Ban Wayfarers, pulled a well-worn black baseball cap down, found a bench and waited. To anybody walking by he looked just like any other man, probably a foreigner on a break, enjoying the late afternoon warm weather.

Morgan was following the threads that led from Dobrashin Petrović – formerly known as Đurađ Lazarević aka Interpol's star informant – straight back into the bowels of the Serbian mafia machinery. Or so he hoped.

When Intrepid uncovered that Petrović was his actual identity and that he'd been a soldier in the Bosnian Serb Army serving under Drago during the war, a spotlight immediately fell upon the information he'd provided to the Interpol case officer in Tirana regarding Milivoj Šerifović, not to mention his motives. The fact that his deposition led to the arrest and delivery of Šerifović to the ICTY certainly added weight to his legitimacy and supported his claim that it was the increased reward that had brought him out of hiding. Adopting the false identity of Đurađ Lazarević, he claimed, was to protect himself from retribution. But none of that was holding water any more. His active participation in the kidnapping of Charlotte-Rose Fleming had changed everything. At that point, Dobrashin Petrović's raison d'etre had become very gray. It was Morgan's job to make it black and white.

What was clear was that he was a double agent, on the

payroll of the Serbian mafia. The challenge now was to determine just how involved he was and with whom.

The paucity of information regarding how Petrović had actually made himself known to Interpol Tirana in the first place had alarm bells clanging back in London, and now the attention was directed to Petrović's Interpol case officer, Lorenc Gjoka.

Davenport had done everything but kick over furniture in his office after discovering there'd been almost no due diligence conducted by Interpol before Intrepid was given the green light to arrest Šerifović. The possibility that the arrest had been part of someone else's grand plan, potentially even a factional power play within the Serbian mafia, had almost sent the general into a fit. Morgan recalled his last, very clear mission brief from his chief. It was the only time Morgan had ever heard the old man utter an expletive.

"Whoever his case officer was, I want a microscope over every aspect of his miserable life, from the day he was born until right fucking now. If there's any possible chance that he's linked to the Wolf or the *Zmajevi*, or whoever these bloody animals are, then stay with him and don't come back until you have him and Dragoslav Obrenović in chains."

Satisfied that there appeared to be no unexpected supernumeraries buzzing around, Morgan moved around to the north-eastern corner of the park and took up the agreed position on the low white wall, with his back to the monument, facing the Ethem Bey mosque, the government buildings and the clock tower on the other side of the street. As planned, he put his day sack down upon the wall to his left, indicating to his contact that the coast was clear. If he'd placed the day sack to his right, it would indicate that they'd been compromised and the meet would be aborted.

Bang on schedule, his contact arrived. Moving in from

the south, she stopped just short of Morgan, feigning the delight of an aunt catching her first glimpse of a much-favored nephew after an extended separation.

"My dear boy," she said. Both hands came up to her face and a broad smile shone through the shutters. "It's so nice to see you."

Morgan immediately stood, leant forward and gave his faux aunt a warm hug and peck on the cheek.

"How are you, Aunty?" he said. "Mum says hi."

The approach had been agreed well in advance of the meet. It was simple and appropriate given their respective ages. Above all, it was totally normal.

After exchanging obvious pleasantries and Aunty taking a let-me-look-at-you moment, they sat down on the wall and fell into comfortable, familiar conversation. A few minutes in and they changed tack.

"Therese St Marie," she said. "Pleased to meet you."

"Alex Morgan," he replied.

Therese was in her early fifties; her accent made her Belgian, he thought. Her long hair, which she wore tied back into a ponytail, was naturally auburn and she liked to keep it that way. Her dress was casual, loose fitting to the ground. Underneath it she wore ankle boots. She had dark brown eyes, a fair complexion and a warm, genuine smile.

It was not common practice for the paths of agents and surveillance crews to cross out in the open, far from it. But time was against them today and things had to get done. Besides, the moment this meeting was over, Therese St Marie was booked on the next flight out of Albania.

Therese was one of Intrepid's most experienced covert surveillance operatives. A couple of weeks ago she'd been leading the crew supporting Hermann Braunschweiger's operation across the other side of the city. Their work had been critical to the success of the operation that resulted in Charly's rescue. This time, Therese and her team had been covering the movements of the Interpol case officer who first brought Dobrashin Petrović in from the cold.

"So, what do you have for me?" asked Morgan.

"Our man is Mr Lorenc Gjoka." She pronounced it perfectly – Morgan knew he'd struggle with it. "He's an ethnic Albanian, in his mid-fifties and married with a couple of young adult children. A small man, a little under 5-and-a-half feet tall in the old currency. Fair-skinned and bald on top but consistent with the vanity of many older, conservative men, he insists on preserving a ridiculously fat ribbon of gray hair around the sides and back of his head – all that he has left. At least he's resisted the comb over." They both laughed as she continued: "He walks very quickly, always forward and up on his toes; trying to get himself more height, you know. His hands are small like a child's and he constantly rubs them together. Other than that, there are no particularly remarkable physical attributes. Due to his size he is very easy to lose track of in a crowd, which he uses to his advantage. Unprofessional of me to say but he's a slippery little weasel. So, you must be on your toes, too."

"Got it," Morgan said. He liked her style. "When can I expect to see him?"

"He's due out of his office soon. The Interpol Tirana office is five minutes' walk from here, but don't worry. He leaves at precisely 4.45pm every Friday afternoon. He has an apartment with his wife here in the city and normally he dutifully goes home to her every night after work; but not on Fridays. Today he'll walk across this square at approximately 4.50pm and get into his car, that old white Mercedes back there." She gave an almost imperceptible nod behind her. "You parked where I told you?"

Morgan nodded. It was also close by.

"Good. He moves the Mercedes there during the lunch hour to avoid the peak-hour traffic crush near his office. As soon as he gets into that car he heads straight out of town to a chateau. He has a mistress, a local woman. All we know is that the chateau is hers, and it's just outside a small town called Petrelë, fifteen kilometers due south of the city along the E852 route."

"OK, great," he said. "Got any pics of this guy?"

"I'll send some to your phone," she replied. "Other than that, it's up to you. Once I leave here, the team will begin a staggered withdrawal from this task. We're all leaving Albania tonight, so you'll be on your own. You'll receive a call shortly from Amir, a member of my team. Amir will hand over to you by phone when the target is here in the square and when you confirm with Amir that you have eyes-on. Clear?"

Morgan nodded.

"OK, give your aunty a hug then," she said. They both stood and embraced as warmly as they had in greeting. "Good luck," she said finally, turned and, in seconds, disappeared into the mob.

For the next couple of hours, Morgan played tourist, acquainting himself with the local area and stopping for coffee at a little café off the square. Eventually, as time ticked by toward H-hour, he received the call from Amir, spotted the target and the handover from the surveillance crew was complete.

As he kept his eyes locked upon Lorenc Gjoka, scuttling across Skanderbeg Square toward his dilapidated old Mercedes and off to his weekend squeeze, Alex Morgan was seized by the reality that he was in fact, once again, on his own. And while normally that wouldn't be a problem, since he'd been taking on the Serbian mafia he'd learnt to expect the unexpected.

Never underestimate your enemy, he reminded himself; *even a little rodent like Gjoka*. He had a feeling he'd be reminding himself again before the night was out.

No backup. No lifeline.

No second chances.

Chapter Fifty-Four

MAHDIA, TUNISIA

"Am I able to see him now, doctor?" asked the police district director, impatiently. "It's been two hours already. I must speak with him."

"Very well," replied the doctor, older than the policeman, but only just. He was not in the least bit rattled by this blustering, oafish, self-important man. "You may see him for ten minutes, that's all. Then my staff will ensure he gets more rest and you will be out."

With that the doctor turned smartly on his heel, the edge of his long white coat flaring out wide like a cape and, clipboard in hand, he disappeared down the corridor.

"Asshole!" exclaimed the exasperated policeman to no-one in particular. He removed his cap and marched briskly into the room where they were treating the foreigner.

Youssef, who had been diligently keeping watch over his charge while the medics fussed about, leapt to his feet as his district director appeared. Youssef had recognized him from the photograph in the station office.

"Who are you?" demanded the director.

"Police Officer Youssef Ali Hassan, sir," he answered with parade ground snap. "From the Sécurité Publique division in El Djem. I was instructed to bring the gentleman here and remain with him until you—"

"Very well," the senior man said abruptly. "You have your notepad?"

"Yes, sir," Youssef answered, and produced it from his tunic pocket.

"Excellent," the director replied. "Be seated. You will transcribe my interview with this man. I will let you know when to begin."

Youssef Ali Hassan saluted and sat down.

A nurse finished taking the patient's blood pressure and left without a word.

"I am Colonel Habib Ali Bach Hamba of the Sûreté Nationale," he announced haughtily, his monstrously festooned uniform similarly trumpeting his position and status. "I am the district director for this area, and I am responsible for your safety and wellbeing while you are under the protection of the Tunisian Republic."

"Thank you, colonel," Demaçi responded from the bed. "I'm honored to have such an important host, but it is not necessary. I don't intend to be here long. I really must be getting home. There are people waiting for me; wondering what has become of me ..."

"That is all in hand, I assure you. I have advised Interpol," the colonel lied, "that we have you under our protection and they will dispatch a representative from their office in Tunis first thing in the morning to begin the arrangements for your repatriation. In the meantime, there are some details I am obliged to discuss with you. I'm sure you understand."

"Very well, colonel," Demaçi said.

Chapter Fifty-Five

TIRANA, ALBANIA

Sitting behind the wheel of a late-model VW Passat hired at the airport, Morgan kept his eyes glued to the pigeon-toed figure of Lorenc Gjoka, scurrying nervously across Skanderbeg Square toward his Mercedes. It was almost dusk. Soon he'd lose all the natural light.

Never in a million years would anyone walking past suspect this ordinary-looking, harried little man of being at the center of an attempt to subvert the course of international justice. Exactly the extent of his involvement and just where he sat in the criminal hierarchy was yet to be determined, but from what Morgan and the Key had pieced together from Simović—the big Serb, and informant-turned-double agent—Petrović, this guy Gjoka was up to his neck in it.

They knew that in his guise as Interpol case officer, it was Gjoka who had manipulated acceptance of Petrović as a reliable informant, including passing him off under the assumed name Lazarević; and that he had orchestrated the subterfuge to bring down the fugitive war criminal and leader of the Serbian mafia in the Mediterranean, Šerifović, who Morgan subsequently arrested in Corfu. Straightforward enough, but the big question was: Why? Some internal Serbian blood-letting? Retribution for some past wrong? Or a management reshuffle Balkans style?

Intrepid was leaning toward the latter.

Lorenc Gjoka now knew that his so-called reliable informant, Petrović, had been outed as a double. He would have found out through official Interpol channels long before his criminal network reported the arrests of Petrović and the crew in Albania. He also knew that the microscope had now swung toward him. In fact, with a less-than-gentle nudge from General Davenport, pressure to explain his association with Petrović had already been brought to bear upon Gjoka by his Interpol superiors in Tirana. As expected, he hadn't reacted well and so he'd been put on notice that an internal investigations team was being sent in from Interpol headquarters in Lyon. He was forced to surrender his passport. The strategy worked. Gjoka panicked and Therese St Marie's surveillance team confirmed that he was preparing to skip the country.

Now it was Morgan's job to bring him in.

Alex Morgan never ceased to be amazed at how inaccurate first impressions could be.

His own initial take on Gjoka was that of an anxious schoolboy type who struggled every day with being illtreated and undervalued because of his diminutive size, driven by the need to prove that he could outdo the big boys.

The official intelligence on Gjoka read of an ambitious,

dedicated man who, after completing his twenty-seven months of compulsory military service, joined the Directorate of State Security in 1978, aged twenty-one. Surviving the fall of the Iron Curtain, his career continued unabated with the establishment of the Albanian State Police. The scant information available suggested a career-obsessed individual who stopped at nothing to further his purely self-serving interests. Personal friendships and loyalties were of little importance to him.

Clearly, in Morgan's view, it was the attraction of promotion and power associated with entrée into the elite Interpol club that would have given Gjoka his sense of ultimate recognition and acceptance. But simply making it all the way to the hallowed halls of the Interpol headquarters in Tirana would not have been enough. Backstabbing colleagues and stepping on subordinates without compunction was like rolling over in bed for him. Morgan had come across his type before. They were treacherous because they were so petty, always looking for the next opportunity to feather their own nests. Morgan's skin crawled at some recollection and he mentally shook the memory away.

Watching Gjoka now in his car and turning over the ignition, Morgan wasn't surprised to see him suddenly pull into the busy traffic, causing those behind to stand on their brakes, honking horns and cursing from their windows. There was no reaction from the Mercedes. To Gjoka, these people didn't exist.

Well, Morgan thought, still with the mental picture of a nerdy little kid dressed up in loose-fitting grown up clothes, the time had come to give Mr Gjoka some long overdue payback.

Chapter Fifty-Six

MAHDIA, TUNISIA

Colonel Habib Ali Bach Hamba had no intention of reporting to Interpol the sudden appearance of this foreigner who claimed to be the victim of a kidnapping along with some famous American woman. Besides, Hamba had never even heard of this Fleming woman – how famous could she be? The whole thing sounded too far-fetched, even a little suspicious. No, Hamba would not risk the embarrassment of bothering his superiors until he was absolutely sure of the facts. Then, if the man's claims did stand up, Hamba would be praised for his meticulous handling of the situation. He would make the report once he was satisfied with the man's story.

And so he began, gesturing for Youssef to commence the transcription.

"Perhaps we could begin by confirming your name," said the colonel. "For the record, you understand."

"Of course. My name is Raoul Demaçi and I am a proud citizen of the Republic of Montenegro. Unfortunately, my passport was taken from me, I presume by the kidnappers, so I have no way of formally identifying myself."

"Don't concern yourself, Mr Demaçi. We've made arrangements with your embassy and they have confirmed your citizenship details." Another lie. "A new passport is being prepared for you as we speak. In the meantime, I must talk to you about the abduction. Do you feel prepared to discuss this now?"

"Yes, I'm fine. Please ask whatever it is you need to know."

"I must say, Mr Demaçi, you seem very well adjusted for a man who has spent almost a month as a hostage." It was more a question than an observation. There was not much that got past Colonel Hamba.

"Well, it may seem that way, colonel," Demaçi replied uncomfortably. "To a large extent, I am in reasonably good shape. But I feel as though I came to terms with my captivity when I realized that my kidnappers were more interested in my lady friend than me."

"How do you mean?" Hamba asked.

"It became apparent early on that my friend, Ms Fleming, was the target of their terror. I initially thought they had targeted me, given my financial situation, and that they would be seeking some kind of ransom in exchange for my safe return. I was wrong."

"How did you know?" asked the colonel. "Did somebody give you this information?"

"Not at all," Demaçi answered. He was wary of the line of questioning and the intense gaze of the policeman. It seemed a detailed physical appraisal was being conducted as he spoke. "For some reason, I don't know why, they presumed from the beginning that I was French. Obviously, you and I know that I'm not. However, I do speak French, along with a dozen other languages. It's important in my line of work to accommodate a variety of languages and cultures."

"I understand that," said the colonel, unimpressed by the man's arrogance. "But how did you know they only wanted Ms Fleming?"

"It didn't take long to work out that my kidnappers were a mix of Serbs, Maltese and Tunisians. I thought it would be wise to disguise the fact that I could understand them, so I allowed them to keep thinking I was French. As a result, all of their communication with me was in French, a very basic form, I must say. Meanwhile, they conversed among themselves in their native languages and, depending on who was talking, I could understand almost everything that was being said around me without their knowledge."

"Remarkable, Mr Demaçi," replied the colonel, unmoved. "You are a very resourceful man."

"That's kind of you."

"Now, if we could discuss—"

The door flew open and the doctor came bustling back in.

"Colonel, I was quite clear when I said 10 minutes," said the doctor. "And you have already been much longer than that. I must insist."

The doctor gestured to the door he was holding open, but Colonel Hamba had no intention of leaving. He'd been made to wait for 2 hours and the interview was yet to bear fruit, other than confirming Hamba's suspicion of Demaçi. He was not about to be put out into the street by this doctor. Hamba had the vital ground and he was not about to give it up. He turned to the patient.

"Mr Demaçi, if you feel you are unable to continue ..." The policeman's expression was all empathy and encouragement. "However, we are progressing quite well. It would be a pity if I was required to come back and forth over the next few days."

"Colonel, for the last time," ordered the doctor.

From the bed, Demaçi raised both hands to appease the men.

"Gentlemen," he began. "Doctor, I'm appreciative of your concern for my welfare. However, it is doing me good to finally convey the details of my abduction and captivity to the authorities. I am happy to continue with the colonel and promise that I will rest this evening. It is my hope that I will be released tomorrow, so that I may return home as soon as possible."

After a few moments of consideration the doctor eventually acquiesced with a "humph", and disappeared out into the hall, his white jacket flapping angrily behind him.

"Thank you, Mr Demaçi," said Colonel Hamba. "Now, if we could return to the beginning. Please take me through what happened from the time you first became aware of the kidnappers until your presentation at the police station in El Djem earlier today."

Raoul Demaçi took a moment to gather his thoughts. He poured water into a glass from a jug beside the bed, drank the glass empty and refilled it. Then he began.

Sitting invisibly in the corner, with painstaking thoroughness, Youssef transcribed every detail.

For the next 2 hours, Demaçi led the colonel through the kidnapping step by step, followed by the period of his captivity.

According to his best recollection, he said, when security onboard the *Florence* announced that they were about to be boarded by pirates, they began herding the crew and guests below decks for their protection. Of course, Demaçi said, there were only two guests on board: himself and Charlotte-Rose Fleming, and in the noise and chaos they were separated. Soon after, the pirates had begun firing upon the yacht and the security men were returning fire. During this time, the security man closest to Demaçi was wounded. So he picked up the man's gun and began to shoot back at the pirates. Sadly, he said, by this time they were almost aboard, and the second security man was killed and Demaçi was taken hostage.

This aspect intrigued the colonel.

"How did you know what to do, Mr Demaçi?" asked Colonel Hamba, interrupting the flow of the account. "I don't imagine there is much call for a successful businessman to be adept in the use of machine guns."

"That's right, colonel," the man replied, his jaw tightening. "However, I undertook a short period of military service during my younger days – an obligation in my country at the time. Like riding a bicycle, I suppose."

"I see," said Hamba. "The body of the security man who, according to your statement to my officers earlier, was at the front of the vessel and was retrieved by the Maltese authorities. It was, you said, riddled with bullet holes and floating face down in the water. Unfortunately, it is hard to verify exactly what became of the other security man, the one nearest to you, as his body has yet to be found."

Demaçi appeared to be giving this issue some consideration.

"I expect they probably threw his body over the side, too, colonel," he said.

"Yes." Hamba's response was non-committal. "Carry on."

"You understand, colonel, it was all happening very

quickly. I can only remember the main things from my perspective."

"You are doing extraordinarily well, Mr Demaçi," replied the colonel.

As Youssef continued to scribble furiously, Demaçi went on to describe his horror at realizing they were being kidnapped. He had no way of getting to Ms Fleming, he said, because he was bound by the wrists, a rag pushed into his mouth and a sack pulled over his head. After being transferred from the yacht to the pirates' inflatable boat, they were taken ashore. He was aware that Ms Fleming was still close by on the boat: he could hear her whimpering, but was unable to console or reassure her because he himself was gagged. Once they reached the shore – he had no idea where that was – he was put into a vehicle. From then on, he did not see or hear Ms Fleming again.

How convenient, thought Hamba.

Demaçi took another drink of water and stared at the wall. The two policemen remained silent.

"I'm sorry," Demaçi said after a few long moments in reflection.

"Not at all," said the colonel calmly. "Continue when you're ready."

By this time, Youssef had been forced to resort to his second pen.

Demaçi described the trip in detail. Once transferred, he was held down on the floor of what seemed to be an old truck. Then he found himself back on another boat, still bound and gagged, for what seemed like a very long time, days even. He couldn't recall exactly how long.

"You say you were transferred to another boat. How do you know it wasn't the same boat?"

"Well, it felt bigger than the inflatable one," Demaçi

answered, somewhat riled, then added, "and it smelled of fish."

Eventually ashore, he was moved into a building of some sort. Rural, he gathered, due to the sounds of the animals nearby. And that, he said, is where he remained, until being released this morning.

"Nothing of your period in captivity?" asked Hamba. "I realize it must be …" he searched for the word, "trying for you to revisit the experience."

"As I told your men earlier, colonel, it was unremarkable. I was kept in a small dark room of an old … farmhouse, I suppose you'd call it. I slept on the ground. I was fed occasionally and otherwise left alone."

"And what of your treatment? Were you beaten? What about things like the ablution arrangements?"

"No, I was not beaten, although I was roughly handled. As for toilet arrangements, when I needed to go I was escorted with a bag over my head."

"And then, for no apparent reason, this morning you were once again bound and gagged with a sack over your head." The Colonel raised his eyebrows. He received a nod. "And you were driven for some considerable time, taken out of the vehicle and then the bindings on your wrists were cut and you were left by the side of the road." Another nod. "You relieved yourself of the sack and gag, realized you were free and made your way to the nearest police station. Would you say that is an accurate summary?"

"That's it, colonel," Demaçi answered cautiously.

Colonel Hamba could not take his eyes from the man.

He had no reason not to believe the account Demaçi had just presented. The Mediterranean provided unlimited opportunities for criminals and organized groups operating across continents, and the kidnapping for ransom of wealthy foreigners was not uncommon in North Africa. Human trafficking was also prevalent. If the object of the kidnapping was the young lady rather than Demaçi, then it made sense that the two of them would have been separated early on. And it was very possible that the underlings holding him panicked, probably due to lack of communication from their masters, and let him go. Better that than be shot.

But something was not quite adding up.

Hamba had spent his entire adult life in law enforcement and thought he'd seen it all. But, for the first time in a long time, he found himself genuinely astonished at the extent of this man's composure. *Yes*, he thought, *this Raoul Demaçi is a very cool customer indeed*.

"Well, I'll leave you to get some rest, Mr Demaçi," he said with finality. "Your embassy should have someone along in the morning with your new passport." Well, they would when Hamba decided to contact them.

"I see. Would I be free to go then?" asked Demaçi.

"It's best that you remain here in the hospital tonight so that we can get hold of you if we need to, but I don't see any reason why you couldn't leave once we have your citizenship and passport details sorted out."

"Yes, of course," Demaçi replied, relieved that the interview was over. "Is something wrong, colonel?"

"Wrong? Why do you ask?"

"You seem distracted."

"No, nothing," Hamba lied. "It's been a long day. Anyway, I'm pleased that you're safe once again, Mr Demaçi. Good night."

"Good night, colonel."

Colonel Habib Ali Bach Hamba left the room with a heavy frown. Youssef shuffled out obediently in his wake.

As they walked out through the hospital reception in silence, the colonel stopped. Outside the rain was hammering down and the roof of the old hospital rumbled under the deluge.

"Give me your notes," he demanded.

Youssef handed over his notepad. He'd always been praised for his neat writing. Today of all days he felt more lucky than ever that it was so neat. He watched in silence as the colonel scrutinized page after page of his transcript.

"And you took down every detail, as I asked?" said the colonel without looking up.

"Yes, sir. Every detail."

Youssef saw a change in the colonel's face, as if something that had eluded him suddenly appeared.

"Good work, young man," said the colonel. "Get those typed up this evening and have them on my desk by first thing tomorrow morning. We must ensure our report is as accurate and detailed as possible for our superiors in Tunis." He was bluffing. Nothing would go to Tunis until Hamba was ready.

Absently looking up into the appalling weather, Colonel Hamba knew he had stumbled upon the glaring gap in Demaçi's account. How, if he was where he said he was during the attack by the pirates, would Demaçi know that the body of the security man was retrieved by the Maltese authorities? Or even that the man's body was full of bullet holes, face down in the water? Most importantly, not once throughout the entire deposition did Demaçi make any inquiry or display any concern whatsoever as to the whereabouts of this Charlotte-Rose Fleming, who he claimed to be the other victim.

"I've got you," Hamba said to himself. He would return first thing in the morning to continue his interrogation of

Demaçi and he would get to the bottom of the foreigner's story then. Meanwhile, food and wine was required and there was a particularly attractive, buxom and very lonely divorcée waiting for him at his favorite restaurant in downtown Mahdia.

Striding purposefully around the reception desk, Hamba pulled his cell phone from his pocket and dialed.

"This is Colonel Hamba," he said, awaiting acknowledgment. "Send my car around to the reception area of the hospital and tell the duty officer I want a guard placed outside the foreigner's hospital room immediately. Mr Demaçi is not to leave until I return in the morning."

Chapter Fifty-Seven

PETRELË, ALBANIA

As last light fell into step with the thousands of tired workers spilling out onto Tirana's sidewalks and the city's peak hour got into full swing, Alex Morgan followed Lorenc Gjoka's Mercedes at a discreet distance through the rapidly congesting streets. Like any other city in the world, Friday night had arrived in Tirana and anticipation of the weekend ahead had begun. But for Morgan, it was highly unlikely that his Friday night was going to be anything but dangerous. His anticipation was driven more by a desire to make it through alive than just getting through Saturday and Sunday without a hangover.

Morgan was amazed at how recklessly Gjoka drove, stopping and starting unexpectedly, changing lanes at speed, weaving erratically through the busy traffic. Red brake lights blazed like distress flares, drivers executed aerial dog fight maneuvers to get clear of him and horns blasted relentless broadsides in his wake. Jesus! The guy was a moving disaster zone. It was obvious he was using his cell phone while blindly negotiating his way through the melee. Who was he calling that couldn't wait? His mistress? An airline? The railway? Or what if it was backup? Had Morgan been compromised? Instinctively, the Intrepid agent dropped further back into the traffic to reduce his chances of being seen. Regrettably, this also made it harder to keep track of Gjoka in the early evening peak, but Morgan knew where they were headed. He'd pick him up again on the outskirts of town if he had to.

Despite the aggravating demeanor of this annoying little rat, Morgan kept reminding himself not to underestimate the man. Morgan had no idea what to expect at the chateau. What if the whole mistress thing was just a ruse? A guy with Gjoka's experience would have to have an extraction plan. He'd be a fool not to. No, whatever else he may be, one thing he definitely was not was a fool. Gjoka was a survivor.

Morgan shifted his mental image of Gjoka from annoying little rat to irritating cockroach.

Up ahead the erratic attack against other drivers continued. If his driving alone was anything to go by, Gjoka was rattled. Nobody would drive this badly normally, especially not a cop. The man was feeling the pinch. The surveillance team were right to call forward the arrest. Morgan had the distinct impression that this was a man in a desperate hurry, and not just to get laid by his mistress in the mountains.

Before long they had crossed the aqueduct that fish hooked around the bottom of the city, and were heading south along the E852 route. The traffic crush eased and the narrow road became a meandering snake through the hills, not much more than an old horse track that had at some point been widened and sealed. In no time it became dark and Morgan strained to keep the old Mercedes' red tail lights in view, as houses and shopfronts close by the road's edge shot past in a blur. He raced through one settlement after another, while in the distance the lights from lonely villages up on the hillsides sailed slowly across the blackened landscape like the lights of distant ships at sea.

Approaching the village of Lundër, Morgan saw a Euro Drin services center and felt hungry. Food would have to wait, he realized disconsolately. It'd be close to midnight, he reckoned, before he'd even get a chance to eat. More importantly, he'd scoped Lundër on the GPS and had stored it as a mental trigger to remind him that the road would soon do a long sweep around to the south-west before a natural left turn near Stërmas would bring him back to a heading due south.

The road toward and beyond Stërmas ran around a long finger of land that ran back up into the mountains, its tip pointing ominously in the direction Morgan was heading. He had to contend with the frustration of regularly losing sight of the old Mercedes through all the twists and turns that led into Petrelë. Where there were straight stretches he'd chance a bit of extra speed to keep up. It helped, marginally, but soon he was across the Mulleti Bridge, and the road closed in and trees with white-painted trunks and low stone walls appeared on either side. He took the right-hand fork toward Petrelë and as the car climbed the hill into the village, Morgan could see from the lights in the distance just how high and remote he was up here: Tirana was now a flat cluster of sparkling gold. The road continued in a series of tight hairpin turns up to the center of the village and as he finally reached the top he saw the silhouette of the castle tower Therese St Marie had told him to look out for.

"It was built in the fifth century, you know. In fact the whole place is pretty much all that's left of an ancient castle," she'd said when she called to check that he'd received the images she'd sent through.

Made sense to build a fortress up here, he thought with a soldier's instinct for defenses; dominate the high ground. In daylight you'd be able to see for miles in every direction. How appropriate for Gjoka to establish his little hideaway up here, albeit one with a distraction.

Driving carefully through the streets of the centuries-old village, Morgan saw the tail lights of the Mercedes extinguish up ahead. He pulled into a parking bay for sightseers. There were a few people about, so his presence wasn't unusual. Through his wing mirrors, he watched Gjoka lock his car and stride into a small local restaurant. Turning in his seat to get a clearer view, he saw the man approach a thirty-something woman at a table by the window. As she stood to kiss him, Morgan noticed that she was quite a bit taller than Gjoka.

The two of them sat down at the window table, chatting. She traced bright pink fingernails seductively along his forearms, he squirmed excitedly in his seat and then they started to peruse the chef's specials. Morgan wondered if Gjoka would order from the kids' menu.

Perhaps he was going to ditch the wife, and the mistress was going to flee the country with him instead. This guy just got lower and lower on Morgan's snake scale.

Chapter Fifty-Eight

MAHDIA, TUNISIA

Raoul Demaçi was sitting up in the hospital bed, agitated and impatient. Where was he? It was taking too long. The trip back to Tunis International Airport would take them two hours. There wasn't time for delays.

A policeman had been placed on guard duty outside the room. According to the idiot colonel, the policeman was there to keep Mr Demaçi safe from any possibility of reprisal or second thoughts by his kidnappers.

But Demaçi was no fool. He knew Hamba was suspicious. Waiting around until morning was too dangerous and, besides, it was never what Demaçi had had in mind.

"Excuse me, officer," he called weakly from the bed.

After a few moments the door opened and a middle-aged, overweight policeman with iron-gray hair and a full, walrus-style moustache wandered in. His expression was one of disinterest and mild annoyance. He didn't like having his working day extended without notice just to babysit a wealthy foreigner.

"Yes, sir?" the policeman said.

"Would you please tell me the time?"

"Yes, sir. It is—" he consulted his watch, "—4.45pm."

"Thank you. It's possible that a person from my company may arrive soon. I'd be very grateful if you would show him in."

"I wasn't aware that any visitors had been authorized by Colonel Hamba, sir," replied the policeman.

"It's all been arranged," answered Demaçi, smoothly dismissing the man's concerns. "I was allowed to put a call through from the police station in El Djem, before we left to come up here. I've asked that some clothes and toiletries be brought in. That's all."

"You know this person?"

"He's from our office in Tunis," replied Demaçi. "He's a young man, dark hair, average height and build. His name is Dmitri. He should be here very soon."

The policeman looked warily at Demaçi. The duty officer had been clear that this man was to be treated with utmost caution, but the policeman also didn't want any complications tonight. He was sure that this foreigner would be the type to cause trouble over every little thing. Besides, if he just had some clothes being brought in, what harm could there be in that?

"OK," he said. "I'll keep an eye out for him. But you know that you're not to leave the hospital."

Demaçi's face suddenly became fierce and his blue-gray eyes blazed like a fanned flame. His deep voice cut across the room like the delayed report of heavy artillery firing on the horizon.

"What did you say? I cannot leave? Am I now your hostage?"

The words hit the old policeman with a crack, unnerving him. He stood quietly dumbfounded. The ferocity of the man was completely unexpected. On the surface, it appeared that the foreigner was simply making an inquiry but, in reality, he was issuing a warning.

"Well?"

"No. No, sir," the old man replied unconvincingly. "It's just that my superiors want you to remain safe … here in the hospital, where we can take care of you."

A stony silence crept into the tiny room and felt like ice. The old man found himself riveted to the floor, unable to move.

After a while Demaçi said, "Fine, show Dmitri in when he gets here. I'd like some coffee."

The old cop turned on his heel and headed for the staff kitchen.

Watching the empty doorway, Demaçi forced himself to take a deep breath. The urge to lose control was overwhelming. He had to remain calm for just a bit longer. Soon Dmitri would arrive; then he could start getting everything the way it was always meant to be.

As he heard footsteps echoing along the narrow corridor, the tranquility of the moment was callously invaded by the face of his old mentor forcing its way into his thoughts.

"Yes, Drago," said Demaçi to the empty room. "I will fix everything, but you better be prepared for when I come back to fix you."

There was a knock on the half-open door, a man appeared and Demaçi threw his arms up with relief.

"Dmitri," he exclaimed. "What has taken you so long?"

"I'm sorry, *šefa*," Dmitri replied deferentially. "There was a bad accident on the outskirts of town. The news broadcast is blaming the weather; it's terrible out there. Just as I was attempting to get through, the police blocked the roads to allow for ambulances and fucking fire trucks. Is there a problem?"

"Yes, I can't wait until the morning. These fucking cops are suspicious, so my plan to get them to legitimize my return from captivity has gone to shit." He grabbed the bag of clothes from Dmitri and began to dress. "We must leave tonight. The only thing that matters now is that I get to Seattle before they have time to warn her. Have you booked the flights?"

"Yes, *šefa*," Dmitri said eagerly. "Just as you ordered; I've booked one at 8.30 tonight and another, the last flight, leaves at 2.45am. We still have time to fly this evening if we hurry. It's an Air France flight. Two stopovers: Marseille and Paris. Arrives in Seattle at 1.10pm local time tomorrow. I've also booked the midday flight and two more tomorrow night, to be safe. All booked and paid for."

"Good, we don't need to worry about those other flights; we'll take the Air France at 8.30 tonight and you will go as far as Paris. I will travel on my own from there."

"Yes, *šefa*. Here's your new passport. It's an EU, in the name of Adolfo Mendosa. Spanish."

"Excellent work, Dmitri. Quickly, let's—"

They turned to find the old policeman standing in the doorway holding a steaming, hot cup of coffee. His face smothered by uncertainty.

"What is happening?" he asked. "Why are you dressed? I said—"

"Now, now, officer," Demaçi responded, full of charm as he walked over and relieved the man of the coffee. "Thank you for this and, as you can see, my friend, Dmitri, has arrived with my things."

It only took a matter of seconds but those seconds were the last few in the old policeman's life. While Demaçi talked and skillfully distracted his attention, a thin blade appeared in the palm of Dmitri's right hand.

Chapter Fifty-Nine

PETRELË, ALBANIA

Morgan checked the time on the Passat's dashboard clock. It was 9pm.

He'd been forced to wait, impatiently, while Lorenc Gjoka and his mistress whispered sweet nothings at each other over dinner and, rather than looking obvious by sitting in his car the whole time, Morgan had found a small café on the other side of the square where he could keep an eye on them. He was pleased that he actually had time to eat something – he'd been on the go ever since he'd left Berlin at midday. In this job, he mused, if the jetlag didn't kill you, starvation was always just a few steps behind. But now he was back in his car again; Gjoka was paying their bill over in the restaurant and his mistress was waiting by the Mercedes.

The dinner had been innocent enough and the two of them appeared to be in high spirits throughout – albeit with an undercurrent of nervous tension, which supported Morgan's prediction that they were going to take off together. What did bother Morgan, though, was that during the meal, he'd noticed a large black van doing randomly timed drive-bys of the restaurant. It had driven past three times that he'd seen. It was impossible to be sure if the two were related, but it kept him on his toes. He'd made a note of the registration plates.

Morgan watched as the Mercedes pulled away from the restaurant and drove out of Petrelë, heading south along Rruga Durishtit, the road leading to the chateau. He waited. He knew the house was only a few hundred yards along the ridge line. If he followed straight away he might as well have asked them for a lift. He was confident that they would be returning to her house to collect personal effects and either leave immediately or get a good night's sleep and take off first thing in the morning. Otherwise, why would Gjoka drive all the way up here and stop for a private, romantic meal? Morgan's money was on them leaving immediately. He checked the dashboard clock again and, satisfied that a few minutes had passed, he drove off.

Cruising with excruciating slowness along Rruga Durishtit, there was absolutely no other traffic and, importantly, no lights. As he drew closer to the house, Morgan switched off the headlights of the Passat and kept the speed around 5 miles per hour. The tires crackled and popped along the loose gravel surface of the unsealed road. It was only one lane wide and at some of the hairpin turns along the way, old car tires had been stacked in low walls three or four layers high to warn of the dangerous conditions beyond. *Nothing but world class safety standards out here*, he mused. It took all of Morgan's concentration to negotiate the road in total blackout without going over the edge.

When he finally reached the last bend in the road before the house, his heart almost stopped.

In the pitch darkness of a moonless, starless night with a

gentle breeze whistling through the treetops on the hillside, Alex Morgan heard a blood-curdling scream.

Chapter Sixty

SUNSET HILL, SEATTLE, WASHINGTON, USA

It was almost lunchtime when Charlotte-Rose Fleming sat down to the piano. But today the music eluded her. Her fingers lay dormant upon the keys, unwilling to cooperate.

Charly felt utterly conflicted over her feelings about Raoul Demaçi and her escalating interest in the elusive man from Interpol, Alex Morgan.

She'd never known such confusion. Truth be told – and despite the views of the tabloids – she was not the type to gavotte from man to man; quite the opposite. More than anything, her interest in Raoul was a curiosity born more from end-of-tour fatigue and a desperate need for escape; that, and the fact that the relentlessness of his platinum-laced pursuit basically wore her down. At a time when she normally would have shunned such an overbearing approach, she found her misgivings about him vastly outweighed by the prospect of a couple of weeks of seclusion, floating around on a luxury yacht in the Mediterranean.

She hadn't actually taken the time to consider how she

felt about Raoul Demaçi and now it was too late. If anything had happened to him, she'd never be able to forget it. His death would always be inexplicably linked to the first and last time she would ever throw caution to the wind and allow a foolish, selfish whim to take control of her. And then along came Alex Morgan.

She smiled and a warm feeling enveloped over her.

Charly gave up on the piano and went back to the sofa she'd shared with Morgan that night. She took up the small Union Jack cushion he'd commented on – a souvenir from a visit to Windsor Castle years ago – and nestled into the corner where he'd been sitting. Holding the cushion affectionately against her chest, Charly allowed her memory of him to consume her thoughts.

"My God," she whispered, "what the hell are you doing to me, Alex Morgan?"

Chapter Sixty-One

PETRELË, ALBANIA

Alex Morgan found a gap in the trees off to his left and drove the car down an overgrown track, masking it from sight. He pulled on a black sweater, lowered the window and eased himself out into the darkness. The moment his feet touched the ground, Morgan knew he was on enemy turf. There'd be no turning back.

With the SIG Sauer P226 in his right hand, Morgan moved cautiously along the edge of the gravel road, stopping every few feet to listen. He could just make out the mumbling of men's voices close by. No more screaming. He thought he heard a sob, so he stopped to listen some more. Still incoherent mumbling, but the tone spoke volumes. This was a one-way conversation, a monologue with no emotion or room for negotiation. He pressed on slowly, silently, until he found a small track to get him off the roadside and up to a vantage point closer to the house.

Morgan crept through the low-lying shrubs, careful not to disturb any of the branches, leaves or twigs littering the track. As he approached the crest of a small mound he could see the dim glow of an overworked light globe from the house. He was less than 20 feet away and the voices became clearer, with one in control and the other pleading for clemency. Morgan had never heard Gjoka's voice, but surmised that it was him doing the pleading.

Morgan realized they were speaking English. Second language, he thought. So, the unexpected visitors were not Albanian. Otherwise, they'd be dealing with Gjoka in his native tongue. That told Morgan two things: they were not local police and Gjoka was in serious trouble.

Morgan flattened himself to the ground and slithered upward inch by inch. When he got there he positioned himself with only the top of his head close to the base of a shrub so he wouldn't be seen. It took a moment for his eyes to adjust to the light.

The house was a converted two-story farmhouse, a hundred years old by the look of it, built from locally mined stone with old wooden window frames that were faded and worn. The driveway and the small area by the side-door entrance to the house was dry gravel, much like the road. But Morgan's review of the house ended there.

A single low-wattage globe barely lit the area but he could see the Mercedes and right behind it the black van he'd spotted doing laps in the village. Not good. It was only a short, very narrow driveway up from the road and once that van had come in, Gjoka and his mistress were blocked in with no way out.

Morgan could see four men, big guys with too much time for the gym. They were dressed in standard-issue black everything, heads shaved to the scalp. *Don't fuck with the baldies*, he thought gloomily. Then he realized that they all had identical goatees; thick and well maintained, like some kind of membership badge. One of them had Gjoka by the collar, pushing him inside the house. Gjoka was trying desperately hard not to go. He must have known he wouldn't be coming out alive. When Morgan eased forward to get a clearer view of the house, he could see why.

Lying on the ground in front of the Mercedes was the mistress. Her throat had been cut and blood was gathering in dark pools in the wheel ruts of the driveway.

Morgan stayed where he was until he was confident nobody had been left outside on sentry duty. He pulled away from his position, crawling backward until he reached the base of the mound and then, moving furtively through the shrubs, he made his way toward the mistress. He froze. As he reached the driveway, Morgan heard movement within the black van. A shuffling sound. Fuck! Then the handle of the van's sliding back door clicked. Morgan leapt back on his toes and vanished into the darkness nearer to the main road. His hand tightened reassuringly around the grip of the SIG.

The door eased back and a man emerged. He stepped out onto the gravel and idly lit a cigarette. He was so close that the smell reached Morgan in a second. Taking a long draw to fill his lungs with the muck, he turned and walked toward the house. Morgan watched him step around the body of the mistress. The only interest he displayed was to avoid stepping in her blood. As he reached the light by the front door, Morgan saw him properly, but only for a few seconds. Average height, he looked solidly built; big, but not as big as the others. Unlike the baldies he had hair, thick and jet black, slick with oil; like the baldies, he also had a goatee. Although somehow, Morgan felt that the others wore theirs because of him, not the other way around.

As the man disappeared inside, Morgan waited a few

seconds, gave the spare magazine pouches on his belt a reassuring tug and then crept into the house behind him.

Chapter Sixty-Two

PETRELË, ALBANIA

"Do you know who I am, Gjoka?" asked the man who had entered last.

"No," Gjoka replied, shaking. "I'm sorry. Should I? Have we met?"

Morgan managed to infiltrate as far as the base of the stairwell. He could see up through the stairs to a mezzanine level where the conversation was taking place. Gjoka was sitting in an armchair, the slick-haired man asking questions in front of him and two of the goons in partial view. Morgan couldn't see the others.

Deciding it would be prudent to listen in, Morgan remained hidden. He could be up the stairs in three bounds if need be.

"No," the man scoffed, "we've never met. I only meet people like you once."

"People like me? What do you mean?"

"People who cause problems. People who become greedy. People who should know better." The accusations rolled off the man's tongue as he stalked menacingly around the insipid creature in the chair. "People like that."

Gjoka remained silent, looking from side to side, not knowing where this was going or what he was being accused of.

"My name is Obrenović," the man said calmly. "I am the son of Dragoslav Obrenović. My father asked me to pay you a visit."

Gjoka's blood turned to ice. Downstairs, Morgan's did, too. His radar went into overdrive.

"You've been a bad little man, Gjoka," Obrenović began. "You have shown that your loyalty is for sale. My father is very unhappy about this."

"But what on earth have I done to Drago?"

"You have forgotten already, Gjoka. You have forgotten who made all this—" he waved his hand around, "—possible. This chateau, your bitch downstairs, your position in Interpol; you owe my father your life."

"I don't understand. I have done what I was asked—"

Obrenović exploded. "Following the orders of that fuck the Wolf, over my father's? Selling out Šerifović, one of my father's oldest friends?"

The young Obrenović stepped forward, stood over Gjoka and punched him hard. Gjoka's nose erupted blood and he bounced in the chair, screaming in agony. His hands flew up to fend off a second blow. But it came in from the opposite side, and Gjoka didn't have a chance of blocking it. Obrenović struck the already broken nose again. Tears of pain streamed down Gjoka's bloodied, smashed face.

"I thought this was what Drago wanted," Gjoka sobbed. "Wolf told me this was Drago's wish. That it was time for Šerifović to go. I did as I was told."

"I don't believe you, little Gjoka. Those bags over there

tell me I'm right." He flicked his head at the his-and-hers luggage in the corner, ready to be loaded into the car. "You were about to run. Fortunately, I arrived just in time. I would hate to have missed you."

"No, no, I'm running from Interpol," he said, blubbering, pleading his case with every word. He looked in disbelief at his hands, covered in his blood. "They already have the Wolf's brother, Dobrashin, and Ivan Simović, too."

"And they have one of my men!" Obrenović snarled. Morgan surmised that he was referring to Muscles, who'd been shipped back to Belgrade to face organized crime charges. "He was there to make sure the Wolf's operation went ahead as agreed. Now he will rot in Požarevac!"

"An investigation has been launched against me. A team is being sent from Lyon to investigate me. It was only a matter of time before they had me, too. What else was I supposed to do?"

"You ask Drago for help," was the reply. "But you didn't. You didn't tell anybody what you were doing. Instead, you made arrangements to escape Albania. Let me see, what was it? By boat from Durrës to Bari in Italy, and then from Italy you were booked on the high-speed train to France; correct?"

The look on Gjoka's face confirmed the allegation.

"Would you like me to talk about these too?" Morgan saw two passports thrown into Gjoka's lap. "Not the actions of a loyal man."

Gjoka looked down at the passports.

"Your bitch told us everything, little Gjoka," Obrenović said. "We visited her before you'd even left your office. She told us everything, even handed over your fake passports to save her own miserable skin. What? Didn't she warn you over your sweet little dinner in the village?

Of course she didn't, you stupid fuck. Do you know why?"

Gjoka shook his head, numbed by the revelation.

"Because, I offered her a deal: her life for yours. I told her if she breathed a word to you, I'd kill you both. But if she got you back here nice and quietly, I would only take you. The stupid bitch believed me."

Gjoka's face was in his hands now. His head shook in disbelief; blood streamed down his wrists into his shirt sleeves.

"I tell you – I tell you it was the Wolf and his brother. They convinced me that it's what Drago wanted. I was only doing what I thought was part of a plan. I thought Šerifović must have done something to piss Drago off."

"That's not the way my father sees it, Gjoka," Obrenović said. "For some time, Drago has suspected the Wolf of having designs upon his position as *šefa* of the *Zmajevi*. His betrayal of Šerifović, which you made happen, was the final straw. And, despite numerous chances to prove his loyalty to Drago, the Wolf has done little to remove the threat of these fucking judges from The Hague."

"OK. OK," said Gjoka, buying time. "Let me make my case to Drago. I'll come with you, back to Serbia. I'll prove to Drago that I'm not to blame. I'll do whatever he wants me to do."

"Wrong again, little man," Obrenović replied. "There's nothing you can say that will sway me. My father's orders were clear."

Morgan looked on in silence as the impact of it all seeped into his skin.

General Davenport's instincts all those years ago had been spot on. Nothing much got past the old man. The Wolf did exist. He was an enforcer for the Serbian leadership, had been since the Balkans War, and his name was Vukasin Petrović; the brother of the former Interpol informant, Dobrashin Petrović.

Vukasin, as the Key had said, meant wolf. Not such a coincidence after all.

On top of that, this confirmed there was a management reshuffle underway. The Wolf, a once-trusted apprentice, had grown tired of his position as enforcer. He was older now, ambitious, and being held back by his mentor, Drago, was not what he had in mind for his future. Possibly, his efforts over the years to support the old guard were not being recognized and now, this young Obrenović was emerging as the one most likely to succeed his father. That would be counter to the Wolf's aspirations. Whatever it was, enough was enough and the Wolf was making his move.

It was a situation as old as time – greed, ambition, the thirst for power – and as far as Gjoka's part was concerned, Morgan felt there was some long overdue karma tied up in it all. That said, Morgan couldn't stand by and watch the young Obrenović and his crew of muscle-heads kill Gjoka in cold blood. How would he explain that to Davenport?

Morgan decided to move in. He had to do something.

But as he started toward the first step, a pair of hands like clamps gripped his ankles and yanked his legs out from under him.

Chapter Sixty-Three

Morgan hit the stairs face first. The SIG fell from his hand.

The baldy at the end of his ankles had come in the front entrance. Morgan was so intent on the interrogation of Gjoka that he'd missed it. Baldy had obviously gone out through an exit on the other side of the mezzanine to do a perimeter sweep and then backtracked from the driveway. Fuck!

Morgan's crash against the stairs caused everything around him to stop. The interrogation process froze, replaced by a stunned silence.

"What the fuck?" cried Obrenović.

But Morgan had fallen from view and Obrenović and his crew's shocked, undisciplined inaction bought him precious fractions of a second.

Morgan's subconscious instantly triggered what his friend and hand-to-hand combat proponent Tom Rodgers once termed total violence. In the movies they called it kill or be killed; the place where primal instinct and lethal force meet, when your survivability has reached absolute zero. At this point, anything less would result in his death.

Morgan's face became a mask of unrestrained rage.

Baldy was still clasped to the Intrepid agent's right ankle but he'd removed one hand to reach for Morgan's dropped gun. It was a fatal mistake. Morgan flipped onto his back and relinquished control. In that split second, his left leg withdrew like a piston and fired into action, kicking relentlessly at the gangster's face. The heel of Morgan's boot connected again and again with flesh and bone. The man cried out, struggling to hang on.

"Fuck!" boomed Obrenović. "Check it out!" he ordered.

With the gangster still attached, Morgan pulled his right leg back and at the same time spun around to face the threats from the mezzanine. The movement wrenched the gangster forward, positioning his forearm perfectly, elbow and wrist braced on the edges of alternate stairs. Morgan needed only to twist slightly to be standing directly above the exposed forearm, then he slammed his left foot straight down with everything he had. The man howled in agony as both bones snapped like dry driftwood. The other hand let go.

Amid the agonized screams, Alex Morgan looked up and saw two men appear above him on the mezzanine tearing guns from shoulder holsters, confusion written all over their faces.

Morgan dived down the stairs over the screaming gangster with the broken arm back to where he'd been hiding in the darkness watching the interrogation. He spotted his gun, the SIG Sauer P226, and threw himself at it. Landing in a slide, he grabbed the SIG as a barrage of 9mm rounds from the Serbs followed him, hammering the stairway. Most of them struck the howling baldy; caught in the crossfire, he was helpless to stop them. He fell silent.

Under their onslaught Morgan couldn't get a shot at anyone but he had a clear line of sight at a ceiling light up on the mezzanine level that cast a beam like a search light down the stairwell. He fired and got it and everything went black. He kept firing as close as he could to where he knew the other two had been standing. In the midst of the gunfire and darkness he heard nothing but chaos and lots of yelling, underscored by the noise of retreating footfalls on stairs across the room.

Morgan moved fast, driven by survival, knowing they'd be splitting up to circle around, close him in on the stairs and kill him. He launched up to the mezzanine level like a freight train, firing on the move, but the two gunmen had gone. Without missing a beat, he drove himself across the dark room straight for a large oak table. He had it on its side just in time to receive a hail of incoming fire. The rounds boomed as they struck and splintered the heavy table top. He couldn't afford to get bogged down. He had to get clear of this room.

He could hear Gjoka screaming somewhere.

Morgan changed mags then blindly fired off a mad burst to get their heads down. In a bound, he made it to the darkest corner at the back of the room. It was away from the table and there was no cover, but he was flat on the floor, and as the gangsters all fired at once, he caught their muzzle flashes in the darkness.

Right, Morgan thought, *there's just two of them: one down in the back stairwell leading to the rear exit, and the other behind a sofa at the top of the same stairs*. They were lined up like shooters at a carnival shooting gallery and Morgan's head was the bullseye. But the stupid bastards had missed his move and were still wasting their ammo on the table.

Morgan set his sights on the sofa first. It was low and thin, offering zero protection. Cover from view but not from fire. He unleashed a rapid stream of rounds at the spot where he'd just seen the guy's head duck down. The rounds punched straight through the fabric and wood with the devastating impact of a prize-fighter knocking the shit out a second-rate opponent. Every one of them landed where he needed them to and above the explosions from the SIG, Morgan heard a string of strained expletives as each round found the target. But the swearing lasted only seconds. The last rounds in the stream finished the job. The dull thud on the floor told Morgan a gun had been dropped.

The guy on the stairs opened up again, firing anywhere and everywhere, but Morgan was already moving. *Fucking amateur*, Morgan thought; he should have been firing to cover his offsider but he was too busy keeping his own head down. Morgan dived back behind the table while rounds from the stairs zinged past, up into the ceiling and into the walls and furniture. Pots and windows and picture frames shattered all around him.

Morgan kept going across the open space of the shooting gallery, heading straight for the sofa he'd just shot the hell out of. He had no idea where the other guy's rounds were going but miraculously, so far none had hit him. Every shot from the other man's gun thundered through the room searching for him. Christ! Heavy caliber revolver, Morgan realized. His intuition, honed by years of training and experience, told him then that the guy was due for a reload any second now. The sofa was near the top of the back stairs and Morgan made it in two more paces. He threw himself down and launched into a slide across the polished floorboards, firing wildly down the stairs as pure momentum carried him forward. The bark of the SIG was constant as Morgan kept pulling the trigger until the second man was finally down.

The revolver fell silent.

Back on his feet, Morgan checked both men were dead. Habitually, he kicked their weapons far from reach. Then he caught sight of Gjoka, sheltering beside a large bookcase, trembling uncontrollably, hands over his ears. He'd pissed himself.

Morgan didn't have time for Gjoka right now. He had three dead up here. That left Obrenović and one other still at large, somewhere nearby; both armed and most definitely dangerous.

"Stay here, Gjoka, and you might just stand a chance of surviving," Morgan said. "I'll be back for you."

With that, he headed for the back stairs.

Chapter Sixty-Four

Outside, the night was black with the breeze rustling eerily through the trees, and the stars and moon nowhere to be seen.

Morgan got himself away from the doorway quickly, crouched down in shrubs at the back of the house and listened intently, allowing time for his night vision to adjust. He waited a full minute, his senses in overdrive, before moving cautiously around the edge of the graveled area that bordered the entire house. Staying close to where the vegetation started and the gravel stopped, he minimized the sounds of his footsteps upon a strip of soft sand. Every few feet he'd stop and listen again. Still nothing.

Then, diagonally opposite the corner of the building where the cars were parked, he stopped dead in his tracks.

It was barely perceptible, but he could just make out the sound of shoes crunching on gravel less than 10 feet from him.

Morgan got the oxygen going again, filling his lungs to pump blood to his already dog-tired limbs. He slipped easily out of his RM Williams boots with the elasticized sides, moving in silence across the last few feet of gravel separating him from the house. Standing in his socks with his left shoulder hard up against the rough-hewn stone of the century-old wall, Morgan brought the SIG back up to his chest, clasped in both hands, barrel pointing forward and close against his body. He craned his neck forward until his face was as close to the corner of the building as he dared. His breathing was deep, calm.

Around the corner the two remaining Serbs – Obrenović and the last of the baldies – were in a tight huddle by the side door they'd all gone through earlier. The two of them were mumbling in Serbian, he guessed, but Morgan could tell it was basically an "on three, we're going in" discussion. He braced himself, waiting.

"*Jedan*," came the first muffled count. They were ready to rush inside, find the unexpected intruder and kill him.

"*Dva*," came the second. Both men's shoes shuffled on the gravel in dark anticipation.

"*Tri!*"

Before they disappeared inside, Morgan leapt from his corner and faced directly across their flanks. In a fluid movement, he closed one eye to protect his night vision, fired twice, then threw himself back behind the cover of the wall.

In the short, explosive lives of the SIG's muzzle flashes, Morgan knew that both rounds found their target. One went through a shoulder and the second, miraculously, through the side of his head. It was the last of the baldies.

From the doorway, Obrenović unleashed a shocked burst of obscenities in Serbian, screaming in frustration, no doubt, as what was supposed to have been a simple take down of the little worm Gjoka quickly turned to complete shit. All his men were dead, he alone had survived and only because he was already through the door and halfway inside when Morgan opened up. Now desperate, Obrenović fired chaotically in every direction from the doorway.

Then he broke from cover and ran for his life, heading for the van.

Morgan risked his neck beyond the corner of the wall again and fired in the general direction of the fleeing footsteps, but it was impossible to see Obrenović as he ran away. Morgan heard the driver's door of the van open and the engine cough to life. The headlights blazed, filling the blackness with football stadium lighting. The suddenness of it was blinding. Morgan clenched his eyes shut tightly and rubbed them with the back of his gun hand.

Behind the wheel, Obrenović revved the engine and wrenched the gearshift into reverse. The vehicle screamed backward out of the driveway.

Already, Morgan was sprinting.

Chapter Sixty-Five

In the moments it took Obrenović to get the van back out onto the road, Alex Morgan was propelling himself forward, desperate to get there before the Serb escaped. As the van skidded to a dusty halt, pointing back down the hillside road toward Petrelë, he leapt at it.

Obrenović struggled at the wheel, full of shock and tension. He fumbled with the gearshift, unable to make the change from reverse into first. The more he forced it, the harder it became, not realizing that due to his nervous energy, he still had one foot planted flat on the accelerator. The engine revs were in the high reds as the gears crunched and whined helplessly.

Meanwhile, his SIG back in the holster, Morgan launched at the van long-jump style from the sprint, catapulting forward from his right leg. Still in his socks, Morgan's feet protested with every painful, jarring impact upon the sharp stones of the graveled driveway, but he pressed on. There was no way he could stop now.

Morgan's left foot found the top of a low-lying stone

wall that bracketed the driveway, giving him the extra height and leverage he needed to make the remaining few feet to the top of the van. He hit the roof with a thunderous bang and the metal buckled beneath the impact of his 200 pounds. The Intrepid agent's fingers madly searched for a purchase point.

Down in the engine block, the gears found their groove and the van lunged forward with all the grace of a runaway train hurtling through a station. The gangster heir apparent stamped his foot flat to the floor again and the van sped off down the hill. The sudden momentum nearly saw Morgan slide uselessly off the back but he managed to find the lip of the roof's edge on both sides and grab on tight, his fingertips pressed white against the metal.

Obrenović surely knew Morgan was up there, but in his rush to escape he'd thrown his gun down on the passenger seat beside him. Panicked but not beaten, Obrenović wrenched the steering wheel left and right, over and over again, slewing the van recklessly across the narrow dirt road. With every deliberate pull to the right, the rear wheels skidded across the loose surface of the road, causing the back of the van to fishtail perilously close to the edge of the road that fell away to nothing.

With deafeningly cold wind racing across his body and his fingers slipping along the metal work, Morgan saw the lights of Tirana and the surrounding villages far off in the distance. The thought of what normal people might be doing right now flashed through his mind.

Obrenović's driving became even more drastic. He knew this was his only chance to dislodge the madman on the roof. He tore the wheel so hard that he was in danger of toppling the van and himself over the edge.

Morgan struggled to stay on as each swerve threw his

legs over the sides of the roof, relentlessly alternating port and starboard like a crazy pendulum. Soon, it was one too many times.

Obrenović tore the wheel to the right once more, the back of the van went hard left and Morgan was thrown into the black emptiness of that steep, bottomless hillside.

Chapter Sixty-Six

Blubbering incoherently, Lorenc Gjoka broke from his petrified stupor on the floor and crawled slowly across the room, past the dead body by the sofa, toward the packed suitcases in the far corner. Tears, snot and blood streamed down his face, accompanied by the pungent stench of urine from his soiled trousers. The debris of the gunfight littered the entire area and he cut his hands and knees on bits of broken pots and light bulbs before he risked standing up to sneak the rest of the way on his feet.

Reaching the cases, not daring to switch on a light, Gjoka fumbled around in the darkness until he found and opened his. A few minutes later he'd wiped himself down with his dirty shirt, extracted a fresh shirt, trousers and underwear, and was dressed, once again ready to go. Lumbering awkwardly with his luggage down the stairs, struggling to avoid the body of Morgan's first opponent, Gjoka came across a discarded automatic on the floor near the corpse. He picked it up with a still-shaking hand, heading warily toward the driveway.

When he reached the doorway and looked outside, everything was in darkness. The exterior light had been switched off and the big black van was gone. There was no sign of life. Gjoka took a first tentative step forward out into the unknown when the toe of his shoe caught on something and he fell. Both arms instinctively shot forward to break his fall, the suitcase and gun tumbling from his grip. As he fell, his knees landed on something soft and he realized that it was another body.

On the edge of a complete meltdown, Gjoka scuttled away from the body of the last baldy. He located his suitcase, dragged it over to his Mercedes and shoved it in the back seat. As the interior light came on he saw that the keys were still in the ignition. *Thank God.*

He turned around and tried in vain to find the gun but soon gave up. In a second he was seated behind the wheel and the engine was running. It was then that Gjoka broke down. His face fell into his hands and his shoulders shook as he sobbed.

Minutes later Gjoka was beginning to recover his composure when a set of headlights appeared behind him, filling the interior of the Mercedes in brilliant white light. 'No! No!' he cried, but then, just as he thought all hope was lost, the lights from the car behind him showed him exactly where his gun had fallen. It was less than 5 feet from his door, his only chance. Gjoka thrust the door open and lunged for it.

On all fours, he was scrambling across the gravel when the cold pressure of a gun barrel was rammed into the cleft beneath his ear. Gjoka knew exactly what it was. His hand froze in its last-ditch effort to reach the automatic and he came back onto his haunches, hands in the air in supplication.

"On your feet, Gjoka," said a rough, tired voice. The gun didn't budge from beneath Gjoka's ear as he slowly stood. "Turn and face your car."

Gjoka found himself completely under the man's control. His arms were pulled behind his back, plasti-cuffs fitted tightly around his wrists and he was dragged by the scruff of the neck to the back of the house.

"What are you going to do? Are you going to kill me? Please—"

"Shut up, you sniveling little turd," the voice barked harshly. "I need to find my boots."

Gjoka fell silent and did exactly as he was told.

PART IV
A Wolf in Sheep's Clothing

Chapter Sixty-Seven

INTREPID HQ, BROADWAY, LONDON

"I've just heard from him, sir," Mila Haddad replied, walking into Davenport's office. She sat down in front of his desk. He looked tired already – it was only midday.

"And?"

"Early this morning he handed Mr Gjoka over to the internal investigations team at Interpol Headquarters in Tirana; even waited with Gjoka personally until the team arrived from Lyon. And—" she consulted the general's wall clock, "—they're an hour ahead of us in Tirana, so it's about 1pm over there. I expect he's about to meet with senior members of the Albanian State Police regarding the wash-up over last night's incident at Petrelë. Then he's booked on a flight to Seattle late this afternoon. He's going to follow up with Ms Fleming regarding her report that a possible association exists between her male companion, Mr Demaçi, and the Serbian gunman, the third man, who was arrested in Tirana alongside Ivan Simović and Dobrashin Petrović."

"I see," said Davenport. "Why didn't we know about this connection earlier?"

"Well, I believe the concussion she suffered when she was being forced upon that seaplane, along with the very real possibility of post-traumatic stress, resulted in short-term memory loss; very common, under the circumstances. She's had no option but to piece it all together as it returns to her."

"Very well," Davenport replied gruffly but his eyes betrayed the deep-seated concern and affection he held for his goddaughter.

"Ms Fleming reported seeing the Serbian gunman posing as a bodyguard aboard the *Florence*, and then again later when she was being relocated via seaplane to Albania. Unfortunately, there's still no word on the whereabouts of Mr Demaçi."

"Very well. Hopefully, Interpol internal investigations will manage to extract some useful information from Mr Gjoka; something we can actually make use of," Davenport replied. "Anything more from Morgan?"

"He did say that he could do with some leave; asked me to put in a good word." She smiled.

"He can take bloody leave when he's finished doing what I sent him off to do," Davenport replied gruffly. "I've read the operations update on Morgan's activities in Petrelë last night, sounds like he's damn lucky to be alive. Make sure he gets appropriate cooperation from the local authorities; and when I say appropriate, I mean maximum. Let me know immediately if there are any problems."

"Of course, sir," Mila replied. She got the impression that the piece of Iraqi shrapnel embedded in the general's right knee during Desert Storm was giving him more than a little grief this morning. He was unusually tetchy.

"Now, XO, I need you to ensure that I am absolutely up to date on everything we currently have relating to the hunt for Drago Obrenović. Let's start with the murder of Judge de Villepin. My recollection of Commander Sutherland's last report from France was that the French authorities had no luck in identifying any suspects. By the way, where is Commander Sutherland?" he asked. "I don't recall hearing from him lately."

"He's currently in the United States. You sent him off to do field trials of some new equipment the US Special Forces are using."

"Of course, must have slipped my mind," Davenport said. "Lucky I have you to keep me on track."

"You'll recall we had him wrap up in France, sir," she answered. "He'd exhausted every avenue with the French police and Interpol Paris has now taken point on that. Although Commander Sutherland did manage to cut through some bureaucratic red tape and, let's just say, *secured* some digital surveillance footage that may come in handy."

Davenport's eyebrows raised. "If not secured, what else would we call it?"

"I believe the word he used was pilfered, sir," she said, holding back a smirk.

"God forbid," said the general.

Mrs Jolley entered with a tray. Davenport took the opportunity to stand and stretch his leg. He struggled as he left his chair and Mila had to stop herself from leaping to his aid. Of course, Margaret Jolley, who had been the general's personal assistant for many years, knew better than to even consider offering help. Instead, she proceeded to set the tray down between them on the general's desk, pouring green tea for Mila and coffee for Davenport. Noting Mila's thanks, she quietly withdrew and closed the door behind her.

Davenport was pacing the room slowly, deep in thought. With great courtesy, Mila continued to peruse her notes and drink tea, outwardly unperturbed by the general's brief absence from the desk, inwardly wishing there was something she could do for her boss. After a few moments he returned, resumed his seat awkwardly and took up his coffee; black, two sugars.

"Please keep a steady watching brief on the de Villepin investigation, XO. That one will eventually come back to us, I'm sure of it."

"Of course, sir," Mila replied.

"Now, do you have anything further regarding the Wolf?"

"There's a fair bit going on, sir. Where would you like to start?"

"Let me see where I'm up to and perhaps you can take over from there," he began. "If I recall correctly, during their interrogation of Dobrashin Petrović, Major Morgan and Hauptmann Braunschweiger discovered that Mr Petrović has a brother or, more accurately, a cousin, by the name of Vukasin, Vukasin Petrović; which you have subsequently confirmed through the Serbian births and deaths registry. And as we've previously discussed, and Mr Braunschweiger has more recently identified, both the Serbian word Vuk and the name Vukasin translate to wolf. How am I going so far?"

"Perfectly," Mila answered.

"As yet we do not know the whereabouts of, nor do we have any way of definitively identifying, Vukasin Petrović. However, he has, in absentia, been escalated to the top of our list of candidates for the Wolf?"

"That's correct," Mila replied. "Based on Major Morgan's assessment of the conversation he observed between Mr Gjoka and Drago's son at Petrelë last night, it is the Wolf who has been pulling the strings from the outset. During the conversation, Gjoka referred to the Wolf's brother, Dobrashin, being in custody along with Ivan Simović. This alone confirms Vukasin Petrović as the Wolf. Later in the conversation, Gjoka blamed the Wolf and his brother, Dobrashin Petrović, for the plan that resulted in the Šerifović arrest in Corfu. Gjoka claimed that he was innocent of any betrayal or wrongdoing against Šerifović. He said that the Wolf had convinced him it was what Drago wanted. I suspect that the Wolf had also convinced his younger brother to do it in order to collect the reward, which they would split later. But it was much bigger than that."

There was a long silence as Davenport considered it all.

"So, the Wolf does exist," he said finally. "It seems we were working our way inevitably toward him from the very beginning. Even as far back as my service in Bosnia all those years ago, which you uncovered, XO; how extraordinary. What was it that Morgan referred to it as in his report?"

"A management restructure, Balkans style." She smiled. "The Wolf's objective is to seize total control of the Serbian mafia by systematically clearing the decks of the old guard. Ascending to the position of chief of the *Zmajevi*, via a bloodless coup, avoids a direct challenge against Drago."

"No better way to ensure solidarity across their various factions than by unifying them in the hatred of a shared enemy."

"The ICTY."

"Precisely," Davenport said, with a tinge of respect for the strategy behind it all. "It's both incredibly infuriating and brilliant at the same time. Do we have any way of linking the Wolf to the arrests of Karadžić, Mladić or Hadžić? That would be worth pursuing."

"Not yet, but we'll keep looking into that," she said.

"So, where is Mr Braunschweiger at the moment – staying on the Petrović brothers?"

"Yes, sir. He's still in Berlin debriefing with the German authorities over the interrogation of Dobrashin Petrović, and arranging for him to be moved to The Hague. He'll continue to investigate Vukasin Petrović; specifically anything that can categorically prove him, from an evidentiary perspective, to be the Wolf."

"Unfortunately," Davenport said, "without a known location for Vukasin Petrović, or even a current physical identification of him, it seems all we've done is add another name to our list of fugitives."

"Not necessarily, sir," Mila offered cautiously.

"You have something?" he asked eagerly.

"It's more of an idea at present," she began. "I've been intrigued by the connection of the Serbian name Vukasin meaning wolf and the criminal persona he may have adopted and, it seems, at the very least actively cultivated in his guise as the Wolf."

"Yes," he replied. "But, it's not such a stretch for him to have become notorious under his own name."

"Not necessarily, sir," she said, not to be put off. "While Vukasin is actually quite a common name in the Balkans, not everyone called Vukasin goes around beating their chests, passing themselves off as the great and noble wolf. No, I think we need to explore the possibility that there's more to the psychology of the man."

"OK, XO, you have my attention." Davenport poured more coffee for himself and tea for Mila as she continued.

"Knowing what we know about the Wolf, he presents all the classic tendencies of the narcissist: self-obsessed, ambitious, delusional, manipulative; with no compunction about using others to get what he wants. Of course, we also know that narcissists are incredibly fragile and sensitive creatures, prone to erratic swings in behavior: jealousy, insecurity, rejection and so on. And while there's no proven cause of narcissistic behavior, historical or environmental factors can play a part."

Mila stopped for a moment, drank some tea and collected her thoughts. The general remained absolutely silent.

"I mean, imagine this scenario, sir: a very young boy suddenly loses both parents in a tragic accident. He is then adopted by relatives who can't have children, who take him under their wing purely out of a sense of familial obligation. When the boy eventually becomes established and secure within his new family, he's derailed again when the adoptive parents unexpectedly have a child of their own. It's not a great stretch to surmise that a deep-seated fear of rejection may have sent the over-compensatory characteristics of the narcissist — self-obsession, competitiveness, a predisposition to creating fantasies and so on — into overdrive."

"I see," Davenport replied. "But is that enough to have triggered the levels of unrestrained violence that we are associating with this creature? These homicidal tendencies, multiple executions and so on. How on earth has he managed to last this long and avoid detection?"

"I would say the Balkans War was the ultimate catalyst. It gave Vukasin Petrović the perfect environment to vent his anger and frustration while being supported, even encouraged, by the military leadership. With the appropriate guidance, a mentor, he would have been ideal 'enforcer' material."

"Drago," said Davenport.

"It seems that way, sir. But this is just my unqualified observation. In all honesty, confirming any of it would require formal assessment of the subject by an experienced professional. And, of course, for that to happen, we have to catch him first."

"I wouldn't discount your theory so readily, XO," said Davenport. "I concur with what you're saying and I suspect you have some idea about how we might go about catching Mr Petrović. So, let's have it."

"It's just a hunch, sir," said Mila, somewhat tentatively, although she was confident she was on the right track. "On the basis of my assessment of Petrović's narcissistic qualities, and returning to my thoughts about his attachment to the persona created by his name, I believe he has established and used the title Wolf to great effect, a personal brand, if you like. His ego and hunger for power and control would revel in the way the name Wolf would conjure both fear and legend throughout the criminal underworld. In his mind he would be so intrinsically connected with the enigma as to believe it to be true. He is not just wolf by name; he is the Wolf. To that end, I suspect that his ego does not allow him to shed the Wolf title or persona at any time, even when he assumes alternate identities in order to avoid the authorities. I mean, he's obviously a master of deception and every moment that he remains at large, despite the horrendous crimes he has committed right under the noses of the international community, only serves to reinforce his sense of supremacy over others. Ultimately outwitting even the ICTY and Interpol."

"So, what are you suggesting, XO? What exactly do you

mean by him not letting go of the Wolf persona? I don't quite follow."

"I think it's possibly as straightforward as the names he uses when adopting false identities. Petrović needs to remain, in some fundamental way, connected to his ultimate persona, the Wolf. If we include other names that also mean wolf, we will refine our search parameters and, therein, extend our chances of actually finding him. I'm confident that we'll find him hiding right out in the open, under our very noses, behind a very simple wolf-related alias. I'm going to start by compiling a list of names that mean wolf then take a look at the list of all the names currently associated with our investigations into Obrenović and the *Zmajevi*, to see if any red flags pop up. I've already arranged it with Scotland Yard; I need access to their experts and their database."

"Well, XO, I never would have thought to approach it that way, but it definitely warrants every effort," he said. Davenport would never discourage any avenue of investigation that was based on a reasonable and structured argument. "Let me know when you're leaving, I'll wander around with you and catch up with Commissioner Hutton. It'll do my leg some good to get moving."

Mila Haddad could not have been more pleased with the general's reaction to her theory. She knew that, at his core, he was a man of action who looked for tangible results from his people in all their endeavors. But importantly, she also knew he wasn't closed to any idea that had merit. In fact, she knew that he encouraged everybody in the organisation to think outside the box.

Pleased to be, in a small way, the catalyst of the reinvigorated search for the Wolf, Mila was determined to ensure they left no stone unturned in tracking him down. And, as far as her responsibilities were concerned, she was sure she'd find something that would bring them closer to him. Even if the general did initially think the name angle was a stretch.

As he always said: Sometimes the simplest things were the key to opening the most complex issues.

Chapter Sixty-Eight

OFFICE OF THE DISTRICT DIRECTOR HEADQUARTERS
SÉCURITÉ PUBLIQUE, MAHDIA, TUNISIA

"Do you realize what you've done?" Hamba barked across the room.

"I thought I was following your orders, sir," answered Youssef honestly. He was shaking with fear.

"My orders, Officer Ali Hassan, were for you to ensure that the transcript of my interview with the foreigner Raoul Demaçi was on my desk first thing this morning. Nothing more."

"But it was, sir," he replied meekly. "I brought it personally at 8am. You weren't here. I sat outside all this time to ensure you received it the moment you returned."

"Don't you dare take that impertinent tone with me, boy!" Hamba bellowed. "I was investigating the brutal murder of one of my officers; killed last night in the hospital room of the man who is the subject of this very transcript."

Hamba had Youssef's transcript in his hand and threw it down upon his desk in exasperation. His shoulders slumped. Turning his back to Youssef, he looked out of the window, lighting a cigarette.

"Now, it appears that Mr Demaçi has fled the country." Hamba spoke to the window. "With an accomplice."

Youssef remained absolutely silent.

"Who or what on earth coerced you into dispatching a copy of this report direct to headquarters in Tunis?" Hamba asked tiredly, still facing away from Youssef. "Answer me that, Officer Ali Hassan."

When Hamba turned around, Youssef's face was perplexed. His eyes, mouth, nose and cheeks twitched and squirmed as he tried to comprehend the extent of the grave error of judgment he was being accused of.

"But, I ... I..." he stammered, "I was following protocol."

"What?" demanded Hamba. "What protocol?"

"In accordance with station operating procedures and Sécurité Publique standing orders, any report submitted directly to a district director must be copied to the chief of staff, care of Headquarters Sécurité Publique in Tunis, sir," Youssef answered, searching for reassurance that he had actually done the right thing. "I thought this is what you would have expected."

Protocol.

Hamba took a long draw on the cigarette that was already nearing the end of its short, contemptible life and blew the smoke across the desk at the young, inexperienced officer. He thought about the night he'd been having with the busty divorcée before the peal of his cell phone tore him from her clutches and saw him standing over the bloodied corpse of a dead cop in the room he'd been in just hours before.

He should have immediately looked into this apparent kidnapping of the pianist Fleming. Obviously, now he knew all about it, knew who she was and that her kidnapping had occurred but, on the orders of Interpol, it had been kept a closely guarded secret. Had Hamba taken the time to actually read the daily operational updates that were disseminated to district directors by headquarters in Tunis, he would have known. But now his desire to avoid ridicule and get to the bottom of the foreigner's story in his own time had cost him dearly. The humiliation was unbearable. His lack of judgment no doubt career ending. He had been summoned to Tunis to explain his actions while this snotty-nosed kid was supposed to be commended for his initiative.

Meanwhile, the lines of communication between his office in Mahdia, the Sécurité Publique headquarters in Tunis, and Interpol headquarters in Lyon were running hot.

For Hamba, hindsight was a cruel mistress.

Chapter Sixty-Nine

SUNSET HILL, SEATTLE, WASHINGTON, USA

"So, how long do you think you'll be gone?" asked Charly.

"Only one or two nights, honey. Three, tops," Madeline answered.

"Couldn't I come along?" She really wasn't comfortable about her mother's impending absence, but Charly knew she had to go: Great Aunt Dominique had taken a bad tumble. Now in her late eighties, she was very particular about whom she wanted around her at a time like this. So, childless – she'd never married after the love her of life was killed in action at Normandy – Dominique had called for her favorite niece, Madeline Clancy.

"I don't think that's a good idea, darling," replied Madeline, handing Charly a cup of tea from a freshly brewed pot. "You enjoy some peace and quiet. Besides, you've got your very own US marshals protection detail out there, watching over you 24/7. And you can keep up your sessions," she said. "I'm sure you'll be fine."

"But I thought they'd be going with you?" Sitting at the

kitchen table, looking across Puget Sound, Charly suddenly thought of Alex Morgan. She found herself wishing he was around.

"Some will go with me and some will stay here. Don't worry, it's all arranged." Madeline caressed her daughter's face the way she had throughout Charly's life whenever her girl needed comforting. Charly tilted her head against her mother's warm hand. "I'm only going to Ellensburg. Two hours' drive, literally down the road. So, not far at all. I'll go down, check on Aunt Dominique and, if need be, I'll get her back into the hospital for proper care. Then I'll be straight back here."

"So, what will I do around here for the weekend?" Charly asked, feigning adolescent obstinacy.

"Play the piano, read a book, get some rest," Madeline replied. "I'm sure you'll think of something. But absolutely no boys!"

They laughed.

There was a knock on the back door. A US marshal was standing there looking in apologetically.

Madeline opened it.

"Good morning, Stacey," Madeline said.

"Good morning, Judge," replied the marshal. "Sorry to interrupt. We're all set out here, ma'am. So, whenever you're ready to roll …"

"Thank you so much," Madeline replied. "I'll be out in a few minutes."

The door closed again, and mother and daughter hugged and said their goodbyes.

As Charly watched her mother disappear to collect her final bits and pieces and heard the front door click shut behind her, she couldn't help but feel anxious at the prospect of being left alone in the house, despite the protection detail.

The big house felt very empty.

Chapter Seventy

OFFICE OF THE COMMISSIONER OF THE METROPOLITAN POLICE, NEW SCOTLAND YARD, LONDON

"It's good of you to see me, Sinclair," said Davenport as he entered the office of his old friend. "Thought I'd drop in while my people are downstairs ransacking your database; I realize it's short notice."

"Not at all, Nobby. Glad we could be of assistance," replied Sinclair Hutton, commissioner of the Metropolitan Police. The two men had known each other for many years. They trusted each other implicitly. "I understand they're doing some profiling and looking for particular name references?"

Hutton headed straight for the emergency scotch, as he called it, which he kept discreetly tucked away. It usually came out when Davenport visited. It was well past 7pm anyway.

"Yes, that's right," said Davenport. "Ms Haddad, my executive officer, has a theory. Initially I thought it was a bit thin, but, in light of latest developments and her developing a profile of our principal person of interest, I want her to see it through. It's a strong line of inquiry and working with your people will not only shave hours off the process of trawling the databases, it will contribute significantly to the profiling work she's commenced."

"I take it this is about Tunisia?"

"You've seen the Interpol Blue Notice, then," Davenport replied.

"I have."

He handed Davenport a glass and the two of them slumped into lounge chairs away from Hutton's desk. Outside, the early evening had settled in across Westminster and the lights of the city were taking their place in the nightscape. The relative austerity of Hutton's office compared to the warmth of Davenport's was no reflection of the man. It was firstly an inheritance, but also a consequence, of the building's postwar, utilitarian design, which began in the late 1950s and continued into the Sixties, when the old-world traditional architecture of surrounding Westminster was surpassed by the urgent need for functional office space. The straight lines, stainless steel and one-way reflective glass made the New Scotland Yard complex a standout in the area. More obviously, however, it was the simple revolving sign out on Broadway bearing the location's name that had become the real landmark; a beacon of British law enforcement.

"So, how badly is this affecting your operation?" asked Hutton.

"Well, it's not insignificant," the general offered with his trademark understatement.

"And when did it all happen?" While Hutton was aware that Interpol had issued a Blue Notice, he wasn't yet across the details. It simply wasn't a matter for the Metropolitan

Police. "All I know, so far, is that a Blue Notice has been issued in relation to a Raoul Demaçi who, as I recall, was the man kidnapped alongside your goddaughter, Charly. Now I know from our last chat that your men recovered her from Albania, thank God, but this Demaçi chap was supposedly still missing. So, if he's been a victim in all this, then why now is there suddenly a Blue Notice out for him?"

Interpol notices were standard fare for Davenport and Hutton. Urgent alerts dispatched to law enforcement agencies around the world, they covered an extensive range of issues and were color coded to instantly alert international authorities to the significance of the subject matter – red, black, blue, yellow, green, orange and purple. The Blue Notice just issued regarding Raoul Demaçi meant he was a person of interest urgently wanted in relation to a criminal investigation.

"It all happened yesterday in Tunisia," Davenport began. "From what I can gather, Demaçi – who's been missing for weeks now, ever since Charly's kidnapping – appeared out of nowhere at a police station in a small town called El Djem. He told local police his name, that he was a kidnap victim and that he'd been released by his kidnappers just outside the town. He was taken straight to a hospital in Mahdia, the closest city, for treatment and observation, where he was eventually interviewed by police."

"How extraordinary," said Hutton.

"It gets better. According to the police report that accompanied the Blue Notice, a police officer who'd been guarding Demaçi was killed some time around 5pm yesterday, in the very hospital room where Demaçi was situated; exactly the same time as it is here in London, by the way. So, a little over twenty-four hours ago. Nobody saw anything and the hospital doesn't even have CCTV, so there's nothing we can check there either. The only thing we do know is that the policeman made an entry in his notebook indicating that Demaçi had told the officer he was expecting a visitor, named Dmitri who, surprise, surprise, was expected to arrive around 5pm."

"And then this Demaçi chap just vanished again? Without a trace?"

"Correct," said Davenport.

"Whatever became of the police report or the statement Demaçi made? Wasn't any of that fed to Interpol?"

"No," Davenport replied. "Apparently the senior officer who questioned him at the hospital – a Colonel Hamba – suspected that Demaçi's story didn't add up and decided to sit on it overnight with a plan to resume questioning the next morning; which would have been this morning. A simple tactic, I suppose. If he thought the man was a fake, then he'd want to give Demaçi the time to stew and think again about what he was saying, before their interview carried on. However, in the interim, the police officer was murdered and Demaçi vanished."

"Do you think Demaçi's implicated in the officer's death? I have to say, straight off the bat, it sounds like he may be."

"I'm afraid I have to agree with you, Sinclair, but we've had to look at it from both angles. I mean, for all we currently know, he could have been snatched back."

"It may not have been your Demaçi, at all. Have you considered that?"

"The thought had crossed my mind."

"And it's taken twenty-four bloody hours for this critical information to reach you," Hutton noted angrily. He had no involvement in Intrepid's current operations, but he knew and shared the frustration of his friend. It was part of the job.

"Astonishing, isn't it," Davenport said, somewhat despairingly. "I've been trying to speak to both Madeline and Charlotte for the best part of an hour but haven't had any success getting through. Although we've already advised the US marshals who are protecting them both around the clock. They'll advise Charlotte of Mr Demaçi's reappearance … and subsequent disappearance."

"You think he might make contact with Charly?"

"It's hard to say. At this stage, as you've already noted, we're not even sure whether or not he was involved in the murder of the policeman, or if he has once again been taken captive."

"How are Madeline and Charly?" Hutton asked. "I haven't seen them in years."

Hutton had met Madeline, her late husband, Peter, and their daughter, Charlotte, via Davenport many years ago, and their three families had often socialized together while the Flemings were based in England. But as the years passed, Peter had been killed, Nobby had divorced, Charly had gone on to become an international star, and the family get-togethers had sadly become few and far between.

"They're much better now," Davenport replied. "But they've been through a great deal in these past weeks."

"I can only imagine." Hutton took another drink; the scotch bit hard at the back of his throat. He changed tack. "Now, tell me about this theory of your XO's that necessitates you and your people storming into the Yard and ransacking my world-renowned database."

"Well, it's quite interesting," Davenport began. "My XO, Ms Haddad, actually began unraveling all of this when she identified – within the pages of my notes from the war, mind you – a Serbian enforcer known only as the Wolf. His name is Vukasin Petrović and, as the Wolf, he is now one of only two outstanding fugitives of the ICTY remaining in our sights. The other one, of course, being Drago Obrenović."

"Big fish, indeed," Hutton said.

"For years, dating back to the Balkans War, Petrović has been known in the underworld as the Wolf." Davenport finished his drink and shook the empty glass at Hutton who, as any genuine friend would, rectified the crisis immediately. "Now, based on her profiling of Vukasin Petrović, Ms Haddad's theory is that for a variety of reasons, the man would be inclined to stick with aliases that also mean wolf."

"It's quite a stretch, Nobby," Hutton scoffed.

"Less than an hour ago, I would have been in total agreement with you, Sinclair," Davenport replied. "However, her explanation of it in terms of his criminal psychological profile converted me and that is the element I expect she is discussing with your people right now. But it doesn't end there."

"I'm listening," said Hutton.

"Just minutes before we left the office to come here, the news of this Raoul Demaçi debacle finally reached us from Tunisia in the form of the Blue Notice. She immediately checked the meaning of the name Raoul; a curiosity, more than anything—"

"Don't tell me," said Hutton.

"Raoul happens to be an old French form of the German *Radulf*, meaning wise wolf."

"Bloody hell," he said. "So, what does she hope to achieve by trawling our databases?"

"She's narrowed down our search parameters to focus on airline passenger manifests of flights that left Tunisia over the past twenty-four hours, looking for male passengers with any names that could even remotely be associated in meaning with wolf."

"I can see where she's going but it's still a bloody long shot, Nobby."

"It's all we've got, Sinclair."

Chapter Seventy-One

DOWNTOWN SEATTLE, WASHINGTON, USA

At 4pm on Friday afternoon, the man who'd fled the hospital in Mahdia as Raoul Demaçi and boarded the Air France flight from Tunis to Seattle as Adolfo Mendosa, surrendered a Danish passport in the name of Ulric Sørensen to the reception desk. When he checked into the Paramount Hotel on Pine Street his appearance had markedly changed, although the transformation was much less complex than the end result suggested.

As Raoul Demaçi, everything about his demeanour and appearance reflected precisely the persona he intended to convey: a wealthy businessman from Montenegro who could afford the sort of lavish lifestyle others could only dream of. In the guise of Raoul, with his actual personal fortune underwritten by the considerable financial reserves of the *Zmajevi*, he gained entree into a select strata of international society that instantly propelled him into the social circles of the rich and famous. It was too easy then to appear as part of an exclusive entourage being introduced to the beautiful American pianist at a post-performance reception for her in Rome. How pathetic that she so easily fell for the treacle he would pour upon her, lavishing her with gifts and feeding her hungry ego. Never once did she stop to ask questions of him or delve into his past; blindly accepting, instead, the shallow character of Raoul that he chose to present.

Adopting the pretext of Adolfo Mendosa, a middle-aged Spaniard of modest but comfortable means, tired of the extensive travel required for his work but nonetheless engaging and humble, had been a breeze. It enabled him to both enter and exit Tunisia unnoticed by the authorities. The moment the American bitch's abduction had been successfully carried out, he left her to the babysitters and turned his attention to the task of preparing for her movement through Albania and then, as per the plan, on to Serbia, never to return.

During the weeks that followed his own faux abduction, he'd allowed his hair to become unruly and his beard to grow, while dramatically reducing his food consumption, relying largely on a protein-only diet to reduce his weight, resulting in a gaunt and weary facade. The ruse had worked doubly well when it had been necessary for him to once again adopt the persona of Raoul Demaçi – post kidnapping – in order to pass general inspection by the Tunisian cops.

Ten minutes alone in a gas station men's room halfway between the airport and downtown produced the transformation from Adolfo Mendosa to Ulric Sørensen. With his head shaved to the scalp, beard trimmed to fashionable stubble and an outfit change that included stylish contemporary wear for an outgoing man in his forties, he emerged confidently into Seattle's late afternoon and hailed a cab to the hotel.

Ulric Sørensen flirted outrageously but respectfully with the young woman on the counter and within minutes, his room had been upgraded from a standard to an executive king.

When his luggage finally arrived and the door closed behind the bellboy, he walked over to the large corner window that overlooked Seattle, along Pine Street and down toward Pike Place Market.

Standing there quietly taking in the significance of what he'd achieved already, Vukasin Petrović allowed himself a broad, self-satisfied smile.

The Wolf had returned to America to finish what he'd started.

Chapter Seventy-Two

INTERPOL HEADQUARTERS, LYON, FRANCE

Hermann "the Key" Braunschweiger found himself once again buried deep within Interpol Headquarters in Lyon, this time surrounded by floor-to-ceiling state-of-the-art technology. Somehow he'd managed to convince the techno-boffins of Intrepid's Intelligence, Investigations and Communications Section to allow him into their inner sanctum without proper adult supervision. From what he'd heard, it was absolutely unprecedented for field agents to be allowed back here without a grown up. Maybe it was because it was a Saturday morning. Who knew? Whatever the reason, true to their word, they'd found him a mini-operations room, given him the soldiers' five on how everything worked, showed him where the coffee was and left him to it. Most importantly, there was plenty more room in here than there had been in the surveillance van in Albania. That was enough to celebrate on its own.

Braunschweiger had quickly become the point man on everything to do with the Petrović brothers. Of course, now everyone's attention had shifted dramatically from

Dobrashin Petrović, who was in custody, to Vukasin Petrović, aka the Wolf, still at large.

Braunschweiger had been working through the night, trawling through hundreds of pages of Interpol reports from the past two decades relating to the Serbian mafia and organized crime figures, but still nothing surfaced on Vukasin Petrović or the Wolf. His task now was to search the endless gigabytes of images and CCTV files Intrepid had managed to piece together since the operation commenced.

Overnight, Mila Haddad had confirmed a number of possible hits on passengers traveling out of Tunis in the past forty-eight hours with names meaning, or associated with, wolf. Of particular interest was a passenger by the name of Adolfo Mendosa, a Spanish citizen traveling on an EU passport. According to Mila, the name Adolfo meant noble wolf, which, given that the final destination on his travel itinerary was Seattle, suddenly made Mendosa a person of interest. Mila was in the process of chain sawing through red tape to access CCTV footage from Tunis International Airport in the hope that airport surveillance would assist in identifying him. The moment she had it, she would patch it through to Braunschweiger.

The details of Adolfo Mendosa's itinerary put him on a flight out of Tunis late on Friday night, via Marseille and Paris. He was scheduled to arrive in Seattle early Saturday afternoon – yesterday. What added to the serious interest in him, apart from the fact that he happened to be traveling to Seattle, was that the age on his passport was reasonably consistent with the actual age of Vukasin Petrović, give or take a few years, and that the departure time from Tunis would have allowed sufficient time for him to leave the hospital in Mahdia, travel the distance to Tunis International Airport and still make the flight.

The efforts of the XO and the New Scotland Yard team in London to examine the passenger manifests of every flight leaving Tunis since Friday notwithstanding, identification of the name Adolfo Mendosa and the discovery that Adolfo meant noble wolf did not occur until well after the flight had landed in Seattle.

The Key looked at his watch: almost 10am; about 1am in Seattle.

So far, there'd been no reports of anything untoward occurring at the Seattle residence of Judge Clancy – whose daughter, Charlotte-Rose Fleming, was also staying there. And once the red flag regarding Mendosa had been raised, Intrepid had immediately contacted the US marshals who were protecting the judge and Ms Fleming, alerting them to the arrival of Adolfo Mendosa in Seattle and, importantly, the reasons for Intrepid's interest in him. In turn, the marshals advised Intrepid that Judge Clancy was visiting a sick relative in Ellensburg, two hours' drive away, while Ms Fleming had remained at the main residence in Sunset Hill. US marshals were on station at both locations.

Despite all the cross-pollination of information, including the fact that over eleven hours had transpired since Mendosa's flight had touched down at Sea-Tac International Airport, none of the local law enforcement agencies in Seattle had managed to locate him for questioning.

Braunschweiger left the control room to make more coffee. When he returned, he dropped heavily back into the seat in the center of the console surrounded by digital screens, rubbed his eyes, took a long drink of the strong brew and began.

He started by uploading images of all the key players associated with the hunt for Drago Obrenović and placed them on the screen directly in front of him. He grouped them in a kind of family tree structure, Drago at its pinnacle. Bit by bit he added additional images of each person under their respective names until he had run the image sources dry. The whole process took the best part of three hours. He sat back and studied them all.

There were dozens of Drago, although none of them recent. And there were numerous images of Ivan Simović, Dobrashin Petrović and Lorenc Gjoka, all of whom were in custody. There were even police mug shots of those now confirmed as *Zmajevi* foot soldiers, like Muscles and the other baldies, all of whom had criminal histories. Although the most recent of those, excluding Muscles, were post mortem.

The only blank spaces sat beneath the file names Vukasin Petrović aka the Wolf, Adolfo Mendosa and Raoul Demaçi.

Braunschweiger moved all the other image files across to the high screens on his left and kept Petrović, Mendosa and Demaçi open in front of him. Something occurred to him and he turned his attention to the emails he'd received from Mila Haddad. Increasingly he found himself drawn to this beguiling Ms Haddad he kept hearing about. He was fascinated by her wolf-name theory, which she'd convinced the general to see as more than just a theory, enabling her to put it into operation. He re-read some of her emails to him and smiled.

Concentrate, Braunschweiger. Concentrate.

Going through them again, he found the attached files he was after and brought them up on the center monitor. In front of him were two passport photos: one was Adolfo Mendosa and the other Raoul Demaçi. He peered intensely at the screen until his brow furrowed. Then he enlarged both images and brought them up on separate screens above the center monitor. Another thought occurred to him and he returned to his emails, scrolled to the group listed 'Morgan, A,' and found what he was looking for.

Alex Morgan had emailed him an image recently provided by Charlotte-Rose Fleming. According to Morgan's email, Charly said that Demaçi always avoided having his photograph taken, but she'd managed to find one taken at a party in Rome in which Demaçi was clearly captured in the background. She'd been happy to provide it to Morgan to assist in identifying him. Morgan's final comment on the email said: "Good-looking bloke. Bastard. Maybe it's better if he stays missing! Joking, mate. Joking."

Braunschweiger laughed to himself, enlarged the image and flicked it up onto the screen alongside Demaçi's passport photo. He picked up his coffee, rolled in his chair to the back of the small room, placed his feet up on the console and stared at the faces of Adolfo Mendosa and Raoul Demaçi looking lifelessly back at him.

Hermann Braunschweiger remained fixated on the images for five full minutes until he had finished his coffee. By then, the intensity of his examination began to play havoc with his eyesight and his objectivity. There were definite similarities, he thought, but there were also enough differences to make a definitive match impossible. Still, he kept them up high and turned to phase two of his search: CCTV footage.

"Let's see," said Braunschweiger, as he began tapping out commands on the keyboard, "if we can't smoke you out, Wolf man."

Chapter Seventy-Three

SUNSET HILL, SEATTLE, WASHINGTON, USA

The Wolf parked the hire car in 34th Avenue, got out noiselessly and went the rest of the way on foot. It was 1am. The place was pitch black and stone-cold quiet.

He couldn't afford to come this far and blunder in without knowing the lie of the land. He'd already paid for a local crew to spend a week driving by the house and reporting back, so he knew there were cops on point at the Clancy house. He just needed to see the layout of the place and the street approaches for himself.

He'd decided that, once he'd dealt with the cops as covertly as possible – and he wasn't quite sure how he'd do that yet – he'd reduce the chances of an incident and lots of screaming at the house by playing it natural, walking straight up to the front door and presenting himself as Raoul Demaçi, returned safely from captivity. She'd buy it; he knew that already. Once inside, he would get them both together, mother and daughter, kill them quickly and leave. It was important that both should die. Killing the judge was crucial to successfully achieving the original objective: to force the ICTY and Interpol to back off. Killing the daughter would make the Wolf a legend, not only of the underworld, and the only rightful successor to the role of *šefa* of the *Zmajevi*.

That left only Drago to contend with.

Drago. He spat on the ground as he moved along 34th Avenue, comfortable in the darkness. The time had come to kill the old fuck and be done with it once and for all, rather than fucking about with keeping the factions onside. That ship had sailed. Once Drago was dead he would deal with the fallout. The son had to die, too. That was a given. Deflecting the blame would be a challenge, but not impossible. Maybe he could make it look like a murder-suicide between the two. A power struggle between father and son. That would keep the factions at bay.

He turned left, down Northwest 67th Street. He knew where he was headed. He'd done his map reconnaissance. Part way down 67th was a cul-de-sac backing onto the street that the Clancy house was situated on.

At the right spot, the Wolf found the laneway he needed that branched off from the cul-de-sac. He knew that once he'd made it past that last house and got to the end of the laneway, he'd have a clear view to the Clancy house. Then he'd take his time, get as close as he could, scope it out for as long as possible and backtrack to the car.

With that, the Wolf checked his surrounds, listening intently for dogs or any human activity. There were neither.

He moved in for the final recon. With luck he'd be back in his hotel room by 4am and would manage a few hours' sleep.

Tomorrow was going to be a busy day.

Chapter Seventy-Four

INTERPOL HEADQUARTERS, LYON, FRANCE

By early evening, Braunschweiger had sifted through literally days of CCTV footage.

He'd forgotten how many times he'd reviewed the scenes captured from the apartment block in Albania, where the *Zmajevi* had taken and held Charly. He found himself constantly tracking between the vision of the guy who, at the time, they'd referred to only as the friend of Lazarević – really Dobrashin Petrović – and the stuff Dave Sutherland had obtained of the guy who had murdered Judge de Villepin. Despite the deliberately altered appearance, it was definitely the same man, thought the Key, although neither his brother, Dobrashin Petrović, nor the big Serb, Ivan Simović, had willingly identified him as Vukasin Petrović. That said, there'd been enough in their reactions to questions about the friend in Albania and de Villepin's killer in France, to create a sufficient level of certainty in the minds of the Intrepid agents that it was in fact, the same man: Vukasin Petrović, the Wolf.

France. France? Braunschweiger was in France, so what the hell was bugging him about it?

Time for more coffee and some food, he thought. He dialed up to the cafeteria and arranged for a meal to be brought down. Then he went out to the coffee room and fixed another strong pot. Walking back into the mini-operations room that had been his home away from home for the past twenty-four hours, Braunschweiger couldn't get his mind off coffee or food. Was there something there?

Sitting back down at the console, his eyes caught a name listed within his email inbox: Sutherland, D.

That was it. Dave Sutherland had managed to acquire from the local authorities in Bordeaux some additional CCTV footage that clearly showed Judge de Villepin out and about. The Key immediately began tapping on the keyboard and brought it up on the screen.

The digital location stamp on the top right corner of the screen, next to the date-time group, said Rue Sainte-Catherine #13, Bordeaux. The scene was a long shot taken along a section of Rue Sainte-Catherine from a camera that must have been situated on a pole 12 feet up, around the height of the awnings along the shop fronts. Perfect. It showed a strip of small restaurants, cafés and shops and, in the middle of the shot, having coffee and reading a newspaper at an outdoor café, was Judge de Villepin.

Braunschweiger spent the next forty-five minutes watching the footage in real time, enduring the infuriating stop-start of the time-lapsed digital images. Occasionally he would stop and scroll back to check something that had caught his attention before resuming again. But it was toward the end of the footage that he stopped suddenly, rewound and then paused. He leant forward to the screen to get a closer look before transferring the detailed snapshot up onto a much larger monitor to his right.

He'd paused the footage on a man, tall, dark, good looking and well dressed, who had been speaking into a cell phone and then turned away from a shop front. In the action of turning and walking away, his face had been captured perfectly for a split second by the CCTV camera. Gold!

With an expression somewhere between disbelief and elation, Braunschweiger's gaze switched back and forth between the CCTV image from Bordeaux on one screen and the passport photo and the picture Charly had provided of Raoul Demaçi on the other.

"*Scheisse*!" he said. "No fucking way."

There was no doubt in his mind – they were a definite match.

Chapter Seventy-Five

SUNSET HILL, SEATTLE, WASHINGTON, USA

Early on Saturday afternoon the weather in Seattle was sunny, albeit cool. A strong wind was blowing across Puget Sound and the yachts down at the Shilshole Bay Marina bobbed up and down on the swell, their hundreds of masts tipping erratically left and right like a bunch of unsynchronized, out-of-control metronomes.

The Wolf parked his car on 34th Avenue. He was now familiar with the street and the approaches to the Clancy house because he'd memorized the map and walked the ground during the night. As planned, he'd made it back to the hotel by 4am. He slept deeply and untroubled until mid-morning, ate breakfast in his room, checked emails, slept some more, then showered, dressed and headed out. He dressed casually but well, with expensive jeans, sweater and a tailored sports coat. His shoes were made for trekking, with reinforced toes and good traction. Not in the same league as his clothes but expensive for what they were. Necessary, too. You never knew when you'd need to stomp on a head, kick the shit out of someone or just shoot and run.

With hands thrust inside the pockets of his coat, walking in the general direction of the house with affected nonchalance, he felt through the coat's lining for the pistol grip of the Accu-Tek HC-380 semi-automatic shoved into the belt of his jeans. It had been left for him at hotel reception by a local Serbian underworld contact. He'd decided against the pancake holster that came with it because he didn't want to have to explain it in the first few seconds of reuniting with the woman. Without the holster, he could dump the gun anywhere and retrieve it when he was ready.

As he approached the house, he saw a cop sitting in a smart-looking black SUV in the driveway facing out into the street. That's number one, he noted. Number two would be stationed at the rear of the house.

He saw the SUV was parked under a balcony to the right of an enclosed porch and so wasn't visible from within the house. The cop was checking him out from behind the wheel.

The Wolf maintained his casual indifference and kept walking, all the while whistling as he walked.

Both the US marshals on station at the Clancy house that day could hear the strange whistling from the easy-going guy strolling down the street, but neither were familiar with the tune. If they had been, it might have saved their lives.

As the Wolf prepared to enter the rear of the Clancy property through a cluster of trees that had overgrown the back fence, he reluctantly brought to a close his personal rendition of the inspirational and movingly patriotic "Bože pravde". It was the Serbian national anthem, "God of Justice".

Chapter Seventy-Six

SEA-TAC AIRPORT, SEATTLE, WASHINGTON, USA

From the moment he set foot inside the US frontier at Sea-Tac Airport, Alex Morgan had a taste of the celebrity treatment.

Met in the customs arrivals hall by a US marshal, he was waved straight past the customs formalities. His luggage, along with his gun, was retrieved from stowage and delivered to him on a trolley by a US Customs officer. At the same time, an officious and very respectful young guy suddenly appeared, introduced himself as airport customer service, and took control of Morgan's trolley.

Morgan signed for his gun, leaving it within the sealed, reinforced travel case, and handed the paperwork back to the Customs officer, who countersigned it. After shaking hands cordially, the marshal led him through the labyrinth of the airport's back corridors and office spaces, only accessible to those officially authorized to be airside. Eventually they arrived at a nondescript exit door at the end of a long corridor and walked out into the cool of late afternoon. Morgan was comfortable enough in his suit, but he was glad that he'd thought ahead and carried the trench coat with him rather than pack it into his luggage. Speaking of luggage, the kid with the trolley seemed to be struggling; he was nowhere to be seen, though Morgan soon heard a squeaky wheel approaching from behind.

The marshal handed Morgan a set of car keys and walked him over to an immaculate white Dodge Charger SRT8 waiting for him directly opposite the door. The trolley guy finally caught up with them, his jaw visibly dropping at the sight of the Charger. "Sweet wheels," he said. But with a stern look from the marshal, he shut his trap and began packing Morgan's luggage in the trunk.

"Now, who do I have to thank for this little beauty and the red carpet?" Morgan asked the marshal. They'd barely spoken a word throughout the entire rigmarole.

"The car is courtesy of the United States Marshals Service, major," answered the marshal genially. There was military bearing in the guy, Morgan noted; looked like he'd done some time. "As for the red carpet, I think someone big in London called someone big in Washington and, well, it's all way above my pay grade, sir." He smiled. "I just do as I'm told."

"I get it," Morgan replied, slightly embarrassed. "I really appreciate your help, mate. Sorry if you got dragged away from duty just to come out and shepherd me around."

"Don't mention it," the marshal replied. "My partner and I are due out at the house in about an hour for shift change with the other team, Joe and Sam. I'll check in with you then."

"Sounds good."

Morgan shook the marshal's hand warmly and jumped behind the wheel, instantly withdrawing his SIG Sauer

P226 from the travel case and reinstating it to operational readiness.

The marshal's cell phone rang in his pocket; he took it out.

"It's my boss, I better get this. Ah, major. About the car," he added as the phone continued to ring. "I was told to tell you one very important thing."

"Go ahead," Morgan replied.

"If you break it, you bought it."

"No worries," Morgan replied with a laugh. "If I mess it up, tell 'em to send the bill to my boss."

A huge toothy smile appeared on the man's face. He banged the roof twice and said, "Keep your powder dry, man," and then answered his phone.

With that, Morgan shifted the Dodge into gear, the 470 horsepower V8 roaring a warning at the road and peeling away from the curb side. As the huge surge of unleashed power pushed him back into the sports seat, Morgan had to remind himself to drive on the wrong side of the road. He changed lanes immediately. He was looking forward to seeing Charly. Talking about the Serbs was officially why he was back in Seattle but it was more than that. He just wished he'd been able to get hold of her sooner to see how she was, but she'd been off the radar for a while. He was surprised to find himself suddenly thinking of Arena, again. *Jesus*, he thought. *Get over it. Not going to happen, mate.*

He set the GPS for Sunset Hill and his sat phone started to ring.

"Morgan," he answered.

"*Guten Tag, Herr* Major," came the deep, familiar grumble of Hermann Braunschweiger. There was concern underpinning the big guy's salutation. Morgan listened intently. "I take it you are now on the ground in Seattle. On the way to Sunset Hill, I hope."

"What is it, Key?" said Morgan. "Something's up."

"I'm afraid so," answered the Key. "Before I begin, I suggest you step on the gas—"

Wasting no time, Morgan jammed his foot hard to the floor, the Seattle traffic raced past and Braunschweiger took him straight to the headline: Raoul Demaçi was confirmed as Vukasin Petrović, aka the Wolf. The Key rapidly summarized for Morgan the complex stream of events, including Mahdia, Marseille and Paris, that had brought the Wolf – as Adolfo Mendosa and Ulric Sørensen – to Seattle, ultimately, back to Charly and Madeline.

Morgan's hands gripped so tightly around the wheel he was in danger of ripping it from the steering column. As the Key briefed him, Morgan scrounged with one hand through the center console and the glove compartment until he found what every well-equipped, official, US law enforcement vehicle was guaranteed to be fitted with. The siren was already howling as Morgan slapped the magnetic blue light onto the roof above his head. He'd always wanted to do that. With his foot planted upon the gas pedal, the Dodge surged onward.

"Does Charly know, Key?" he yelled above the noise of the siren and his own speed. "Has she been warned?"

"The US marshals on station at the house have been warned. We contacted them the moment we had the first hint of a problem, when Mila discovered Adolfo Mendosa was traveling to Seattle. Of course, he was just a suspect then, but we weren't taking any chances."

"I was just with one of the marshals at the airport," Morgan said. "He didn't mention anything."

"It's probably just filtering down."

"Has anyone spoken to Charly or the judge?"

"Charly wasn't taking any direct calls and, I believe, neither was Judge Clancy."

"Fuck me! Why not?" Morgan yelled. "Second thoughts, scratch that. No time. Just give me the latest from the house."

A large intersection was coming up ahead and all the normal people were slowing down to abide by the road rules. Fortunately, most at the back of the queue could hear Morgan's siren and were shuffling their vehicles aside to make as much room for him as possible. But Morgan didn't have time for staying in his lane. Besides, he was more comfortable on the opposite side of the road.

He wrenched the sports steering wheel hard to the left and fired the Charger directly across the intersection and into the oncoming traffic. The tires of cars and trucks crisscrossing the four-way screeched and burned as their drivers blared their horns in unanimous protest at the crazy bastard cop in the hot new Dodge. Morgan's only option was to power through, fishtailing through the jumble of vehicles and racket, a huge plume of rubber smoke trailing behind him.

"Latest update to the house was via a sitrep and comms check with the marshals about thirty minutes ago—"

"Thirty minutes! Fuck!"

"Wait," barked Braunschweiger. "I'm not the only one on this, you know. Right now, Mila Haddad is talking directly to the US marshals team leader on the ground in Seattle and the general is talking to Tappin to ensure you have US top cover no matter what you need. Right now Seattle PD SWAT are gearing up and sending a team to RV with you at the house in Sunset Hill. A second team is en route to Ellensburg by chopper—"

"Ellensburg! Why the hell does anyone need to go there?"

"Short version: the judge is visiting a sick relative. Leave that one to the marshals and SPD SWAT. We expect the Wolf wasn't aware that the judge had gone away for the weekend either. So, he'll be focused on Sunset Hill. How far away are you?"

"Two minutes."

Chapter Seventy-Seven

SUNSET HILL, SEATTLE, WASHINGTON, USA

The US marshal on station at the rear of the Clancy house heard the whistling stop. The guy must have kept walking down toward the water, he guessed. But he decided to check in with his partner anyway.

"Four-five, this is three-seven," he said into the radio mike clipped to his left sleeve cuff.

"Go ahead, three-seven," came the reply.

"Joe, did you see some guy walking past just now?" he said, wandering off the back porch to kick some small pebbles that had been bugging him off the grass and back into the garden. "I couldn't see him but I heard him whistling; sounded kinda Russian, or something."

"Yeah, bud, I saw him. Cool dude, dressed in Gucci gear. Looked like one of these rich locals. He kept going."

"Probably heading to his yacht."

"Roger that," replied the marshal in the SUV. "Like I said before, Sam, since this Wolf guy's turned up in Seattle, there's a whole lotta backup on the way over here right now.

I've just been inside and told Charly. So, all we gotta do is sit tight and hold the fort till they get here. You know."

"Roger. I'll keep my eyes peeled."

"Good man. Check in again in ten. Out."

As his left hand dropped back to his side, Sam gazed reflectively once again toward the boats down at the marina. Hell, most of them would be easily worth more than five years' salary. He'd never have a hope of owning one. Still, he was happy with his 15-foot aluminum runabout. It meant he could get his two sons out on the water for some fishing now and then. The boys loved the water as much as he did; and it gave his wife some much-deserved free time, too, once the testicle festival – as she called their posse – got out of the house for a few hours.

The movement that occurred behind him was so sudden that he wouldn't have stood a chance of fending it off, even if he'd had a split second more warning. A large hand appeared around the left side of his face and clamped hard over his mouth, jolting his head and shoulders back against another man. He smelled expensive aftershave at the same time as he felt the hard tubular end of a muzzle suppressor push into the small of his back. The first shot fired soundlessly into his flesh, lost amid the usual background sounds of any suburb on a Saturday afternoon. The second followed immediately, straight into the base of Sam's brain.

The Wolf dragged the body further underneath the overhang of the balcony, out of sight of the upstairs living area of the house, and into a small garden, rolling it over so it would bleed into the dirt.

He made sure there'd been no backsplash against his clothes from the wounds and retraced his steps, concealing himself all the way. He jumped back over the fence under the cover of the overhanging trees and headed for the marshal on duty in the SUV.

Joe, the marshal in the SUV, was just checking a text message on his cell phone. It was the latest update from his team leader downtown, letting him know that their USMS relief team, SPD SWAT and an Interpol liaison officer were inbound within five minutes. *Great*, he thought. Couldn't happen soon enough. It was then that a tap on the windscreen in front of him pulled his eyes from the phone. The sudden, unexpected sound startled him. It was the whistling Gucci dude.

"Can I help you, sir?" he asked cautiously through the open driver's window. But it was too late. The Accu-Tek HC-380 appeared, the trigger was squeezed and the .380 caliber round exploded through the suppressor, straight into the marshal's chest.

The Wolf pulled the body from the SUV and pushed it unceremoniously down a small set of bricked steps that led through a wooden gate to the backyard. He straightened his sweater and coat and walked calmly to the front door.

Chapter Seventy-Eight

Charly was sitting at the piano, tears streaming from her eyes.

She wriggled her shoulders within the loose-fitting rugby jersey that had been her dad's and put her iPhone down, glad to have finally spoken to her mother and relieved that she and Great Aunt Dominique were both OK. The marshals were with them at Ellensburg and a SWAT team was also on the way.

A SWAT team!

In addition to the team heading to Ellensburg to protect her mother, the marshals protecting Charly had told her just ten minutes before that another SWAT team was on its way right now to Sunset Hill. God, what was happening?

Charly couldn't believe she'd been so stupid as to have left her cell phone off. The fact that she'd also turned the home phone to silent so she could sleep was another disaster. But it was what she and her mother had agreed. Everything had seemed OK at the time Madeline left to visit Dominique. Charly needed peace and quiet; time to get her head right. That meant distancing herself from all she'd been through, including the fear and uncertainty she was now reminded of by the constant presence of the protection detail. When her father had been killed, Charly had locked herself away in a bubble of self-imposed, solitary lockdown. It was the only way she was able to survive the inordinate levels of grief she'd experienced when they'd lost him, and strangely this situation felt no different. It was the powerlessness she felt at being so out of control.

On top of it all, her attention had been distracted, if not consumed, by her feelings for Alex Morgan. That was until just a few moments ago when the marshals had broken the news to her about Raoul.

The shocking revelation that the supposed dashing European millionaire Raoul Demaçi was actually a Serbian assassin and fugitive war criminal made her physically sick. Her face was red and swollen from the anguish and humiliation she'd felt since hearing the news. Now, she was repulsed by every memory of him. Those warnings from her nearest and dearest, all of whom had seen something behind Raoul's mask when she, Charly, had been so blinded by the prospect of new love came back to her. She could only put it down to the fatigue and loneliness of relentless touring. He'd targeted her and exploited her vulnerability when her guard was down.

The wolf in sheep's clothing. Hadn't someone already said that to her?

God, Red Riding Hood didn't even come close to this mess. But it was too much to even process. Her entire body was numbed by the realisation of what could have happened between them but, thankfully, had not. Strangely, she suddenly remembered at one point aboard the Florence, her instinct had twinged when some mannerism or reaction of his suggested that he might not have even been interested, despite his overtly manipulative attempts to seduce her. *Oh God*.

"Why is this happening?" she whispered.

She had to talk to Alex. Just to hear his voice would make her feel safer, somehow.

She began dialing his number.

Chapter Seventy-Nine

The Seattle Police Department squad car powered down Northwest 85th Street, heading south toward Sunset Hill; red and blue lights blazing and sirens blaring, clearing the road ahead. At the wheel, Officer Michael Connelly of the SPD's North Precinct. His heart was pounding.

Along either side, houses, shop fronts and telegraph poles flashed past, cars pulled aside to let him pass and pedestrians stopped to watch the squad car as it screamed through their normally quiet corner of town.

The call had come in through the SPD 9-1-1 Center and was the first task dispatched to Connelly as he commenced his shift. He recognized the address the moment it appeared on the car's onboard computer: Madeline Clancy's house. Connelly and his partner had been the first officers on scene the day the first attempt had been made on Judge Clancy's life outside Picolinos. And it was all happening again, only this time it wasn't local hoods hired to kill her. It was much worse than that. This was fucking intense.

SPD SWAT was inbound but the call had gone out to any available units in the immediate vicinity to get to Judge Clancy's residence ASAP and lock down a perimeter for SWAT. A hostage situation was likely. The judge was not at the residence but her daughter, Ms Charlotte-Rose Fleming, was. A description of a Serbian national with a string of aliases followed. An Interpol Red Notice had been issued for his arrest. Officers were advised to approach with extreme caution. The man was known to be armed and dangerous. First responding officers were to make contact with US marshals at the scene.

Connelly grew up knowing Judge Clancy and her family, after they'd returned from England and before she'd become a judge in The Hague. But still, his mother and Madeline went way back. They were old college friends and during this recent situation – while the judge and Charly were back in Sunset Hill – the two friends spent a lot of time together again, catching up on the good old days. Charly. Jesus. Connelly hoped she was OK. Not that he'd ever admit it, but he'd had a crush on Charly since he was in short pants and she was a hot teenager.

God damn, she was mighty fine even back then, he thought. Now, she was totally off the Richter; light-years out of his league.

The hail of the sirens reminded him where he was and what he was doing. Connelly shook his head clear of Charly and kept pushing the car south.

Reaching Caffè Fiore, he spun the wheel and the car screeched into 32nd Avenue Northwest. He was seconds away.

Chapter Eighty

Alex Morgan was charging through the final mile of traffic in Sunset Hill at breakneck speed. The big Dodge tore up the road ahead of him, its 470 horsepower responding effortlessly under the crop of Morgan's urgent driving. He had to get to Charly. He had no idea what to expect when he got there or even if she was in any actual danger. But something told him he had to be there, right now. Intuitively, he silenced the siren, figuring he was close enough not to need it any more while also not wanting to herald his imminent arrival. But the moment his siren fell silent, he could hear another blaring nearby. Jesus!

Clumsily, he fumbled with his sat phone, trying desperately to dial her number again. He almost hurled the phone from the car when his third attempt still failed to connect them.

Chapter Eighty-One

With an exasperated shout, Charly threw her iPhone at the sofa and saw it devoured by the cushions. She still couldn't get through to Morgan. Where was he anyway? Immediately, she reconsidered discarding the phone so soon, and decided she should probably check her messages and emails, perhaps he'd tried to get hold of her that way. As she went to retrieve it, she heard a sharp double knock at the front door.

Oh God, the marshals had probably heard her scream at the phone and thought there must be a problem.

"I'm OK, Joe," she called, making her way to the door to let him in. "I just got a bit angry at my damn—"

But the door was already open. Standing there with a self-satisfied smile on his face and the last breaths of daylight waning behind him was the man she knew as Raoul Demaçi.

"Charly, how delightful to see you, darling," he began smoothly, playing the charming millionaire Demaçi to the hilt. "I'm so relieved that the police have been looking after you for me all this time." He walked further inside and, closing the door behind him, said, "Have you missed me?"

"Stay away from me," Charly threatened, her body rigid, her eyes darting in every direction, looking for the marshals. Any second now, they'd come flying in, all guns blazing. But they didn't. "I know who you are. You're a killer. A war criminal. After lying to me from the beginning, now you've been found out."

"I don't know what you mean," he said, playing with her, but underestimating her. "I've waited so long to see you. Suffered at the hands of the kidnappers. Not knowing from day to day whether or not you were still alive."

"Where are the marshals, Joe and Sam?" She stepped back a pace as he moved further inside. "What have you done with them?"

"Oh, you mean the two dead bodies outside." The face of Raoul Demaçi was vanishing before her eyes and the full monstrous scowl of the Wolf was taking its place. The transformation was surreal. Charly's mouth was agape as she witnessed the metamorphic rotation from one persona around to another. "You don't have to worry about them any more. Perhaps you could play at their funerals. Then again, perhaps not."

Charly gasped. Her hand clutched at her throat. "What have you done?" she whispered.

"You don't understand, little girl," the Wolf replied, his voice chilling. "I was never interested in you. It's your mother I'm after. She's upset a lot of people since she became top dog in The Hague. But that's all about to end. You're just what I like to refer to as a bonus kill."

"You're finished ... whatever pathetic name it is that you call yourself, Wolf!" she sneered bravely, tears forming in her eyes. "The police are on their way. Lots of them. They'll be here any second."

"You're bluffing. Call her to join us," he ordered dismissively, but there was bite in his tone now. "Call her, or I'll kill you right where you're standing and I'll find her myself." He produced the gun and menacingly twisted the suppressor firmly into place.

Charly's sky-blue eyes became a firestorm of rage. The fear was still there too. But this anger was channeling her primal responses to his sudden appearance in her family's home. She was not going to run from this man. He had invaded her life, threatened her mother and tainted the precious memories of her father in this house merely by setting his poisonous feet upon the threshold. She felt her father's warrior spirit at her side and the image of her mother on the judicial bench, staring down the world's worst criminals, giving her new strength.

"She's not here. You've got it wrong. She's visiting our aunt, literally hours away from here. You're a fool and you've walked into a huge trap."

"You're lying. Madeline Clancy!" he called out. He raised the gun and pointed it straight at Charly. "Judge Madeline Clancy! Come out from wherever you are hiding or I will kill your daughter. Now!"

But there was total silence. Charly remained standing, defiantly staring him down. The gun barrel was all she saw. Her chest heaved with the effort of retaining control despite being terrified. Then, just as it looked like he was going to speak again, the blessed sounds of a police siren grew to a crescendo outside. The flashing red and blue lights streamed in through the entrance windows, bouncing off every wall. The car screeched to a halt. The sirens stopped but the lights kept flashing.

A car door opened then slammed shut.

"Fuck!" the Wolf exclaimed, poking a finger through the sheer curtains to see into the street.

"I told you, you bastard!" Charly said. "You're done. You're surrounded."

The Wolf had lost the casual indifference he'd arrived with. The caged animal emerged as he searched through the windows to see what he had to contend with.

"One car is far from surrounded, you stupid fucking whore," he said.

He turned from the window and lunged at her. Grabbing her by the hair, he took her to the floor and sat on her chest. His legs pinned her arms to the floor, one hand had hold of her hair and the other, the gun. It pointed directly at her face.

"Where is your bitch mother? Quickly!"

Chapter Eighty-Two

Officer Michael Connelly pulled the SPD squad car to a screeching halt diagonally opposite the Clancy house. Blocking off the street so he could divert traffic approaching from the east or west, he left just enough room for SWAT to gain access. He shut off the siren but left the lights on. A police emergency was now in progress and he was the first responding officer.

Connelly called in his position from the squad car then, switching to the Motorola portable police radio on his belt, he stepped out, zipped up his fleece-lined jacket and pulled his cap on.

Moving across the street, Connelly observed the black Chevrolet Tahoe SUV sitting in the driveway. He'd been advised it belonged to the US Marshals Service, although he couldn't see anybody behind the wheel like he was told there would be. Connelly approached the house with caution. Technically, he wasn't supposed to. But the direction was to link up with the US marshals, establish a perimeter and await SWAT. So, to do that, he had to find the marshals. Strange that no one had even waved him over yet.

As he reached the path where the Wolf had walked along earlier whistling "Bože pravde", instinct and training told Connelly that something wasn't right.

His right hand moved straight to the handgrips of the .40 caliber Glock duty weapon on his hip.

Chapter Eighty-Three

Inside the house, the urgent red and blue flashes from the lights of the squad car pulsed like a manic strobe across the Wolf's malignant features. He needed to resolve this fast and get away before the cops came through the door. It wouldn't take them long to stumble over the bodies of the other two. He was holding Charly down, below the level of the front windows, threatening her with the gun, but she wasn't giving in. The Wolf was losing patience. The unexpected absence of her mother and the sudden appearance of the squad car had scuttled his plan completely.

He needed to know where the bitch Clancy was. And he needed to know now.

His movements became jerky, tinged with desperation. He crouched down upon her, his face almost touching hers. The warmth of his stagnant breath fell heavily upon her fair skin. Charly cringed, trying to turn away as he grabbed her chin.

"Listen," he demanded, his deep voice full of malice, his position absolutely clear. "I'm going to start counting and if you haven't told me where she is by three, you'll be without a pulse by four. Understand?"

Eyes clasped shut, Charly nodded her acknowledgment against the sinewy grip of his deadly fingers.

"One." The voice was a snarl. He checked the window, craning his neck to see if there was any activity going on out in the street. Nothing yet.

"Two." The spit from his tongue sprayed her. Charly's breathing labored under his weight upon her arms and chest. She recoiled, tossing and squirming against him but she couldn't budge; fear, anger, exasperation all strove for first place. She had to do something.

"Three!"

"OK! OK!" Charly said. "But, I'll take you there myself. If you're going to kill us both, then I want to be with her. Otherwise, go fuck yourself."

In the darkness, the Wolf eyed her suspiciously, wary of this woman he might have underestimated. Her blue eyes blazed up at him defiantly, despite her struggle to breathe. He squeezed her face harder in annoyance and frustration, sizing her up, weighing up the pros and cons of what it would mean to escape with her and get to the mother.

"Where is she?" he whispered hurriedly. "Tell me!"

"Bellingham. Eighty miles due north of here," Charly answered under his grip, deliberately misleading him – Ellensburg was to the south-east. "You'll never find her without me."

"OK," he said, reluctantly. "But make a sound when I release you, and I'll kill you and hunt her down on my own. Make no mistake, her final moments will be more terrible than you can possibly imagine if you fuck with me. Understand me, bitch?"

Charly nodded.

"On your feet, not a sound." Charly obeyed. He shoved her toward the back of the house. "Downstairs, move!"

Charly had him right where she wanted him.

Now she had a chance

Chapter Eighty-Four

Officer Connelly crossed the path, edging closer toward the house. The light of the sun was fading, yet no lights were on inside. Looking around he saw the burgeoning glow within the other houses on the street. Strange.

He reached the marshals' Chevrolet Tahoe. Touching the wide, flat metal surface of the hood with a tentative hand, he discovered it was cold and there wasn't anyone behind the wheel. Why was the driver's window down and the vehicle left unsecured, he wondered, a dark pit forming in his stomach. With the Glock in its holster but his right hand still resting warily on it, he inched slowly along the front of the vehicle. Avoiding the large wing mirror, he saw the keys were still in the ignition. *What the fuck?* A dark, wet shine on the upholstery caught his eye. Connelly released the weapon retention device on his holster and gave the gun a twist, hearing the creak within the hardened plastic sheath, feeling the gun loosen, ready to be drawn. He reached in through the open window with his left hand, fingers outstretched. The moment he made contact with the seat, he knew what he'd found. The thick, red goo of congealing blood was unmistakable and sickening.

Instantly, Connelly's Glock came out and was aimed into the SUV.

Quietly, he opened the driver's door. The cabin light came on. Bullet hole through the driver's seat. Damn! Connelly checked the vehicle for any sign of a victim. Not a thing. Then, backing up, he almost tripped down a set of brick steps behind him. Turning to check his footing, his heart began racing as his eyes fell upon the crumpled body of a US marshal. Connelly jumped down to the man, a colleague but unknown to him, a fellow law enforcement officer. He checked for a pulse. Dead. *Sweet Jesus*.

"Get down there and don't make a fucking sound."

The Wolf had Charly by the very roots of her thick red hair. On his orders, she'd taken him downstairs, out of sight and away from the front porch, heading to a side door that opened onto the driveway. The US marshals' Chevrolet was there.

"You're hurting me, you bastard," Charly cried, her eyes raw with tears, her face taut with tension.

"Shut the fuck up and move."

Charly squealed in protest and pain as he yanked on her hair. But despite the outward fear and submission, Charly was resolute. She had made up her mind to act and the moment was upon her.

Alex Morgan wrenched the Charger's steering wheel left then right, tearing through the final streets on approach to the house. He'd only been to the house once before, with Davenport, so he was relying on the GPS to get him there. Throughout his high-speed race to Sunset Hill there'd been no time for him to be guided by the infuriatingly calm narration of the GPS module and he couldn't find the button to mute the fucking thing. By the time one instruction had been issued, he was already moving onto the next.

He checked the screen for the hundredth time. He was so close.

"Come on. Come on!"

With both hands gripped to the weapon, breathing deeply to control the inevitable shaking, and with his mouth open to counter the thumping of his heart in his ears, Officer Michael Connelly's training kicked in. Calling the situation in to the police operations room via the Motorola on his well-worn belt, he whispered every detail as calmly and clearly as possible, while continuing to scan the front of the house. An officer was down and he needed back up, pronto. He found an access door from the driveway that led into the house and tried it. Locked. Damn! He needed to assess what was going on inside and he couldn't do that from down here in the driveway. There was a short flight of stairs that led up to the front porch. If he could get up there, he'd have a better chance of seeing inside.

"How far away is that SWAT team, over?" Connelly asked, making his way to the stairs.

"ETA four minutes. Withdraw back to the squad car and await SWAT. Acknowledge, over."

"Roger." Then Connelly heard something from deep within the house. "Wait!"

What the fuck was that?

It had to be Charly. Was it a scream? He couldn't be sure. Fuck!

A combination of adrenalin overload and the rapid onset of dusk channeled his attention straight to the most obvious entry point, the front door. His heavy patrol boots thundered upon the three flat wooden steps that led to the porch and, with his face set in stony determination, he charged at the door.

---

20 feet away, the door in the driveway opened and Charly was thrust into the half light of the early evening, tears streaming from her eyes. The Wolf still had her by the hair and was pushing her toward the marshals' SUV. As the cool air hit, she knew her only opportunity had arrived. If he got her into that car she didn't know what chance she'd have. This was it.

Now upstairs on the porch, Connelly threw himself behind the cover of the wall next the front door. With a deep breath, he pounded a fist on the woodwork.

"Seattle PD. Open up!"

"What the fuck?" hissed the Wolf, drawn to the demand from the policeman upstairs.

His attention distracted, Charly made her move; the self-defense sessions she'd been having with the marshals flooding back. Keep it simple. Nothing fancy. That's what they'd said; just get it done, fast and hard.

Charly stopped dead in her tracks and the Wolf, with the gun in his right hand and her hair in his left, stumbled into her.

Without hesitation, Charly threw her arms behind her head and locked both hands around the Wolf's left wrist. Holding tight, Charly stamped her heel down hard, as hard as she possibly could, on the top of his right foot. His grip in her hair loosened immediately and this time he cried out in pain. With her hands firmly clasped around his wrist, she pulled his arm over her left shoulder, as far forward as she could until his feet left the ground. Then, with a twist of his arm and all the strength she could muster, she thrust her hips backward, flipping him straight over her shoulder in a textbook judo maneuver. It took less than three seconds.

The Wolf hit the driveway in a crumpled mess at her feet. His head cracked on the paved brick surface and the wind whooshed from his lungs as his back slammed down hard.

Charly ran to the porch.

A blue flashing light appeared down the street and the engine beneath it roared toward them. Charly could hear tires squealing as she ran.

Connelly was sure it was SWAT, but out of the corner of his eye he saw a man standing in the driveway.

"Charly," Connelly yelled from the porch, moving to her. "Get down!"

The Wolf had already recovered himself and his gun was up.

Connelly saw it but Charly was in the middle, running up the stairs toward him. The Wolf's Accu-Tek HC-380 semi-automatic was pointing straight at Charly's back as she fled to the police officer for safety.

Michael Connelly didn't flinch. He took the three steps he needed to get to her and threw himself between her and the Wolf.

Morgan's Charger screeched into the street, right next to the squad car as Charly hit the deck.

Connelly opened fire.

Chapter Eighty-Five

As Morgan flew into the middle of the scene, within the beam of his own headlights and the crazy red and blue flashes of the squad car emergency lights, a man with a shaved head, dressed in a sports coat and jeans, sprinted across the front of Madeline Clancy's house firing wildly up at the front porch; a policeman bravely returned fire, only to be struck in the chest and tumble down the stairs. There was Charly, cowering helplessly in the midst of it all.

Morgan was out of the car before it even stopped, the SIG in his hand. The man in the sports coat sprinted toward the far end of the street. The Wolf? It had to be!

Morgan's first instinct was to respond to the man down. It was a given. He bolted from the car straight for the cop lying in a crumpled heap at the bottom of the stairs, hands clutching at his chest. Up on the porch, Charly was collecting herself, terrified out of her mind, but something that looked like recognition came over her as her eyes fell upon the cop.

"Michael?" Morgan heard her call, just as he arrived at the cop's side.

"How bad are you hit?" Morgan asked urgently, tearing the zip down on Connelly's jacket, checking for entry wounds. He called out, "Charly, you OK up there?" Morgan didn't have time for any of this, he had to get the Wolf, fast, but his immediate priority was to make sure they were both stable. The cop was gasping for air, but his eyes were open and he was responsive. "Talk to me, mate."

"Alex?" Charly sniffed, barely believing what she was seeing. "Is that you?"

"Yeah," Morgan replied urgently. "Get down here."

"Vest," Connelly wheezed. "He hit my vest. I'm OK."

Morgan realized the Wolf had failed the moment he had the cop's jacket open and saw the Kevlar ballistic vest: two definite impact sites sat right above the guy's heart.

"You're a lucky man," Morgan said. "Sit up and settle your breathing. Emergency Medical Services are en route with SWAT. I can hear them now. Hang in there. Charly?"

She was already by his side, shaking with the distress of it all. She knew the cop, Morgan realized. Locals. Morgan grabbed her by the shoulders. He wished he had time to console her but he didn't. He'd already lost precious seconds.

"Charly, listen. Is that him? Is that the Wolf?"

"Yes," she said meekly, nodding. "That's him. That's Raoul."

"OK, stay here and look after Michael," he said. "When SWAT arrives, give them a detailed description of the bastard. Tell them I'm going after him."

With that Morgan was gone.

Up ahead, the Wolf was already at the end of the cul-de-sac, racing from the scene. He could hear the sirens of a dozen cop cars heading into the area – it sounded like it was reaching saturation point. He had to get away. He got the cop, saw him go down. He just didn't know if he'd managed to shoot the bitch or not. But he couldn't hang around to find out. It was all too close; the closest he'd ever been to getting caught. The Wolf reached the house he'd snuck through earlier that morning in the darkness and clambered over the six-foot-high fence into the backyard.

The moment his feet hit the ground on the other side of the fence he heard the deep growl of a big dog somewhere in the backyard. Fuck! The dog hadn't been in the yard this morning. It was dark alongside the house, but suddenly a light blazed ahead, illuminating the backyard. Motion activated, no doubt, by the fucking dog. Before he'd even reached the open end of the strip of land between the side of the house on his right and the property boundary fence on his left, the dog appeared.

Positioned like a mythological sentinel with golden light streaming behind in ethereal menace, a big-shouldered Rottweiler defiantly blocked his path. Facing down the Wolf, its booming bark ricocheted down the confined space of the strip with a crazed bloodlust that only intensified with every step the Wolf took toward the snapping, salivating jaws.

The Wolf slowed but didn't stop, instead raising his gun. Once within the final 10 feet, he howled back at the wretched mutt in a twisted parody of his predatory canine namesake and began firing relentlessly.

Morgan saw a light-colored sports coat disappear into a yard at the far end of the street and heard the cavernous salvo of a big dog's bark, followed by a howl and, immediately, rapid gunfire. He ran straight for it. Lights came on in every house along both sides of the street as curtains were pulled open and snatched shut by residents who did and didn't need to see what was going on outside. Thankfully, no-one dared step out into the middle of it. Most importantly, the dazzling red and blue explosion of light behind him that heralded the arrival of SWAT and EMS couldn't have been better timed.

Morgan ran on. The firing had stopped and so had the barking. Christ, to finally be this close to the guy who'd been behind everything, ever since Morgan first set foot in the Greek Islands to take down Šerifović; however long ago that was now. The SIG was ready, his finger was lined up along the trigger guard, the moment he had a clear shot at the Wolf he was ready to fire. But it wasn't going to be that easy. He knew that. This animal needed to be in shackles for the rest of his days. Dead was just the easy way out.

Morgan reached the house where he'd seen the Wolf disappear.

In a perfectly executed vault he launched upward, waist on top of the fence, right arm thrown down to counterbalance his momentum on the opposite side, and legs flipping over behind him. He sprang forward from the maneuver and down to the ground without skipping a beat. After all these years, the basics he'd learned as a new soldier flashed back without even thinking about it. Closing the gap on the Wolf, he saw the Rottweiler in the light, whimpering on its side, blood gushing from the wounds inflicted on it by the Wolf's gun.

This guy had to go down.

Chapter Eighty-Six

The Wolf made it through the yard and laneways, and ran up the center of a side street toward the junction with 34th Avenue, where he'd parked the hire car. Right now, that was his best option for escape. If he got there quick enough he'd be out of the way before the cops even had time to get their shit together and spread out to search the immediate area. He'd become invisible again. The ability to vanish off the face of the earth and reappear at will was his specialty.

He chanced a quick look behind him. Nothing. He thought he'd seen someone following from the Clancy house but it looked like he'd shaken them. Good. With this many cops after him, the sooner he got out of America the better. He'd already made up his mind to write off the Clancy plan. He would now have to find another way of getting the ICTY off his back. But that could wait. It was no coincidence the American cops were all over him. The Wolf was convinced he'd been set up and in his mind there was only one person who could have arranged a tip-off like that.

The time had come. Drago was next to go and he would pay for this betrayal.

Morgan rushed through the yard and with another vault he was over the back fence and into a long laneway. Without all the obstacles he could sprint, powering like an Olympic 100m champion, bursting onto the street with the same explosive power. In the dim light ahead, he could just see the light-colored sports coat running up the center of the road, but the Wolf was too far away for Morgan to risk a shot. Besides, a stray round in the middle of suburbia had too many unthinkable possibilities.

In lieu of shooting the shit out of the entire street, Morgan took to the sidewalk. He was keen to avoid what any experienced ex-soldier worth his salt would see as an obvious fire-lane – the center of the road – but it also meant he could gain vital ground while minimizing the chances of being seen by the Wolf until he was right on top of him. Morgan's legs were burning with the effort of the uphill sprint. Still, running was one of his core strengths, ever since his school days back in Western Australia, so now all twelve cylinders were kicking in.

The Wolf made it to 34th Avenue, rushing through a sudden line of cars buzzing by in both directions. Horns blasted and a couple swerved but he made it across the narrow road unscathed.

Meanwhile, hurtling forward at top speed, Morgan was almost at the intersection when a vehicle appeared from nowhere, reversing fast out of a driveway to his left, oblivious to Morgan's rapid acceleration across the front of the property. Fortunately, the Intrepid agent marked the sudden red hue of brake lights followed by the white flash of reversing lights just in time. As the old driver of the equally old sedan stamped on the gas – as he had thousands of times before – powering the car backward into the road, Morgan leapt, skidded across the trunk and slid off the other side, landing perfectly back on the sidewalk.

He kept running.

Morgan hit 34th Avenue and turned into it with the speed of a passenger train perilously close to derailing around a tight bend. 60 feet away he saw the swerving cars, heard their blaring horns and, there, on the far side of the avenue, caught the Wolf wrenching at the driver's side door of a late-model Nissan Maxima. Fuck!

"Petrović!" Morgan bellowed. "Vukasin Petrović!"

The Wolf stopped cold. He had the driver's door open, had thrown the gun onto the passenger seat and was a breath away from getting in. With a hand on the door, one on the roof and one foot inside the vehicle, he turned his head a fraction, keeping his body partly shielded behind the door. His eyes fell upon Morgan across the street. Morgan's SIG Sauer P226 was up, aimed straight at his head.

"Do not move!" Morgan barked, moving slowly, closing the gap between the two of them, getting as close as possible before crossing the avenue. He was thankful that, for now at least, there was no more traffic in sight. "Step back from the door. Kick it shut and spread your arms out on the roof."

The Wolf didn't budge. He was holding out; buying time to work out a plan – Morgan knew it.

A stalemate ensued with Morgan on one side of the street and the Wolf frozen on the other.

Morgan fought every instinct to just shoot the bastard down in cold blood. He had every reason to kill Vukasin

Petrović purely by virtue of what he had done to Charly, let alone his track record of violence and murder. But it wasn't the Intrepid way. It wasn't *Morgan's* way. The carnage in Albania had been brutal and bloody but there it had been kill or be killed. This was different. The world deserved the opportunity to deliver justice upon the Wolf and his twisted mentor Drago, and Morgan was determined to get them both before the judges of the ICTY. If there was any way to avoid bloodshed today, he had to try.

Morgan needed to maintain a covering position diagonally across from the Wolf. If Morgan was directly behind, he wouldn't be able to see the Wolf's hands if he tried anything. But staying where he was also meant that the Wolf was partially covered by the car and Morgan was exposed. He had to get across the road.

"Arms on the roof, Petrović! Right now!"

No sooner had Morgan placed his foot upon the road and was advancing toward the Wolf than a VW Kombi van pulled from a side street, driving straight toward them. The flash of headlights momentarily blinded Morgan. It was all the distraction the Wolf needed.

In the moments the Kombi was between them, the Wolf got behind the wheel of the Nissan and got the engine running. After the VW passed a hail of gunfire erupted from the Nissan. Morgan threw himself to the right behind a parked car, instantly returning fire. The SIG found the Nissan but missed his target. Petrović stamped on the pedal and tore away down 34th.

Morgan was back up, firing at the retreating Nissan. The rear window shattered and bullets ricocheted off the body work but Morgan didn't stop. He could hear sirens again. The cops had regrouped. Thank fuck! They'd be heading out to help him stop the Wolf. He ran on, harder than he'd ever run in his life. Morgan watched the tail lights of the Nissan get further and further away. The police sirens got thankfully louder. In a matter of seconds they'd meet the Wolf at the same intersection. *Go, boys!* Morgan willed them on.

But the Nissan vanished across the intersection ahead as the cops turned right, missing the Wolf completely. Instead, the red and blues rushed straight toward Morgan down 34th.

"No! No! You're going the wrong way. Turn around!"

From the middle of the road Morgan waved at the blinding headlights, urging them to turn around. There was no use. With a gut-wrenching sense of utter exasperation and failure, Alex Morgan could only watch as the Wolf slipped through his fingers while the police charged toward the only man they could see with a gun.

Seconds later Alex Morgan was surrounded by SWAT, a dozen gun barrels pointing at him, and being ordered to drop his weapon and get on the ground.

PART V
The Dragon's Cave

Chapter Eighty-Seven

NATO AIR BASE, GEILENKIRCHEN, GERMANY

FIVE DAYS LATER

General Davenport stood patiently waiting while the ramp of the NATO MC-130E Hercules Combat Talon I was lowered.

The hangar had been selected for its distance from the main operational area of the base and was perfectly situated for the purpose of both maintaining the anonymity of the Intrepid personnel and enabling the process of preparing the aircraft for their mission to occur in secrecy. Davenport knew that a second identical aircraft was also inbound. Once on the ground it would join its brother within the hangar and the giant barn doors would be closed.

To an experienced eye, the distinctive nose configuration of these particular aircraft would be a dead giveaway as to their purpose. Therefore, it was best to minimize any local speculation by getting them within the hangar and out of view of the base as quickly as possible.

The hangar was brilliantly lit by an array of huge lights

high in the scaffolded ceiling. Davenport watched with interest as trucks carrying equipment and petrol tankers emerged, while ground crew prepared to load and recondition the aircraft in readiness for the next, much more dangerous leg of its onward journey.

This was to be a quick turnaround. It had to be.

Davenport considered the grave significance of the hours that lay ahead for his agents. This operation would be their last opportunity to drop the net on the ICTY fugitives. If Intrepid missed them this time, the general knew in his gut that the Wolf would vanish forever and Drago, if he survived the Wolf, would die an old man, living in luxury, albeit in self-imposed exile, never to be punished for his crimes against humanity.

No, Dragoslav Obrenović and Vukasin Petrović had dodged the hangman's noose long enough. They must be caught and brought to justice. Of course, he mused, the ICTY could never impose so barbaric a punishment. But for Drago and the Wolf, if Davenport had his way, ending their miserable lives at the end of a rope would be an appropriate conclusion and he would happily release the trapdoor beneath their feet.

With the ramp finally down, Morgan and Sutherland walked out of the aircraft clad in black combat parachute jumpsuits with dive bags thrown over their shoulders, full of the same banter and camaraderie of shared experience that had so marked Davenport's own early years of service.

"Gentlemen," he said, shaking their hands as they reached him.

"Good evening, general," said Dave Sutherland. "Good to see you again."

"Sir," Alex Morgan responded. How like the boss, Morgan thought, to make a field visit resplendent in his finest navy blue pinstripe three-piece courtesy of Somerville & Son. Impeccable as ever.

"I'm afraid I can't overstate the urgency involved. It's imperative we get you back in the air the moment the aircraft and the equipment are ready to go."

"Understood, sir," said Morgan.

"I expect Commander Sutherland has brought you up to speed during the flight," Davenport began, "and you've had a chance to go over the new equipment?"

"Yes, sir. Dave's brought me up to speed on all the main points and the new gear he was trialing with the special forces back in the US." The two agents exchanged conspiratorial glances. Sutherland looked like the cat that got the cream.

"I think this is the perfect system for the extraction," Sutherland said, barely able to contain his enthusiasm. "And I can't wait to personally strap those bastards into it."

"Well, let's hope they're still there so you can have your chance," said Davenport cautiously. "On that note, let's get underway. The pilots are advising me that they're planning on a three-and-a-half hour flight time. When you factor in the additional half an hour you'll need once they've dropped you in, we don't have a moment to spare. As soon as this briefing is concluded you'll be on your way. Come with me."

The general walked them to the back of the hangar where a huge shipping container bearing the logo of an international frozen foods company sat ominously upon an eight-wheeled trailer attached to a Volvo truck. A set of metal steps provided access to a door in the middle of the facing side of the container and the hum of activity from within told the two agents it wasn't designed for hauling refrigerated peas.

Like a captain returning to his ship, Davenport led them both inside and turned left, toward the back of the trailer. Hot on his heels, Morgan noted that the front half of the trailer was divided from the back by a heavy canvas curtain that, at this time, was zipped shut. There was no sound or light emitting from that end.

The rear section was a different story.

A surveillance operations console for remotely piloting an Unmanned Aerial Vehicle, or UAV, ran a quarter of the length of the trailer along the opposite wall. Half-a-dozen large digital screens, a couple of keyboards and joysticks, and an array of communications and navigation gear filled the space from floor to ceiling. The screens were already relaying live infra-red footage from a UAV somewhere over the target area, while color stills taken during daylight of a remote mountaintop villa were displayed on the top right-hand screen. In front of it all sat two operators, who Morgan immediately recognized from the Intrepid Intelligence, Investigations and Communications Section in Lyon. Morgan knew them both to be former military surveillance experts.

He tapped each on the shoulder as he walked behind them.

"Pilot," he said to the first one, and, "mission commander", to the second. Both nodded. "And two more consoles like this back there?" he added, jerking his thumb toward the sealed-off front section of the trailer.

"Yes, sir," said the mission commander. "Not needed this time, though."

"Understood. So, what are we using," Morgan asked, "Reaper or Predator?"

"MQ-1/9 Predator," answered the mission commander

keenly. "Fitted with the Raytheon multi-spectral targeting system; on loan from the Italians."

"When you're ready, gentlemen," the general summoned.

The last quarter of the container was fitted out as a state-of-the-art briefing and operations room. More digital screens filled the available wall space, depicting not only the live-feed full-motion video from the Predator, but also satellite imagery and detailed map sections of southern Europe; specifically the south-eastern corner of Serbia, with Kosovo to the west, Macedonia to the south and Bulgaria to the east. A round table sat in the middle of the room with seats along one side. Davenport was standing to the front of the screens, ready to commence proceedings.

"Right," said Davenport. "Pull up a pew, you two, and let's get started."

Chapter Eighty-Eight

"Firstly, Alex, perhaps you could start us off and give us the headlines regarding the Wolf's escape from the United States. Then I'll take you both through the interrogation of Lorenc Gjoka, which gave us the location of Drago's hideout, recently confirmed by the Predator, thanks to the efforts of our chaps out there."

"Well, the short version is that in those last moments in Seattle, Petrović and I had what I can only describe as an extremely short-lived exchange of gunfire across the street. Regrettably, Petrović escaped by car." The frustration Morgan felt was palpable. His fists clenched in unison and his jaw was tight. "In the confusion of the situation around Judge Clancy's house and subsequently through the streets of Sunset Hill, SWAT responded to the first man they saw in the vicinity waving around a gun: me. In the time we lost resolving the fact that I was one of the good guys, our ability to rapidly redeploy police resources to find Petrović evaporated and, as we've come to expect, he disappeared."

"I guess, like I said on the plane, bud, the cops had no

choice," said Sutherland. "They see a well-dressed guy running through their streets with a gun when they've got an APB out for a well-dressed guy running through their streets with a gun, what are they going to do?"

"Yeah, I know, Dave," replied Morgan. "I would have done the same thing in their shoes. And, you know, it made no difference that we resolved it in less than thirty seconds once they found my ID. Petrović was already a ghost. Two days later his hire car was found abandoned a mile from Judge Clancy's house. He'd obviously stashed it early on, then either got himself a new set of wheels or jumped on public transport and skipped town."

"So, where did he go, boss?" asked Sutherland. "And how do we now know that both he and Drago are together at this house?" He gestured toward the screen.

"We believe Petrović made his way north into Canada," said Davenport. "Then, no doubt with an identity change, he escaped North America, most likely out of Vancouver or Calgary. As for his current whereabouts ..."

General Davenport took the agents through the key aspects of the Interpol internal affairs interrogation of Gjoka. Faced with a string of serious criminal charges and the prospect of his remaining years spent behind bars, Gjoka was ready to bargain from the time they sat down. According to the general, who had observed the entire interrogation process via live video feed to his office in London, information literally hemorrhaged from Gjoka.

"There is no loyalty among thieves and killers," the general noted wryly. "Gjoka would have given up his own mother just to shave a few minutes of a sentence or to push for a minimum-security prison anywhere other than southern Europe. Of course, there were no deals on offer, then or now. Still, he gave up contacts, radio frequencies and codes, processes used to confirm meetings, cell-phone numbers, dead-letter boxes, details on the *Zmajevi* foot soldiers who guard Drago at his residence, Drago's son; the list goes on. So, while we all share your frustration over the Wolf's escape from North America, Alex, you can rest assured that the cumulative effect of your endeavors to date on this operation, including the assistance of Ms Haddad and Messrs Braunschweiger and Sutherland, has brought us closer than we have ever been to finally taking Drago down; with the bonus of also having identified a Serb enforcer who has remained at large for over fifteen years. I have absolute confidence that the two of you will bring this matter to its appropriate conclusion tonight."

Morgan and Sutherland nodded their acknowledgment that success tonight was critical: nothing was going to get in the way of that.

"But what's most important for our purposes," the general continued, "is that the Interpol interrogators managed to extract the location of Drago's secret hideaway."

Davenport directed their attention to a screen behind him displaying a map reference in southern Serbia, specifically the mountains due east of the city of Vranje, south of Lake Vlasinsko.

"This, gentlemen, is your objective," he said gravely, pointing at the map. He then indicated two other screens, one playing a video loop captured in daylight by the Predator UAV thirty-six hours earlier, and another playing an infra-red video loop of the same location taken at night twenty hours earlier. "This is Drago Obrenović's villa. He calls it *Zmajeva Pecina*—the Dragon's Cave. He is there now and the Wolf is expected to arrive at 10pm this evening."

The general paused, allowing the agents to study the images now of such significance to them.

"It appears that the Dragon's Cave is serviced by workers from the nearby village of Božica. The village has a population of around 300. Apparently, due to cell phone network coverage in the area being negligible at the best of times, cell phone sales to the good people of Božica would not have been a necessarily lucrative business. As a result, according to Gjoka, for many years Drago was completely reliant upon VHF and UHF radio comms with his immediate people, mostly to the north in the city of Niš. However, he'd been fed up with that arrangement for some time and recently managed to coerce local authorities to install cell phone towers in the center of Božica. Made them an offer they couldn't refuse, I expect. Needless to say, at this moment, 99 per cent of the traffic to or from those towers is associated with Dragon's Cave. So, we've spent most of the last three days targeting the cell phone and radio frequencies in and around Božica. Sure enough, Gjoka's claim that the Wolf would make contact with Drago to arrange their routine fortnightly meeting proved to be true."

"And that's happening tonight?" asked Morgan, knowing already but still barely able to believe it.

"Confirmed," the general replied, "by voice recognition software."

"What are we expecting of this meeting?" Sutherland asked. "Correct me if I'm wrong, boss, but isn't this Wolf character likely to kill Drago now that their plan to destroy the ICTY has gone to shit? I mean, from the beginning this has been about a hostile takeover."

"That's exactly what we're expecting, David," answered Davenport. "Which is why we must exploit this opportunity and recover them both, as soon as we can get you two on the ground."

Davenport checked the iPad he was briefing from as a young woman in a NATO pilot's flight suit entered.

"Excuse me, general," she said with an Eastern European accent. "The second aircraft has arrived. We'll be ready to take off in fifteen minutes."

"Excellent, Colonel Rodanski. Thank you very much."

As she left, with Morgan's and Sutherland's eyes following her all the way out of the trailer, Davenport wrapped up their briefing.

"Right, Alex, this has been your investigation, so you'll lead the insertion and recovery; and, David, I know you're itching to try out the new gear, so I want you to take care of the extraction arrangements." He walked over and handed Morgan the iPad. "Detailed aerial surveillance video, along with maps and stills of Dragon's Cave have been loaded onto this iPad to assist you with your onboard preparation. Go and get kitted up immediately. Develop your final plans once you're airborne; and, David, I know you've worked through it already with Alex, but make sure you're absolutely clear on employing the Fulton surface-to-air recovery system before you hit the ground. Once you get to the extraction point, you won't have time to be giving lessons."

Chapter Eighty-Nine

"I can't believe I let you talk me into this, you know, Dave," said Morgan. "I thought the Key was crazy with the whole garbage disposal chute down the side of the building trick in Albania, but this extraction plan of yours has got knobs on it!"

Morgan had just been up with the pilots going over the final details of the insertion while Sutherland stayed down in the fuselage doing the equipment checks.

"Hey, don't blame me, man!" Sutherland replied jovially. "Take it up with the chief. It was his idea."

"Bullshit," said Morgan, incredulous.

"Seriously. He did it years ago, during his SAS days. When I told him US Special Forces were planning to re-introduce it and I'd just completed trials with them, he loved the idea."

"He's as crazy as you are." Morgan laughed. "Makes sense though. If we want to get these guys out of the country without any chance of interference on the ground, there's no better way."

"You got that right, bud," Sutherland replied, securing a final strap on an equipment platform with the NATO loadmaster, who would also be their dispatcher when the time came. "You want to go over the jump now?"

"Yeah, Dave, this is the way it will go," Morgan began. "We'll make the jump at 25 000 feet. That'll keep us around the same height as most commercial airliners, so we won't look out of place on anyone's radar. We'll deploy 15 miles from the target and fly in under canopy all the way to the drop zone. I've already programmed the GPS units on our command panel with the exact location of the DZ; a clearing on the edge of the Dragon's Cave. The Predator UAV will maintain visual on the DZ until we're on the ground. They'll keep us advised of any hostiles when we're on approach. Good so far?"

Sutherland nodded, his attention focused intently on the iPad images and maps Morgan was briefing from.

"We'll fly in a stack, 20 feet up, 20 feet back. I'll lead and you'll follow me in. Once the Predator confirms the DZ is secure and we're on the ground, we'll do a comms check. From there we'll move straight into the recovery phase."

Again, Sutherland acknowledged.

"Half an hour before jump time, we'll mask up, attach to the aircraft's oxygen console and pre-breath pure oxygen for thirty minutes. Three minutes out, we'll disconnect from the console and transfer to the oxygen tanks on our gear. The pilot will let me know when we're close. Once that ramp's down and the green light's on, we're out the door."

Chapter Ninety

Minutes away from the green light the two agents stood shoulder to shoulder, ready to jump.

Each man was cocooned in standard covert insertion gear: helmet, night-vision goggles, high-altitude oxygen supply, Raider Hi-Glide high-altitude/high-opening parachutes, wrist-mounted altimeters, as well as a navigation command panel with GPS and compass fitted to their chests. In addition, each carried two multiband inter/intra team radios – one set to VHF for internal comms with each other, the other providing the crucial UHF link back to the aircraft and the Intrepid ops room, including the Predator operators, back in Germany. Their SIG Sauer P226 sidearms and Heckler & Koch MP5 SD sub-machine guns were strapped to the remaining available space.

When they'd concluded their checks of each other's gear, the NATO dispatcher stepped forward and began to lower the ramp. Buried beneath helmets, NVGs and oxygen masks, the two agents exchanged good luck nods and punched each other's fists as Morgan's radio buzzed in his ear. It was the pilot, Colonel Rodanski.

"One minute," said Morgan over the VHF internal comms. He held up a finger.

"Roger that, bud," came Sutherland's reply.

The ramp split like the jaws of Hellmouth, yawning open in front of them, presenting unequivocally the stark reality of what they were about to do. The huge black void of space beckoned. There was no turning back now. Each man knew that the next 2 hours of his life were likely to be the most intense he'd ever experienced and each was glad to have the other in his corner. There were no guarantees; there never were. But they knew they had to try.

The green light blazed and Alex Morgan disappeared into the night sky. Sutherland instantly followed.

Chapter Ninety-One

Out in the icy darkness, the insertion underway, the agents soared from the aircraft, racing through the mental checklist for the seconds and minutes ahead. The high-altitude, high-opening – HAHO – jump required perfectly timed deployment of the parachute. If they didn't deploy their 'chutes within three to seven seconds of leaving the aircraft, the combination of low air pressure and rapid descent would disintegrate the canopy. And if that happened at this height, you needed to have your shit together.

They both went out hard, but Morgan, so full of the task ahead, realized he had his head down too far. In the crucial first seconds of his descent, he'd become unstable, fighting against his own body position, air pressure and velocity. The rush was incredible but he couldn't prolong it. Morgan lost critical seconds he couldn't afford but then, in a microsecond, he was there, his body stabilized. His right hand shot to the ripcord and, with a wrenching forward motion, he punched out. The canopy deployed with a massive crack and Morgan felt the whiplash snap through every joint in his body, from toes to neck.

"Jesus, man! You OK?" It was Sutherland via his headset. "That looked rough."

"Tell me about it," Morgan replied breathlessly. "Came out too steep. All good now."

"Roger, bud," Sutherland replied. He'd been there. He knew exactly what it felt like.

The Intrepid agents set to flying under canopy for 15 miles overland toward their target. They maneuvered into position to form a stack; Morgan in front with Sutherland 20 feet up and 20 back from him. They'd jumped out over the south-eastern corner of Serbia, north of the border with Macedonia, with the winds on their backs, flying due north. For ten minutes the agents flew in silence, expertly manipulating the toggles to steer their parachutes toward the target. Through their NVGs they could make out some of the prominent buildings and landmarks they'd identified via map reconnaissance to ensure they kept on track in the event that the GPS units failed and to assist them in getting ready for landing. It was unlikely that the gear would fail, but knowledge of the terrain around any target was invaluable, particularly if the extraction plan was compromised and they needed to resort to escape and evasion. *Live by your wits!* as General Davenport would say. *Prepare for success without the technology.* Morgan could almost hear the boss now.

In minutes they would be above the objective: Drago's secret hideaway, the Dragon's Cave.

Their headsets buzzed with activity.

"Alpha Mike, this is Predator, over."

"Predator, this is Alpha Mike, go ahead," answered Morgan.

"This is Predator. DZ is green. I say again, DZ is green. You are GO for mission insertion."

"Roger, Predator," replied Morgan mechanically. "Any sign of the second package?"

"Negative, Alpha Mike. You're ahead of schedule. Second package is due in five minutes. Will advise when we have visual on approach. Good luck."

"Thank you, Predator. Alpha Mike, out." Morgan switched to the VHF internal radio so he could talk only to Sutherland. "Dave, those lights on our right are Božica," he said. "We're about a mile from the drop zone. Standby."

Sutherland acknowledged and they each prepared for landing.

Chapter Ninety-Two

Vukasin Petrović was decided. Today was the day that the great, all-powerful Dragoslav Obrenović would tumble dead from his throne.

The time for kowtowing to his crazy whims and fucking about with judges was over. But the Wolf wasn't going to make it easy on Drago. No, that was not the way this had to go. First, he would kill the son. He'd watch the little shit squirm right in front of his father before pulling the trigger. Then, and only then, would he turn the gun on *šefa* himself.

Petrović had played second fiddle to Drago for longer than he could remember but in recent years, as the old man began to rot, the Wolf was the one who had maintained control of the *Zmajevi*. The one who kept the factions, all of them, in line. The threat of Drago was no more. It was the threat of the Wolf that carried the fear. Now, the Wolf had had enough. America was the last straw. By the end of the night there would be no doubt in anyone's mind that the Wolf was finally the real *šefa* of the *Zmajevi*.

Driving south from Lake Vlasinsko along the 122 route,

he knew this would be the last time he would ever be summoned to Drago. It would be the last time Drago summoned anybody. The hatred coursed through the Wolf's veins, so much that he was barely able to contain his own violence. But he had to. He could not enter all guns blazing. The timing had to be perfect.

Maintaining a safe visual distance behind Petrović's Mercedes-Benz SLS AMG, the Predator UAV followed his approach as he turned off the 122 route and began the uphill climb along the zigzag of side roads that led to Drago's hideaway. Above the beautiful noise of the Mercedes' AMG 6.3-litre V8 engine, the Wolf was oblivious to the UAV's presence. Meanwhile, back in Germany, 900 miles away, the Predator's mission commander reached for the radio.

"Alpha Mike, this is Predator, over."

"Go ahead, Predator," said Morgan.

"Second package is on approach. We have clear visual. Red Mercedes-Benz. ETA your location: five minutes."

"Acknowledged, Predator. Thanks, out."

Chapter Ninety-Three

On the ground, the operation moved from insertion to recovery.

With their parachute gear cached, the agents regrouped off the DZ and crouched behind the cover of an old stone wall, overlooking the house 10 yards away. Under the NVGs, the position, layout and setting of the building and its surrounds combined to produce an eerie, foreboding atmosphere that both agents found unsettling. There was a cemetery-like lifelessness to it, despite it being occupied, and Morgan wondered how many bodies were buried around them right now in shallow graves.

The Dragon's Cave.

"This place gives me the heebie jeebies, bud," Sutherland whispered. "Feels like the goddamn *Amityville Horror*; remember that movie?"

"Yeah, mate," Morgan replied quietly. "Blood out of the walls and all that. Fucking horrible."

"We should have brought an exorcist."

It was large, designed in split levels across three stories

and, during daylight, would have sweeping views of the surrounding countryside. It was built to dominate, like a fortress, upon large stone foundations that looked to also contain a cellar or store area at the end closest to the agents. The brick work had been rendered with cement and painted white, common to the area, with wooden window and door fixtures and roof tiles of the red clay variety.

Scanning through their NVGs, they saw that the whole place was neglected and overgrown. Vegetation around the house was out of control and, to the trained eye, had blocked many of the locations where they spotted long-outdated CCTV cameras sitting dormant and useless where previously they would have provided excellent coverage.

"I bet he doesn't even realize how bad his security is," said Sutherland. "This place is a goddamn jungle."

"Might have been OK once," Morgan replied. "But not now."

Lights were on in only two areas of the house: the upper floor on the southern side, which, according to Gjoka's testimony, was Drago's personal living area – it would command the greatest views of the area; and the lower floor on the north-western corner, which faced back into the forest behind the house, and was, according to Gjoka, where the guards lived.

Morgan and Sutherland were on the southern side. Drago's living area was directly in front of them.

On the plane, the two agents had used Davenport's iPad to review the intelligence summaries that had been pieced together from Gjoka's confession and the video surveillance captured by the Predator. The UAV had provided invaluable detail and confirmed many of the descriptions and layout provided by Gjoka.

Now the trick was to identify the exact location of the

bodyguards; specifically, where they were right now. The guards were the primary threat and had to be neutralized first, before the agents could even consider moving against Drago and the Wolf.

Sutherland tapped Morgan's arm, gesturing toward the lights in the back corner.

"Guards?" he said.

Morgan nodded.

According to Gjoka there were normally three and due to Drago's continuingly erratic bouts of impatience, usually resulting in violence, the guards had been relegated by Drago's son to staying away in the far corner of the house. Basically, as far away from Drago as possible. The son's strategy was designed to protect his father's reputation by minimizing the exposure of the foot soldiers to his increasingly self-destructive and uncontrollable behavior. In any professional security environment, pushing guards out to the extremities of the perimeter would still be effective if they were expected to constantly patrol the premises. However, the obvious decline of Drago's personal influence, evidenced by the dilapidated exterior of the place and lack of any visible presence or deterrent, mirrored the lack of skill and discipline among those expected to protect him. The naive plan to protect his reputation among his immediate people only had the effect of leaving him exposed and vulnerable.

So it was that the Intrepid agents raised their weapons and headed for the back section of the house.

It was in that moment that the lights of the Wolf's Mercedes flared into the driveway on the far side of the house.

"We better get this done quick, Dave," said Morgan. "I

don't know how much time we'll have before Drago and the Wolf try to kill each other."

Chapter Ninety-Four

With NVGs now flipped up and away from their eyes and Heckler & Koch MP5 SDs at the ready, the agents prepared to assault.

Using the cover of the vegetation at the edge of the forest that grew close to the house, they'd split: Sutherland took the main back-door entrance to the guards' living area and Morgan took a secondary door he discovered on the way around. He tried it. Unlocked. Perfect. It was a side door that also led into the guards' living area but, by the look of it, most likely gave access into the main part of the house, too. Morgan couldn't afford to have anyone get past him and raise the alarm. So he'd be the cut-off as Dave flushed them toward him.

"What can you see back there?" said Morgan into the radio mike on his helmet.

"I've got two here, bud," Sutherland responded. "Muscle dudes; T-shirts and jeans, with shoulder holsters draped over the backs of the chairs. Watching TV. Not much activity. Can't see any others."

Morgan confirmed that he was in place and that there was no sign of anybody else. "OK, mate. Standby," he said, wondering for a moment if there was actually one out patrolling. But they couldn't wait. They had to move now.

Out in the driveway on the far side of the house, in a brazen display of adolescent testosterone, the sound of the Wolf's Mercedes skidding to a halt on the loose gravel was followed by a series of high-pitched revs, no doubt designed to announce his arrival and unnerve his hosts.

"Let's use the noise," said Morgan rapidly as the revving happened. "Go!"

Under the momentary cover of the V8's high-pitched squeal, Morgan and Sutherland burst into the guards' area from opposite directions.

Without time to determine whether the door was unlocked or not, Sutherland put his foot to it and kicked it open. One of the guards, sitting with his back to the door, eyes glued to the TV, stumbled from his chair as he twisted to see what was happening behind him. Sutherland headed straight for him.

At the same time, the guard to the left lunged for the large-caliber revolver in the holster on his chair. He was fast and got the gun out quickly, bringing it up to aim at Sutherland, but Morgan was right there. The guard hadn't seen him come in from the other door.

There was no time for barking orders to drop the gun. At this range, if Morgan delayed a second, Sutherland would be dead. With thousands of hours of precision training and experience behind the move, Morgan's MP5 came up, and with a single cough from the suppressor, he put a 9mm round directly into the guy's temple. He fell to the floor, dead. Sutherland didn't see it. He didn't have to. He knew Morgan had his back.

Meanwhile, in the scramble to reach for a gun, the guy now missing his favorite TV show had fallen from his chair. On all fours, he was about to scream the alarm when Sutherland's size ten boot caught him under the chest and lifted him off the ground. Winded, he fell into the fetal position, gasping for air that wouldn't make it to his lungs until his diaphragm regrouped. That was going to take some time. As he continued to struggle, Sutherland wrenched his arms behind his back, fixed plasti-cuffs to his wrists and ankles and, as the lungs began working once again, applied a liberal amount of duct tape to the guy's face.

Turning to look for the third guard, Morgan heard a toilet flush in the narrow passage that linked the room where they were to the back corridors that led to the house. *Christ! Why do I always end up with the blokes coming out of the fucking toilet?*, he wondered, remembering Malta. At least this guy flushed. Morgan was outside the toilet door in two strides. The moment it opened he launched. The confined space made it difficult to maneuver but Morgan was fast. With the HK ready if he needed it, he retracted the top half of his body and, as soon as the door to the cubicle opened, he fired an explosive helmet-enhanced head butt straight down upon the bridge of the guard's nose. Blood instantly flowed and the guy threw both hands up to protect his face from a second attack, stumbling backward onto the toilet in the meantime. Morgan flipped the HK around on its sling and set to work with the plasti-cuffs and duct tape.

Two restrained and silent. One dead. It all took less than thirty seconds.

"You OK?" said Morgan.

"Yeah, bud," Sutherland replied.

"Pity about this guy, though," Morgan said, gesturing to the body at his feet. "No choice."

In silence, Sutherland and Morgan finished tying the two survivors to separate chairs, facing them away from each other, then Sutherland walked over and gave the former paratrooper a grave but very grateful pat on the back.

"Hey, bud, you saved my life," he said. "Don't ruin the moment by regretting it."

"Piss off, Dave."

Chapter Ninety-Five

Drago studied the Wolf carefully, imagining that his son was dragging the dog in on the end of a leash after having kicked the shit out of him, rather than ushering him in on his own two feet looking so smug.

But there was something different about the Wolf this time.

Drago noted his gaze, unflinching and uncompromising from the moment he'd entered the sanctum of Drago's private office. The dog moved in with the confidence and cunning of a predator. There was no respect shown. No fear of any kind. Despite himself, Drago felt the sudden shift in their dynamic and the realization unsettled him. But was this change sudden? Had he not been fearful of the Wolf's growing influence over the *Zmajevi*, his *Zmajevi*, for some time? Drago knew most men better than they knew themselves, and this one, he knew, had come here tonight to kill. Or be killed.

Moving in silence up the central stairs of the villa, Morgan and Sutherland headed toward the lights on the top floor.

They'd watched the Wolf's arrival from the shadows below the entrance foyer and Morgan recognized Drago's son from his time stuck in the stairwell in Albania watching the heir-apparent interrogating Lorenc Gjoka. Unlike that night, this time Morgan had backup.

When the Wolf and junior Obrenović moved upstairs with barely a word exchanged, the Intrepid agents followed behind, albeit one floor below. Now, as they came closer to the top floor, they could hear the deep mumble of voices from a room at the top of the stairs.

"You've been a busy boy, Wolf," Drago said from behind his Alexander Roux desk. "You're lucky to have made it back here at all, from what I hear. Lucky you're not rotting in an American cell getting fucked by some big black gangster."

Both Drago and son broke into unrestrained laughter at the Wolf's expense. But the Wolf didn't bite. He remained silent, positioned so that he could access them both when the moment arrived; the squirming sycophantic son to his left and the fat fuck father to his right. Ignoring Drago's laughter, he turned his attention to the son.

"You should be very careful, little Obrenović, and learn to show some respect," the Wolf began. "One day, Daddy won't be around to wipe your ass."

The laughter stopped immediately and the rage that rippled beneath the surface of junior Obrenović's skin was enough to bring a broad smile to the face of the Wolf; he knew the little shit wouldn't dare take him on – not even in front of his father. At the desk, Drago had also fallen silent, watching carefully, considering his options. Junior's eyes flashed between his father and the Wolf, looking for a green light. A hand ran through his thick black hair and scratched at his goatee, anything to keep his hands from his gun.

"You see," the Wolf continued calmly, noting the son's inaction, "you could never be *šefa* of the *Zmajevi*. You're paralyzed by indecision. You are someone who needs to be told what to do. Without your papa, you are nothing."

"You are the one who should be careful, Petrović," said Drago. "You forget, once again, where you are standing, who you are talking to. That is my son. You speak to him as you would to me."

"That's exactly what I'm here to discuss, Obrenović," he replied, deliberately dropping the traditional deference of *šefa*. He noted immediately how much it rattled the old fool. "But, I'm afraid you will not be very happy with the outcome."

The Wolf instantly produced two automatics, one in each hand and each pointing directly at an Obrenović – senior and junior. Drago Obrenović rose from his desk with both hands on the edge of his desk to steady him, the anger and effort purging from him like steam from a locomotive. Junior Obrenović stood dumbfounded, shaking. The black eye of the Wolf's gun was pointing straight at his face. In any other circumstances he would have shot the man dead, but with less than 10 feet between them, he knew he couldn't outgun him.

"I'm taking over as *šefa*, Obrenović," the Wolf began, directing his attention at Drago. "Effective immediately. That means you and this piece of shit have to go."

The threat was too much for the son. He was watching

as his father stood silent, frozen in shock – or supplication. The junior Obrenović saw his only chance of becoming *šefa* barreling away from him at breakneck speed. This wasn't right. He was so close. He knew his father was in decline and he had positioned himself as the rightful successor. He was poised, but now this.

Something snapped in him and he reached toward the waistband of his trousers.

The Intrepid agents were at that moment moving silently but swiftly toward the partially opened door leading into Drago's private office, his war room, at the top of the stairs. With weapons braced in their shoulders, creeping stealthily forward, one foot after the other, Morgan and Sutherland faced the door.

"OK, this is it," Morgan whispered. "I'll go left, you go right. Whatever we do, we have to try to take Drago and the Wolf alive."

"Ready, bud."

On the other side of the door, the standoff between the Wolf and Drago and son had reached detonation point. Each one of them knew before the meeting had even commenced that there would be bloodshed. Just how long it would take to move from greeting to killing was unknown, although it was clear now that the fuse had been lit.

"Wolf!" Drago bellowed furiously. "You dare to come in here and threaten me! I will shoot you down, cut your body to ribbons and serve you to my guests for fucking dinner, you piece of—"

Junior Obrenović could no longer contain himself. A gun appeared in his hand, it was up and pointing at the Wolf, his finger was on the trigger.

There was an eruption of gunfire.

Chapter Ninety-Six

Alex Morgan kicked the door in. Dave Sutherland followed. They burst into the room with ferocious, determined intensity, not knowing what to expect on the other side.

MP5s high, standing shoulder to shoulder, Morgan covered left and Sutherland right. In a moment, Morgan took in the scene that confronted them.

First there was the prize, Dragoslav Obrenović. He was directly in front of Morgan, captured in the sights of Morgan's gun, standing at a huge ornamented desk, dumbstruck by the unexpected appearance of the Intrepid agents. Behind Drago was his portrait, a monstrosity that took up most of the wall space behind the desk. The vile display of arrogance by the mass murderer, war criminal and fugitive was grotesque in the extreme. Shadowed beneath his former glory, the old man was dead still, eyes wide open, long hair wild, hands clasped to the edge of the desk.

On the right-hand edge of Morgan's vision was Vukasin Petrović, the Wolf. Sutherland had him covered but still he remained defiant with a gun in each hand, one pointing straight at Drago, the other at the floor.

Wrapped around them all were dozens of digital screens interspersed with the most bizarre collection of oil paintings depicting sexually explicit nudes. There were no windows and the place stank. At the epicentre, in a crumpled mess at the Intrepid agents' feet, was the body of junior Obrenović, bleeding from a catastrophic head wound. There was blood everywhere. The body was twitching. That would stop soon.

The Wolf's expression mirrored Drago's: shock and incredulity. His eyes flickered as he considered his options. He went for it. The left-hand gun moved upward from the floor in an arc toward Sutherland. At the same time, he began firing blindly in the general direction of Drago.

The priority of Intrepid was to bring these two in to face the ICTY to answer for their crimes against humanity. That objective was paramount in the minds of both agents. Dave Sutherland responded faultlessly. The ex-Navy SEAL countered the Wolf's action in less than a heartbeat. He threw himself in a roll to the right behind a heavy chair. The MP5 was thrust to his side on the sling and from a holster on his left thigh he drew an X26 ECD Taser. The weapon appeared above the chair, clasped tight in both hands and before the Wolf had the chance to react to the moving target, Sutherland fired.

With a sudden crack, the Taser shot two bullet-shaped electrodes, which trailed wires that connected the electrodes to the weapon. Both hit the Wolf perfectly, one in the torso and the other in the chest. He dropped to his knees, contorting in uncontrollable spasms, fists clenched, elbows bent, face locked in a jaw-breaking grimace, as 50 000 volts seized his body.

In the midst of the spasms, Sutherland went for him,

holding the trigger down to maintain the charge, ensuring the bastard enjoyed the full experience. When he reached him, Sutherland released the trigger, punching the Wolf hard in the face, dropping him to the floor. Compliant, the Wolf received the plasti-cuffs treatment, followed by duct tape.

A simultaneous confrontation was happening across the room.

As the Wolf's rounds shattered the lamps and ornaments that adorned Drago's desk, Morgan leapt across the room and hurled himself through the gunfire to take Drago down. The Wolf's rounds ricocheted but not one of them found their target.

As Sutherland brought the Wolf under control, Morgan was sliding across the desktop only to see Drago suddenly descend from view.

Crashing through the piles of debris that littered the mile-wide desk, Alex Morgan arrived on the other side to discover an open trapdoor and a set of narrow steps that disappeared into a void. He flipped his NVG down on his helmet and threw himself down the stairs.

Chapter Ninety-Seven

A dozen wooden steps confronted Morgan as he rushed down into the darkness.

Through the NVG the space was alive but it didn't discount the threat. Drago may have been old but he was still dangerous. As Morgan's foot was about to hit the last step, a burst of rounds from a machine-pistol came from the left and ripped through the air directly in front of his face, crashing into the wood panels at the base of the stairs and sending splintered shards in every direction. Morgan spun toward the shooting and dropped. He brought the SIG around and fired two rounds high into the ceiling to get Drago's head down. Morgan didn't want to kill him – Davenport was expecting he'd be brought in alive.

Morgan chanced a look around the bottom of the stairs. It was clear. He rushed into a narrow dogleg on the stairwell where just three steps remained. A door was open at the bottom step. Beyond the door was the outside world.

Morgan weighed up his options. He couldn't afford for this to become protracted. There were two aircraft on station overhead ready to pick them up and if it took too long, they could lose the aircraft to a greater priority.

He launched out of the doorway.

The NVG took him to the left behind an old water pump. He scanned. Nothing. He moved fast, across to the right to a large tank that once must have serviced the pump and scanned again. Still nothing. Fuck it! Slowly, he moved away, putting himself in Drago's shoes. What did he want to do? He wanted to escape.

Morgan began to work his way around to the front of the house, toward the driveway. He knew for sure the Wolf's Mercedes was there. Possibly other cars, too.

As he moved across the wide expanse to the front of the house, working his way through overgrown bushes and clusters of rock, he heard heavy breathing coming from just around the corner. Slowly, quietly, he reholstered the SIG. He took another pace forward and his boot kicked a cluster of rocks on the uneven surface. Another hail of bullets from the machine-pistol crashed into the rocks a few feet ahead of him. Morgan stood his ground.

"Stay where you are!" Drago yelled, short of breath, coughing a phlegmy, heavy-smoker's cough before spitting a gobful of the muck out. "I'll fucking kill you if you take another step."

"It's all over, Drago," Morgan replied calmly from the side of the building. "Your son is dead, Petrović has been captured and you're next." Morgan had eased himself hard up against the wall and, through the NVG turned his view toward the voice. *Got ya.*

"Fuck you!" Drago bellowed, still coughing. His body heaved from the effort of unexpected physical exertion. "I'll kill myself before I'll be taken in. Have you thought of that?"

"Yes," Morgan replied and with that, he stepped out into the open, aimed his X26 ECD Taser and fired.

Both electrodes scored direct hits.

Dragoslav Obrenović fell to the ground in a contorted, twitching heap.

Chapter Ninety-Eight

"You enjoyed that," observed Sutherland.

"Yes, I did," Morgan replied with a smile. "A little too much, I think."

They laughed.

"Righto, Dave," said Morgan. Drago and the Wolf were both sitting nearby gagged, cuffed and strapped to separate fence posts on the edge of the DZ. "Leave these two bastards with me and call in the gear. The sooner those Hercs can get us the fuck out of here the better."

"Already done, bud. While you were chasing Grandpa over there, I was on the radio. The gear will be here any second now."

They looked skyward.

"And here we go! You may want to stand back a bit."

On cue, Morgan spotted two large bundles traveling toward them under parachutes. With the accuracy only the best technology can provide, the bundles thudded to the ground right in the middle of the DZ.

The Joint Precision Airdrop System – JPADS – was designed for air-dropping specialist equipment or general resupply gear to an exact point on a map via a GPS-based computer guidance system that steered the parachute straight to the target.

"You think these two are up to it?" Sutherland asked, deliberately trying to rattle their prisoners.

"They don't have any choice, mate," Morgan replied.

Minutes later, Morgan and Sutherland retrieved the gear from the DZ and began getting their prisoners ready. Sutherland had control of the Wolf and Morgan prepped Drago. Meanwhile, two NATO MC-130E Hercules Combat Talon I aircraft were on station high above, flying in a holding pattern, ready to commence the extraction.

"OK, Drago," said Morgan, fighting hard to control his loathing of the man. The darkness helped. "If you want to be able to breathe on this little trip of ours then you're going to need this tape off your mouth. But if you make one sound I'll tape you mouth shut tighter than it is now and it won't come off until you're in the aircraft. Nod if you understand."

Drago nodded submissively, watching with fear and helplessness as, right beside him, Morgan began to lay out two large, heavily insulated, illuminous orange jumpsuits. Sutherland was doing the same next to the Wolf.

Morgan unwound the duct tape and Drago instantly inhaled huge lungfuls of air.

"Who the fuck are you people?" he asked contemptuously, poison in his voice. "And what the fuck are you doing with us?"

"Well," Morgan replied, "as I said to one of your countrymen not so long ago, consider us facilitators. Nothing more. Now get up."

Morgan hauled him to his feet, walked him to the gear, helped Drago step awkwardly into the padded legs of the jumpsuit, and began to pull the suit up over Drago's body.

"Don't forget, bud," Sutherland said. "Leave his wrists cuffed and zip his arms up inside the suit. Strap the suit arms into the harness, so they don't flap around. I'll do the same for this guy."

"Roger that," Morgan replied. "How long we got?"

"Five minutes for the first aircraft and ten minutes after that the second will come through. He nearly ready?"

"Yeah," said Morgan.

"I asked you what you're doing with us," Drago said. This time the voice was less venomous. Fear was starting to play a larger role.

"It's very simple. We're going to put you on a plane," Morgan answered truthfully, pulling on his own suit. "And you'll be pleased to know that there are no queues with our airline. You'll go straight from here to your seat."

Drago fell silent. Somehow he didn't think it was going to be as simple as that at all.

Morgan and Sutherland began shoving their weapons and parachute gear into large bags that they attached to their harnesses.

Two minutes later Morgan and Drago were harnessed in a macabre parody of spooning, with Morgan behind to control the prisoner. Sutherland was just tightening the last few straps on the harness supporting him and the Wolf. They were soon in exactly the same configuration. The harnesses were each connected to 150 yards of high-strength, braided nylon cable. At the other end of the cables were inflatable blimp-shaped balloons that Morgan and Sutherland began inflating from helium gas tanks. Once the balloons were inflated, Sutherland, who was taking the Wolf up on the first lift, released his balloon and the cable pulled skyward to its maximum length.

"Now we wait, Petrović," said Sutherland.

But there was no answer. The Wolf remained totally silent, despite also having the duct tape removed. He was beaten. He knew it.

"Thirty seconds, Alex," Sutherland said via the radio headset. "See you back there."

"I think you owe me a beer for this," Morgan responded. "Good luck."

The deep rumble of the first Hercules came in overhead and before Sutherland had time to reply, he and the Wolf were gone.

"OK, so now it's our turn, Drago," said Morgan.

"What the fuck just happened to them?" Drago gasped, hardly attempting to mask his terror. He was breathing heavily, his head was completely shrouded within the thickly padded hood of the illuminous suit. The drawstring of the hood had been pulled so tightly that only his nose and mouth were open to the air. Drago was completely out of his comfort zone, in the grip of a fear he had never known.

Morgan released their balloon and the cable began to feed skyward.

"Well," Morgan began, "We're using something called surface-to-air recovery. The CIA developed it back in the days of the Cold War. On approach to pick us up right now is a Hercules fitted with a big V-shaped hook on its nose. It'll catch our cable in its hook, balloon gets cut off, and we trail along underneath until the team onboard winches us in. Like I said before, it's very simple."

Drago was speechless. He had no concept of what was about to happen to him and trying to understand it all was overwhelming.

"Thirty seconds," said Morgan. "I hope we can find you a good suit. You're going to need it in The Hague."

PART VI
As Long as You Want

EPILOGUE

Chapter Ninety-Nine

THE INTERNATIONAL CRIMINAL TRIBUNAL FOR THE FORMER YUGOSLAVIA (ICTY)

THE HAGUE, NETHERLANDS

THREE MONTHS LATER

Major General Reginald "Nobby" Davenport CBE, DSO, MC, took his seat discreetly at the back of the public gallery of Court Room 1 and watched with a mixture of great sadness, accomplishment and anticipation as the wheels of international justice began to turn once more.

It was almost impossible to fathom the depth and significance of the hatred, jealousies and private conspiracies that had all given rise to this day, nor the actions that had been necessary to bring these men to justice. Lives had been lost, trusts had been betrayed and personal traumas endured by those burned by the fire of the *Zmajevi*. Despite it all, Davenport mused, none of the events that had occurred recently, which finally brought about their arrests, held a candle to the crimes for which these men were actually here to answer.

During the Balkan wars of the early 1990s, men such as Obrenović presided over many serious violations of international humanitarian law, and perpetrated executions and atrocities on a mass scale, including torture and rape, among their standard operating procedures. Waging a campaign of immeasurable violence, amounting to the systematic destruction of a civilian population, their crimes against humanity and campaign of genocide resulted in the deaths of over 140 000 people, with millions more affected by the bloodshed, driven from their homes into a bleak, uncertain, terrifying future.

But, finally, justice had prevailed.

Through the paneled glass to his right that separated the gallery from the courtroom, Davenport saw members of the prosecution preparing themselves ahead of their opening statements. To his left were the defense team shuffling papers, talking in hushed tones, similarly preparing. He didn't envy them at all. The prospect of genuinely being obliged to mount a defense for a cold-blooded monster like Dragoslav Obrenović was abhorrent to Davenport. But still, justice must follow its course.

Directly ahead of him sat the judges, resplendent in the red-fronted gowns of the tribunal. There were three of them: two men sitting either side of a woman, the chief judge. All three were members of the Trial Division of the International Criminal Court, the ICC. They'd been seconded to ICTY in order to conduct the trial of Obrenović when Madeline Clancy and her colleagues had necessarily recused themselves.

A registry official located in front of the judges stood and addressed the court.

"Your Honors, this is case S-L-0-5-0-6-A; the prosecutor versus Dragoslav Obrenović."

"Thank you, Madame Registrar," replied the chief judge formally. "I'd like to have the appearances please. Prosecution first, followed by the defense."

Over a number of minutes both leaders of the prosecution and defense introduced the respective teams. All were noted officially for the record.

"Thank you, everybody. I note also for the record that Mr Obrenović is present as well," the chief judge announced, looking across to her right at the accused.

Davenport couldn't help but return his gaze toward Obrenović. Many within Court Room 1 that day would not be aware just how much he had been cleaned up prior to his appearance before the tribunal. The long hair had been cut into a neat, respectable short back and sides and the beard was gone. What remained was a tired and aged but still recognizable caricature of the former brigadier general of the Army of Republika Srpska, made infamous the world over by the news footage and press coverage of him taken at the time of the war. He sat behind his defense team in a baggy gray suit, with headphones to assist in the translation process, looking for all the world like a poor old man who had somehow been mistaken for a horrible, calculating, brutal killer.

As Davenport's eyes remained fixed on Obrenović, he heard the familiar tone of Madeline Clancy's voice in his ear.

"I want to hear the prosecution's opening statement," she whispered conspiratorially as she sat down behind him.

"Really," Davenport replied over his shoulder. "Is that the only reason you're here?"

"No," said Judge Clancy emphatically. "I really just want to watch this bastard squirm."

Chapter One Hundred

THE RED LION, WHITEHALL, LONDON

Alex Morgan laughed as he saw a young guy bounce off the Key on the way to the bar. The Key didn't even notice. Juggling glasses, Braunschweiger returned to their high bench by the window, underneath Lord Stanley's picture, and placed the drinks down: a pint of Guinness for Morgan, Pilsner for the Key and Budweiser for Sutherland. It was their fourth round.

Since wrapping up the ICTY mission, their services had been in high demand by Interpol and the UN but unlike that operation, the three of them had been off on solo missions in different corners of the world. They were finally enjoying some much-needed downtime. It was rare for the three of them to be in the same city at the same time and, on the very rare occasions that it occurred, they seized the opportunity to get together over a beer.

"So, Dave," Morgan began, "tell us about that latest railway track down the side of your face. Rope burn?"

Morgan was referring to two parallel lines – one slightly longer than the other – that ran down Sutherland's right cheek. They were healing but still scabbed. Morgan also knew that Sutherland loved to share war stories about his injuries.

"Yeah, man," Sutherland began. "I was fast roping from a Colombian police chopper a week or so ago – when I was picking up that cartel boss, remember? Anyway, halfway down this massive wind hit us and—"

Morgan's head instantly dropped to his chest feigning sleep, snoring loudly.

"Asshole," said Sutherland.

"Ah, I think you have a visitor, Alex," said the Key, gesturing toward the front door of the pub.

Morgan turned to see the spectacular Charly Fleming standing at the door, looking straight at him. She was breathtaking in black: fitted jeans, knee-high boots and a loose-fitting sweater, with a pale gray scarf thrown around her shoulders. A pair of Ray-Ban tortoiseshell Wayfarers were in her hand. As she walked toward him, the three agents fell silent. All eyes in the bar turned to watch her.

"Boys," she said, hardly even looking at Morgan, but she placed her hand on his shoulder before he could stand up. "How are you all this evening?"

"F-Fine," Sutherland stammered, standing. "It's great to meet you finally, Charly."

"I'm guessing from the accent that you're David. Texas, right? And, you of course, must be the Key."

"*Fräulein*," the Key replied, almost knocking over half the bar as he stood and shook her hand. "It's a pleasure to meet you."

"And you," Charly replied. "I've heard a lot about you two from this one. I think we're all very lucky to have you guys in our corner."

"I didn't know you were already back in town," said

Morgan, responding to her kiss on his cheek. "How did you know we'd be here?"

"Oh, I have my ways." She smiled that incredible smile. Her arm was around his shoulders now. "Besides, I wanted to surprise you. I'm in town for rehearsals with the London Philharmonic ahead of my concert series with them at the Albert Hall. I'm in London for an extra two weeks!"

"Fantastic," said Morgan genuinely. "So how long do I get you for?"

"As long as you want," she replied, with a seductive flash in her eyes. Then she whispered in his ear "I want you right now."

"Um, before we need to start drawing blinds around you two," Sutherland piped up, "can we get you a drink, Charly?"

"I'm afraid not, Texas," she replied, cheekily flicking her eyes toward a stretch limousine outside. "I'm double-parked. I just thought I'd try my luck and see if I could entice Morgan here away from you two and all this beer for an early dinner. I hope that's OK?"

Half an hour later, Morgan had been discreetly smuggled into Charly's suite, The Trafalgar, to avoid the paparazzi routinely stationed within prime clicking distance of the Ritz.

He was lying back with his eyes closed and head resting on a towel, luxuriating in the warmth of the water and the sensation of her soft skin brushing against his legs. The oil-scented water lapped at his chest and the aroma soothed his mind of all the stresses and dangers of his profession. This wasn't the first time they'd been together over the past three months and Charly was really coming through after the trauma she'd experienced. She was a fighter. Morgan liked that about her.

"What are you thinking about, action man?" he heard her coo across the surface of steamy water.

Morgan opened his eyes and looked at her. She'd tied her thick copper-red hair back in a loose bun and her face was perfectly framed by thin wet strands that were curling around her chin and dripping into the water.

"I was thinking about you actually," he said. "Thinking about this moment, being with you in this huge bath, naked."

Charly's legs moved slowly against his beneath the surface and a devilish grin broke across Morgan's hard features.

"What is it with those eyes?" Charly said quietly. "I can never work out what color they are and they are constantly full of mischief."

"My eyes are officially listed as camouflage," Morgan responded. "As for the mischief, I guess you see what you want to see. Don't you think?"

"Windows to the soul, handsome," she whispered.

Morgan felt her legs pull away and watched captivated as slowly, enticingly, Charly lifted herself from the water, bringing her body toward him. Streams of water cascaded from her shoulders and over her breasts while, beneath the surface, her fingers danced across the top of his legs, her thumbs trailing along the inside of his thighs.

"You seem to be ready for me," she said, pausing for a moment. Morgan gasped a deep, involuntary breath as her hand found him beneath the water and her full breasts pressed against his chest.

"Alex," she said, serious for a moment as she began

kissing him. "How long do you think we can make this last?"

"As long as you want," he replied. "Any ideas?"

"Do you remember what we did in Tuscany last month?" she said, her warm breath upon his ear.

"How could I forget?" Morgan's hands were gliding across her body now, his fingers lightly exploring those familiar, fabulous curves as he looked up into her eyes.

Charly laughed deliciously at the memory, holding Morgan's gaze with an intensity he found electrifying. Her lips were just inches from his. The water was churning around them, stirred by the simmering energy of their bodies. "Do you remember how it started?"

Morgan looked straight back into her eyes and smiled sinfully. He remembered.

Seductively, Charly peeled away from Morgan, allowing her naked body to slide over him with her arms outstretched and her fingernails running the gauntlet from his shoulders and along his muscled arms. With effortless grace she emerged from the water and sat provocatively upon the edge of the bath. Morgan's gaze remained fixed on her as Charly raised her arms, untied her hair and tousled it until it fell in a beautiful vermillion waterfall over her shoulder. Then, stepping from the bath, she turned from Morgan and walked slowly away across the room, confident in the allure and power of her body. Rivulets of oil-scented water streamed from her skin to the floor, drawing Morgan inexorably towards her with every sodden footprint left upon the tiles. At the door she stopped and glancing over her shoulder at him, she said, "Well, handsome. I hope you remember exactly how I liked it last time."

Next in the Black Ops Intrepid Series

vinci-books.com/avenger

Alex Morgan disappears into the underworld's darkest corners.

INTREPID's top agent, Alex Morgan, faces his most formidable opponent yet: the Night Witch, the mastermind of a global human trafficking network. As Morgan pursues this shadowy figure across continents, he's drawn into a lethal web involving Chinese triads, corrupt officials, and the Russian mafia.

Turn the page for a free preview…

Avenger: Chapter One

MANGOCHI, REPUBLIC OF MALAWI

The retreating rumble of the DC-3's engines was all that remained after the momentary explosion of noise upon exit. Military aircraft, old and new, weren't renowned for their creature comforts and inside, the old Dakota was nothing more than an excruciating din with less than enough room to swing a cat, underpinned by the smell of aviation fuel – leaping into the darkness and leaving all that behind was liberating. Outside it was quiet, there was plenty of space and, above all, fresh air. Alex Morgan sucked in a deep lungful and then another, forcing his chest to rebel against the tightly fastened straps of the parachute harness. He allowed himself a moment to enjoy the adrenalin rush, feeling the fresh blast of cold night air pushing against his face and body as he stabilized his position.

Morgan, an agent of Interpol's deep-cover Intelligence, Recovery, Protection and Infiltration Division – otherwise known as Intrepid – pulled the ripcord of the MC-4 Ram Air Free-Fall parachute and felt the familiar tug as the canopy erupted, unfurling above him. He looked up into the center of the blossoming rectangular canopy as the cells filled with air. He reached for the steering toggles and took control, checking his bearings against the memorized reference points he could see on the ground. There was hardly any wind tonight and the full moon lit the landscape for miles in a serene silver-gray hue. There were the cluster of lights to the south-west of Lake Malawi that was Mangochi and the mouth of the Shire River, then the looming shadows of the hills of the Namizimu Forest Reserve to the north, and there, directly beneath him, was the latticework of tracks and dry creek beds that led to a small enclave of buildings due east of Kwilembe.

Morgan was relieved. The parachute – and the plane for that matter – had been scrounged. He'd needed a means of insertion at short notice; a way to cover some serious miles and get on the ground quickly, and, as a former officer of Britain's elite Parachute Regiment, Morgan knew only too well how best to achieve that. Besides, he was expected to improvise. The effectiveness and success of Intrepid's clandestine operations around the world relied on agents operating, as far as possible, as lone wolves. That was what Intrepid's chief, and veteran of Special Operations, General Davenport expected of them, which meant finding simple solutions to otherwise complex problems.

In this case, a call to a trusted friend and former Parachute Regiment comrade eventually connected Morgan with a retired Portuguese Air Force pilot who, according to Morgan's contact, wouldn't ask awkward questions if the money was right. After the PAF, Captain Henrique Barboza had settled in Maputo with his Mozambican wife and now flew wealthy tourists to nature reserves all over southeastern Africa in a reconditioned war-surplus DC-3 Dakota. Barboza had agreed to assist in any way he could on the basis that Morgan's enterprise was fundamentally righteous and, more importantly, Barboza himself would be paid upfront and in cash. He threw the parachute in for free because he'd apparently won it in a card game and had no use for it. Morgan knew the plane worked, but parachutes had a nasty habit of not letting you know they didn't until it was too late to ask for another. But Morgan liked Barboza. The man was a brigand at heart, which appealed to Morgan's healthy respect for living just outside the rules. He put that down to his own piratical heritage which, according to family lore, made him a direct descendant of Sir Henry Morgan, the infamous Welsh buccaneer. They had reached an agreement, shaken hands and the deal was done. Simple.

Morgan was supporting a joint human, drugs and arms trafficking operation involving various African police forces, Interpol and, covertly, Intrepid. Codenamed Operation Usalama, it was the first time Morgan had been back to Africa in almost three years. He'd been deployed to the fledgling Republic of Malfajiri, West Africa, on his inaugural mission as an Intrepid agent, tracking down gunrunners and evacuating ex-pats, including children, from the middle of a civil war. That time, he'd almost lost his life. Worse still, the brutal torture and murder of his close friend, MI6 agent Sean Collins – whose body had been dismembered, burned and thrown like garbage into the grounds of the British Embassy in the Malfajiri capital Cullentown – had been the catalyst for it all.

This time, Morgan's target was another fugitive from international justice wanted by Interpol for drugs and arms trafficking, and more recently for extending his interests to include trafficking in human beings. Fusani Chomba had eluded the authorities for years but under the umbrella of Operation Usalama the cooperative efforts of the Eastern and Southern African Police Chiefs Regional Cooperation Organizations, EAPCCO and SARPCCO, finally uncovered his location. Chomba had found a safe haven in Malawi near a small village called Kwilembe, eighteen miles north-east of Mangochi and only sixteen miles from the Mozambique border. The intelligence on his refuge indicated that it was deliberately located within a populated area and heavily guarded. Storming it without the high possibility of unnecessary civilian casualties was beyond the immediate skills or resources of local police. With some subtle guidance from Interpol, the involvement of the Malawi military was not deemed necessary. Instead the task of apprehending him found its way on to General Davenport's desk and now, for the fourth or fifth time in his life, Alex Morgan was in Africa.

Morgan prepared for landing. He'd jumped at only four thousand feet, so he wasn't encumbered by unnecessary highaltitude gear – there hadn't been time for anything like that. This job was rough and ready. It had to be. They'd been tracking Fusani Chomba for ages and now they had to get him out.

As so often happened during the final hundred feet or so of a night jump, the landmarks that had been so well lit by the moon disappeared and the ground became nothing more than an endless black void. Estimating the remaining seconds to impact, Morgan pulled down halfway on the toggles to check the parachute's speed and braced. If he pulled down too hard and misjudged his rate of descent he could stall the canopy, which could bring him down like a ton of bricks, or even backward. Moments later, he landed hard among a copse of acacia bushes about a mile from the small cluster of buildings near Kwilembe, where Chomba's house was located. Jumping in at a safe distance from the target reduced the chances of being detected and allowed him to stash the parachute, prepare his gear and approach the location covertly. Morgan felt the landing more than usual and cringed as his knees protested against the collision. He stumbled, his legs tangled in a low huddle of acacia, and fell flat on his back. After sitting for a moment to take stock, he stumbled to his feet, hid the gear around the base of the acacias, and painfully extracted half-a-dozen two-inch thorns from his shins and calf muscles.

Morgan was traveling light, dressed in Helikon SFU combat gear, and armed with only a Sig Sauer P226 and an M4A1 fitted with a suppressor. It took him half an hour to cover the mile to Chomba's location. He made straight for the northern end of the village, paralleling the one and only road through it, scouring the shadows for a vehicle or any sign of disturbance, and working methodically round the back of the settlement. He kept at a low crouch, moving from cover to cover past the ramshackle houses to his right and the open, wild bush to his left, the M4 gripped tightly in his hands, ready to fire. The entire scene was a blur of black and gray, with minuscule flickers of orange light just visible through the occasional flimsy rag of a curtain. It was almost impossible to see, but still Morgan searched, keeping himself to the shadows on the edge of the dwellings.

There were animals and humans to be avoided as he closed in but he eventually reached a poorly constructed six-foot-high whitewashed stone wall that was the reference point he'd been told to look for: the rear boundary of Chomba's house, situated at the end of a long dirt road. It was the only dwelling in the area with such a high wall and, thankfully for Morgan, it backed on to open bushland rather than another property.

He checked the battered TAG Heuer watch he'd worn

on his left wrist for well over fifteen years. It was two minutes to 1am. He was bang on schedule. Right now, Captain Barboza would have the Dakota circling high above, preparing to land. Morgan had two hours to grab Chomba and get him to Mongochi airstrip, so that meant commandeering a car. Barboza would be on the ground from 2am, so if Morgan managed to get there earlier, all the better. Once aboard they'd head straight for Tanzania and Morgan would hand Chomba over to Interpol Dar es Salaam. Sounded straightforward, but nothing ever was in this business. Although, so far, everything had been going a little too easily …

The hairs on the back of Morgan's neck bristled.

He'd heard something, or sensed it. He couldn't be sure. Instinctively, he leaped into the shadows at the nearest corner of the wall. Some stones had fallen out of the wall and he squeezed the toe of his boot into the gap, checked that it would take his weight without crumbling and then stepped up, grabbing for the top. Careful not to make a sound, he got a hand over and held on tight, ready to launch himself into the yard. He remained still for a moment, listening, then raised his head high enough to look over and into the yard. He took his time, scanning slowly, right to left and left to right, searching for any signs of activity. All was quiet. There was nothing stirring in the yard and the house was in total darkness.

"So, where are all these guards then?" he whispered to himself. Something wasn't right here.

Morgan raised himself up until his waist was level with the top of the wall. He reached over, placing his right hand as far as possible down the other side while keeping a firm grasp on the top with his left. Then he flipped his body over and lowered himself quietly into the yard.

Remaining hidden in the shadows, Morgan used the moonlight to assess the house and possible access points. It was a modest, single-story, brick rectangle with square windows, a long porch and a corrugated-iron roof. It was remarkable only for its similarity to the many others like it in the area. Smart. Chomba obviously didn't want to draw attention to himself by living ostentatiously in some grand mansion, which told Morgan the man was keen to maintain his freedom. Between Morgan and the rear of the house was an open expanse of yard. It was about an eighth of an acre, with patches of uneven scrub sprouting from the dirt. A semicircle of milk crates that probably doubled as chairs sat in an expectant huddle near the porch. All in all, the yard was empty but for a lone mopane tree that grew tall and close to the house. Staying put in his dark corner, Morgan turned to the areas the moonlight couldn't penetrate, searching for any sign of a problem, but saw nothing.

He stepped forward, keeping his right flank hard against the shadows of the northern wall. The M4 was slung across his chest and the P226 holstered. Morgan brought his hands up to the pistol grip and stock of the M4, reflexively testing the tension in the sling. It wouldn't do for it to snag if he needed to bring the weapon up to fire. Estimating that thirty feet along the wall would get him as close to the house as possible without being seen from it, Morgan continued, treading carefully, his breathing steady, controlled. He soon reached the end of the shadows. His next move was to cross the yard. It was open, moonlit and exposed, but there was no other choice. Taking a deep breath, he rushed from the wall, leaving the cover of darkness, heading for the mopane tree.

The blow smashed him across the chest, pushing the M4 into his rib cage heavily. It was inflicted by a branch, gnarled and heavy, wielded by someone big enough to put serious force behind it. Morgan stumbled backward, the air forced from his lungs. Stars exploded across his vision as he fell, striking his head on the ground, hard. Morgan was dazed but conscious enough to know that the strike was reactionary, albeit forceful enough to put him on his ass. He sensed the assailant standing over him, raising the branch high, preparing to deliver the death blow on the center of his exposed skull. He had to get back up. With a grunt, the man brought the branch down with the force of an ax used to splinter kindling. Morgan rapidly locked his forearms in a tight cross over his face. The branch smashed into his arms and pain shot ferociously through his entire body. It was just the opportunity he needed.

Using the assailant's forward momentum to his advantage, Morgan grabbed the branch at the second of impact. His legs exploded upward, both feet connecting perfectly with the other man's torso. The move catapulted his attacker up and over Morgan, throwing him into a winded heap flat on his back. As the man tried to regain his breath, Morgan was already back on his feet. The guy sat up, pushing off with his hands to try to stand again just as Morgan leaped to the side and planted a heavily booted kick to the side of the man's head. The guy fell on to his side then pushed up again. He was tough.

But Morgan was on the offensive. He scooped up the discarded branch from the ground and swung it as hard as he could at the guy's face. It was perfectly placed. Morgan felt the jaw crack. The guy fell back to the ground again with a dull thud. Morgan stood over him, still holding the branch, waiting for any further signs of resistance. There were none. He felt for a pulse. It was faint but there; he'd pull through eventually but would need help. General

Davenport's words came back to him: *"Don't go leaving a trail of corpses across Africa. Just get Chomba and get out." Easier said than done, sir*, he thought, but at least he'd managed to achieve the brief on this occasion. Morgan took a second to examine his attacker. The guy was tall and thin, nothing like the physical description of Chomba, who was said to be short and solidly built. So, not Chomba. That was good.

Breathing heavily, Morgan dropped the branch, withdrew back into the shadow of the mopane tree and took stock. Apart from a few grunts and groans, there'd been no noise during the altercation, which had taken just seconds. All was silent again. Jesus, he really didn't see that one coming. How could he have missed it? Morgan spent some extra time watching and listening but there was nothing else happening and, so far, no follow-up goons to take him on or even any lights coming on – inside or out. Just silence. Maybe he'd surprised his opponent, which suggested that the guy was supposed to be on sentry duty but had fallen asleep and then heard or saw Morgan approaching. He must have grabbed for his gun, couldn't find it in the dark, and so reached for the closest weapon.

Morgan felt around carefully at the base of the tree where the man would have been sleeping. It didn't take long before he found what he was looking for. He knew by the feel of it that it was an FN FAL, a *Fabrique Nationale* 7.62 millimeter light automatic rifle. Or SLR, self-loading rifle, as they used to call them back home. Old school. There was no way he was going to carry around the FN. He didn't need it; it was long and cumbersome, and getting rid of it quietly would waste time. So, it would stay where it was but not in a condition for anyone to use it against him. Morgan quietly removed the magazine and pulled back the cocking handle, ejecting the round that was already in the breech.

Then he eased the cocking handle forward again as quickly as he dared so it wouldn't jam, opened the weapon and extracted the rat's-tail breech block, which he threw, along with the magazine, over the wall.

Morgan moved cautiously through the shadows to the porch, which ran along the entire rear of the house. He stepped up on to it and walked quickly to the back door. He grabbed the knob and turned. It was unlocked, for the sentry no doubt. He took a deep breath and slowly pushed the door inward with his left hand, careful not to allow any unexpected squeals from the hinges to warn anyone that he was in town. His right hand was grasped firmly around the pistol grip of the M4 with his forefinger resting on the trigger. The place was in full darkness with only a few slivers of moonlight reaching the interior so it was difficult to see anything, but he soon realized he was in a kitchen by the lingering smells of the night's meal. He crept on through the kitchen, stopping and listening and allowing his eyes to adjust to the darkness. What was that sound? He paused, mouth open and eyes closed, listening. It stopped. Nothing but silence. He moved deeper inside and repeated the process – stopping, listening, vision adjusting, breathing controlled. There it was again. It sounded like 1980s synthesizer music, fast paced, and accompanied by voices and explosions, getting louder and building in intensity. A wry smile broke across Morgan's face as he recognized what he was hearing. No way. He continued for another five paces until he was well inside the house.

His vision had adjusted fully now and he saw through the darkness as well as an average person would see outside at dusk. It was the central living area, sparsely furnished, with nothing more than a long sofa against the wall under the front window to his left, a couple of arm chairs and side tables, and a coffee table, which was low and square; the usual stuff. At the far end of the room was a snooker table and beyond that a door that led into a bedroom. It was the only door on that side of the room and beyond it was the source of the noise he could hear. Through the door, Morgan saw a white light flickering, illuminating the room an eerie gray, occasionally interspersed with flashes of color and darkness in equal measure. It paused, then began again, in the same peaks and troughs of monotonous repetition. He crept on through the empty living area, stepping carefully over the refuse of what looked to be a party – empty beer and wine bottles, bowls, plates, glasses and some clothes. The place stank of marijuana, booze and sex. Each step brought him closer to the bedroom. As he reached the door he could clearly see the room's layout, complete with occupants.

There was a huge bed in the center, basic bedside tables, and a chipped, rickety-looking wardrobe. Morgan approached cautiously but despite all the noise there was no apparent activity. He stepped over the threshold and everything went dead quiet. Christ! His hands tightened around the M4 and he drew the barrel upward ready to fire with the butt pulled firmly back into his shoulder. There was still no movement. Two extra paces into the room told him all he needed to know. A TV screen about half the size of the wall it was bolted to had been left on and filled the room with light. On the screen the menu page of a DVD was going through its looped sequence of spliced highlights. You've got to be kidding, thought Morgan. It was one of his favorites from childhood, a B-grade sci-fi cult classic called *Trancers*, featuring time-traveling cop Jack Deth. The silent moments came and went as the sequence reached its climax and looped to begin again. Morgan grinned. Of all the places. But it was the bed that held his attention.

A man, overweight, not tall, was sprawled naked on the edge of it and bundled beside him were two young women, also naked. A third woman lay sprawled in a heap on the floor between the bed and the screen. She must have fallen off at some stage and got comfortable there. Fortunately, they were all asleep, and judging by the chorus of snores, deeply so. Great! How the fuck was he going to extract Chomba from among the tangle of his brides without causing a ruckus?

"Sometimes, Mr Morgan, you're left with no alternative but a direct assault!" The wise words of the regimental sergeant major from Morgan's days as a young officer cadet came to mind. *Fair enough then, sar' major. Direct it is.*

Morgan took his cell phone from a pocket and moved in close to the edge of the bed. He stood for a while studying the sleeping man's face carefully via the light of the screen, comparing it to images stored on the phone. Yep, he was satisfied. Definitely Chomba. He leaned in close and sniffed. The man stank of too much alcohol and too many joints. His breath was rancid.

Morgan eased the M4 back down to his side, still slung, and extracted the Sig Sauer P226 from the leg holster on his right leg, placing it down on the bedside table. Then he looked around and found a discarded sarong that appeared to belong to one of the girls. He grabbed it and draped it over his own shoulder and back. Given what he was about to do, he didn't fancy the idea of having Chomba's recently engaged tackle dragging all over him and he couldn't very well deliver him naked into the custody of Interpol Dar es Salaam once they reached Tanzania. He took Chomba by the hand, slipped the man's legs over the edge of the bed and dragged him up into a sitting position. Chomba was fat, practically comatose and a dead weight, and lifting him was not easy. Morgan got down as low as he could beside the bed and toppled Chomba awkwardly forward until he fell across Morgan's left shoulder and on to the sarong, in a classic fireman's lift. Morgan stood up and hefted his captive into position. Then he retrieved the P226 from the table, gave Jack Deth and his compadres on the screen a nod of thanks for providing the background noise, and walked out of the room.

No one even stirred.

**Grab your copy...
vinci-books.com/avenger**

About the Author

Chris Allen is an author, senior executive, leadership mentor, public speaker, veteran and father. He is a member of the Australian Crime Writers Association (ACWA).

The formative years of Chris's career began in the Australian Army, initially as a soldier before being selected for commissioning as an officer. His service included airborne forces, military intelligence, attachments to the New Zealand Army, the British Parachute Regiment and deployments to Africa, South East Asia and Central America. After almost fifteen years of military service, Chris was medically retired at the rank of Major.

Chris's post-military career continued to reflect his commitment to service. He led security and logistics operations for CARE International in East Timor during the 1999 emergency. Later, in the wake of the September 11 attacks of 2001, he oversaw the upgrade of Counter Terrorism First Response (CTFR) measures at Sydney Airport. And in 2003 when protestors painted 'No War' on the sails of the Sydney Opera House, he was headhunted to take over the protection of the iconic landmark. In 2008 he was appointed Sheriff of New South Wales, one of Australia's most historic law enforcement appointments.

In more recent years, Chris has continued his career as a senior executive, broadening his experience across a diverse range of roles within Commonwealth and state government departments, and the not-for-profit sector.

Today, Chris lives on the New South Wales south coast with his sons, Morgan and Rhett.